BEHOLD THE MAN

by

Robert W. McKewin

Linda - May Jesus Christ bless your life + Bob McKewin

Macalester Park Publishing Company
St. Paul, Minnesota

10/9/94

Scripture references taken from several
translations, but mostly from
The New English Bible

BEHOLD THE MAN

Printed in the United States of America

International Standard Book Number: 910924-95-3

Macalester Park Publishing Company,
St. Paul, Minnesota 55105

For my beloved wife

Table of Contents

Preface

Have you ever thought about God with dirt on His feet? The feet of Jesus of Nazareth surely got dirty, just as ours would walking in sandals through the dusty roads of Palestine. From His birth to His Resurrection, Jesus lived with us, fully as a human being.

It is easy for me to forget this while reading the Gospels. In truth, I don't think I was even aware of it until I had the privilege of reading the early drafts of *Behold The Man*. The people who saw Jesus from day to day were people full of trouble and doubt just as you and I are today. We know this from the plain words of the Gospels. His Disciples were not sure just who He was. They had trouble understanding His message.

The writers of the Gospels tell us everything we need to know about Jesus of Nazareth, but not one word more. After all, they were aware that every letter would have to be laboriously copied by hand. They wouldn't bother to explain things which were common, everyday knowledge for their readers.

In two thousand years, the message taught by Jesus of Nazareth has not changed. The problems faced by His people have not changed; and the solution to those problems is eternally the same. On the other hand, as I sit typing this into my computer in my air-conditioned town-house, I need help understanding just how the people who walked with Jesus thought about the world.

In *Behold The Man*, we have the opportunity to imagine with Robert McKewin the day-to-day thoughts of four of the people who knew Jesus during His time on earth.

Behold The Man will deepen the understanding of those who already know Jesus. I think it will also be a powerful vehicle for introducing Jesus to the many people of our day who think that He and His message have become irrelevant.

If you are someone whose contact with Jesus has been limited to the celebration of Christmas, you may find a word here and there with which you are not familiar. The glossary in the back of this book is worth reading in its own right and may help you with that unfamiliar word.

J. OTTO TENNANT

Introduction

This collection of four meditations was begun a decade ago with the writing of the portions that deal with the thought of Mary Magdalene. Andrew, Judas Iscariot, and then Pontius Pilate followed. This book presents the meditations in a time frame of before, during, and after the Passion of Jesus Christ. The title of each chapter indicates the name of the individual whose thoughts or words I try to portray.

It is with a deep awareness of my personal inadequacy that I present this book to the public. My life as a Christian has included more than a quarter century in the priesthood of The Episcopal Church, more than thirty-five years as a layman of that denomination, and now a brief time as a Bishop in the Old Catholic tradition. Several trips to the Holy Land in the past thirteen years have helped me with an understanding of the geography as well as the history of the people who have populated that area, and of those who are the present descendants of those people. Though I lived with Christians there, I came to know, love, and have deep empathy for both Jews and Muslims as well. All are neighbors to one another. I pray for the peace of Jerusalem.

It has occurred to me that my reason for writing the book could well be the reason for others to read it. That is, to seek the man, Jesus Christ. I felt totally unable to look directly at Him, and determined the only way I could bear his glorious beauty would be through the reflected light of his presence in the eyes of his contemporaries.

It may be that there are many people who have never looked at the story of the life of Jesus Christ in the Gospels. Perhaps their reading this book will stimulate them to turn to the New Testament and to see how first century writers presented Jesus to their world. My prayer is that such a blessing will come to them, for surely a life without knowing Jesus Christ is empty by comparison with one in which He is known to be a beloved friend and savior.

Much joy found me while I was writing these meditations. I have often read parts of them to small groups, and noted that some of the people gained some insights through listening. May those who read the narrative be blessed.

My gratitude toward those who helped me with this book must include my wife, Patricia, who listened to me read it again and again. She was also most patient and skillful in proofreading, and in offering constructive criticism. Otto Tennant, who has written the preface of this book, must also be thanked for both moral and financial support. Sylvia Lewis became an active member of our little congregation in Cottonwood Shores, Texas, and offered her skills in word processing to prepare the manuscript for printing. To all of these, and to family and friends who have encouraged me to complete this work, I say, "Thank you."

1

Andrew

You ask me to tell you about Jesus? Sit down, then, and listen. I warn you that you have asked about my favorite topic, about the most important person who has ever lived! This could take a long time.

I first met Jesus when I was ten years old, at least fifteen years before I began to follow John. The way I met Jesus was like this. My parents let me go with my friends, James and John, and their parents to visit their cousins in Nazareth. Simon stayed home so that he could help our father on the boat. That is what Simon said, but I knew he wanted to spend the time with his new wife. Yes, Simon is ten years older than I.

It is a two day walk from Bethsaida to the western hills. James, John, and I had much fun playing along the way. Part of the road we traveled was a busy highway. It leads from the great western sea to the north shore of our lake, and then on east to Damascus and beyond. We had plenty of people to see, some traveling alone, most traveling in groups of at least ten adult men. The Romans controlled our lives then as much as they do now, and they had soldiers stationed in every town. But they couldn't protect travelers from robbers along the road any more than they can now. Still, we didn't have any trouble on our journey. My memory of it was of a happy lazy walk.

After we broke our fast in the morning at Bethsaida, we forded the Jordan, and followed the road past Caphernaum, around the fields on the west shore of the lake, and then climbed up to the high plateau. As we were already three hours into our journey, we stopped to look back, have a drink of water, and eat some fruit. James' and John's mother handed each of us a fig, and we plopped down on the ground to look back at where we had been. I think our home valley must be the loveliest in the world. The long lake in its center is surrounded by green irrigated fields, and then by brown hills that lead up and away in every direction but south. South is the route the Jordan River takes as it flows down into the desert.

I can still remember the warm sun soothing my aching muscles as I lay there. Life was good for us when we were children. Our parents' concern about Roman occupation wasn't ours. Just being alive to eat and play and sleep was enough.

We continued our journey, stopping for the night when Zebedee, the boys' father, felt we had traveled far enough. About every two hours of walking brought us to another small community where there was a caravansary available for travelers. When we stopped, we stabled our donkey on one side of a caravansary, the animals' side, where there were several other donkeys and two camels already resting. Then we went into the other side, marked off an area large enough for the five of us to sleep, and then went outdoors to prepare and eat our evening meal.

We ate the usual cold supper for travelers; barley bread and dried fish. Grape wine and conversation helped the digestion. Others on their journeys visited with us. This was one way for us to learn what to watch out for on the road ahead, and to give help to those who were heading to where we had been. It was also a way for us to recognize our unity with each other. It is almost impossible in the

Galilee to find a person who is not a relative. Sometimes you have to go back four or five generations, but you know before the conversation ends that the persons you have met along the road are cousins!

James, John, and I soon tired of the talk. Our stomachs satisfied as well as our curiosity about the other travelers, we went off to explore. The road we had been traveling was barely wide enough for a donkey cart, but at the caravansary it joined the Roman road that leads from Tiberias to coastal cities like Haifa and Caesaria. I was impressed by that road, as I have been impressed by Roman roads all my life since. It was wide enough for chariots and for a flow of traffic east and west. This particular road had been completed only a few years before I was born. It was a guarantee for armies or for couriers to travel rapidly from one major fort to another. Very few thieves were brave enough to attack travelers along the main roads. They were too well patrolled.

We boys played the game we had begun when we left home. We pretended we were Zealots, and that our task was to sneak up on Roman soldiers, steal from them, or even take their lives. The Zealots lived to harass the enemy, and would often kill Roman soldiers whenever there was little chance of being killed in the process. The Roman governors and their puppet kings ruled our country with very firm hands. Anyone caught disobeying our rulers' edicts was tried, sentenced, and executed the same day. Though I had not seen them in Bethsaida or Caphernaum, I knew of bodies that had hung nailed on crosses in several Galilean towns and cities. Often the legionaries would keep the bodies hanging for a few days after their death to teach the people a strong lesson.

The lesson they intended us to learn was that it doesn't pay to disobey Rome. The lesson our people learned was, 'be clever enough to do harm to our overlords, but be sure we are not caught!'

James, John, and I played by the road until darkness was almost upon us. Then we returned to the caravansary to lie down on our blankets and sleep until dawn. I had no warning of the importance of the coming day. That summer morning in the eighth year of the reign of Augustus Caesar, I walked to Nazareth with my friends and met a fifteen year old youth named Jesus.

We broke our fast before leaving the caravansary. Then we proceeded to walk westward toward Nazareth. We boys counted the people who were traveling the other way. It seemed as if the whole world was on the move! In all of Bethsaida and Caphernaum there aren't two thousand people, yet we must have seen that many in two hours. Merchants were traveling in caravans. Soldiers of Rome were walking as units. Holiday travelers like ourselves were strolling along, taking their time, just as we were.

By the sixth hour of the day, the traffic slowed a little. The sun burned down upon us, and we boys began to fall behind. The road climbed higher into the hills, and its steep ascent in several places took much of our remaining energy from us.

When we came in sight of Nazareth, which is a lovely small town perched on a hillside that we could see from our position several miles away, old Zebedee called a halt. We sat down under a pomegranate tree, took some of its fruit, and rested. It was so good relaxing there that I soon dozed off. I have no idea how long I slept, but I don't believe it was more than a few moments.

When I awoke, I was looking into the face of a boy I never saw before. He looked down at me, and smiled. "Hi Andrew," he said. "My name is Jesus. I've been waiting for all of you, and got impatient, so I came along the way to meet you."

That was the first time I met Jesus. He didn't seem very special at the time. He was a good looking youth of about fifteen, clear eyed, straight, clean, much like his cousins, James and John.

Zebedee gave us three boys permission to leave the road and go exploring with Jesus. We strolled off through a field of ripe grain, catching some of the heads in our hands, rubbing off the chaff, and munching the crisp seeds as we walked. At Cana we stopped for a drink of water from the well, and I found myself visiting with Jesus.

"Why are you here, Andrew?" he asked.

"Because this is the way we walked," I replied.

"No. I mean, why are you alive?"

"Because I was born. Because I have not yet died." His question confused me. What was he looking for, I wondered.

"I think you are here because God created you to be here. He has some special reason for you to be alive. He has some special reason for each of us to live. It is for us to listen to God so He can tell us what our purpose is."

I stood confused before Jesus. What he said made sense to me even then. But I didn't know how to respond.

"Have you ever been to Jerusalem?" he asked next. And I replied in the negative. In two years I would be old enough to go and enter the Temple as a man. My brother, Simon, promised he would take me there.

"I was there," Jesus said. "I have been there each year since I was twelve. It was there I talked with God, and knew Him to be my Father."

Jesus left me alone for the rest of that day. I don't mean that he ignored me. I mean he didn't talk to me about things that made me think. We strolled along, walking around hills, through pastures and fields, up to the top of one hill that overlooked Nazareth, and sat in the holy place under the tall tree there. Nearly every town has a high hill that has been set aside for worship by our distant ancestors. The gods they worshiped are not the Lord God Yahweh, but they are dark gods. They are secret gods; gods of water, fire, and earth, gods of love and fertility. Nighttime visits by people from the town can be, and are, made today as much as before. In the high place at Nazareth, there is a prominent tomb, that of one of the great leaders of Nazareth from long ago. A man named Eliud was buried there. Eliud was the father of Eleazar, the father of Matthan, the father of Jacob, the father of Joseph, who was the father of Jesus. What Eliud did to receive the honor of burial at the holy site, Jesus did not tell us. We were not curious enough to ask. Resting by the tomb of one holy ancestor is much like resting by the tomb of any other.

From the hilltop we could see the whole town of Nazareth below us. It was about the size of my home town by the lake, perhaps five hundred cubits square, built along the south facing side of the hill on which we were sitting. The valley below offered the women of the town two wells from which to draw water. Jesus pointed out his home, near the center of town, less than two hundred cubits from the eastern well.

Jesus' house was like the other houses in town. It was built into the hillside, constructed of hewn stones from the local granite. This was quite different from my home that stood on flat ground and was made of dark basalt. We could see Jesus' home was a little larger than most of the houses in town, and were impressed by that — until we walked down the hill and entered to discover Joseph's carpenter shop took up more than half the space! As visitors, we were allotted sleeping space on the floor of the shop.

We were quite crowded when we were all in the house. There were Mary and Joseph, their three sons and two daughters; Zebedee and his wife and two sons, and myself. Since it was summer, we children were granted permission to sleep on the roof of the house, under the stars. It never rains in the summer, and there is such a pleasant breeze most nights that sleeping outdoors is far more pleasant than resting indoors.

During the many days we were in Nazareth, Jesus took us boys to visit local hilltops where we saw other shrines to gods of other towns. He took us to see caves that had been occupied by ancient peoples before the towns were built. We found stone tools and ancient campsites in the recesses of these caves. I was impressed. Jesus really knew his territory.

James, John, and I talked about Jesus. We knew he was different. He wasn't enough different for us to note him as Messiah, you understand. He looked and acted like any youth of our country who was approaching manhood. What made him different was he kept asking questions. He kept studying people and things with an intensity I never knew before.

Let me give you an example. One time I was walking alone and Jesus was sitting staring at a wild lily in the field. He seemed to be totally absorbed in it; so much so, I didn't think he even noticed my approach. I sat down to watch, though I wasn't sure of what there was to see. Jesus and the flower were still as stone. His concentration made me want to see what he saw. Yet all I saw was a common flower in a common field in our common country.

"Look at this, Andrew," Jesus said. "Look at this flower!" I moved up behind him and took a closer look. It seemed no different from any other flower.

"How did you know I was here?" I asked. "You didn't look up. I didn't make any noise."

"I wanted you here," he said. And though that answer filled me with more questions, I was distracted by his persistence about the flower. "Look at this lily."

"I see it. What about it."

"Consider its beauty. God made it that way. He made the world a beautiful place of flowers in the field, birds in the air, butterflies and locusts and ants." He paused and continued to look at the flower. I joined him in really looking. It was a beautiful plant at that.

"It is pretty," I said.

Jesus turned and smiled at me. "Thank you, Andrew. It is pretty." There was no sarcasm in his voice. Yet I know he knew I could not express awe at the sight my eyes were absorbing. And I knew he was absorbing far, far more than I could ever do as he studied the plant before him. "Andrew, do you have any idea of what the Kingdom of Heaven is like?" he asked.

"No," I said. "I never thought about it."

"Yes you did," Jesus corrected me. "You think about it a lot. You are distressed at the bad things that happen to people. You are upset that we are ruled by Rome, and that the soldiers watch and control our lives. If you see what is wrong, you must think about what would be right."

"Yes," I stumbled. My thoughts weren't used to coming out in words. "I think our nation should be free. We need a Messiah to free us and make us a strong nation as David did. We need to obey the Laws God gave Moses. People should be honest, kind, trustworthy, generous."

"Hardworking?" I wondered if Jesus should have spent more of his time helping Joseph in the carpenter shop. I thought about Simon fishing and mending the nets without me. It seemed as if Jesus read my mind. "Let's go back to town. They may be looking for us."

But when we arrived at his home, we found no one had missed us. We found James and John, and spent the time before we were called to supper enjoying a game of ball.

Often during the following years of my growing to manhood, I would see Jesus. I didn't visit Nazareth again until I became his disciple and we stopped there in our travels. But Jesus came to Caphernaum to visit, and to help James and John with the fishing. There we swam and laughed and worked and played side by side.

Looking back now, I see we always had more joy when Jesus was with us than we had without him. But we didn't notice it then, or if we did, we didn't mention it to one another.

As I grew older, I took a greater part in the fishing business. Simon insisted on it. He said it was what kept bread on the table, and a roof over my head, and I had a responsibility to do the work. Fishing wasn't that hard a life really. It was just that most of the time it was quite boring, and all of the time it was dirty and tedious work.

Day after day we would clean fish, sell fish, mend nets, caulk the boat. We never were broke, but we were never far ahead of ourselves either. We went into partnership with the Zebedees so that we could work the nets together. When a school of fish is sighted, it is good to have two or even three boats that will help you cast the nets in a pattern. Sometimes you can trap the whole school! At times like that I had mixed emotions. It was exciting and exhilarating to have a good catch, and it certainly made more money for us when we took our full boats to Magdala where we sold our fish.

But the work was far more exhausting when we were lucky. I remember working twenty hours or more in a day, and then having to be ready to go out and fish again the same night.

I moved out of Simon's house. With his wife and mother-in-law in the place, there didn't seem room for me.

Philip was a good friend with many of the same interests I had, religious interests, that is. As he was living alone in his family house in Bethsaida, it seemed good to move in with him. He and I would take our Sabbath day off and rest according to the law. We would read the Torah, pray at the synagogue, and then just talk until sundown.

The question Jesus asked me years before kept bothering me. "Andrew, why are you here?" That set our minds to asking all the imponderable questions. Why did God make the heavens and the earth? Why did he make animals? Why did he make plants? What use are the rough fish that we catch and throw back? If we men are created in God's image, what is our purpose? What makes us images of God? Do we really look like Him? Or is our nature like His?

As Philip was half Greek, he was a better arguer. He spoke of philosophers from Greece, and of the gods of those people. It was enough to make my head spin.

Philip had plenty of money. His father was rich, a traveling merchant. A man of wisdom, he knew Philip was not capable of being in business with him. He called Philip a dreamer, and gave him an allowance to live on.

We kept hearing of a man named John who was preaching and baptizing people in the Jordan River down by Jericho. Some of the people from Bethsaida went down to hear John, were very impressed by his message, and were baptized. We talked with them about their experience.

"What is this John like?" I asked.

"He is like no other man we have ever seen," replied one, and the others concurred.

A second man said, "He is rather tall. He is unshaven, having a long beard, and the man hasn't had his hair cut in years. He wears skins for clothing. He certainly stands out in a crowd!"

The third man said, "John is a Nazirite. You know that Nazirites take vows not to cut their hair, and never to drink anything alcoholic. The man really is a wild eyed fanatic!"

"When he preaches," the first man said, "he makes us realize that he stands as the powerful natural force of God's Righteousness. He makes us look at ourselves and our soft lives, our well made clothing, our pampered hair and trimmed beards. He makes us see what we are."

"Then he tells us what we already know. We recall how often we have broken the commandments, and we see how empty are our lives. He makes us wish we could wash away our past sins."

"And that is when he calls to us to repent and be baptized in the Jordan."

"It is a strong call. It is hard to turn away. I hate my life as it is. I would rather be cleansed. I would like to be clean in the eyes of God."

As we listened to these men, we noted the things they said were not just words. They began to act differently, giving money for the relief of the poor, spending more time in prayer and study at the synagogue, being kinder to one another. Merchants who had been to see John were fair with their customers. Farmers didn't try to hide spoiled food under good fruit.

My friend Philip was even more impressed than I. He said, "I want to go to see John the Baptizer, and to hear him." I tried to argue.

"Philip, you are one of the finest, most honest young men of this town. You don't have anything to repent of! What reason do you have to see John?"

"I really don't know. Call it curiosity. But I must go. Can you get away from the fishing for a while? I would like you to come along."

It didn't seem like too good an idea. Anything might be better than fishing, but the Jordan River near Jericho can be a hot and uncomfortable place in the summer. It was hot enough by the Sea of Genesseret. I didn't really want to go. But I was almost certain I could not get the time away.

"I will go," I said. "I will go if Simon will permit it." I really hoped that this time I would get a negative response from my brother, and then have a good conscience about staying home.

But Simon was contrary as usual. He gave me four weeks off, and I had no excuse. Philip and I left the next morning, the second day of the week, the day the Greeks call Moon Day. It was a long hot three day walk to Jericho, and I didn't enjoy it. We walked in the mornings, and in the cool of the evenings, and rested under what shade we could find by the river during the middle of each day.

Despite the heat, we found we were not traveling alone. The road down the Jordan valley from Tiberias to Jericho and on to the Gulf of Aqaba beside the Sinai desert has been a well traveled caravan route for longer than anyone can recall. We know Moses led our people through the lower part of this route, and that Joshua led them along that road to the promised land. We traveled with merchants and soldiers and pilgrims on their way to Jerusalem. Those people were making a pilgrimage to the holy city because we were nearing the day of Pentecost, fifty days after Passover. But most of the people who traveled with us, and most of those we met, were people who made the desert journey to see John the Baptizer, and to hear his message.

When we came to the place on the river where John was camped with his disciples, we arrived at a time when things were quiet. We found the shade of a date palm, and lay down to rest. The plant and animal life in this place is quite different from that around our lovely lake. We have much rainfall where we live, and this place where John chose to camp was very dry except for the slow flowing, dirty Jordan River.

The place was a natural ford, with the water barely knee deep except for big holes the stream probably gouged out during its spring flood. The date palms were one source of food when they were ripe, as were many other fruit trees that had been planted as orchards by local natives, and then irrigated with canals from the Jordan. The area was sparsely settled, but those people who lived there made a good living.

Near sunset John came down to the river and began to speak. Almost immediately crowds gathered, from where I cannot imagine, though I assume there were many who had been resting under other trees and in the tall grasses at the edge of the water. His audience must have numbered in the hundreds! Soldiers were there, including many of their officers. Members of the Sanhedrin stood back, trying not to be conspicuous, but determined to watch and to listen. But the peasants, people like Philip and me, moved up to stand close to John to see and hear him better.

There was a welcome light breeze that ruffled the water's surface. The same moving air lifted the water of perspiration from our faces. In the desert we all dressed like the bedouin, the wandering people of the desert, covering our bodies and heads to keep from dehydrating. John, in awesome contrast, stood before us barefoot, bare armed, and free of any head cover.

John didn't speak. He roared! His flashing eyes seemed to penetrate our hearts as deeply as his words. Even the reeds seemed to tremble more before his wrath than the blowing breezes would warrant. No one I had ever heard before impressed me as did John the Baptizer. I listened to every word he said, and found that his words burned themselves into my memory so that I could recall them exactly days, months, even years later.

2

Andrew

"You brood of vipers!" John looked out at the Pharisees and Sadducees. "Who warned you? Do you think you can escape from the coming retribution? Do you really repent? Then prove your repentance by the fruit of your lives."

I looked at the men he was challenging, and saw some of them draw back. They lifted their heads, squared their shoulders, and returned the challenge with biting sarcasm.

"Who are you?" Who gave you authority? Do you think yourself the Messiah? What right do you have to baptize? What do you accomplish by this rite?"

It was easy to see that this argument was an old one. The Pharisees and Sadducees John faced may not have been there before, but John had confronted others of the Sanhedrin before.

"I am only a voice crying in the wilderness, saying, 'Prepare the way of the Lord. Make straight his paths.'" John lowered his voice for this response, but he spoke with just as much assurance. Then he spoke loudly again, "Repent! Repent! The Kingdom of Heaven is at hand!"

"We know who we are," one of the Pharisees said. "We are sons of Abraham! As God's chosen people we are held in His arms. He loves and protects us."

"Do not say, 'We have Abraham for a father!'" John shouted back. "God can make children of Abraham out of these stones here. They would have no more part in the selection than did you!"

He became almost quiet, using his voice as an instrument that could rise or fall, change pitch to higher or lower notes. But that voice urged us to look into our hearts and see how great was our need of repentance. "I call you to repent. Be baptized. Let your sins be washed away."

"Who are you?" The Pharisees asked again. "Why do you baptize?"

"I baptize with water. But there is one who comes after me whose shoes I am not fit to unfasten. He is coming soon. He will baptize with the Holy Spirit, and with fire!"

"What does that mean? We don't understand you!" The Pharisees demanded more information from John. "Are you the Messiah?" The sarcasm in the voice of the Pharisee who asked that question indicated he would not believe it if John should answer with a yes.

"No, I am not." John answered the question as if it had been asked politely. "I came to prepare his way."

"Are you Elijah returned?"

"No, I am not."

"Are you another of the ancient prophets?"

John shook his head, almost wearily, at their inability to comprehend. "I am the voice crying in the wilderness!" Surely we were in the wilderness where John was crying out his message. Surely John was a voice. But even I knew John was quoting the prophet Isaiah when he said this. John was declaring himself a prophet, the prophet who would proclaim the early coming of the Messiah.

He then gave his powerful message. "The Messiah is coming soon. His shovel is in his hand, and he will winnow his threshing floor; the wheat he will gather into his granary, but he will burn the chaff on a fire that will never go out!"

Suddenly his mystical analogies struck home in my heart. I looked no longer at the arguing Pharisees and

Sadducees. I did not look at John either. I looked within myself. If the Messiah was coming as John said, what would he think of me? I was so lazy! Most of the work I did was trying to figure out how to get out of my share of the work in the fishing business.

Looking even deeper I could see more faults. I ate too much. I drank too much. I fought too often over little things. I argued with Simon, complained about how hard my life was, and how little my share of the profits. Still, that wasn't all.

John's eyes were everywhere. I know he looked at the others, but those eyes pierced deep into me, and I was faced with absolute righteousness looking at one who had broken every commandment but 'Thou shalt not kill.' Even that one I was willing to break if I felt I could get away with it.

Yet this man John, the most righteous man I had ever seen, was saying he was not worthy to untie the thongs of the Messiah's sandals!

"My God!" I prayed the ejaculation aloud. "I am guilty of so many sins!"

Philip said, "Me too." I looked at him, and his head hung low. We remembered together some of the unspeakable things we had done.

"Repent!" John roared again. "Repent. Be baptized. Give your lives to God. Let him wash away your past sins, and then you can start anew."

Philip and I walked out into the dirty shallow river. We walked together, side by side until we stood before John. We were the first of the crowd to be baptized that evening. I stayed back while John poured water three times over Philip. There seemed to be no physical change. Then I took my turn.

Water spilled over my head and beard, flowing down and soaking into my clothes. "God is washing away your sins, and they are floating away down the Jordan. You are clean. Stay clean. Obey God's commandments!"

I must say I felt no different at first. Except that I was soaked, and I knew the water that had flowed over my body did help to remove some of the remaining heat of the day. The sun had set, and the cool of the desert evening was upon us. I looked at John, and at Philip, and then back to John. I wasn't sure what I was supposed to do next.

"Go to my camp, both of you," John said. "Wait for me there. There is work for you to do here." Neither of us thought to disobey him.

John's camp was on the east bank of the Jordan. We gathered up our supplies and crossed over. From one side of the river to the other, it wasn't more than fifty paces. Fifty more, up a slight incline, and we were at John's camp, and found ourselves among some of his disciples. They were preparing the evening meal. We sat down near them, and while we waited for John to return, we talked.

"How do you know anything important happened when he baptized us?" I asked.

"I think it has something to do with faith," Philip replied.

"I don't understand."

"Neither do I. But we can assume that all our past sins are washed away as John said. That means we can act as if they never happened. What would it mean to you if you *were* that clean, as if you never once did anything evil?"

"I can't say." I shook my head. Philip's Greek ancestry was coming out. He will philosophize about anything. "I suppose I could look anyone in the eye, even the people I have hurt or cheated in business. I could walk a little taller, maybe."

"Do you remember the fifty-first psalm?" Philip loved to read.

"No." I don't read much, even now. And seldom the psalms.

"It is by David, as most of the psalms are. He wrote it after Nathan the priest accused him of adultery with Bathsheba."

"What did he say?" I wanted to know. I wasn't pretending. Was that evidence something had happened at my baptism? I remembered King David was one of our nation's greatest men, but he was also one of its greatest sinners!

Philip quoted this part of the psalm from memory.

> "Be gracious to me, O God, in thy true love; in the fullness of thy mercy blot out my misdeeds.
> "Wash away my guilt and cleanse me from my sin.
> "For well I know my misdeeds; and my sins confront me all the day long.
> "Against thee, thee only, I have sinned and done what displeases thee, so that thou mayest be proved right in thy charge and just in passing sentence..."

"David was quite a poet," I said. For Philip paused so long I thought he was done. "Did God forgive him?"

"He did, though he punished him." This is what David said in the next psalm.

> "...I am like a spreading olive tree in God's house; for I trust in God's true love for ever and ever.
> "I will praise thee for ever for what thou hast done, and glorify thy name among thy loyal servants; for that is good."

Philip was silent again. And I was silent with him. Maybe, I thought, just maybe God is so good he forgives me and washes away my sins — forgives and washes away the sins of all who repent, as he did for King David.

It was dark, and we had eaten with John's disciples before the Baptizer came back to his camp. A fire was burning, fed by some of the dead branches of trees that grew beside the river. The quarter moon was in the western sky, hanging over the Mount of Olives a hard day's journey away to the west. The stars above shown with an intensity that is often seen in the desert, but that we seldom see around our Galilean lake. The moisture in our atmosphere must interfere with the flow of that starlight. Philip and I didn't talk much with John's disciples. They left us alone, carrying on their own conversation. We were still too caught up in our experience of baptism. We found we had little to say, even to each other.

Then John showed up. First he wasn't there, then he was. It was almost as if he materialized before our eyes. He sat down near us, absorbing the heat from the fire, for it was now really quite cool. John didn't waste time with casual conversation. He immediately began to dig for facts about us.

"I will ask you the same questions the Pharisees ask me," he said. "Who are you? Why did you come here? What did you expect to happen? Why did you choose to be baptized? What do you plan to do with your lives now?"

"I am Philip of Bethsaida. I came to see you — mostly out of curiosity — though I heard you had a powerful message for us all. I expected to listen to you, and try to hear God in what you were saying. I really believe I did hear God, especially when you said, 'Repent.' I believe God made me look inside myself and see what manner of man I had become. I didn't like what I saw. I wanted to be clean, so I was baptized. Now I sit here, obedient to your command."

Philip finished and I sat in silence. I had answers for John too, but I wasn't capable of responding with the precision of the Greek. I am always awed by the mind of Philip.

But John wouldn't leave me alone. He looked at me, and even in the firelight I saw the compelling power of those eyes. "Tell me!" he said.

"I am Andrew, now of Bethsaida, formerly of Caphernaum. I am Simon's young brother, a fisherman on the Sea of Genesseret. Simon and I fish with Zebedee and his sons, James and John." I was rattling along, trying to avoid silence. "I don't like to fish, so I came along with Philip."

My honesty amazed me. Maybe the baptism had taken away my tricky lying tongue? Imagine admitting that I had no real purpose for my journey than to get away from my duty. What would I say next?

"And why did you let me baptize you?" John kept probing.

"I don't know. You are a compelling man. I truly felt the depth of my own depravity, and I surely didn't want to continue in that way."

"I frightened you?" John appeared almost pleased to hear it.

"Yes and no." I tried to speak with real honesty which meant I had to work hard at making the words come out of a part of me I had always kept secret. "I was more afraid of what you said about the one who comes after you. Is the Messiah really coming? Is He coming soon?"

"Very soon. He will come here to me at this place. I know this, for God has revealed it to me." John said this with such assurance that I was unable to ask him the obvious questions. But Philip was not stopped.

"How does God speak to you? Do you see Him? Do you hear Him? Why would He speak to you, and not to us?" Philip didn't pause between these questions. It was as if he had prepared a quiz for John, and required reasonable answers.

"God is with me, and He has made me live as I do since I was a very small boy. I am different. I know no one like me. Even the people with whom I lived by the Asphalt Sea, the Essenes, are not as I am." John looked at Philip, but his eyes were turned inward. "I often speak and hear God's words coming from my mouth before I know what words I will say. Sometimes I try not to speak, for I know what I say will not be liked by the authorities. But I find I can't stop my mouth. The words come out."

Philip didn't pursue the questioning, though this was at best a partial answer. But his asking, and John's careful reply gave me courage to ask a question of my own.

"Why did you ask us to stay, to come here?" I asked.

"God directed me to do so. But I don't know why." He looked at me with a real challenge in his glance. "If you think I am wrong in telling you to stay, then go. Go if you can."

I looked at Philip. Philip looked at me. I tried to make myself stand and walk away. I think Philip did too. But I was not able to move. The power that controlled John seemed to be controlling us too.

Finally I had the strength to look away from John's eyes. I turned to his other disciples who had sat on the other side of the fire, listening to us. One of them looked at me and smiled. "Looks like we have two more disciples," he said.

That was when the conversation ended. Abruptly, John left the fire, and stepped out into the darkness. I had nothing more to say to Philip, and I didn't think I could absorb any more of my own thoughts. I moved away from the fire, stretched out on the ground and covered myself with my outer robe. Whatever discipleship of John the Baptizer meant, I was sure it would be better accomplished if I were well rested.

I stared at the stars for hours. They stared back at me and winked, but gave no clue to my future. What would Simon say about my not coming home? How long would I serve this John? How would we survive? Where did the money come from to keep John and his disciples in food?

I fell asleep knowing that there were many questions someone needed to answer if I were to be at peace in this new life. I remember that as I dozed off I heard Philip reciting another portion of the 51st psalm.

> "Create a pure heart in me, O God, and give me a new and steadfast spirit;
> "Do not drive me from thy presence or take the holy spirit from me;
> "Revive in me the joy of thy deliverance and grant me a willing spirit to uphold me."

I felt my soul respond with a quiet "So be it."

The next day we found that life with John was very simple. Each of us was responsible for our own food, clothing, and shelter. John solved this problem for himself by living off the land. Animal skins covered his torso, and were tied together with a belt of leather. He caught insects as he walked, killed and swallowed them. As there were ample large insects by the river, he more or less munched on them all day. He also consumed honey that he must have gathered when he found a beehive. This was available for us, if we wanted it. Also we could make our supplies available for him and the other disciples if we chose to do so. Our only shelter was the trees. They kept off the brightness of the sun, and would have kept off the rain, though we did not stay with John long enough for the dry summer to come to an end. The lee side of a hill could be found if the wind whipped up the dry dirt and sand of the area.

Our purpose for being with John seemed to be just to be with him, and to teach him and the others what might be useful knowledge of God's intent for us. The disciples there were far more interested in Philip and his talk of the gods of the Greeks than they were in me. I exhausted my store of knowledge in less than a half hour, and none of what I knew was new to them. It was as if I were having a first time at school among students who had spent years in learning. I accepted the role of listener and observer.

But I had one valuable asset of which I was unaware. That was my fellowship with the fishing community, and particularly with Zebedee and his sons. John learned of this, and told me he was related to them. It seems his mother was cousin to Zebedee's wife. He asked a lot about them, and then asked if I had ever met their other cousin from Nazareth, Jesus BarJoseph.

When I said I had seen him often, both in Nazareth and in Caphernaum, he took what seemed to be every spare minute to ask me what I knew of Jesus.

"When did you first meet him?" I told him. "What did you think of him then?"

"He seemed especially bright. He seemed to have a magnetic power. Once I was walking in the hills and came upon him, and he said he had caused me to come to him because he wanted me there."

"What do you think of him now?" John studied me carefully as I replied, and then turned away, almost angry, when I said, "I don't. I don't see him often, and when I do it is by the lake, and I am busy with my work as a fisherman."

John turned back to me after a few minutes. "You will see him here soon. He was here a month ago, and I baptized him."

We didn't have the courage to ask John what he meant by his statements when he was preaching about the Messiah. But Philip approached some of John's other disciples and asked them. "What does the Messiah do? What does John mean by 'His winnowing fork is in his hand,' or 'the ax is already laid to the root of the tree?'"

"We aren't sure," one replied. "But we know that the Kingdom of Heaven is supposed to be coming, and that the Messiah will introduce the Kingdom to us. Those who are fit for the Kingdom, He will bring in, and those who are not fit, He will exclude."

"We see John talking to soldiers and tax collectors. They ask him what they must do, and he has an answer for them. Will the Messiah let such people into the Kingdom? Soldiers? Really? Are they not servants of Herod, or temple guards? What right would such have for the Kingdom?" I nodded my agreement with Philip as he asked these questions.

"John doesn't say any are bound to be cast out or refused entry," replied another. "What he does say is that all must show signs of loving obedience to God and His law."

Philip persisted. "But where will the Kingdom be established? Will the Messiah sit on a throne in Jerusalem? Will he cast out the Romans? Will he overthrow the entire Roman government? How many legions does he have?"

The disciples shook their heads. "We do not know these answers," the first man said. We know that we felt it was right for us to stay here with John, or John felt it was right for him to ask us to stay. We know John will be a part of the Kingdom when it comes. We know he has an inner knowledge that the Kingdom is coming, and that the Messiah is about to appear. Why do you ask these questions? How would complete answers help? Even if we knew them all, you would still need to have faith in the teaching."

Another said, "We saw you baptized. We know you repented before you had that done. You are now in the obedience with us. Be content."

"But we have families. We have friends back home. If the Kingdom of Heaven is at hand, should we not go forth to them and urge them to....to....to...?" Philip was tongue tied at last. He seemed to know that there was no special act one could do to be a part of the Kingdom. The coming Messiah would have his choices made. There would be no hope of influencing him by last minute actions.

But if that were the case, what hope did we have in the repentance and baptism we had undergone?

The disciples smiled at Philip and me with accepting glances. Our short lives and minor influence could do so little. Better for us to watch and wait with John.

A few days later I was faced with an angry brother. He had grown weary of waiting for me to return, and set out to find me. He stomped into camp and stood in front of me with his hands on his hips. He had me at a disadvantage, for he was always larger than I, and I was reclining against a tree. I had to look up at his storm filled face. "Hi Simon," I said, surprised at how much at peace I was in his presence.

"Andrew," he almost shouted. "You have been gone six weeks! Our fishing business is a partnership. You must return home! Now!! What in hell are you doing here?"

I knew he was really upset, for he didn't often resort to profanity. "I am sorry, Simon," I said. "I didn't mean to abandon you. But I cannot come home now. I must remain here to be with John."

"Why?" He stared at me, arms folded across his chest, his entire attitude demanding a sound reason for my not obeying him.

"John commanded Philip and me to stay." I feared the next question.

"Why?"

"I don't know why. He just said to stay."

"What do you do?"

"Nothing. Really nothing at all. We sit around and talk. We talk to John and listen to him. And we talk to his other disciples, and listen to them." Listening to myself, I knew I didn't sound very practical. Also, I knew I wasn't convincing Simon. I tried a new approach. "Look, brother, stay a few days and listen to him. I can't tell you what power he has. But you can listen, and find out for yourself."

Simon walked away from me and stood looking across the Jordan. The heat was really draining us that day. Suddenly he took off his clothes and jumped into the river, splashing water over his body. He turned back to look at me and laughed. "All right, you dreamer, I'll stay and hear this John. I've certainly heard enough about him to make me curious. But I won't stay here in this camp with you. I'll go back across the Jordan and find a place for myself. A little dose of absolute quiet will do me no harm at all."

I thought of Anna, his mother-in-law, and of his small house, where her voice was never still. "Yes, Simon. Take a few days. John will be speaking again tomorrow. He does every day."

Simon jumped out of the water, gave me a hug that drove the breath from my lungs, and soaked me at the same time. He grabbed his clothes, and walked naked across the river. He put his clothes on, when he was across, waved at me, and moved upstream. I saw him on the edge of the crowd once or twice the next day. Then I forgot about him.

3

Andrew

It couldn't have been more than three days after Simon came to find me that I experienced one of the most exciting times of my life. The day began simply enough. Just as on any other day there by the Jordan, Philip and I awoke to the sounds of the other disciples moving about. This was normal procedure, for both of us were used to working at night, netting fish, and preparing them for market, while John's other disciples were daylight laborers.

It is hard to change the habits of a lifetime. Farmers who have risen at dawn to care for their animals and do their other daily chores will continue to get up early long after the necessity for doing so has been taken away. Merchants who have produce for sale must buy it at the market early in the day from those same farmers, and then take it to their place of business. It may have been hard on the other disciples to see us sleeping late, but surely it was harder on us to always be awakened before our bodies were ready to rise. That morning the others seemed even more agitated than usual. I asked them about it.

"You are moving about especially early this morning," I said, glancing at the still dark sky. We had barely enough light to see the outline of our neighbors. The skyline to the east was just beginning to outline the mountains with a golden haze that promised another totally cloudless and stifling day. To the west, the last of the stars was dimming. The moon seemed to hang directly over Jerusalem.

"John is going to speak early today," Stephen, one of the oldest of the disciples, replied. "We are crossing the Jordan to wake the pilgrims. Hundreds of them arrived yesterday evening, and some of them have no supplies. They will have to start back home, and buy food for their journey in Jericho. John wants them to hear his message. So...."

We arose from our places in the sand, and after stretching out some of the kinks in our muscles, we followed them across the river. On the other side we put on our clothing, tied our sandal straps, and joined the crowd. In a few minutes John began to speak.

"The Kingdom of Heaven is at hand," he began quietly. "The Kingdom of Heaven is at hand. Repent. Save yourselves." It was the same message as before. It was always the same message, but occasionally he would give another example of what the Messiah would do to those who failed to be good citizens of that Kingdom. The Messiah would be of the line of David. (Not too hard a task, for each of us claimed ancestry to him if we were of the tribe of Judah. It is a thousand years since David married four wives and sired many children through them, and many more through his concubines. His son Solomon helped spread David's line by siring an untold number. (The history of our people says Solomon had three hundred wives and seven hundred concubines. His children may have been counted, but the records were lost.) The house and lineage of David was not what attracted me to the idea of a Messiah. It was the work of David that excited me.

Though Moses brought our people from Egypt, and Joshua began the work of establishing this land as ours, fighting the natives for it town by town, he never completed the work. The Philistines remained in control of the coastal lands, the best of the land of our country for farming, and the best cities for trading with the world were on our coast.

David gathered the tribes together into a stronger union than they had under our first king, Saul. From the tribes David gathered an army, trained it, and then subdued or destroyed all the other peoples of our promised land. It had taken three hundred years from the time Joshua led our people out of the wilderness until David completed the work of acquiring the land God had promised us. Only under David did the country become fully ours.

What Joshua initiated, and David completed, David's son, Solomon strengthened. It was during Solomon's reign that our people controlled all the land from Egypt to Babylonia, from the South Sea to the mountains that rimmed the north borders of Lebanon. Many cities and nations beyond our borders were forced to pay tribute to Solomon. Ours was a truly great nation then.

It was a great land, flowing with milk and honey, in those days. As God's people, we lived in His Kingdom, with an assurance that our enemies would never triumph over us.

But we lost it all, never to fully regain it, when Solomon's son was unable to keep the union of the tribes. The ten northern tribes set up their own capital at Samaria, and we were never fully unified again.

Occasionally we Israelites had control of our land, and acted again as a united people. When we did, we were able to manage our nation for ourselves. Many of us believed then, as many do to this day, that the times our people were strong and prosperous were the times when we were in obedience to God's law. The promise has been with us for thirteen hundred years. Moses spoke of it, as did the prophets. The Messiah would come, unite us, and we would be a powerful and free people once more.

The prophecies indicated the Messiah would be our king, established as our ruler, and crowned by God Himself.

The Messiah, using God's power, would overthrow whatever enemy held our country captive. The Messiah would correct the evil of the priesthood, as well as of the money changers who made our worship into a profit making venture for themselves and the priests.

These facts were known to John's audience. When John said that all who were not sorry for their pasts, and ready to live according to the tenets of God's Law, would be destroyed by the Messiah when he came, the people paid attention. The Messiah didn't need these weak and disobedient people. He could take a small and disciplined army of three hundred — or even less — as had Gideon, and with the few, and the strong arm of God, overthrow our oppressors. Or, by his power, he could train but a dozen, one to represent each of the twelve tribes of Israel, and the Lord God would make the miracle of the Kingdom a reality.

The message of John was that the Messiah would soon be with us. He promised this in every speech, and he always warned that the weak, the evil, the unrepentant, and the disobedient, would be destroyed.

That morning, as on most other days, his message was very effective. Soldiers of the Temple Guard asked, "What can we do?" and John didn't demand they resign from their work. He knew they had lives to live, and families to feed. "Don't bear false witness. Be content with your wages," he said. And he gave sound advice like this to many others.

I asked one of John's disciples why John had emphasized contentment with wages. The man laughed. "Surely you haven't spent much time in Jerusalem. The guards seek bribes from everyone. Anyone with money need not fear arrest by them!"

When John finished baptizing those who came forward, he walked to the shore, and sat on its bank, wiggling his toes in the water. The hot breeze evaporated the water from his body, helping him to bear the heat of the day. Occasionally

Philip and I would throw water over our heads, or jump in and out of the river, so we too could feel the pleasure of cool air on our skins.

John sat with us as a friend. He reminisced about his past. "When I was with the Essenes," he said, "we had a flowing cold stream that came out of the mountains and bubbled up into the cistern where we were baptized. There we could go to cool off during the day, and we always went there for a spiritual cleansing whenever we broke the Law of God. The men of that community are strong hearted. They pray and obey, and work with diligence at their tasks. I worked with forty others in the Scriptorum where we copied the Law and the Prophets and other documents written by leaders of the community. There we labored diligently for six days, and rested as diligently on the seventh."

He mused as he looked at the people who had come to hear him. Most of them were packing up their camping gear and getting ready to leave. "These people are not required to live in total obedience to God's Law. They have it quite easy. Love God, and keep away from doing things that hurt others is all that is required of them. If they did that only, they would discover that their lives would be almost as happy as if the Kingdom were here already."

Then John grew tense. "Look!" he whispered. "There he is! Behold the Lamb of God who takes away the sin of the world!" We looked in the direction John was looking, and we saw walking slowly through the crowd, his head bent down, as though he were in deep thought, a man of middle years. As he drew closer I recognized him! I was amazed to see the one John was designating as the Messiah was the Zebedee's cousin from Nazareth, Jesus BarJoseph!

"John," I asked, allowing all my doubts to show in my voice, "How do you know that man is the Messiah?"

"God told me." John looked so sure of himself when he said that! "I saw the heavens open, and the Spirit descend like a dove and land on Jesus and stay there. God told me years before that would be the way I would know the Messiah. He assured me I would meet the Messiah face to face." He was silent then, and we sat in silence while we watched Jesus walk to the river, and start to walk through it toward its east bank.

"He looks like any other man," Philip said.

"He is like any other man," I said. "I know him. I've known him for at least fifteen years. He is a carpenter from Nazareth. He works with his father in his father's shop there, and often he goes out to work in other towns. He helped build the palace in Tiberias. He takes his holidays with James and John, fishing with them on our lake."

I poured all this out to fill in time as I examined my own disappointment. The Messiah has to be big enough to fill important sandals. To be the follower of David and Solomon from our distant past, of Judas Maccabeas the great leader from two centuries ago who is the famous ancestor of our foolish and weak Herods, one must demand that the Messiah has to be important and worthy. The thought of the Messiah being a small town carpenter in his thirties was bad enough. But to have the Messiah a man I knew, had seen fulfilling none of the promises of leadership in the decade and a half I had known him was worse. It demanded more faith than I had.

"Jesus BarJoseph? Jesus of Nazareth? Only the first name is right!" I said. Joshua means savior, you know. As Joshua, our leader who served under Moses, and then gained this land for us, was our savior twelve centuries ago, it would be appropriate for another one called 'savior' to be the Messiah for our century.

While I thought my way through to proclaiming my rejection of John's declaration that Jesus was the Messiah, Philip remained still. His eyes followed the figure of Jesus as the man stopped a little up stream, and seemed to look at all the land, the slowly flowing river with its sinuous bends, the trees and reeds along the banks, and we people who were still resting on the shore. Philip watched Jesus, studied him, searched for signs that would make him believe as John did that here was the Messiah.

"If he is the Messiah, we should follow him," Philip said. Then he looked apologetically at John. The thought struck me at the same time. If we followed after Jesus, would we be turning away from John? Would we be disobeying him? Showing disloyalty?

"Go after him," John said. "It is your destiny."

We didn't pause to say 'goodby' to John, or to his other disciples. We simply walked across the stream and began to follow Jesus up the inclining path toward the eastern heights. As the man was walking quite slowly, it didn't take us long to catch him. He turned to us and asked, "What do you want?"

"Master," Philip asked, "where are you staying?" I was glad Philip spoke. Maybe the things John said made me think there would be something different about Jesus than I had known before. Maybe there was a new aura about him. But as we came up to him and he spoke to us, I found myself tongue-tied. How does one address someone you have known all your life, and who now turns out to be the most important person in the world? The chosen one to bring in the Kingdom?

Jesus' look at each of us showed he was fully aware of us, and of who we were. This was neither magic nor superhuman power. It was just good observation. Knowing me, and knowing we had been talking with John, he could deduce we were John's disciples, and that John had sent us to follow. He could know Philip and I were friends by our association, and probably by our dress, for we were both in the garb of the people of the lake country.

"Come and see," Jesus said.

He didn't say anything to us as we walked, sometimes beside him when the path was wide enough to accommodate us, sometimes behind him as we ascended narrow places. We felt comfortable with him, and comfortable with the silence, as if we had known him and been his friends for all of our lives. He demanded nothing of us, our attention, or anything else. When we came to a very small cave in the hillside, an indentation that looked as if it had been carved out of the rock by someone many centuries ago, we sat down with Jesus and looked back on the valley beneath us. The exertion of climbing in the heat of the day used up most of our energy, but the height seemed to provide us some relief from the heat. I estimated we must have climbed to a point at least a thousand cubits higher than the place where we started at the river's edge. It was the fifth hour of the day when we began to follow Jesus, so we had been walking a full four hours.

The haze of heat in the valley gave it an appearance of movement so that the slowly winding river could have been a living snake. Across the valley to the north we could see the mountain on which Saul and Jonathan were slain in their last battle against the Philistines. The land where we were sitting had been our people's for three hundred years before Kings Saul and David. Moses and Joshua conquered the countries east of the Jordan, and two of our tribes stayed on that side, accepting the territory as their share of the gift from the Lord our God.

Syrians, Assyrians, Babylonians, Greeks, Egyptians, and now Romans have attacked us and sometimes conquered us, but none have held us captive for long. We have always formed a resistance movement, strengthened ourselves to become a full fledged army, and have driven the oppressors from our homeland. Though the Romans are mightier than any enemy before them, and have great ability to govern the provinces they claim as a part of their empire, they will be defeated some day. Though their rule is often very fair by comparison to that of some of our own kings and governors, they are foreigners without religion, or with foolish beliefs in human beings as their gods. The Lord God is our King, and by His mighty arm the enemy will be driven out. These were my thoughts as I sat beside Jesus at the close of that day.

Such are the thoughts of most of the men of our land. Our scriptures have promised us the Messiah, the great leader, who will bind us together as did King David, and as a united body under his leadership we will be invincible. We know this will happen. But when? And who will that Messiah be? Those have been the questions, at least until now.

Is it really now? I shuddered a little at the thought. How exciting that is! Is this really the Messiah before us? Would God choose a carpenter as the Messiah? I remembered God chose a shepherd in David. He chose a farmer in Gideon. He chose a shepherd in Moses. Yes, I was sure it was God's choice. God could choose anyone, from any walk of life. I remembered the ultimate proof of God's choice. Twice God chose women to be the instruments of our freedom.

"Jesus," I said hesitantly, "tell us about yourself. Who are you? What plans have you?"

"You know me, Andrew," Jesus said. Then, surprisingly, for I am sure he had never met Philip, and had not been introduced to him as we climbed to this primitive camp site, he said, "You know me too, Philip." That statement certainly caught our complete attention. We waited for him to proceed.

"My name is Jesus, as was the name of Moses' commander who led the people into our homeland, across this very river that we see below us. The name means, 'savior.' My mother has told me an angel visited her and told her to name me this name. The angel told her this before she was ever married, before I was conceived. I am of the house and lineage of David the King. Born in Bethlehem, the village where David was born, and where he lived until he joined Saul's army.

"All my life I have known I have a destiny. My thoughts are not as other men's thoughts. My understanding is not as other men's understanding. As I read the scriptures as a boy in the synagogue, I knew them already. They were burned into my mind, and I comprehended with a depth no one could understand as I offered my understanding to them. Even the priests in Jerusalem, the great theologians in the Temple, were baffled by the questions I asked, and by the answers I provided.

"But it wasn't until I followed my inner direction to seek out my cousin, John, in the wilderness, that I had a confirmation of who I am, and a growing understanding of what my life is to be." He paused for a long time, looking much as he did when we first saw him crossing the stream earlier in the day. It was as if he were listening to someone speak to him, and the voice he heard was so important he had to hear that and concentrate on that only.

"You heard John call me the 'Lamb of God.' You heard him tell you of the dove-like descent of the Spirit upon me." We nodded yes, though he had not asked us, but told us. How odd, we thought it, that he knew what John had told us, though he was far beyond the range of hearing, and had not been looking at any of us. "The Spirit of the Lord is upon me. He has taken me into the wilderness and kept me there several weeks. It was there I met our most formidable enemy, the ruler of the Earth. The Devil is that enemy. He offered me the power to change stones into bread, and I said, 'No.' Then he offered me the glory of being king over all the kingdoms of the world, and I refused him. Then he tempted me to prove I am God's anointed by calling for angels to protect me as I put myself into deadly danger. When I refused that too, he left me. But I know he is near. I know he will be back. Temptation from the Devil is our greatest danger, as he is our greatest enemy."

Neither Philip nor I were used to such deep and emotionally disturbing statements. We were silent before Jesus, studying him. Then he smiled at us, and the whole world seemed to light up though dusk was falling, and the light of the sun was fading beyond the western hills. "Come, let us break bread together," Jesus said. We did that. Our fellowship was great and joyous as we ate our simple meal of bread and honey. Soon we stretched out on the ground where we could look up and watch the stars parade across the sky. I was tired from the long day, and soon closed my eyes, knowing the stars could perform their work without my help.

During the following years I dreamed strange dreams quite often when I slept near Jesus. I know I dreamed that night, and do not know if some of the things I dreamed were a part of our conversation, or if some of the conversation was a part of the dreams. The dreams were not the usual movements of pictures and activities I could not quite share, but had to observe, with an inner knowledge that this was only my soul on a journey that my body could not experience. When I dreamed that night, and on the other dreaming nights in Jesus' presence, all of me participated. I won't tell you of what I dreamed then. I may never tell you or anyone else of those dreams. I haven't the words to tell them. But they were real. Most real.

Those dreams were certainly a part of my decision to accept what John had said. When I awoke early the next morning I was sure Jesus was the Messiah. And, without his telling me, I knew what I had to do. "Goodbye Master," I said. "I have my work to do." Philip said the same, and we departed from Jesus, each of us going our own way after we had descended the path we had climbed only the afternoon before. The time was short. But we knew our lives were changed forever by what we had already experienced with Jesus.

Was it by chance that Simon came to the lower Jordan just when he did? I knew that I had to find him and bring him to Jesus. How long a journey it would have been had Simon not come to find me! It would have been a three day walk each way, walking as far as possible each day through stifling heat. The question could not help but come to me, would Simon be willing to walk so far to meet a Messiah he already knew as a carpenter?

Walking down the pathway was easier than climbing, and I was crossing the Jordan by the third hour of the day. Another hour of inquiring among the other campers, and searching along the riverbank, and I found my brother. "Simon!" I called, excitement filling my voice with a vibrancy I don't recall having heard before from my own throat.

"Andrew!" He mimicked me. "Are you ready to go home with me now? I heard John speak yesterday, and he does have a powerful message. I even let him baptize me. I think I know the attraction he has. But Andrew, you are a fisherman. We have a work to do that is important. If we don't fish, people won't eat. And some of the people who don't eat will be you and me and my family!"

I heard him, but I didn't respond. I stood before him with a feeling of love for him I had not known before, though I am sure it was there. Something in the last day had changed me, and I felt a flow of tenderness for this big bluff demanding man that I know was something of what God felt for him. My silence, and perhaps my look penetrated Simon's awareness, and he let himself be open to me.

"Why did you come?" he asked in a quiet and reasonable tone. "I'm sorry I mocked you when you called. Sitting still by this stream has not done me that much good. The fish jump, and I have no net. The birds mock me. I sweat just sitting still, and I wonder why I didn't go right back home." He would have rambled on, but I touched his arm. "Why did you come?"

"We have found the Messiah." I made the statement, knowing it was the first time I would declare Jesus to be such, but certainly not the last. Simon studied me, looking deep into my eyes. I half expected him to tell me he didn't believe me. But he was silent about that.

He asked, "Where?" And before I could reply, he said, "Take me to him." Without pausing for rest or refreshment, I led him back the way I had come. We didn't talk much along the way, except for me to say what John the Baptist had said about the Messiah, and how he recognized him. I didn't tell Simon the name of the Messiah, or that he was a man we knew already. Perhaps I wanted him to have that as a surprise. Perhaps I feared he wouldn't come if he knew I was leading him to Jesus of Nazareth.

When we came to the little cave, we found Jesus sitting with his back to us, looking into the distance. He turned as we approached, and said to Simon, "You are Simon, son of John. You shall be called Peter."

Simon's face was a study of conflicting emotions. "You? You, Jesus of Nazareth? You are the Messiah?"

"You said it." Jesus' face was still, but a smile played around the corner of his mouth. That was the first time, but often thereafter I heard Jesus use those three words. "You said it." The words implied that the questioner spoke the truth, that he had already answered his own question, and that no more comment need be made.

Simon looked like he didn't believe it. "Can we sit and talk with you for a while?" he asked. Jesus looked pleased to have us. We sat with him and he answered Simon's questions as patiently as he had answered ours the evening before. Jesus broke bread with us, and we shared a skin of new wine.

We stayed the night with Jesus, and I dreamed again. In the morning I asked Simon how he had slept, and a look came into his eyes that indicated he too had dreamed. "Not well," he said. "The wine must have had something in it that bothered my mind."

Jesus told us he was starting for Galilee, indicating that he would be pleased with our companionship along the way. I knew my time with John the Baptizer was over, and it was as reasonable to walk with the Messiah to our destination as it was to walk alone. I had no idea where my life would be taking me. But I knew I really wanted to be with Jesus.

Before long we saw Philip climbing the path with another man as his companion. At first we couldn't make out who the other was, and when I saw finally that it was Nathaniel, I was about to say so when Simon signaled me to be quiet. I knew he had a reason, and decided to go along with him.

When we met the two, Jesus greeted them. "Here is an Israelite worthy of the name; there is nothing false in him." He looked intently at Nathaniel.

Nathaniel's surprised answer was, "How do you come to know me?" It was then I understood why Simon didn't want me to greet them or call them by name. He was looking to see what Jesus would do and if Jesus had the inexplicable power of knowing a man without having met him before.

"I saw you under the fig tree before Philip spoke to you." Jesus spoke this in a matter of fact way as if anyone could see a day's walk, and hear a conversation between two men that distance away.

Nathaniel grasped something I didn't then, and wouldn't come to really believe for at least another two years. In fact, even now, knowing all I do about Jesus' life and death and resurrection, I still don't believe in my deepest being every moment of the time.

"Rabbi," Nathaniel said. "You are the Son of God; you are the King of Israel."

As his exclamation surprised me, Jesus' reply shook my soul.

"Is this the ground of your faith, that I told you I saw you under the fig tree? You shall see greater things than that!" Then he looked at Simon and Philip and me and added, "In truth, in very truth I tell you all, you shall see heaven wide open, and God's angels ascending and descending upon the Son of Man."

My dream! I looked at Simon and Philip and knew it was their dream too. Jesus of Nazareth was surely somebody powerful!

4

Andrew

The next three days we walked together, beginning a way of life for ourselves that we followed for much of the next three years. Jesus led us north toward his home town of Nazareth. Or rather, he chose to go that way, and we to follow. Then we were a group of five men; Jesus, Simon and I, sons of John, Philip the Greek, and Nathaniel. I must say that the experience of walking with Jesus was as normal as any other walk I have taken in my life. Yet it had a quality about it that made it very different. I'll try to explain what I mean by that, but it will be difficult. Life with Jesus was, and is, so much unlike our lives were before we were with Him that one must experience being with Him in order to understand that life without Him is, by comparison, not living at all.

When we left the Jordan River, we walked over to Jericho before we began our hike to the north. There we bought figs, dates, bread, and a wineskin of new wine for the journey. We didn't need to carry water, for though we were walking through the desert, the Jordan would always be near until we began to climb through the fertile valleys into the western hills. Jesus had decided it was time to go home to Nazareth to see his mother, brothers, and sisters. Simon, who liked the nickname, 'Peter' that Jesus gave him, Philip, and I, all decided we would walk with Jesus to the south shore of our lake, and then proceed home to our families and our work. That way we would have two full days with the man we already called 'Master,' and we thought we could part from him, at least for a while, after that. Nathaniel would go on with Jesus, as his home was in Cana, close to Nazareth.

Jesus is like each and all of us. But Jesus is different from anyone I have ever known. He is totally aware. The birds in the air, the insects buzzing, the gentle breeze blowing, the people we meet along the road, the flowers, trees, yes all of the plants, even the rocks and the soil are all a part of His awareness. Nathaniel grasped this when Jesus told him of His awareness of the conversation between Philip and Nathaniel under the fig tree, a day's walk away.

The impact of this awareness on each of us would have been unbearable, if it were not a part of Jesus' total interest in everyone and everything. When Jesus talked with me, he really listened to me, to what I said, and to what I was trying to say. But even while He listened to me, He knew what the others were saying and thinking. Yes! He even knows what we are thinking!

Does it bother you that I speak of Him as one who is here, and who is alive? I must. For I know that He is here. He is alive among us. The fact that we cannot see Him does not remove Him from us.

We didn't know then that our walk with Jesus was the first of many journeys we would be making with Him during the coming years. We only knew we were so impressed by Him that we wanted to be with Him, even if it meant breaking away from the second most impressive person we had ever met, John the Baptizer. As we were walking along, we all tried to walk beside Jesus. But there was only room for one on His right hand, and another on His left. I yielded to Simon, because I always yielded to him. Philip yielded to Nathaniel. We two old friends walked side by side behind the three, and we listened to their talk, interjecting our thoughts and comments occasionally. But even walking behind Him, we knew He knew we were with Him, and His interest in each of us was no less than in the men who strolled at His side, touching His sleeve or His hand from time to time as they moved along the well worn road.

I'm not sure what Simon and Nathaniel had to say to Jesus, or what He had to say to them. My awareness increased immeasurably when I was with Him, and it remains high when I remember I am with Him now. Only when I forget the presence of Jesus, do I fall back into the minimum level of awareness that is the standard for those who do not know Him, who are not His companions in life.

But I remember what He said to me when we were stopped to rest. Walking in the morning hours in the desert, we could cover far more ground than in the afternoons when the heat bore down upon us. But we were in no hurry. We had no schedule to keep. The first day we traveled half way from Jericho to Bethshean at the foot of the valley of Jezreel. We walked, and we talked, mostly asking Jesus questions that would help us to know Him at the deepest level. At least I needed to know who Jesus thought He was.

"Andrew," Jesus said, "your heart is full of questions. You have much you would know of me. Yet you were not so curious about my cousin, John." And He was right! But how did He know?

"How do you know that?" I asked. "How do you know what Nathaniel and Philip say when they are not with you?" I was in awe of Him, yet I knew in my heart that honest questions would not anger Him. "John calls you the Messiah," I said. "Are you the Messiah? What is the work of the Messiah? If you are He who is to come, then what is your plan? Will we have any part in your life and work?"

"The Father of all is my Father," Jesus said. "He has revealed much to me that I cannot tell you now. Even if I were to say it, it would be words that you could not comprehend. Know that John's teaching is true. The Kingdom of Heaven is at hand. As I call you to be ready for it, you must call others. Follow me."

A touch of bitterness filled my heart. "I have been following you the whole day," I said. I have walked in your footsteps in the dust of the road."

"And you wanted to walk by my side?" Jesus asked. "I was as near to you as I was to Simon, as near as to Nathaniel, no further away from you than from Philip." It was true that each of us could have touched Him as readily as the others, but I felt we were not favored for we had seen but the back of his head half the day.

"You and Philip have known what it is to be the first," Jesus said. "You must taste the experience of being the last as well. But last or first does not matter. It is being in the Kingdom that matters. Do not fret, Andrew. I have chosen you."

"Jesus," I asked, "where are you traveling now?" If I couldn't be told of the great plan of the Messiah, the least He could tell me was of his immediate destination.

"Tonight I will sleep in the desert south of Bethshean," He said. "Tomorrow will take care of itself. But Nathaniel has told me of a wedding he plans to attend in Cana." He paused. "You know Cana, Andrew. It is a thriving village in the hill country of Galilee, near my family home at Nazareth. I feel called to go there with Nathaniel. Weddings are joyful occasions, and it is joy that will be the primary sign of the coming Kingdom."

None of my questions were answered. Yet I felt satisfied. His eyes looked deep into mine when He spoke, so I had difficulty concentrating on His words. Then I discovered it was not the words of Jesus I needed to hear, but the Word of Jesus that He was as true as He appeared to be. That information came through so strongly that I set aside my doubts of Him or of the future. Being with Him was enough.

That night I dreamed again of the angels ascending and descending on Jesus. The beauty of the dream was not diminished by having it a third time. The awe of the dreaming experience was as great, and it remained with me even longer upon awakening. Our land is a bountiful and beautiful one, and my home beside the lake is as beautiful as any I have seen on this Earth. But the beauty of the angels, and the glory of the beauty of Jesus in that dream were placed in a setting of such magnificence that I could never describe it to you. As the light of day reveals the colorful landscape about us, so the light that seemed to come from Jesus made everything I had ever seen before glow with a new beauty I had never known. And all I saw of the landscape where He and the angels walked was even more glorious.

Again the next morning I knew without being told that each of the others had dreamed the same dream. We looked with fresh awareness on the Man who walked with us, within reach of us all, and felt a gladness boiling up in our hearts we knew was reality. Jesus looked into our eyes and smiled at us a knowing and gentle smile that captured our hearts.

At the crossroads of Bethshean, Jesus turned to the left and started up the valley of Jezreel. Simon and I looked at each other, and we both looked at Philip. But Philip was not looking at us. He had his back to us as he walked up the road leading to the northwest. He was walking beside Jesus and Nathaniel. I looked at Simon with loving understanding. He had his family back home, and he wanted to be with them. He had his responsibility to provide for them. The decision had to be his.

He could go on alone to the lake, or he could come along with us. I made my choice, knowing in my heart I had no choice. I had to follow Jesus.

It didn't surprise me that Simon followed too, and he did so very quickly. He was walking shoulder to shoulder with Jesus, on Jesus' right as we began to ascend out of the valley. Later we were to hear Jesus say, "He that loves wife or husband more than me is not worthy of me." Even in the third day of knowing Jesus as the Messiah, Simon's love for Him was so great he was ready to abandon all for Him.

As we climbed into the hills we talked. We even sang a few of the psalms. Psalm 148 flowed easily through our lips.

> O praise the Lord. Praise the Lord out of heaven; praise Him in the heights. Praise Him all his angels, praise Him all his host. Praise Him sun and moon; praise Him, all you shining stars; praise Him, heaven of heavens, and you waters above the heavens. Let them all praise the Name of the Lord, for He spoke the word and they were created; He established them for ever and ever by an ordinance which shall never pass away.

That evening I drew Nathaniel aside and asked him, "What was your conversation with Philip that Jesus overheard?" He looked a little embarrassed.

"I was relaxing under a fig tree, just as Jesus said," he replied. "Philip came up to me and said, 'We have met the man spoken of by Moses in the Law, and spoken of by the prophets. It is Jesus, son of Joseph, from Nazareth.' I snorted at that. I knew Jesus, and I have known Nazareth all my life. There is no more common town on the face of the earth. Life there is dull. The people there are dull. They are set in their ways. Nothing has changed there from what it was like before the Romans came. The Greeks didn't change Nazareth. No one ever changed Nazareth. But you know Nazareth, Andrew. You visited there yourself once, years ago."

I didn't reply, but I thought about what he said. He was right. Nazareth is a dull town. In fact, I suspect all of

Galilee is a dull region. When armies have marched through our part of the country, we have simply stepped aside and let them go by. If they stopped and took control over us, we accepted their right to power, for to oppose them meant punishment, imprisonment, or death. If the cities Hazor, Gazor, Megiddo, Jerusalem, and Samaria fought and won, the Jews were in power. If those cities fell, the foreigners were in power. Some of our men joined resistance movements, but most stayed home, doing what their ancestors did before them, living quiet lives, and watching history repeat itself.

Nathaniel continued. "I said, 'Can anything good come out of Nazareth?' I meant it then. I guess I mean it now. The prophets never said anything about the Messiah coming out of the North.

"But Isaiah does say, "He shall be called a 'nezer,' I said, not realizing I had that knowledge in me from my days as a poor scholar in the synagogue. Perhaps the rabbi had taught me more than I knew.

But a 'nezer' isn't necessarily a Nazarene." Nathaniel was a real student. "'Nezer' means 'branch' and the reference, if it is a Messianic reference at all, means that the Messiah will be of a branch of the line of David." He asked, "Did you overhear my questions of Him about His ancestry?" I nodded. "You see, though I proclaimed Him the 'Son of God,' the King of Israel,' I soon had a heart full of doubts."

We looked over to where Jesus was sitting quietly, talking with Simon and Philip. "He looks so ordinary from here," I said. "Yet when He looks straight into my eyes, I am sure He knows me more than ... more than I know myself." Jesus chose that moment to look across at us. He smiled. Somehow He included us in the intimate conversation He was having with the others.

"What of our dream?" I asked Nathaniel. "You had it too. I know you did. What does it mean?"

"It must mean that He is highly favored of God," Nathaniel answered. "I must accept that as I accept the fact that He knows what it is impossible for Him to know."

"But what does He mean by saying 'Son of Man?'" I asked. "He confuses me so."

"Son of Man could mean anything from descendent of Adam to important Prophet. That is the name He has chosen for Himself as 'Peter' is the name He has chosen for Simon. Now surely there is a misnaming if ever I heard one. If Simon is a rock, he is surely a mighty small and useless one." Nathaniel must have thought I would agree with him, being Simon's brother. And I think I did, with far more reason, since I knew most of Simon's faults. But I chose not to reply to Nathaniel's comment, and walked over to join the others. Soon Nathaniel joined us, and we sat at Jesus' feet, listening to Him.

"We walk through the land of our ancestors," Jesus said. "They are as much the ancestors of Philip whose father is a Greek, as they are of each of us who claims to be a pure son of Israel. All of us trace all of our ancestors back to Adam and Eve, the parents of all mankind. But the sons and daughters of Abraham have often mated with other tribes. We claim, each of us, to be of the lineage of David. But what was David's lineage? Was not his great grandmother, Ruth, a Moabitess? And was not Rahab the grandmother of Boaz, the husband of Ruth? Rahab was a Canaanite harlot in Jericho. Our ancestry, in the sense of being in a pure line from Abraham, is not so pure after all.

"We pronounce the coming of the Kingdom of God to the Jews, the children of the tribe of Judah. But each of us has ancestry that leads back to other tribes. And surely, coming from the North, we must assume that some of the ancestors we can name, but not know more than their names, in our individual genealogies, were interrelated to the migrants the Assyrian oppressors brought here. Son of David, I am. But Son of Man I am even more."

I thought of the Greeks who live in Bethsaida where Philip and I have our home, and of the Greeks in the ten towns along the east shore of the lake, and of the Jordan River. They don't look so different from us. And, except for their diet and their worship of other gods, their customs are little different. They dress the same, speak the same languages, buy the same goods, and are as good customers for our fish as any of the Jews.

I went to sleep that night, and on many nights thereafter, thinking this thought. "I am related to Jesus through the same line of ancestors. His kinship to James and John can be traced more readily, but there is no question — we are of one family."

We walked and talked for two more days, basking in the bright closeness of Jesus' companionship. Simon and I were closer to each other as brothers on that walk than we had ever been. I didn't tease him about failing in his responsibility to the fishing business, and he was really courteous toward me. He treated me as an equal, not as the younger brother. It made me more open to the idea of returning to work at his side whenever the day came for us to do that.

The morning of our fourth day together, we arrived at Cana. Nathaniel took us to his home where we bathed in water the servants brought us, and put on fresh clothing. That was certainly refreshing after spending weeks in the desert with only the muddy Jordan to wash out the garments we wore. Washed, combed, fed, rested, and dressed in wedding garments loaned to us by Nathaniel, our host, we left his home and went to that of his cousin where the wedding festivities were well advanced. The wedding had taken place three days before our arrival, with only three days left before the guests would separate themselves from the festivities and return to their own homes. Fruit and vegetables, bread and wine, were on the tables in abundance, and we walked about among the people, sampling what viands suited our fancy. Musicians were playing, and different couples shared in dancing or watching. Over in the corners sat some of the older men, talking about business, crops, politics. In other groups the women gathered to talk about whatever interests women. Men perhaps? Certainly we found ourselves enjoying the beauty of the young women all around us as they moved about, some of them dancing to the music.

The bride and groom moved together through the crowd. Surely all the people of the town of Cana were there, as well as many from neighboring towns. What Jesus said about family was true. Every one of us could trace relationships to everyone else if we went back but four or five generations. All of us have the pride of tracing our ancestry back at least fourteen generations to the time of our people's return from the Babylonian exile. As the bridal couple came close to us, Nathaniel introduced each of us, except for Jesus. Jesus knew them.

As I visited with the bridal couple, it seemed to me there was a look of concern on the groom's face. I was sure there was something troubling him. The fact that I noticed the groom was bothered by something made me realize that I had changed. Before I went into the desert with Philip to see and hear John, I cared little for anyone. People were more obstacles in my path than persons to care about. But there at the wedding I noted I had a caring feeling for the groom. In my heart there was a wish for the man's concern to disappear, and for him to keep the flush of happiness that was his right during this festival in his honor. I said nothing to him, of course. It would be much later in my daily association with Jesus that I would actually speak of my concern for others, and later still before I would offer my personal help.

Late that afternoon, about the ninth hour of the day, I found myself near Jesus. He was enjoying the festivities, speaking with the guests, simply mingling, joking, laughing. He was really attractive, drawing men and women close to him with his joyful personality.

Then a woman approached Jesus. I remembered her from my visit to Nazareth years before. It was Mary, Jesus' mother. She nodded her recognition of me, looking a little surprised to see me so far from home. Then she turned to Jesus.

"Son," she said, "They are out of wine." She said nothing more, just stood looking at him expectantly, and waited for his response.

"Your concern, Mother, is not mine. My hour has not yet come," Jesus said. I didn't understand what He said then. I barely understand anything more now. I think Mary understood his reply. And I feel she knew her part was over. It was her task to tell Jesus of the need. Once she had accomplished that, she could stand back.

I saw Mary turn to the servants and say, "Do whatever he tells you." Then she walked away to join some other women. I walked away too, thus missing an amazing occurrence. Nathaniel told me about it later. Somehow Jesus provided the wedding feast with almost eighteen firkins of wine — enough to provide everyone all they wanted of the juice of the grape as they continued to feast, eating and drinking until the end of the week long party.

Where did the wine come from? I don't know. Nathaniel said Jesus performed a miracle by changing water into wine. I tasted some of that wine later, and found it to be very good. Everyone else liked it too.

When the marriage feast ended at the end of the week, Simon, Philip, and I took our leave of Jesus. "It has been good walking with you, Jesus," Simon said. I concurred by a nod, and so did Philip.

"I will see you soon again," Jesus said. My heart rejoiced at that word.

We disciples have often wondered when it was that Jesus began his ministry. Some say it was the day He walked by the sea of Galilee and called Simon and me, James and John, to follow Him. Others say it was the day He came to John the Baptizer, and after being baptized, received the gift of the Holy Spirit. If starting in ministry begins at a specific time, then I would agree with their thinking, for I know the Jesus I saw before I met Him at the Jordan was somehow different from the Jesus I have followed since. Always assured, He became somehow the only man I have ever met who was totally certain of His direction. Always warm, outgoing, friendly, He became something more than that, displaying a loving concern for each person He met. Always intelligent, and capable of learning all subjects with ease, He became a great teacher, an ability, that if it were in Him before, had been sleeping, awaiting the right time for Him to show it.

Simon, Philip, and I returned to our homes by the lake. Simon was in such a hurry we made it in one day, and arrived home after dark, nearly exhausted. We left Simon to explain to his wife and mother-in-law where he had been, and Philip and I walked on to row ourselves home to Bethsaida in the fishing boat.

We started rowing along the lake shore, then stopped and watched the stars overhead. Philip wanted to talk, and I was not against sitting and listening. My friend was too deep for me to understand, but I knew he developed his ideas by speaking. I tried to help by asking intelligent questions.

"What do you think of Jesus?" Philip asked. I sat silent. I thought so much of this man who was quite probably the Messiah, that I didn't know how to begin to verbalize my thoughts. "I have never been so impressed with a man in my whole life," Philip continued, as I knew he would. Philip does not endure silence well. "He seems to shine! He seems to know my every thought before I speak it! Yet, knowing me so completely, He offers all of himself in friendship."

"Do you think Jesus is the Messiah?" I asked.

"You know I don't know much about the Messiah," he replied. "The Hebrew teaching is not an area of learning for me. I never went to a Rabbi for instructions. My teachers were at the Greek schools, and I wasn't too apt a pupil. We Greeks have a great history, one in which our nation once conquered almost the whole world. Greek athletes are adept at any sport. Our art and architecture cannot be matched by artisans of any other nation. Scientists, Mathematicians, Philosophers, writers of poetry, plays, and great epic stories are all a part of our heritage.

"But we have not developed our thinking about the Creator of the Heavens and the Earth as have you. Nor have we had the experience of communication with that Creator through Prophets and through Temple worship. Of course, we have temples and priests and priestesses who offer us favors from any of a hundred gods and goddesses. But in our hearts we know them to be charlatans. Their gods are myths created by fogged minds. What they really offer is self-indulgence in a hundred forms.

"I like to visit the synagogue, and am glad my mother insisted on my circumcision as a child. Thus I am forever one of the people of Israel. But I know little of the Books of Moses, and the wild history of my Hebrew ancestors. Though I have studied the psalms and love them, as you know, there is a vast amount of the history of the Jews I do not know, and what I do know, I don't understand." He paused and looked to the sky, lost in contemplation of the beauty above us.

"My teachers have said that there is a theory our sun is only one of the stars, and that this place where we live is turning slowly about our sun once each year. I don't understand that either, but if it is so, how can a creator so great as to make all these suns and earths be interested in man? How can He choose a people to be His over all the other people of the earth? Does He really care about who rules the little nation of Jewish people? Does He have a moral law that must be obeyed for people to be obedient citizens of His kingdom?"

I quoted the first of the books of Moses. "'God created man in His own image; in the image of God He created Him; male and female He created them.'" To me that expressed all that needed to be said in the matter. God created us. He made us to be like Him. He cared for us. He would take care of us if we obeyed Him. The people who did not obey Him, who did not follow His Law, were His problem, not ours. In our life of obedience, we would have control over the promised land. It was His promise to Moses. The day of our glorious victory over our oppressors would come soon.

"What do you think of Jesus?" Philip asked the question again.

Looking up to the heavens, my mind confused about so many, many things, I answered. "I think He has been sent by God to bring us what we truly need," I said.

"And what is that?" Philip asked. For a while we were both silent, and then, without speaking, we rowed on to Bethsaida, and walked up the bank, through the sleeping town, to our home.

5

Andrew

The things you read in the scroll written by John Mark are as nearly correct as anything that has been written about Jesus. The Good News about Jesus really began when John baptized Him in the Jordan, and He went into the desert where He was tempted. Our meeting with Him, and going with Him to Cana is something Simon didn't tell, probably because he left the wedding feast early and didn't see the miracle of changing water into wine. He was off by himself feeling guilty about not being home and at work.

That first time we were with Jesus, it seemed to me that He was waiting for some event to take place before He began teaching and preaching. I don't know what that event was, but I know it was after John the Baptizer was arrested by Herod and put into prison that Jesus began proclaiming the Good News of God.

"The time has come! The Kingdom of God is upon you! Repent, and believe the Good News!" That was the Word Jesus had for all mankind, not just for us Jews.

What we were to expect from the King, God Himself, we were not sure. Each of us had his own ideas on that. But we were certain the King of the Universe would not permit the Roman's Caesar and the half Hebrew Herods, Caesar's puppet kings, to rule over us. We would be free from oppression, and that was good news indeed.

One day, it must have been several months after we were with Jesus in Cana, He came by the lake. He called to Simon and to me. I remember we were fishing unsuccessfully, as often happens to every fisherman. "Come with me, and I will make you fishers of men!" Jesus called. Immediately we rowed ashore, left our boat, and walked along with Jesus. "How good it is to see you!" we each said. He embraced us each in turn — Simon first, of course. Simon is always first. We strolled along the lake shore toward Caphernaum, Simon's home.

As we walked, Jesus called out to his cousins, James and John. "Follow me!" He said, and they left their father in the boat with the hired help mending the nets for the next day's fishing. They didn't stop to say 'goodby.' Surely they knew they would be coming and going, and could make their farewells later. But maybe they knew they were to choose Jesus and never look back, and were both totally obedient from the first. All I can say is that they joined us, and that we went on together.

That day Jesus took us up into the hills toward the town of Chorazim. There we sat in fellowship while Jesus renewed acquaintance and visited with James and John. The Zebedee brothers had not been with us by the Jordan, nor in Cana, so there was much for us to tell. Jesus listened to us as we told of the events as we had seen them. He did not interrupt us, nor offer any explanations for the things that had occurred. Of course we had told James and John and hundreds of others about our experience with Jesus before this day on the hillside. But telling it again in Jesus' presence added much weight to what we said.

After a while, I excused myself and hurried home to Bethsaida to bring Philip back. He was eager to come. Together we composed a note to Nathaniel in Cana, asking him to hurry to be with us. "Jesus has begun to preach the Word as John did," we wrote. "Come be with us and hear

Him." I believe it was on the second day of the week we wrote him, and he arrived among us on the eve of the Sabbath. He must have left home immediately after receiving the note.

Then we were eight. Simon and I, James and John, Philip and Nathaniel, and a younger cousin of Nathaniel named Jesus BarTholomew. BarTholomew came from Nazareth, Jesus' home town, and Jesus knew him well. James, John, Simon, and I provided the food we needed, as our homes were nearby. Those first days we were never more than half a day's walk from our homes by the lake. I remember the night before the Sabbath we slept on the hillside just west of Caphernaum, less than a Sabbath day's walk from the Synagogue. Then, in the morning, we walked to the synagogue for prayers. There we knew Jesus would preach His Good News message to the people of Simon's community.

How exciting it was to hear Jesus preach! He didn't quote from the doctors of the law, or sound like his throat was dry from the dust of the scrolls he read. He spoke with a freshness and assurance. His teaching was like pronouncements from one who had absolute authority to give his message. It was at the synagogue in Caphernaum I first heard Him use one of his analogies as to what the Kingdom of Heaven is like. It was a homely thing He said, one that all had experienced. A woman lost a piece of silver and searched her house for it. Finally finding it she called her neighbors to rejoice with her that the lost was found. Surely each of us knew there was something precious in life that we did not have. We all have spent our lives searching for it, or trying out substitutes. How splendid, we thought, if the lost coin in our lives was found, and we could rejoice with all our neighbors.

It was then, while Jesus was preaching, that a disturbance occurred that changed our lives forever. Up to that moment Jesus was a charismatic person, outgoing, learned, and friendly. Once He had done something peculiar that provided beverage for a wedding feast, but we had no inquiries about what He did there, or how He did it. What happened in the synagogue in Caphernaum was a dramatic public experience.

A man in the middle of the synagogue began to shout at the top of his voice, "What do you want with us, Jesus of Nazareth?" The man's shout was more like a shriek. He seemed to be tormented by the Devil himself. Then he cried out, and the cry was even worse. Was it the sound of the Tormenter screaming in fear?

"Have you come to destroy us?"

Then the man continued in a more fearsome voice than ever, but this time it was almost a whisper of conspiracy. "I know who you are!" It was as if an enemy spirit within the man knew Jesus did not want His identity revealed at that time. Jesus walked rapidly toward the man, and it was apparent He would not stop until He confronted the enemy face to face. "You're the Holy One of God!" It was the last word that came out of the man's mouth.

"Be silent!" Jesus commanded, and there was no longer a sound from the man's lips. Still, those of us who were close enough could see terror in his eyes. Some of that terror must have been the man's, for surely he had no way of knowing Jesus could drive the madness out, and free him without doing him harm. Too, he may have felt the spirit of madness within him and believed himself and it were somehow bound together for eternity. He may have thought he would not ever be himself again if he were separated from the evil power that controlled him.

Jesus looked absolutely sure of himself. "Come out of him!" He said. The spirit made a desperate effort to remain there, throwing the man into convulsions on the floor. Then, with a loud cry it left the man. The poor fellow lay exhausted before us until Jesus lifted him up. Though the man was very weak, he appeared to have changed dramatically from what he had been only moments before. It was as if he were suddenly at peace. A look of surprise and of dawning awareness of his new freedom came to his eyes. He grasped Jesus' hand to thank Him.

The synagogue was in a turmoil. "What is this?" some of the people were shouting to one another. "Is it a new kind of teaching?"

Others commented, "He speaks with authority. When He speaks, even the unclean spirits submit." We disciples knew that news of this day's worship at Caphernaum would be spread throughout the region. We were right. Thereafter, wherever we went there were people who came to hear us, but many brought the wild ones out of their homes, the ones who had no control over themselves, hoping for a cure.

The time for worship was over. We left the synagogue and walked the short block to Simon's house. It was a nice home, that had once been mine until I felt it too crowded and moved away. Still, Simon kept a corner bed for me in the sleeping room, and I knew I was always welcome there.

Arriving, we entered the home to discover Anna, Simon's mother-in-law, was ill with a fever. Sarah, Simon's wife, was caring for her mother as well as she could. But the day was warm, and there was no breeze. Sarah washed her mother's face and arms with a damp cloth, and then fanned her gently, helping the water evaporate and thus, hopefully, cooling the sick woman. It was obvious that Sarah was concerned. This was not the time for several hungry men to come into that house.

I was about to say just that when Jesus stepped forward. He took Anna by the hand, and helped her to a sitting position. Then He helped her stand. By the time she was on her feet, the fever had left her, and she was strong enough to go about her function as a hostess to us all.

Anna laughed, and we laughed with her as we enjoyed the simple Sabbath meal she and Sarah had prepared the day before. Though I am sure they had not been planning for us to be there, we found ample bread and wine and other viands to meet all our needs.

That evening, after sundown, when the Sabbath was ended, the people brought their sick to Simon's door. For nearly two hours, until long after dark, Jesus healed many who were sick and drove out many devils. He wouldn't let the demons speak any more than He did the one in the synagogue that morning. I am sure He held them to silence because they knew who He was. We disciples knew something of Him, and were beginning to guess. Messiah? Yes. But far more than the Messiah we envisioned before. This one brought the Kingdom of Heaven with Him.

When we awoke the next morning, Jesus was gone. He had been provided a mat and an area on the floor in the room with all of us. That room was quite crowded, so we assumed He had moved His pallet outdoors, perhaps down by the lake, or up on the roof of our house. We searched in those and other probable places for Him, but could not find Him. So we set ourselves to search for Him beyond the edge of the town. It wasn't long before Simon found Him, and called to us. We came running.

"I found Him here. He was praying," Simon said. A quick glance, and we could see Jesus was still at prayer. None of us was brave enough to disturb Him. But we waited nearby watching Him. He seemed totally absorbed in a conversation with Someone. Perhaps I have an overactive imagination, but it appeared to me that as I watched Jesus I could see power flowing into Him. But later I asked Philip about it, and he agreed with me. Jesus gained strength while at prayer.

We were certain Jesus had used a tremendous amount of power in His activities of preaching and healing the day before. Somehow that power needed a source, one that would have to be tapped if Jesus were to continue the ministry He had begun.

When He was ready, Jesus turned to us. I don't know if He had stopped praying, or if He ever stopped. It is probable He and the Creator God talked with each other constantly. But Jesus did seek solitude often after that, and when He was alone His prayers may have been more intense.

"The people are looking for you," Simon said. He sounded like he was accusing Jesus of neglect of duty. "They are all looking for you."

"Let us move on to the country towns in the neighborhood," Jesus said. "I have to proclaim my message there also. That is what I came out to do."

That was the beginning of our itinerant ministry. We followed Jesus all through Galilee. In every town He went to the synagogue, and the people gathered to hear Him preach. He preached every day of the week, from the first through the Sabbath. We never had a day of rest. He not only spoke, but He healed every day. And He cast out devils.

Jesus hated evil in any of its forms, whether illness or deliberate disobedience to the law. He wouldn't let it exist in His presence without challenging it, and it would always yield to Him. Every creature under Heaven is built by God to live free from pestilence. Somehow we lose the power to fight off illness, and then we are subject to enemy occupation that threatens to take our very lives, as well as our peace. For instance, one day a leper came to Jesus, knelt before Him, and said, "Sir, if only you will, you can cleanse me."

Jesus looked angry, whether at the man's doubting if Jesus would use His power, or at the illness, I don't know. But He spoke with the usual authority. "Indeed I will. Be clean again." As He said this, He stretched out His hand and touched the man.

You know that no one is permitted to touch a leper! If they do, they are declared unclean. It is the law! But Jesus touched him. I saw it. And the man was made clean immediately. Jesus said, "Go show yourself to the priests, and make the offering laid down by Moses for your cleansing that will certify your cure." He also urged the man to say nothing of the healing to anyone.

But of course the man proclaimed his healing as had all the others. And, of course, he named the man who had touched him to make him whole. It wasn't long before we couldn't go into any town without drawing crowds. Jesus had to stay in the country and we disciples would take turns going into towns to buy the articles we needed for daily living.

Still the crowds came. They gathered about Jesus from morning until evening. They came from far away, as far as Jerusalem. Some of the men of Jerusalem were priests, spies sent out by the Sanhedrin.

Perhaps two or three weeks went by, perhaps it was a longer period of time. Those days passed quickly, I assure you. But after this first preaching mission we returned to Caphernaum, and the news spread that Jesus was again at Simon's house. A crowd gathered and grew until there was no way of gaining entrance to the house. The things Jesus said that day were relayed to the people outside the door, and they passed the words back to others behind them. How many were there because they had an illness, I don't know. But I know I was disturbed by the continuing experience of being caught in crowds. The business of following Jesus was much harder than any work I had ever done as a fisherman of fish. Even though I did little more than listen and watch, and occasionally run errands, I was drained most of the time. Perhaps I needed to find a quiet spot for prayer, but I knew I had no skill at that work. When I talked to the sky, there was never an answer.

As Jesus talked that day, there was a commotion on the roof of Simon's house. We looked up to see the tiles over our head being removed one at a time. Then down came the cross beams in the center that held up the dome. Simon and I tried to stop the men who were doing this. What right had they to tear down our home? But the men kept at it, and we had no way to get to them. We were incapable of getting out to them as anyone was of getting in to us.

When enough of the roof was removed to get a person through, four men lowered a man on a mat to the floor directly in front of Jesus. The man looked at Jesus and said nothing. Jesus looked at the man, and saw what we saw. He was terribly crippled. Jesus looked up at the men on the roof, and I believe He questioned them with his eyes. No words needed to be passed between the Master and these four friends of the man on the mat.

We looked again at the poor fellow before us. I didn't remember having seen anyone in worse condition. Arms and legs were twisted, back bent, and the poor man appeared unable to move. He lay there looking up at Jesus, unable to speak for himself. Perhaps he had no faith, and was there simply because the others carried him there. Perhaps he was in such awe of the Master, and of the circumstances of being center stage in a huge crowd, that he couldn't get his wits about him.

Jesus looked at the man with a look of deep compassion. The man must have felt the love that came from that look was warmer and stronger than any he ever had before. "My son, your sins are forgiven," Jesus said.

We knew there were scribes and Pharisees from the Temple present in the crowd. They had been informed of the healing Jesus did on some occasions on the Sabbath. We had not thought of it, but Anna, Simon's mother-in-law, was healed on the Sabbath. So was the demon possessed man in the synagogue. Of course, none of the others who were healed that day were healed on the Sabbath. The sun had gone down when they were brought to Jesus, so they were healed at the beginning of the first day of the week. Still, we were sure the Temple officials among us were there to get evidence against Jesus. Our Master had broken religious laws by doing forbidden work on the Sabbath.

I overheard the scribes talking among themselves. "Why does the fellow talk like that?" "This is blasphemy!" "Who but God alone can forgive sins?" I would have tried to defend Jesus, but I had no way of speaking to such highly educated men. I forgot that Jesus didn't need my help.

"Why do you harbour thoughts like these? Is it easier to say to this paralyzed man, 'Your sins are forgiven,' or to say, 'Stand up, take your bed, and walk?' But to convince you that the Son of Man has the right on earth to forgive sins, Jesus turned to the paralyzed man and said, 'I say to you, stand up, take your bed, and go home.'"

The man stood up! Even though I saw him do it, I didn't believe my eyes. He took his stretcher and walked out in full view of us all, right past all the people who were jammed outside the door. Everyone fell away from him as he walked out. The men on the roof shouted their joy. One called down, "Thank you, Jesus." Then they rushed down the outside stairway of our house to embrace the man and walk away with him. Simon and I looked at each other. We were not quite as happy as the others. We knew who would have to repair the roof before we slept that night.

The people were in a turmoil. Fevers healed were one thing. Emotional problems or demons driven out were something that might be possible. But the man they saw healed of his paralysis was too far gone to recover. No one, perhaps not even God, could heal such a devastated body. But the healing had taken place! "Never before have we seen the like," was said by many. We could only agree, for this was

— up to that moment — the most powerful of the miracles Jesus performed.

What the forgiveness of the man's sins had to do with his healing, I didn't know then. I'm not sure I know now. I know Jesus equated forgiveness with healing on this occasion, and later on some others. But He didn't always do that. With the leper, for instance, He merely said, "Be healed." Whether Jesus had the power to forgive sins, we didn't know, nor try to fathom. We knew He had the power to heal, and that knowledge we acquired from seeing. Who can see forgiveness?

Let me assure you of this. Jesus lived what He taught. We walked with Him to the shore of the lake, at the junction of the Jordan as it flows into the lake. This stream that rushed out of the side of the mountain at Caesaria Philippi, and twisted down hundreds of feet before arriving at our lake, was tamed and quiet before us, and quite filled with sediment. There at the shore line sat Levi BarAlphaeus, the tax collector. The man was a known thief, worse than most of his fellow customs officers. He had ways of extracting money from travelers that were really ingenious. For instance, he could postpone an assessment of the value of a camel caravan for days, causing loss of time and profit for the merchants. Or he could speed up the process, helping some while hindering others, thus providing an unfair advantage to those who bribed him to hurry, or gave him a share of their profits.

Simon and I knew Levi well, for often our catch of fish, once processed and dried at Magdala, was sent on to Damascus and other eastern communities past this point of entry and exit of our nation's borders. East of us was the territory of Philip. Bethsaida was a part of his domain. Caphernaum was the first major town on the west bank of the north Jordan. Levi collected taxes for our Herod, as well as for the Roman Governor. But neither government fared as well as

Levi. I disliked that tax collector with an intense dislike. Simon went further. He hated the man.

It was almost as if Jesus had chosen to walk that way so he could see Levi. Almost all of us were with Jesus then; Simon, James and John, grouped around Jesus, almost as a body guard, for even then in the beginning they were an inner circle. The rest of us followed. Philip, Nathaniel, and I, and another cousin of Jesus, a man who looked so much like Jesus we called him 'Thomas,' 'the twin,' though his first name was Judas.

Jesus called to Levi. "Follow me," He said. I tell you, I was shocked! Jesus was choosing Levi to be one of His followers! People couldn't help making an unfavorable comparison. We other followers would all soon be considered as evil, as wicked as the publican!"

Levi left his place of customs, and joined us. Jesus stopped near Levi's place of business, and began to teach the people who had followed us. As always His message included concepts of the Kingdom that He said 'is at hand.' The Kingdom is like a man who..." I can't remember what Jesus said that time for the message wasn't directed particularly to me. I sat and stared at the lake, thinking of how difficult it would be to be a disciple with Levi among us. I may even have offered a silent prayer that Levi would not obey Jesus' call.

That prayer, if I offered it, was not answered with a 'Yes.' When we moved away from the shore, Levi called for another tax collector to take his place. Then Levi walked along with us! Worse still! The thieving tax collector was given the place of honor by Jesus' right side. Levi looked happy, nearly ecstatic. We who were Jesus' first and deeply loyal followers were critical. We thought Jesus was wrong. Levi was a very bad choice.

"Come to my home for dinner," Levi said. "Bring all your friends." Jesus agreed to come.

That gave each and all of us a choice. We could either continue to follow, accepting Levi as one of us, or we could ... There was no alternative.

Later, when we sat down to dine, we shared in a sumptuous dinner Levi had ordered prepared and served by the lake shore. Around us were many people of the town, eating their meals, or enjoying the quiet evening's cool breeze that wafted down from the nearby hills. Levi had invited his co-workers, other tax collectors and customs inspectors. In spite of myself, I enjoyed my meal, for it was almost a banquet. And, to my surprise, I found the tax collectors to be really good fellows. Their wives and children were with them, and I could see little difference between these people, and we who worked at other tasks.

Scribes and Pharisees gathered near us, ostensibly on a casual walk along the lake shore. More and more of these men were to be seen wherever we went. A few of them walked over to visit with me and Philip. "We see your master eats with tax gatherers and sinners!" they said.

I hung my head, for I was ashamed of Jesus. And I noted that Philip had nothing to say in Jesus' defense. We had already come to believe everything Jesus did was right. Yet here we were criticizing Him by our silence. I forgot that Jesus heard everything, no matter how far He was away from the speakers. I am certain He heard our thoughts, even when we did not speak. Certainly He looked at me and Philip with a glance that registered His sorrow at our being critical of Him. Then He spoke.

"It is not the healthy who need a doctor, but the sick. I did not come to invite virtuous people, but sinners." Philip and I knew we were among the invited. I looked into my heart for the sin that made me qualified. It wasn't hard to find. Of several, I chose my jealousy of the other disciples' time with Jesus, and my being critical of Jesus' choices and decisions. The fact that I had repented past sins and been baptized by John came to mind. Had I not been a sinner, baptized by the man of the desert, I would not have been present when John said, "Behold the Lamb of God."

I looked at the scribes and pharisees to see how they would respond to Jesus' statement. Certainly they would have an answer. But they didn't. They looked at each other, each perhaps wondering if those about him knew of his own inner character faults, his own words and actions that qualified him to be one of the called. Silent, they walked away from us. I believe they learned something from Jesus that evening. But Philip and I learned more. We went back to the feast Levi had prepared for Jesus and us. There we shared in real fellowship with Levi, and with all his friends in the tax business. I wondered then, and have wondered since, would the Kingdom be here finally when all tax collectors and all tax payers were honest with one another?

You should know we feasted often with Jesus. We were nearly always included in invitations to sumptuous meals. Our hosts were usually people who were grateful for Jesus' message, or for His healing ministry. But, as Jesus grew more famous, he was invited to homes so that people could say, "Jesus of Nazareth ate with me at my house."

We disciples enjoyed several months of such feasting, and basked in the reflected adulation of our master. But the day came when we were embarrassed again. John's disciples fasted often. The tradition of fasting on special occasions has been with our people from the time of Moses. On the special Day of Atonement, when all the people were fasting but Jesus and we who were blessed to be his constant companions, some of the men of the Temple chose to test Jesus with this question. "Why do your disciples not fast as John's disciples fast?"

Several things were inferred by their question. But the primary one was that Jesus was less of a spiritual leader than was John. Jesus' reply showed He understood their purpose, and He challenged them by declaring Himself the most honored one at a perpetual wedding feast.

"Can you expect the bridegroom's friends to fast while the bridegroom is with them? As long as they have the bridegroom with them, there can be no fasting. But the time will come when the bridegroom will be taken from them, and on that day they will fast." He told a parable after that about patches and wine skins that you already know. Apparently now the Kingdom had come with Him present as the Messiah, the old patch of a day of repentance was no longer needed. We were like bubbling and frothing new wine that had to be put into a new container that could expand with us!

There are so many things I have to tell you about Jesus. But I know His other friends are telling of their first hand experience with Him, so I will try to speak only of the highlights of my shared ministry with Him.

One day He called us to follow Him up a hillside, and He selected twelve of us to be his Apostles. Simon, my brother, who we were all learning to call, 'Peter,' was first. James and John, the sons of Zebedee, were next. Then me, Philip, BarTholomew, Matthew (Levi), and Thomas. Four others I have not mentioned, were James BarAlphaeus, a brother of Jesus; Nathaniel, also called Thaddaeus; Simon of the Zealot party; and Judas Iscariot, a man from Judah who none of us knew, who was later to betray Jesus. Jesus began a process of close instruction in which He took the first three I have listed, and trained them, and then each of them took three of us and taught us. Often I was jealous of my brother, and of James and John as they trudged off alone with Jesus to learn directly from Him. But I did not envy them their responsibility of being our teachers in turn. Those were the days when we were not filled with the Spirit of God, and we had to rely on our own resources.

6

Andrew

If I were to pick one incident in my life that convinced me of Jesus' infinite power, I would choose the time when we had thousands of people gathered in the plain near the Sea of Galilee. It was a busy time, and we had much work to do, lining up the people so that they could see Jesus, or touch Him, or ask Him to touch them to heal them. His purpose, He told us, was to teach the people, giving them the Good News of the Kingdom. His healing of them was secondary, or a proof of the truth of His teaching. Many times such a large crowd gathered that we found ourselves overwhelmed by them. Jesus had trained us to help Him in several ways. In fact, He had given us authority to do some of the things He did.

The week before the event I will soon describe to you took place, Jesus sent us out two by two to towns and villages. There, following His orders, we preached the Good News of the Kingdom, and we actually healed many sick persons in the Name of Jesus. When this first happened, we were surprised, even though Jesus had told us to expect it. But by the end of the week, it became a matter of personal confidence for each of us, and we spoke with authority. We came to know the sick would be made well, the lame would walk, the lepers would be made whole, and the deaf would hear. If the Kingdom was coming, Jesus had assured us, there would be no illness within it.

As usual, my traveling companion was Philip. Our destination was a little village south of Nain, and we stayed there with a family that welcomed us and fed us. The local Rabbi welcomed us as well, and we were invited to preach in the synagogue. When our time with them was over, we returned to the lake to find Jesus, and told Him of our experience. He was pleased. The others arrived in due time and made their reports, and Jesus told us it was time for us to have a time of rest. We climbed into a boat, and rowed to the west bank, climbing out of the boat, expecting to walk a few miles up into the hills.

But too many people had seen us leave, and they hurried around from the north side of the lake, telling others along the way that Jesus was heading for the western shore. When we landed, there was already a crowd waiting for us, and that crowd grew rapidly as the day progressed. Jesus said to us, "Look at these people. They act as if they were lost sheep who had no shepherd." So He began to teach them, to bless them, and to heal their sick. We began to help when and as we could.

As the day grew warmer, Jesus called us to be with Him. He said, "How is the day going for you? What would you do now?" He was always teaching us, often by asking our opinions, and frequently He took our advice.

"This is a lonely place," Philip said. "And it is getting very late. Send the people off to the farms and villages round about to buy themselves something to eat."

"Give them something to eat yourselves," Jesus countered.

One of the men, perhaps Judas, who had the purse that contained all our traveling money, said, "Are we to go out and spend two hundred denarii (almost a year's wages for one man) to give them a small meal?"

"How many loaves have you?" Jesus asked. "Go and see." So we went obediently to see what we could find. Soon it was obvious that not one of the twelve of us had any food. The people we asked claimed they had no food either, though it is possible many lied. But I kept searching until I found an enterprising boy. He had guessed that where there was a crowd, there would be empty stomachs. So he had filled a basket with bread and smoked fish, and brought it along, offering it for sale at a good profit.

By the time I found the lad, all he had left were five small barley loaves, each the size of one of my fists. Also he had two small dried fish. I said to him, "Jesus needs some food for the people." The lad said, "He can have this. I sold all the rest."

So I brought the boy to Jesus, and said, "Here is a lad with a few loaves and fishes. But what are they among so many?"

I assure you there were as many as five thousand men on that plain, and most of them had brought along their families. I expected Jesus to say something about it being best after all to send the people home. But He didn't.

Instead, He said, "Make the people sit down in groups of fifties and hundreds." The twelve of us set about organizing the crowd. It was one of the few grassy spots beside the lake, a lovely place to sit and rest. We had no difficulty getting the people to do what Jesus asked.

But when we returned, Jesus took the bread and the fish, said a blessing over it, and told us to distribute it to the people. I was one of the first to reach into the basket, and I decided I may as well take two of the loaves and one of the fish. Let the other apostles squabble over the remainder. But as I turned away, I looked back to see the basket had more bread and fish in it than before I took out the part I planned to distribute. I was a little shocked, but not too surprised. one's eyes can play tricks occasionally.

I stepped away to the nearest group of fifty people with my basket, and handed a loaf and a fish to one of the men.

That should have left me with no fish and one loaf. But it didn't! I looked in my basket and there were three loaves left, and two fish besides! I gasped, and handed them another loaf and another fish, and went on to the next group. By the time I got to them, my basket was overflowing with loaves and fish. I handed out five loaves and four fish, and then decided to hand out five more loaves and three more fish.

My basket grew heavier each time I gave away some of the food! I looked around to see how the other apostles were faring, and saw that each of them was in the same quandary. How to unload a never emptying basket? The faster we worked, the faster our supply grew, until every one of the groups of men and their families had been given all they needed — even more than they needed. Only then, after we ourselves had a loaf and a piece of fish apiece did we find our baskets empty.

When we returned to Jesus, we were both surprised and confused. "How?" "What does it mean?" "We read of the oil jar the widow had in Elijah's time, Lord. But this?" "How does material grow in our hands?" "How can so little be made to do so much?"

Jesus sat and smiled at us, and ate His share of the bread and fish. "Now the people are finished, go out among them and bring back the leftovers," He said.

I heard Thomas mutter, "What leftovers?" But I didn't dare ask the same question. I just took my basket and went out to do what I was told. When I came back, I had a full basket of broken loaves, and some small pieces of fish as well. Jesus thanked us, and told us to give our baskets full of bread to people who were from the nearby towns. "Tell them to take this food and give it to the poor."

One miracle after another Jesus did that I cannot explain. But the miracle of provision of food for thousands out of a supply that should have been barely enough for three of us, changed my heart. I no longer believed Jesus might be the Messiah. I somehow knew He was the Messiah! I knew the Kingdom was really with us. I rejoiced.

Jesus gave us further proof of Himself that night. When we got into our boat to return home, He remained behind. He said, "I must be alone for a while. I shall go up the hillside and pray to my Father." We were getting used to His calling God His Father. It sounded a bit too intimate, because He used the term in its diminutive form, the name a child would give his father, 'Daddy.' Perhaps one could say that the creator of all things and of all creatures, including mankind, could be called our Father. But to think of the Creator of the Universe as 'daddy,' someone who would pick us up, play with us, hug us, care for us, and love us as our own dads did when we were infants was very difficult to accept. At least it was difficult for me.

We were tired, and ready to get home to our beds. Two weeks out in distant towns, caring for the sick and preaching were tiring enough, but then to have a long day of being with Jesus as He preached and healed, as well as doing some healing work ourselves added to our exhaustion. My own heart needed solitude as much, I was sure, as did Jesus. As He went to talk to his 'Daddy,' to replenish His power, I needed to get away from all people so I could have time to concentrate on the miracle of multiplication of the food.

But it was not to be, not for a while. We had hardly set out on our journey when a strong east wind came up, blowing us back to the west bank of the lake. Several of us struggled with the oars, fighting a battle that we knew we could win in time. Holding our own against the wind, and making a little headway, we knew the wind would die as quickly as it began. That was the way with our lake. But this time we rowed for hours, and the wind continued against us. We spelled each other at the oars, so that half of us rested while half pulled hard keeping the boat straight into the wind.

We were nearly exhausted from this last challenge of the day. There was little left in us, and the wind continued strong against us. It was then that Jesus showed up. He was walking on the surface of the water, seemingly with no difficulty, as the waves swept toward Him, under Him, and on out of the way to be replaced again and again by more waves. The waves were almost as high as His waist, and some of them crested as they approached. But He walked as if on dry land, never sinking, never thrown off balance.

Some of the other apostles shouted, "A Ghost!" They screamed their fear as several of them let go of the oars.

But Jesus called, "Don't be afraid. It is I." He came to us and climbed into the boat. As soon as He was with us, the wind stopped, the sea became calm, and we pulled on to shore at Caphernaum. All were amazed.

Some said, "Who is this that even the wind and the waves obey Him?" But I didn't say that. I knew how the lake could change suddenly from calm to storm, and storm to calm. My thoughts were on one who could walk across that sea when the water was so high no one could survive swimming in it.

Once on shore on our side of the Jordan, Philip and I hurried to our house ostensibly to rest. But neither of us could sleep. We were too full of the events of our lives with Jesus. We had to take our experiences out, air them to each other, study them in depth, before we could 'sleep on them,' and let our souls try to make acceptable but incomplete sense of them.

"How could five loaves and two fish feed so many?" Philip asked.

"Perhaps they didn't," I said. "Surely some of the people there had the foresight to bring along something to eat. It is reasonable that they should share when they saw us sharing so little. If a hundred had food to share, their food could have been shared with all the others along with ours." I said this, knowing it could be but a partial answer. Philip's Greek mind caught the flaw immediately.

"If a thousand had food, and the thousand shared, there wouldn't have been enough for all." He was right, of course. Few would have brought baskets of food larger than what they needed for themselves and their families. Most had seen us rowing to our destination and had hurried away from their homes unprepared for more than a few hours, if they were prepared to be gone at all. It had been a headlong and impetuous charge to get to the shore ahead of us. "You know, too, that what happened to my basket happened to the baskets of each of us." Philip looked at me until I raised my eyes to his, acknowledged his statement with a nod, and looked away.

"What did happen, then?" I countered.

"I don't know. We have no stories of our Gods doing anything like this for themselves, or for us. But you and I have read of how Yahweh, the God of the Jews, who we claim is God of all the Universe, created all things."

"He spoke and said, 'Let there be...' and each thing he called for came into complete existence at His Word." I said this as if I were reciting to my Rabbi. It was one of the first lessons a child learns as he reads the first pages of the first book of Moses.

"Jesus spoke and said, 'Feed them yourselves,'" Philip said. "He really did much less than Yahweh in this instance. He only fed thousands, and he started with some bread and fish that were already in existence. Yahweh created out of nothing. Jesus multiplied out of what Yahweh created."

"Why were the people healed when we commanded they be made whole in Jesus Name?" I asked. I knew I was changing the subject for what Philip said about the food was beyond me. "How did Jesus walk on water?"

"Who is Jesus?" Philip responded. He was difficult to talk to when he began to answer questions with questions.

Talking wasn't helping. Our dilemma was too large for our small minds. "I have to agree with the demons Jesus drives out of people. Jesus is the Holy One of God." I knew what was coming next.

"And what does that mean?" asked Philip.

He had the last word. I had no answer for that then, and the answers I have now only partially satisfy me, even though I rest in assurance that the Spirit of God dwells within me. Then I only had myself, Andrew the fisherman, inside, and I was very lonely, really quite frightened, and terribly confused.

"All we can do is keep following Him," Philip said. "Surely we will learn more tomorrow." He turned away and lay down on his pallet.

"Tomorrow," I thought. "Ah yes, tomorrow we will be with Jesus again. I am grateful for that thought. Amen. So be it. Amen."

It was the next day that word came to us that John the Baptizer had been beheaded by Herod. Judas Iscariot, who had been away for some time, brought us the news. This was one time that it seemed Jesus had not known of the event before the rest of us. Perhaps He had been so busy with His teaching, preaching and healing and feeding the people that He blanked out the awareness He must have of all events in the Kingdom. He was deeply affected by the news, and went off for several days by Himself into the hills north of Caphernaum.

When He returned, He took us on a journey to Caesaria Philippi, the capital of Philip's Kingdom. We walked slowly into the hills, discussing the death of John, and the life we were living. What danger were we in? John's disciples had not been arrested or killed. Would we be in as much trouble as John, perhaps more?

Simon the Zealot was eager for trouble to begin. He saw no way for the Kingdom to come in, and for Jesus to ascend the throne than for armies to be formed and joined against the enemy.

Jesus didn't seem to be listening to us at all. At camp that night He asked, "Who do men say that I am?"

"Some say one thing, some another," the Zealot replied. He was as sure Jesus was the Messiah as any of us. He was betting his whole life on it.

"Some say you are Elijah," BarTholomew said.

"Some say you are John the Baptizer come back," John said. This seemed to be the most ridiculous of the things we had heard, for Jesus had been with John the Baptizer, and had begun his ministry months before John's death.

"Some say you are one of the other prophets, perhaps even Moses, or Isaiah, or Ezekiel, or even Malachi," Judas Iscariot said, and we recalled Judas had come from Judah near the Temple. The Order of Melchizedek, the long line of priests from before Aaron had one of its greatest spokesmen in the Prophet Malachi.

We discussed each of these possibilities almost as if Jesus were not there to hear us. The idea of the dead living again in another generation was not new to us. We all knew we were representatives of our ancestors. Had they not lived and reproduced, we would not be alive. Each had had to be successful enough in the business of living to carry on the race, our line of life. Sometimes I would feel the presence of those ancestors very close to me, helping me to make decisions in my life. Sometimes this comforted me. Sometimes it irritated me too, for I wanted to live by my choices, not theirs.

The stories of Elisha acquiring the spirit of Elijah on the day Elijah was taken up in the chariot of fire were part of our heritage. Could Moses who was a member of the tribe of Levi, be the power and strength of Jesus, a descendant of the tribe of Judah? Again we remembered the frequent intermarriages between the tribes, and wondered if the female line would carry as well as the male. When most of the men of the tribe of Benjamin had been killed in a bloody battle with other Hebrew tribes, men of those other tribes married the widows and daughters of the Benjaminites so they could reproduce their tribe. That would indicate women were capable of carrying on the line of tribal heritage.

How confusing it all was! Yet I wondered what difference it made. I knew who Jesus was. John the Baptizer had told me and Philip months before by the Jordan River. "Behold the Lamb of God," he said. "Behold Him that takes away the sin of the world."

"But who do you say that I am?" Jesus asked. Each time He said, "I am," he repeated the name of God. When Moses asked God His Name, God replied, "I am that I am. Tell them I AM has sent you." Moses used that name and the power of the Spirit God gave him to confront Pharaoh, and to lead the Hebrew people out of Egypt. The name of God, 'I AM' that we pronounce 'Yahweh' is not to be taken in vain. We Jews have almost dropped using the two words, 'I' and 'Am' together for fear of breaking that holy commandment. But Jesus used them together frequently. Was He challenging the authorities? Or was He proclaiming Himself?

I knew. I was certain. Though that sort of certainty comes and goes. I believe every one of the twelve Apostles, and many of the other disciples, who were following along with us knew as I did. But I didn't have the courage to say the words.

My brother spoke up, and he spoke for all of us. "You are the Christ. You are the anointed one. You are the Son of God."

Jesus said, "Blessed are you Simon, son of Jonah. Man did not reveal this to you. It was revealed to you by my heavenly Father. And I say this to you. You are Peter, the rock. And it is on this rock I will build my Church. And the powers of death shall never conquer it."

It was then Jesus told us for the first time that He would have to suffer and die. It was what we all feared, for had not that happened to John the Baptizer? But we did not want to think of it. My brother spoke for us all again, "Oh No, Lord! This shall never happen to you!"

Jesus spoke harshly, hurting us all by saying to Peter, "Away with you Satan! You are a stumbling block to me. You think as men think, not as God thinks.

How else could we think?

Jesus talked to us for some time after that, but I wasn't listening. My mind went into a private fog, and remained there for some time.

7

Pontius Pilate

Late Spring, Year of Tiberias — XVII

Sire -

I send you greetings, and greetings too to your new wife. Also, please greet my brother if he is presently in Rome.

These past three years of my assignment here in Judea have, on the whole, been pleasant. The climate here is gentle and warm most of the year, only January and February offering occasional damp or chilly days. Tiberias' subjects here, the Jews, are a rebellious people, as I have mentioned in earlier letters.

Life here in Caesaria continues to provide little stimulation. Procula is bored with it, and I have urged her to travel home for a few months so that at least one of us can enjoy again the excitement of civilization in Rome. But she refused, as usual. She is a very jealous woman, and thinks that as soon as she is two miles at sea I would be in bed with a Jew girl. She's right, of course, but her not going doesn't keep me from getting a little exercise. Opportunities arise almost daily, and I choose to accept them occasionally.

Still, I am discreet. I say this, knowing your concern that I be aware of the political nature of my position. Perhaps you are the only man in the empire that considers me naive and foolish. But that is your right, my dear father.

The years of my administration here have been quiet ones. That incident with the Jews during my first year would not happen now. I have good relationships with all the puppet kings but one; that is Antipas, the Tetrarch of Galilee. He is a real fool. He not only seduced his brother's wife, but then he was party to her divorce. He let himself be talked into marrying her. Such a shrewish woman I have never seen! Only last month, Procula and I and a few officials of our occupying army accepted an invitation to Antipas' birthday party in Tiberias, the city he had constructed to honor our present emperor. The four day journey from here was pleasant, as we traveled through some of the most fertile hills of this lush land. The road leads us north along the shore of the great sea, past the flowing streams Herod had diverted half a century ago when he needed water for this, our capital city of Caesaria. (I have had our engineers develop a system that parallels the old one, doubling the water supply here. That project is almost completed.)

Then we turn inland, just south of Mount Carmel, and follow an ancient caravan road to the shores of the beautiful inland lake the natives call the Sea of Galilee. Herod renamed that lake after Tiberias just as he named the city on its western shore. I admit Herod Antipas is a fairly competent politician. But he is a fool as well.

The quarries that supplied the stone for Herod's home are of flawless rock that glistens an almost pure white. The whole little city by the lake is truly lovely, and the climate there is quite tropical. Antipas' house is high on the hill overlooking the lake so any breeze that comes will help cool the guests. We enjoyed three days of rest there after our journey, and then were informed we were to travel down the Jordan valley to the fortress Hyrcania where the party was to be held. Hyrcania, if you will look at the map of this territory, is about ten miles south by west of Jericho, on the northwest corner of the Asbestitis lake.

I wish I had known that the celebration would be there. I would not have accepted the invitation. There is no place on earth hotter or with a worse stench than that valley, especially by the lake these Jews call the Dead Sea. The sickening sweet smell of sulfur and other unknown, but vile salts from the earth can cause one to feel real nausea.

Ah well! One does what one must. We rode south with Antipas to the party. There we were given adequate rooms, a good steam bath, followed by a leap into relatively cool flowing water that had been diverted through the fortress. These Jews are really quite clever in their use and conservation of water! But they have to be so. Their dry season is much longer than ours, even along their sea coast. And the desert region by the Jordan is so dry, nearly a year can go by without any rainfall at all. The Jews have arranged their forts along their borders to be in good military locations, but also where known supplies of water can be tapped. Then they have added fantastic cistern systems to supplement their wells and aqueducts. I understand this process has been going on for hundreds, perhaps thousands of years here.

Excuse me, father. You know my interest in water supplies. I'll get on now with the story about the party that showed Herod's foolishness.

The celebration began the evening after our arrival at Hyrcania. It was held by lamplight in the elaborate gardens outside the walls of the main house where we all slept. The soldiers of the fortress were really there to function as prison guards, for it is in that hellish place that Antipas keeps his prisoners. The prison building was separate from our quarters, of course, and it housed both the prisoners and their guards.

It was obvious that Antipas has traveled to Rome. For the party was very like the happy revellings we have enjoyed at the royal court of Tiberias. Superb food and drink were offered us, and both in abundance. These Jews do know how to make good wine, and we were gratified by the taste and quantity provided. The servants were young Jew girls dressed for the hot weather in very skimpy costumes. Procula did her best to ignore them, but I found pleasure in noting their obvious charms.

We were seated, probably by some sadistic whim of Antipas, beside the High Priest of the Temple. Annas, and his son-in-law, Caiaphas were both there. They were the ones, you will remember, father, who led that near revolt against me shortly after I arrived in this country. You remember the reason they gave for surrounding my home in Caesaria and raising their cries of protest that I had Tiberias' name emblazoned on shields at our headquarters in Jerusalem. I backed down that time, and they have made the mistake of thinking me a weakling ever since.

The six of us, Procula and I, the priests and their wives, sat around a low table from which we could take our choice of fruit, bread, meat, or wine. For a time we kept up a pretense of polite conversation. Fortunately Herod had entertainment provided. Therefore we could look at and listen to that rather than force courteous small talk.

The last dancer of the evening was Herod's stepdaughter, Salome. She proved herself to be remarkably competent, almost as good as some of the erotic dancers I have seen in Rome. We applauded her performance. Even Procula recognized the child (Salome is barely in her teens) was competent in her portrayal of erotica.

But Antipas was more than appreciative. He was aroused! He called Salome to him and in thanking her offered a price for her favors. I heard him say, "Up to half my kingdom." Now what girl could possibly be worth that?

It was then we saw how foolish this man was. His sexual appetite put him in trouble. His promise to Salome got him in deeper.

The girl ran to her mother and asked her what she should demand. You remember that Herodias was once the wife of Antipas' brother. That woman! Apparently she made Antipas arrest a wild preacher for calling her a whore, and her husband an adulterer. The wild man, named John, was one of the prisoners there at Hyrcania. I knew of him, of course. He had drawn crowds by the Jordan River for the past few years, and some of my soldiers were there to be sure no rebellion was coming from that source.

The wild man, John, was harmless enough. He preached a new kingdom was coming with a new king, and that all should watch out as the time for that king was near. He even scared some of my men into more honest ways of soldiering, less stealing from the people, and less raping of their wives and daughters. (As you know, our occupying armies have never been easy to control. Our work of occupation would be far easier if we had better disciplined soldiers, men with families assigned to our frontier.) I came to appreciate this John, called the Baptizer, because he had his converts symbolically wash away their past guilt in the river. His preaching made my work easier.

Herodias spoke to Salome, and she went back to her step-father where she asked in a voice that carried through the garden, "Give me the head of John the Baptizer on a platter."

Salome is surely her mother's daughter. She knew what her Galilean Tetrarch wanted. She shook off her dancing costume, an almost unnecessary thing to do as it was nearly transparent, and showed him the merchandise. All of us watched Antipas squirm, but I took interest in the priests with me. I wondered what their reaction was to this display.

Neither Annas nor Caiaphas seemed the least shocked by Salome's action. But they were leaning forward, looking almost hopeful, as we awaited Antipas' response.

The king sentenced his wild man subject to death with a nod to one of his attendants. Then he looked at Salome. "Your wish is granted. Dress now. Go to your mother." We watched the young tart turn into a child again, appear confused for a moment, then grab up her clothes and rush out of the garden.

"Don't go too far," Herod called. "Your reward will be here very soon." He lowered his head, not wanting to look into the faces of any of us. Somehow his birthday party was no longer any fun for him. "Come back to me, Salome," he called. She returned, dressed again in her costume to stand before us all. We sat in silence, not wanting to speak.

The soldier returned carrying a man's head on a large plate. I watched him hand it to Antipas, who refused it. "Give it to her," he said, indicating Salome. The girl took the plate, gingerly , in her outstretched hands. Then she turned, walked to where her mother was sitting, and dumped the head in the woman's lap. Without a word, Salome left the room.

Herodias was strong. She took the head by the hair, held it up, smiled first at it, then at Antipas, then walked out, the head dangling from her right hand, drops of blood dribbling on the floor behind her.

Of course, the party broke up then. Herod sat there, gazing at us all, but not focusing on any of us. Some made excuses. Others paused to extend good wishes, but the smart ones, including me and the two priests, simply left. I took Procula to our rooms where she was promptly sick. I called for a maid to clean up, and to help Procula to her bed. Then I went out for a private walk about the grounds.

You see why I called Antipas a fool? Of course you do. You who have been a diplomat in or for Rome over forty years, serving under three emperors, know that rulers must rule, not allow anyone, not even petulant children in their own families, to stop them from doing the politically wise thing. Herod had a man killed who was greatly loved by the people of his territory. Their anger toward him has been growing for a long time. Now the anger will grow to unreasoning rage. Someone will form a band of rebels and try to overthrow him; or more likely to assassinate him. Ten to one the fool will come within three months to ask for a guard of Roman soldiers to help protect him.

Perhaps, should he ask this, it would be better to refuse him, to let him die. But there are few any better than he who could succeed him.

That night I strolled through the gardens at Hyrcania, and watched the servants cleaning up the remains of the feast. It seemed to me that much of the leftover food was carried out to the periphery of the lamp light. It looked like shadows of people were out there to take the food and wine from the servants, and I must assume the poor people of the valley ate better that night and the next day than they usually did. There is a bond among the poor I envy sometimes. They seem to care for one another....

I was about to go back to my quarters and see if Procula was feeling better when I noticed Caiaphas, the young priest I had dined with, walking toward me. "Good evening. Are you having trouble sleeping too?" I asked.

"Your excellency," Caiaphas addressed me formally. "I love the desert. But I love it better at night after the heat has left. The earth and the air cools. The stench of the Sea is less. My thoughts are clearer." I could almost see him smile as he said with calculated concern, "Did something at the party disturb you, Governor Pilate?"

"I know little of your religion, young priest," I said, not trying to be diplomatic with him. "Tell me how many of your God's commandments were broken by Antipas and his family tonight?"

"None that haven't been broken before," he replied instantly. "God will punish Antipas and Herodias and Salome in his time, and in his way."

"Do you priests of the Temple approve of the Tetrarch?" I persisted. "Why do you permit such a man to be over the Jewish people?" I thought I could shame him.

"Ah, your excellency," he replied, and I discovered the tempered brilliance of the man in his next statement. "We have little power over the selection of our rulers. We did not choose the Emperor. We did not select the puppets that rule here for him. We were not even asked to help select our governor."

I was silent. That is a move in the diplomatic game of life that you taught me, father. When your opponent has an advantage over you, don't let him know it by a foolish word. Rather, wait for him. Silence has to be filled with confidence, or with empty angry words. The power of Rome was my confidence. The weakness of the Jews and their terrible frustration as vassals for all but fifty of the last two hundred years was Caiaphas' weakness.

"Even our God chose us," he mused. "We did not choose him. He has made us his people. He has given us a burden of law we cannot obey. And then he has punished us with oppressive rulers. We are no better off today in Jerusalem than our ancestors were in Egypt before Moses came to tell us of God's gift of freedom in a new land."

Perhaps Caiaphas is smarter than I thought him to be. His answer goaded me into an apologia for our empire. "Our rule is fair. It is lawful. It is just. We don't condemn a man to death without cause."

"Yes, your excellency." Caiaphas' answer sounded sarcastic. And, of course, it was. "Only last month your soldiers entered our Temple and slew twenty Galileans at worship. Tell me about their trial. What was their crime? What law of Rome permits your uncircumcised soldiers to walk on the holy ground of our Temple?"

"Some of those men were Zealots," I said. "We know we weakened that clandestine movement by attacking them when we did. Had we waited...."

He interrupted me. "Had you simply surrounded the Temple, and called for the Temple Guards to bring the men out to you, perhaps you could have interrogated them all and let the innocent ones go? Or perhaps you knew them all to be guilty?"

"You would not have cooperated. You know it. Annas would have found a hundred excuses... Besides, we both know the Jews would not tell anything, even if we tortured them until they died!" I knew I had lost the debate when I said that. Forgive me, father. I am still learning.

"I am confused," said Caiaphas. "You speak of justice and law, and of torture and indiscriminate slaughter. Tell me how Rome can make such concepts compatible?"

I changed tactics. "You and Annas showed your joy in the decision of Antipas tonight. Did he do your dirty work for you? You wanted the Baptizer dead, but didn't want to arrange it yourselves." I knew the Sanhedrin, the body of governors of the Temple, had been bypassed often by the high priest's henchmen. Assassination is not just a Roman tool for eliminating troublesome people. There are ways of getting the people to do your work for you too. A few key people can get a crowd to become a maddened mob, and then get them to stone someone to death before they can stop to ask why. Caiaphas' hands were no cleaner than those of Antipas, or of me, or of you.

"Of course we wanted him dead, or at least silenced. He was a wild shouter, always accusing without understanding the need for compromise." This time Caiaphas saw his error. Honest answers may occasionally be good politics.

But admitting John the Baptizer's accusations had an element of truth in them was not the thing for him to do. Certainly he shouldn't be admitting such to the governor of the territory.

We had tested each other, and each had found weakness in his opponent. That may have given Caiaphas reason to hope. It gave me reason for greater caution in dealing with the Pharisees. I determined to have my men in Jerusalem keep a close eye on this man. We wished each other a good night's rest, neither meaning what we said.

As I returned to my quarters, I saw Salome slipping down the hallway toward Antipas' suite. Perhaps the exercise he was about to have would clear his head, I thought. But I doubted it. He is such a fool.

The next day we left Hyrcania, and returned to Caesaria, traveling directly west through Jerusalem. Our Roman road climbs at a very steep angle from the desert to the top of the Mount of Olives, and then just as steeply descends down and into that old city. But our horses were strong, and we only had to spend two nights on the road before we were enjoying the sea breezes on our own patio.

It is here on that patio that I complete this letter to you, father. What can I do with these Jews? They are wily, and very difficult to manage. They demand so much that is unreasonable! My servants will not work on the seventh day of the week, even if I have them beaten! Every baby boy has his penis cut on the eighth day of his life, no matter how often we insist that they are being cruel to helpless children. The Jews won't eat pig meat, and their diet excludes many other excellent foods.

They say their God has made a law. They must obey that law. Did you ever have one of our gods talk to you, father?

This letter has grown long enough. Now I am writing foolishness.

Procula sends her love with her greetings. Perhaps in my next letter I will tell you more of my frustration with the Jews and their God.

In Filial love,

Pontius

8

Pontius Pilate

Autumn, Year of Tiberias — XVII

Father,

Thank you for your letter, and for the presents. Procula particularly likes the dresses. I expect the local dressmakers will get fat off the copies they make and sell during the next few months.

I am surprised my letter about Antipas reached you, and that your reply returned so quickly. The winds must have been favorable! Even for summer, four months is exceptionally rapid transit. I wonder how long it will take for a return letter to this epistle I now write?

You asked me about the Jews, the nature of their Gods. I am prepared to answer that question now much more readily than before Antipas' birthday feast. Of course I had to be aware they were monotheistic, and that the Temple to their God whose name is Jah or Jahweh, is at Jerusalem. I knew too that they have a profound hatred for any statues or pictures that portray any god, even their own. Their governments through history, when they were not a vassal state of the Syrians, Assyrians, Greeks, or Egyptians, approached that of a Theocracy. Their God is their true ruler, and any king appointed over them is there by the consent and approval of Jah.

This Jah speaks to certain of the Jews, and has done so for perhaps thousands of years. (That is the Jews' claim, and they have scrolls to prove it.) Jah created the first human beings after creating the heavens and the Earth. Jah walked in a garden with the first two of these people, and gave them directions on what they could and could not eat. The story is that they disobeyed Jah and he had them thrown out of the perfect garden. Since then all mankind has had to shift for itself. You recognize, of course, that this tale is similar to other tales of origins from other regions, especially Babylonia.

When peoples lived over the whole earth, the Jews' God chose their tribe. Apparently they were called Haiberews then. The Haiberews' common ancestor was a man called Abraham. Abraham moved his people to this land after Jah directed him to do so. Some of them have been here ever since, though most of the descendants of Abraham were dispersed by the Assyrians hundreds of years ago.

In fact, the reason these people are called Jews now is that most of them are descended from one of Abraham's great grandsons, a man called Judah. A few of eleven other tribal names are mentioned from time to time, especially Levi's descendants, for the tribe of Levi was the tribe that produced priests for all the Haiberews.

One of the Haiberew Levites was a man called Moshe. He was born a slave in Egypt, perhaps fifteen hundred years ago. Can you imagine, father, a nation of people with a history that extends back two thousand years? It makes our two hundred year old Roman people look like an infant nation by comparison!

This Moshe somehow became a powerful priest of the Egyptians, and then he killed a man. The Jewish scrolls tell the story, something about intervening when the man was whipping a slave. Moshe ran away, escaping capital punishment, to live in the desert.

The life of Moshe is divided into three equal parts. The first forty years he spent living in Egypt in the home of the King, reared by the King's daughter. The second forty years he spent in the desert, working as a herder of sheep that belonged to a priest of Midian, a small nation that existed at that time. So Moses was first a priest of Egypt, probably worshipping their sun god, then a servant of a Midianite priest who must have had a great deal of influence over Moshe. Moshe married the priest's daughter, and had children by her. The third stage of Moshe's life is what has made him the principal hero of the Haiberew people.

The Legend is this. Moshe, while attending sheep on a mountain in the desert south of here, actually saw and talked with Jah, their God. Jah was a fire in a bush that did not consume the bush! Moshe talked with Jah, and was told to free the Haiberew people from Egypt.

Moshe obeyed Jah, and after a series of miracles, brought all of the slaves out of Egypt into the desert. There he trained them for the last forty years of his life. It was there in the desert that Moshe talked regularly with Jah, and was given the rules of life for Jah's chosen people to live by. Those laws include the dietary requirements of what these people can or cannot eat, and the rule of circumcision I told you of in my last letter.

The fascinating part of all this is that when the Jews have a ruler they feel is cruel or foolish or oppressive, they assume their God has been just as reasonable in selecting the bad one as He was in selecting the good ones. They get the bad ones when they have been bad. They get good when they have been good.

This is as true of their puppet kings and high priests as it is of Caesar or of his appointed governors. Presently the Jews believe they are having a mixed blessing. Antipas is hated. His brother, Philip, is tolerated, though his territory is really outside the area where most of the Jews live, being north and east of Lake Tiberias. I have become 'reachable,' that is, they believe I can be influenced by their political actions. I am still hated, of course, but they think any successor here could be much worse. So they tolerate me. The reason they believe this is probably that I acceded to their demands about those shields shortly after my arrival here.

Procula has become very interested in the Jews and their faith. She has made friends with the wife of one of my most trusted centurions, Cornelius. That woman, Ruth, is a native of the area, having lived in Joppa from the time of her birth until she married Cornelius. I know that the emperor frowns on fraternization and intermarriage of our soldiers with the local populations. I did not permit this marriage. Cornelius was here and married before I arrived four years ago. They have three children. I think Procula visits them as much as she does because she loves children and we have none. Yet, I know she has developed a strong friendship with Ruth.

But Ruth is a good evangelist for the Jews. She loves and trusts her God, Jah. And she sings lovely songs she claims were written by one of the Jews' great kings, David, who reigned in Jerusalem a thousand years ago! Apparently the man was a poet, great general, and competent administrator. (He was also a ladies' man, having several wives and more concubines. Everyone in the land claims David for an ancestor.) I copy now one of the songs Ruth sings. She translated it into our language for Procula.

"The Lord is my shepherd;
I shall not be in want.
He makes me lie down in green pastures
and leads me beside still waters.
He revives my soul

and guides me along right pathways for his
Name's sake.
Though I walk through the valley
of the shadow of death,
I shall fear no evil
for you are with me;
your rod and your staff, they comfort me.
You spread a table before me
in the presence of those who trouble me;
You have anointed my head with oil,
and my cup is running over.
Surely your goodness and mercy shall follow me
all the days of my life,
and I shall dwell in the house of the Lord
forever."

The song says much about what many Jews believe their God is like. Anyone who has seen a kind shepherd caring for his flock can understand the analogy. Apparently David was a shepherd before he was anointed by a wandering priest and became the second king of this land. Of course, the song says much about what the Jews think of themselves. How many of us Romans would compare ourselves to a smelly sheep?

Procula has thought about secretly becoming a convert to Judaism which is the name their faith is given. But I don't believe she has done so. She knows our multiplicity of gods, and accepts the deity of Tiberias. But she is ambivalent enough to believe in their God too, and I think she prays to Jah with Ruth, and may even do so when she is alone.

No matter Procula's faith. She is a great blessing to me in my work, and she provides me a tranquil bed where she can draw out my frustration, surrounding me with her deep love. This would be a terribly lonely place without her, despite the beauty of this land.

Maybe I'm not the man you are, father. The older I get, the more contented I am with Procula. The lovely young women here are just as available to me now as ever before, but all they really provide is an hour's diversion in the bedroom. Procula is fully capable of gratifying that need, and of giving me so much more! I'm not in any way saying the choice you made in divorcing mother and marrying an eighteen year old was wrong for you. All I say is that at this time in my life I would never consider such a change.

Well, as you can see, it is more pleasant for me to write about women and sex than about religion. But I will continue with my description of the Jewish faith. You might think from what I have written that there is but one religion in this land, that of the Jews. That is not true. There are many religions here, some of them quite disgusting, some of them happily erotic.

A number of my soldiers have told me about participating in sexual orgies with prostitute priests and priestesses as a part of the worship of a god named Ba'al. Such worship is conducted on high hills near small towns in the northern areas of the country. I am told that this religion dates back to times before the Haiberews came here.

Some of the communities off the regular routes through the country still worship a god called Molluck. That god demands the firstborn male son of each couple. These babes are thrown into the mouth-like orifice of a red hot furnace. The reason for this is that all Molluck's people must love him so much they will give up their most precious possession to him. That most precious possession is, of course, their firstborn son.

Molluck was worshipped here, as was Ba'al for perhaps thousands of years. The Haiberews who came here were introduced to those gods, and had to find a way to obey the laws of their own God, Jah. Jah said no one was to fornicate with anyone to whom they were not married. Jah said no one was to kill anyone. They have been fighting against ritual prostitution ever since, but probably they have won the battle against Molluck for their own people.

The way they did that was to offer substitute sacrifices to their God. These sacrifices were killed and burned, showing God they loved and wanted to obey Him, but they were assured God did not want to kill their baby sons. In addition, they set aside one whole tribe of Haiberews, the sons of Levi, one of the twelve great grandsons of Abraham. These sons of Levi were called Levites, and were not given any of the land. Instead they were to serve as priests and have the people of the land support them. As that whole family became servants of Jah and of the people, Jah did not require the children of the other families for His priesthood. Firstborn sons were, and are still, dedicated by the descendants of Judah, but a lamb is sacrificed, or even a pair of doves, as the people's offering.

I note too, that Jah does not 'eat' the food burned at the Jews' sacrifices. Rather, the meat is cooked, and then it is eaten by the priests and their families, and the balance is distributed to the poor — the widows and orphans of the land.

There are two other things you might want to know about the Jews. There are many people living north of Jerusalem who believe Jah wants them to worship on Mount Gerizim near the city of Samaria. These people are called Samaritans and they have a priesthood that is descended from an ancient Levite named Eli. These people sometimes refer to their god as El. So Eli's name indicated that he belonged to that god. Ancient texts of the Jews indicate that Eli and his sons failed the people, but that one of Eli's servants, a boy named Samuel (note the name 'El' in that boy's name) was elevated to the priesthood after Eli's death. Samuel was the one who anointed the first two kings of the Haiberew people.

The Samaritans maintain that El never appointed Samuel, and did not want the ancient place of worship on Mount Gerizim to be abandoned. They have built a beautiful Temple on that mountain where they worship on the same feast days as do the Jews in Jerusalem. The Samaritans hate us as much as the Jews do, and we have to have part of our standing army watch them constantly. So far they have not formed an alliance with the Jews against us. But that doesn't mean they won't! We must be constantly alert here on the frontier.

Don't misunderstand me. The principal religion here is Judaism. And the Jewish leaders would be powerful indeed if they weren't constantly debating with one another. The priestly leaders are called the Sanhedrin. That body is made up of two nearly equal groups, the Pharisees, and the Sadducees. When they are in agreement, they establish laws, and govern the people fairly well. When they are in disagreement, they sit and argue interminably. The arguments are always on subjects they cannot prove.

The primary difference between these two factions is their believing — or not believing — in an after life. Remember all the myths you and mother taught me about our gods, and how the good people went to live with them, gaining immortality as a special favor from Zeus? Such childish teachings! I suppose you went along with that prattle in order to assure us children we had nothing to fear from the dark.

Well, the strongest of the two parties, the Pharisees, believe that Jah will give them eternal life providing that they obey all of His laws. They argue from the holy scrolls that date back to Moshe who was apparently not only a priest and shepherd and general, but also an historian. The Sadducees argue from the same writings, and believe they have proven their point. They believe they are a line of priests maintaining the same concepts of the faith as one

Zadok, a priest who ministered during the time of King David.

One thing both sets of priests agree on, and that is they must maintain the worship and businesses of the Temple. It is from that work the revenues come that support all of these priests on a very high scale of living. They have fine homes, well furnished, are well fed, and they parade their corpulent bodies about the land, especially around the city of Jerusalem, in beautiful garments. Most of the priests keep slaves and pay other servants too. The people of this land would be so much better off if they would get rid of the priests, tear down their Temples in Jerusalem and Samaria, and let themselves relax under our rule.

Greet my brother and your new wife. The autumn rains have begun to fall. The Jews call it their new year. They have shed their past guilt (all the evil they have done during the past year) in their day of atonement. It is possible that for a while things will go well for all of us here in this troubled land.

In Filial love,

Pontius

9

Andrew

I said before that Jesus often took Simon Peter, James, and John with him for special instruction, leaving us behind. Later these three would teach the other nine. Perhaps this pattern is what Jesus wanted us to follow until the entire world was brought into an awareness of God's Kingdom. Though some strife developed about which of the Apostles was the greatest, the problem was more between the Zebedee brothers and Peter. We who were the second rank of Apostles were almost certain we had no chance to be elevated to so high a position.

Still, Jesus said things that encouraged us. "The last shall be first, the first last," he said often. And "He that would be greatest among you must become the servant of all."

On one occasion we were all impressed by His teaching as it affected us very much. One of the men who had been following Jesus for some time, Matthias, came from a wealthy family. Often he gave generously to help support us, for we seldom had any time to work at our trades, and the daily cost of food and other traveling expenses had to be met somehow. Matthias wasn't the only one to give funds for Jesus' work. There were members of the Zealot party who thought Jesus might be the one to lead them to victory, so they contributed frequently. One of those zealots was Simon of Nazareth, whom Jesus had picked to be one of us twelve!

Other zealots gave money to help us, because in their cynicism they wanted to use Jesus as a foil to annoy the Romans while they continued to plot a strong military offense.

Matthias was sincere in his giving. He really wanted to help, and had come to love Jesus and Jesus' teaching of the Kingdom. Matthias rejoiced in the miracles of healing that he saw nearly as often as did the twelve of us. A shy man, he kept well back in the crowds, and seldom imposed himself on Jesus or any of the rest of us. But the day came when he approached Jesus with a personal need.

"Jesus, Good Master, what must I do to win eternal life?" He asked the question all of us hold in our hearts. We all want our lives to continue on forever, and for our lives to be worthwhile, with no illness or other suffering.

Jesus responded with a question as He often did. "Why do you call me good?" He asked. "No one is good except God alone."

Matthias was silent at this. He didn't take back the word, which indicated he was either unable to speak, or that he truly felt he was talking to God Himself as he talked to Jesus. I believe it was because he was afraid to change the title. The thought of Jesus as God was different from that of thinking of Him as being God's son. Nathaniel's comment in the first days of our fellowship with Jesus, and Peter's statement on the road to Caesaria Philippi were not spoken of very often among us. It was enough for us to have Jesus for our Rabbi, our beloved teacher, our companion on the road. Our minds couldn't contain the thought that we walked the hills each day with God!

After waiting for Matthias to respond, Jesus continued. "You know the commandments: 'Do not murder; do not commit adultery; do not steal; do not bear false witness; do not defraud; honor your father and mother.'"

"But Master," Matthias replied (we noted he left out the word 'good' in the second address), "I have kept all these since I was a boy."

Jesus looked straight at him; and He gave him that look that we have each received often, the look that searches the depths of one's heart. I watched Jesus' face, and saw it change to the look of deep affection He had often bestowed on each of us. "One thing you lack: go sell everything you have, and give to the poor, and you will have riches in heaven; and come, follow me."

At these words, Matthias face fell, and he turned and walked away. As I said, he was a man of great wealth. The price Jesus asked was too high for him to pay.

Jesus looked around at us and said, "How hard it will be for the wealthy to get into the Kingdom of God." I'm sure my own face fell at this comment, for many of the followers who traveled with us, or came often to where we were, as well as helped keep our purse full, meeting our needs, were quite well to do people. The other disciples looked surprised or uncomfortable too.

Jesus called us children then. He often did this when He saw how little we understood, or determined we really needed to listen to what He would say. "Children, how hard it is to enter the Kingdom of God! It is easier for a camel to pass through the eye of a needle than for a rich man to enter the Kingdom of God."

This really astonished us. It didn't matter whether Jesus was talking of a sewing needle that was too small for an insect to pass through, much less a camel, or the pedestrian gate of a city after the main gates were closed. Probably He meant the latter, though we didn't ask Him. Camels could go through the several sharp turns in the wall of a fortified city where people could only walk single file. But they would have to move slowly, and the load they carried would have to be removed before they entered. No merchant would separate the camel from its load in a place where the goods could be stolen. Instead, he would wait outside the town, protecting his property, until the gates were opened. Then he could proceed safely into the town.

I understood this statement of Jesus. A rich man was like the camel, unable to proceed into the safety of the Kingdom while carrying the burden of his wealth.

"Then who can be saved?" I asked Simon Peter. And as I asked, I heard others of the twelve asking the same question.

Jesus looked at us and said, "For man it is impossible, but not for God; everything is possible for God."

(After Jesus' death and resurrection, we had an election, and Matthias was given the place that had been Judas Iscariot's. We all wanted Matthias to enter the Kingdom of God. Later in his life, he sold or gave away all of his possessions, and when he stopped living this life, he left no estate.)

Then my brother spoke up. He was always either more brave than the rest of us, or less able to keep silence. "We here, have left everything to become your followers."

Jesus said, "I tell you this: there is no one who has given up home, brothers or sisters, mother, father or children, or land, for my sake and for the Gospel, who will not receive in this age a hundred times as much — houses, brothers and sisters, mothers and children, and land." He paused and looked at us with a look of sorrow. "And persecutions besides; and in the age to come, eternal life." Then He said again what He so often said, "But the first shall be last, and the last first."

That was one of the many things that puzzled us. I guess it puzzled James and John more than any. They knew they were among the leaders Jesus had chosen. Perhaps they feared Jesus would make Simon Peter the leader, finally, or perhaps He would name Judas Iscariot as the leader of us all. Judas was the one who kept all the money for us.

A time came when Jesus decided to take us to Jerusalem for the Passover Feast. We were reluctant to go, for the priests, Pharisees and Sadducees, as well as the scribes, were determined to stop Jesus' ministry. We felt safer in the country, and we liked being close to our homes. Sometimes Jesus would give us time off and we would go to our home towns, visit with our families, even work a few days at the old tasks that had bored us before. But they took on an aura of home and safety after we had endured long periods of following Jesus. I can't speak for the others, but my mind can absorb only so much at a time. Some of the things Jesus said disturbed me terribly.

For instance, Jesus led the way toward Jerusalem, and He set a fast pace. Then we were reluctant followers. The ones who followed behind us were really afraid. Jesus took the twelve of us aside and said, "We are going to Jerusalem, and the Son of Man will be given up to the chief priests and the doctors of the law. They will condemn Him to death and hand Him over to the foreign power. He will be mocked and spat upon, flogged, and killed." We were horrified.

If He really believed that would happen to Him, why was He going? And why in the name of the Kingdom was He hurrying? Many asked themselves why they were following, and more than a few turned back.

"And three days afterwards, He will rise again," Jesus added. I heard Him say it. Most of the others heard Him too. I know Simon Peter, my brother, heard it, for he dictated it to John Mark as a part of his recollections of our life with Jesus. But I know I didn't understand. Now, years later, I still know I don't understand. All I do is accept. And rejoice. I accept and rejoice.

What of the twelve? Did any of us have second thoughts? I know my mind was in a turmoil. Once before, when we were in Jerusalem, Jesus taught the people they would have to eat His flesh, and that if they did so, they would live forever. Nearly all the crowd walked away that day, shaking their heads. Some, I am sure, considered Jesus to be a madman, and determined it was foolishness to listen to Him. That day Jesus asked us, "Will you leave me too?"

Simon Peter answered for all of us with the question, "Where shall we go? You have the words of eternal life." We didn't understand Him then. Our understanding is not clear now. One of Jesus' later followers, Saul of Tarsus, says, "Now we see through dark glass. Someday we will see Jesus face to face." When we saw Him face to face, while he lived among us, and we loved Him, and were loved by Him, we knew that to leave Him was to go nowhere.

The mother of James and John walked part of the way with us. She didn't often come along, but they had relatives in Jerusalem, so I suppose she thought this to be a good time to go visit. When we were stopped for a rest one day, she sought Jesus out, bringing James and John along with her. I don't know if she thought of asking Jesus a favor, or if her sons put her up to it. But she said to Jesus, "Master, will you do a favor for my sons?"

"What is your wish?"

"I want you to give orders that in your kingdom my two sons here may sit next to you, one at your right, and the other at your left."

Jesus knew it wasn't just their mother who wanted this. He looked thoughtfully at James and John for several long moments. "You do not understand what you are asking," He said. "Can you drink from the same cup from which I drink, or be baptized with the same baptism with which I am baptized?"

They answered together, as if they knew the question was coming, "We can!"

He continued to look at them thoughtfully, first at one, then the other. Their mother withdrew, leaving them to face Jesus without her. "Yes," He said finally. "The cup that I drink from you shall drink, and the baptism I am baptized with shall be your baptism; but to sit at my right or left is not for me to grant; it is for those to whom it has already been assigned by my Father."

James and John grew up knowing Joseph, Jesus' father. They knew the old carpenter had not made such an assignment, had not had any part of Jesus' ministry. They knew Joseph to be dead.

I watched them digest the information Jesus gave them, and I saw them leave Him without further comment. I was the only one who overheard this conversation, and before I walked away too, I asked Jesus if He would explain to me what He meant by drinking from His cup, or having a special baptism.

"You will learn in time, Andrew," He said. "Your faithfulness will be tried, and in the end you will drink fully of my cup. Your strength will be as great as that of any of the twelve because you will have accepted my baptism." He put his arm around my shoulders, and I felt a flow of love come from Him that made me content. I was at His side at that moment, and I knew I was still one of His chosen twelve. What more could I ask?

I was quick to go to the other nine and tell them. "Do you know what James and John got their mother to ask Jesus?" I asked. Of course they responded in the negative. "They want Jesus to set them on His right hand and on His left when He establishes His Kingdom!" I was quite proud of myself for being able to pass along this bit of news, and they were all certainly very interested in what I said.

Maybe some of them were put out that James and John and Simon Peter had the inner circle already, and this gave them a chance to bring their anger out in the open. "What do you think of that, Peter?" BarTholomew asked. "Which of the three of you is number one after Jesus? It looks like the Sons of Thunder are trying to squeeze you out!"

"What about the rest of us?" Simon the Zealot said. "We are of the twelve. We go out on missions two by two just as they do. We have sat and learned from Rabbi Jesus. What about us?"

Philip said, "I thought He chose twelve as a symbol of the twelve sons of Jacob, the tribes of Israel. Which of the twelve tribes was the strongest? Which of us represents that tribe?"

"We all trace our ancestry back to Judah, except for Levi who claims his ancestors were the priestly tribe," Judas said. "Surely the one He will pick is the best educated of us, someone who can walk in dignity through the courts." We didn't know much about Judas then, but he had an air of pride about him that made him look like he was accustomed to luxury.

Each of us had something to say, but the underlying mood was one of dissatisfaction. We were vying with one another for position, and were very unhappy with James and John. We went over to them and started to give them a verbal barrage. Would they learn from such? Probably not, but they would be more careful in their maneuvers for power thereafter.

Jesus continued on ahead of us as we bickered. When we came to a small town with a tree shaded well, he stopped to rest. Then He turned to us and said, "You know that in the world the recognized rulers lord it over their subjects, and their great men make them feel the weight of their authority. We nodded, knowing He had caught us in our petty arguments. But they weren't really so petty. Jesus' Kingdom would start out small, and even after we had captured the whole of our land, there would be only one or two really high places in His court. The rest of us would have to be subject to those appointed.

Jesus made another of His enigmatic statements. It stopped our argument about who would be first, but provided us reason to discuss the meaning of this teaching. "That is not the way with you; among you, whoever wants to be great must be your servant, and whoever wants to be first must be the willing slave of all." He looked on us with great love, and drew water from the well, passing it to each of us to drink, and then drawing more so that we could wash some of the dust from our bodies.

"For even the Son of Man did not come to be served, but to serve, and to give His life as a ransom for many." That ended the conversation in Jesus' presence. But we continued it that evening in small groups. Judas, Philip, and I sat together.

"I don't know what to make of it," I said. "How can we know which of us is the greater servant of the others? We don't wait on each other very much."

"Well," said Judas, "I've heard that from Herod's stewards before. 'Those of us elevated to high places have great responsibilities,' they say. 'We are really the servants of everyone.'" Judas could really sound sarcastic sometimes.

"But what does He mean when He says He must give up His life as a ransom?" Philip asked. Judas didn't reply to that, nor did I. We learned from Jesus what it means to be 'servant of all' by His actions that day. I determined to try to offer simple kindness to the others. I could help prepare the evening meal that night, and I could help clean up after the meal. It was a little disconcerting to discover as I confided this to Philip that he had the same thoughts, and the same anticipations. If we all struggled to wait on one another, the right hand of Jesus was still in dispute.

We continued on our way the next day. When we arrived at the outskirts of Jericho, we were met by a blind man named BarTimaeus. It was significant that he had no name, but only that of his father. BarTimaeus' only work was to beg, and in a small town where all knew him there was no hope of his getting much from his neighbors. Each day someone led him to the gates of Jericho where he sat and waited for the travelers who came along the road to take pity on him and throw a few coins into the basket he had before him. Blind beggars are a common site. Eye problems afflict many of the people of our land. Some lose their sight in battle, some from diseases of aging, but many like this blind beggar are born blind. Some say it is the sins of the father that are visited unto the sons, as is written by the prophets.

We had been through Jericho before on our way from the north country to Jerusalem, and on our way back to Galilee. The Jericho road is the best route to follow during the winter months as it is so much warmer in that deep valley than it is through the hills of Samaria. We had often seen BarTimaeus sitting with the other beggars at Jericho's gate as we passed, but we never once thought to bring him to Jesus, or to offer him money. We simply ignored him. Perhaps, if we had been rich, we might have given him something. There are so many beggars in the world...

Jesus' reputation over the two years of His teaching and healing ministry had grown. All the beggars of Jericho knew of Jesus, and apparently BarTimaeus knew what he would do if Jesus ever came near again. This time, as we passed by, he learned that Jesus of Nazareth was among us. A crowd gathered about us while we were still some distance outside the gates, and they were cheering Jesus. Some of them were calling Him 'Son of David,' and bowing before Him as if He were already the King of the country. It made us proud to be with Him, for the twelve of us to be known as His Chosen men.

As we came close BarTimaeus called out, "Jesus, Son of David, have pity on me.!" Many people near him told him to be quiet. He was very loud! I am sure the crowd didn't want this beggar's cries to disturb the welcome they were providing this possible Messiah.

But the more they tried to quiet the man, the louder he called out. "Son of David! Have pity on me!" We began to wonder what Jesus would do. How could He possibly ignore this disturbance? Jesus didn't try to ignore it. Instead, He sent me and Philip to get the beggar.

One thing I have hated about our discipleship under Jesus was working with the sick and the crippled. Those of us who have made our living as fishermen on the beautiful Sea of Galilee have always been clean. We have enjoyed a midnight swim almost every night of our lives, and we have had clean clothing to wear. The smell of fish was about us, we know, because many of the town's citizens teased us about that. But the smell of dirt was never there. The smell of old sweat, and of draining wounds, sometimes of vomit dried on the clothes of the sick who came to Jesus, was something I hated.

When we reached BarTimaeus, I noticed right away the man didn't smell bad. He showed evidence that either someone cared for him, or he had a sense of responsibility to care for himself. Philip and I came to him where he was still calling out, "Son of David, have pity on me."

"Take heart; stand up; He is calling you," I said. At that the man threw off his cloak, sprang up, and we led him to Jesus.

"What do you want me to do for you?" Jesus asked. It was a question I would have asked. And I have seen Jesus heal blind people on other occasions. This man's eye sockets looked empty. Other blind people Jesus had healed hadn't looked as physically without hope of sight as this man. Surely he wouldn't have faith enough to ask to have his sight!

But he did. "Master," he said. "I want my sight back."

Jesus didn't even touch the man. "Go," He said. "Your faith has cured you." Jesus used that line often. "Your faith has cured you." Jesus didn't take the credit, he gave it to the one who believed a cure was possible, and sought it.

It didn't surprise me that the man instantly gained his sight and began to follow in the crowd as we moved along the road.

"Jesus," I asked, "Why did he ask to recover his sight? All in Jericho know him, and they say he never was able to see."

"He has always had the light of knowledge within him," Jesus said. "All men are created in my Father's image, and all know deep within themselves that sight is their gift from the creator. BarTimaeus knew this too. That is how he found the courage to ask. Though he has never seen before today, the gift of sight has always been his, as it has been yours. He was right to ask for it to be restored to him."

The number of people traveling with us increased by BarTimaeus, and by many more. As we walked into Jericho, we may have numbered hundreds. Hundreds more stood along the wayside to get a good look at Jesus. We were half way into the city when Jesus looked up and called to a man in a tree. "Zachaeus, make haste and come down. I must stay at your house today."

The man climbed down the tree as fast as he could, and hurried up to us. He welcomed Jesus joyfully. "You will be most welcome in my home, Master," he said. He fell in beside Jesus. It was then we noted Zachaeus was at least a head shorter than Jesus. Matthew Levi moved up from the rear of our inner group and embraced the little fellow as if he were an old friend, and walked beside him too.

Several people in the crowd complained out loud. "Is Jesus going to that sinner's house?" one asked. "Doesn't He know the man is the worst sinner of all the tax collectors in this area?" For once, Simon Peter and I held our own counsel. We remembered how we had complained when Matthew

Levi was called to join us. We learned then that we had no right to judge others unless we were sinless ourselves.

As Jesus walked along with Zachaeus, the voices of the people in the crowd became angrier. "He is going to stay at that sinner's house!" I watched the man who said that reach down to pick up a stone. Philip and I walked between the stone carrier and Jesus, and we stared hard at the man until he turned away, dropping the stone. I was quite concerned for the safety of all of us.

But Zachaeus stopped and stood before Jesus and spoke clearly so that the crowd could hear him, "Sir, I am going to give half of all I have to the poor." Then he looked about him, taking in the entire crowd with that glance, and said, "And if I have cheated anybody, I will pay him back four times the amount!"

Then we arrived at Zachaeus' home. Before we entered, Jesus said to him, "Today salvation has come to this house, because this man too is a son of Abraham." He looked at the crowd, and rested one hand on the shoulder of BarTimaeus, and the other on the shoulder of Zachaeus, and said, "The Son of Man has come to seek out and save what was lost."

Which was the greater miracle, we asked ourselves, the healing of the blind man, so that he could see, or the healing of the thief and miser, so he could be numbered as a good neighbor? The Kingdom of Heaven might well be a joyful place if Jesus could heal the hard empty hearts of the wealthy.

We dined that evening with Zachaeus and his family. Jericho is one of my favorite places. There is a greater variety of fresh fruit and vegetables there the year around than anywhere else in our land. The process of irrigation of the land was begun here thousands of years ago, and continues to make this a huge oasis in the driest of deserts. We rested under sycamore trees as we ate, and we watched the sun set over the mountains to our west. The city of Jericho was filled to overflowing with pilgrims on their way to Jerusalem. The Passover feast would be celebrated in another week, and anyone who was not sure of lodging in the Holy City needed to be there before the coming Sabbath.

Zachaeus was a wonderful host, seeing to it that his servants filled our trays and bowls with fish, lamb, goat, and chicken meat as well as good bread to dip in a variety of tasty sauces. Our cups were kept full from wineskins that held a variety of choices to quench our thirst. We were not Zachaeus' only guests. Travelers and local citizens were invited to join us, and we participated in a fellowship with the community that night that was at least equal to any we had experienced throughout our journeys.

The next day we climbed the steep hills out of the Jordan valley, up and up again to the east side of the Mount of Olives. There, in the little village of Bethany, we stayed at the home of Lazarus and his sisters, Mary and Martha. Earlier, Jesus performed two miracles for that family, and again I can't tell you which was greater. Mary, He cured of possession by demons early in His ministry in Galilee. She had lived a terrible life in the village of Magdala. We who were fishermen knew her there, some of us sexually. We often were in Magdala with our catch of fish, for there we sold what we had netted, and were free from having to sell it on the market in the nearby towns. The main industry of Magdala was the drying of fish, and then exporting it to distant places.

Once Mary was cured by Jesus, she was befriended by Joanna, the wife of Chuza, Herod's steward, and by Suzanna, a young woman of Herod Antipas' court. We were surprised to learn on our next journey to Jerusalem that Mary came from Bethany, and had a brother and sister living there. When the reunion took place, Jesus was introduced to

Martha and Lazarus, and we were invited to use their home whenever we came to the Holy City.

The second miracle Jesus did for that family was to raise Lazarus from the dead. That statement sounds surprising in my own ears, so I am sure it causes you to question, even to doubt the truth of what I say. Still, it is true that Jesus did just that. It was about three months before this journey that we were called from the River Jordan to go to Lazarus. Mary and Martha sent word that Lazarus was very ill. Jesus chose to linger by the river for some time after that, two or three days at least. Then He said He would go to Lazarus, and informed us the man was dead.

When we arrived at Bethany two days later, we were told Lazarus was indeed dead, and had been in his tomb four days! Now, when Jesus raised the dead on other occasions, it was only moments, or no more than hours, after the person died. The young man at Nain was being carried to the cemetery. The little girl in Caphernaum was dead no more than an hour.

But Lazarus was certified dead four days. His body had been prepared for final rest. Ointments had been rubbed into his cold flesh. Linen wrappings were wound around his body, so his rotting flesh would mingle with the ointments, and the aroma near the grave would not be so offensive. The stone had been rolled against the hole where his body was entombed with the mortal remains of his ancestors. I saw the grave, and can assert there were shelves inside where at least four skeletons lay, with fragments of linen still resting over and under the bones. Lazarus' family was obviously wealthy to own such a large tomb. The stone that rolled over the entrance was at least four cubits in diameter, and almost a cubit thick. Levers were used to move the stone in a track prepared for it. The workmanship was superb, and must have been completed well before the time of the first King Herod.

When I say Jesus raised Lazarus from the dead, I must also say that He did not touch Lazarus. He directed the stone be rolled away, and then called to Lazarus in a loud voice — directing him to come out of the tomb. There must have been a hundred people standing there watching as this miracle took place.

All twelve of us Apostles shared in the rejoicing at Lazarus' home thereafter. We saw the man who had been dead, who we were informed had died of a wasting disease, his skin yellow, his flesh hanging loose. We saw him in robust health, laughing, joking, eating, and somehow free from the fear that grips most of us, the fear of what life there might be, or might not be, on the other side of the grave.

Leave it to others to explain the value of a miracle. I know that Lazarus alive meant joy for his sisters, as well as for us, his friends. I know that neither Mary nor Martha had any other man they could depend on for their protection and care.

Some of the other Apostles will argue, now that years have elapsed and we have seen other friends die, and not return, that passing through death is the way to being able to see and touch Jesus again. That death is the way to be with God, our heavenly Father, in His Kingdom. For Lazarus to be brought back then, would be for him to lose paradise for life here on earth. Some say that would be worse than the fate of Adam and Eve when they were driven from the garden. If that is true, they could argue that Jesus did harm to his friend Lazarus by bringing him back to life. Such arguments confuse me. I know I was glad to see Lazarus alive again, and I rejoiced in my friendship with him; until he died a second time not long ago.

I am sorry for the diversion. Where were we? Oh yes. We came up from Jericho to Bethany to stay with Mary, Martha, and Lazarus...

We spent the sixth day of the week, and the Sabbath with our friends in Bethany. The night of the sixth day we were invited to a feast in the home of a Pharisee, Simon the Leper. Now the law says no one who is a leper may associate with the people, but must be outcast. This is to protect us all from the dread disease of leprosy. But Simon was able to stay in his own home, and to have servants wait on him, for he was not only a priest, but came from a wealthy family. Even then, he could not have lived at home if his disease was severe, and if open sores showed as they often do on lepers. He was not permitted to serve in his profession at the Temple, of course. But he continued to receive his portion of the Temple revenues, doing some service for the Sanhedrin when asked.

It is most probable that Simon invited us to his home so that he could learn more of Jesus, and pass on his observations to Caiaphas, the high priest. Whatever his reason, we were provided good fare, and pleasant surroundings. The priest's home was built higher on Bethany's hill, with a view looking eastward to the Jordan valley. We rested in an open courtyard where people of the town could enter or leave as they chose while we ate.

Mary, sister of Martha and Lazarus, formerly Mary of Magdala, came into the courtyard and stood behind Jesus as He ate and talked with Simon. Her gratitude for her own new life free from her past was always great, but since her brother's miraculous return from the dead, she was overflowing with the desire to show how much she appreciated Jesus' kindness to her and to her family.

Once, after her deliverance, she came into a room where Jesus was dining with this same Simon, and on that occasion she poured oil on Jesus' feet, wiping them with her hair. Then she was weeping, and so grateful she kissed Jesus' feet. This had embarrassed Simon, as he remembered

Mary's past. Jesus rebuked Simon then, and both remembered the occasion.

This time Mary carried an alabaster jar, filled with perfume. She broke the thin neck of the bottle, and poured out its contents on Jesus' hair. The perfume's scent filled the area quickly, wafted past our nostrils by a gentle easterly breeze. This time Simon said nothing, merely watched the drama unfold, as most of us did.

You must know that three years of walking with Jesus made us as full of love for Him as was Mary. We too looked for ways to express that love, and our gratitude for having been chosen by Him. The power he gave us to preach, teach, and heal changed us. More, it made us able to understand and appreciate Him in greater depth than we could at the beginning. Mary's act of anointing Jesus was one in which we shared. It was her doing, but most of us rejoiced that it had been done. We remembered that Samuel anointed David in much the same way. Also that Elijah anointed Jehu and Elisha hundreds of years ago. Mary's act was one that God approved, and that we witnessed.

But there was at least one of the twelve who objected, and perhaps there were others. Judas Iscariot spoke up, demanding an explanation. He asked Mary, "Why didn't you sell that perfume on the market and give the money to us for distribution to the poor?"

Mary was silent for a moment. "Because I wanted to do with it what I have done," she replied quietly.

"But it must have cost at least three hundred..." Judas sniffed the air. "At least three hundred!" He was almost speechless, a condition unique for him.

"Leave her alone," said Jesus.

"But its pure oil of nard!" Judas exclaimed again. "Do you know how expensive that is?"

"Leave her alone," Jesus said again. "She has anointed me in preparation for my burial." Again we heard the haunting sound of his personal prophecy of death.

Judas would have spoken again. But Jesus rested his hand on Judas' arm and quoted Moses. "The poor will be with you always. You will not always have me."

We left Simon's home shortly after that, and enjoyed our Sabbath rest at Lazarus' house. Perhaps the others had some premonition that the most awful week in our lives was about to begin. But I didn't. I simply relaxed, resting as the Lord commanded us to do on the Seventh day. In Bethany it was easy to find joy in the beauty of God's creation all about us.

10

Andrew

The first day of the week started rather quietly. Our Sabbath rest the day before was totally within the law. No Pharisee could find fault with us that day. We visited with one another. We read or listened to Scripture. We offered our prayers to Almighty God, ate the food the women had prepared for us before sundown on the sixth day, and relaxed, enjoying the warm sunlight that beamed upon us. In that warmth was the promise of a joyful spring season.

As we broke our fast that first morning of Jesus' last week, He asked Judas Iscariot and me to go together to Bethphage, the small town west of Lazarus' home, and to bring him back a donkey. "Go off to the village facing you, and as soon as you enter it you will find a tethered colt that no one has yet ridden. Untie it and bring it here. If anyone says to you, 'What are you doing?' say, 'The Master needs it and will send it back here directly.'"

Of course we went as He directed us. I was always glad to obey Him. Judas wasn't most of the time. He certainly had grumbled a lot about the perfume Mary spilt on Jesus, for instance. But this time, he was almost ecstatic! "Do you know what this means?" he asked me. He didn't wait for my reply, seeing perhaps that I looked confused by his question.

"It means that Jesus is proclaiming Himself King!" Judas did a little dance on the dusty road. "He is proclaiming Himself King of Israel." Judas looked at me, his eyes gleaming like those of a wild fanatic. "More," he whispered. And he looked around to be sure no one heard but me. The road was empty. "More! Do you remember what Zechariah said about this?"

I didn't. I was a fisherman, not a scholar. But Judas seemed to know whole passages of the law and the prophets, and he seemed to take pleasure in educating any of us who would listen. Probably his most apt pupil was Levi, but apparently I would do if there was no one else to listen.

"This is what Zechariah said," Judas persisted.

"'Rejoice heart and soul, daughter of Zion!
Shout with gladness, daughter of Jerusalem!
See how your king comes to you;
    he is victorious, he is triumphant.
    humble, and riding on a donkey.
He will banish chariots from Ephraim
    and horses from Jerusalem;
    the bow of war will be banished.
He will proclaim peace for the nations.
His empire will stretch from sea to sea,
    from the river to the ends of the earth.'"

"I don't believe I understand all that," I said. Judas looked upset, even angry for a moment. Then he laughed and relaxed and gave me a gentle, almost playful shove.

"I don't understand it all either," he said. "It sounds like the great king will rule the world, all of it, and that he will have the power to proclaim peace for every nation." He shook his head as he thought about what he said. "But the first thing for the king to do is to proclaim himself, and that is what Jesus is doing today! He is going to ride a donkey into Jerusalem! Let's go get that donkey." He hurried on ahead of me into Bethphage. There we found the donkey as Jesus had said we would.

I sometimes wonder if Jesus set that up, or if it was something he knew would happen without his making arrangements beforehand. But it doesn't make any difference in the outcome of the day. We started to untie the colt, and some men nearby asked us what we were doing. We replied with what Jesus told us, "The Master needs it, and will send it back here directly." They gave us no argument, but turned away to continue their conversation.

When we brought the donkey to Jesus, He stood beside it, and was still. Judas took off his cloak (the morning on the Mount of Olives was quite chilly, we were all wearing outer garments). With a flourish, Judas lay his coat on the donkey's back. I decided to do the same. Then Jesus mounted and sat there quietly. Suddenly there were many people around us, including all ten of the other Apostles, and the people we had dined with in Bethany. I saw many of the travelers who had climbed the road out of Jericho with us as well. Several took off their cloaks and lay them before Jesus, making a pathway of cloth for the donkey to walk upon. Then many more went to the trees nearby, and cut down branches to wave, or to straw before the advancing animal.

They and we began to shout, perhaps at Judas' urging, but more likely out of a growing spirit of enthusiasm for the moment.

"Hosanna!" we shouted. "Hosanna! Blessings on the coming KIngdom of our Father, David! Hosanna in the highest heavens!" We danced and sang and shouted for Jesus all the way down the Mount of Olives to the valley opposite the gates of Jerusalem.

We were all shouting, singing, rejoicing. We were a mob as we approached the gates of the city. First we were numbered in the tens, then in the hundreds, and then there were thousands upon thousands of us. Pilgrims coming south and north converged on us as we and the hundreds who were arriving from Jericho came down the side of the Mount of Olives into the Kidron valley. The body of Jesus' followers swirled around Him and slowed His progress, bringing Him almost to a standstill.

We were crossing the Kidron that was running a little water down its often dry bed that day, when several Pharisees stood in front of the little donkey and stopped our progress completely.

"Jesus," I heard one of the Pharisees say, "Make these people stop all the shouting."

"I tell you if my disciples keep silent, the stones themselves would shout," Jesus said.

What a glorious day it was! Jesus was right. The people, the trees, the other plants along the way, and even the stones of the earth God created were sharing in that joyful moment. Our voices echoed against the walls of the city, and the people came out to meet us; residents of the city as well as pilgrims who had arrived in the city before us.

Then we were subjected to one of Jesus' mood changes. He sat and looked at the city before Him and spoke to it as if the city itself were alive. He wept as He said, "Jerusalem, Jerusalem, you that kill the prophets and stone those who are sent to you! How often I longed to gather your children as a hen gathers her chicks under her wings, and you refused! So be it! Your house will be left to you desolate." He wept, surprising many of the people who were celebrating the glorious event of the Messiah's arrival in the city. I saw many turn away then, shaking their heads as they left.

I heard one say, "This couldn't be the Messiah. He hasn't the quality of a great leader."

Jesus continued talking through His tears. "Jerusalem, if you in your turn had only understood on this day the message of peace! But alas, it is hidden from your eyes! Yes a time is coming when your enemies will raise fortifications all around you, when they will encircle you and hem you in on every side; they will dash you and the children inside your walls to the ground; they will leave not one stone standing on another within you — and all because you did not recognize your opportunity when God offered it."

I watched as Judas Iscariot and Simon the Zealot tried to stir up the crowd's enthusiasm again, but the excitement was over for most of the people. They stopped being a part of a movement under one will, and became separate members of an audience. They looked again, and saw there was nothing important going on any longer. They melted away by small groups of twos and threes, and before long we were the twelve plus the usual followers. Together, we walked into Jerusalem behind Jesus, who still rode the donkey. He stopped inside the gate, dismounted, and a young boy, probably from Bethphage, took the animal's halter and led it away. Then we followed Jesus up the steps that led to the Temple. What would happen next, we didn't know, but we were loyal, and wanted to be with Him. The stairs that led to the Temple Mount were jammed with pilgrims, and with peddlers and vendors offering food, beverages, souvenirs, as well as animals and birds for sacrifice. There was an abundance of spring lambs, tethered to each other, and tied to convenient pillars. Bird cages filled with doves and pigeons filled openings that had been passageways for people the week before. Money changers, calling their price of exchange for Temple shekels, filled the balance of the space. There was hardly room for two people to pass on the staircase, and where they walked was fouled by animal droppings. The noise of the animals was rivaled only by that of the vendors. The combination of bodies and noise packed within the confined area was made almost totally unbearable by the stench of all.

Jesus stood in the narrow passageway left open for pilgrims and others to pass through this temporary market. The crowds moved about him, jostling Him and us as they went their separate ways. It is interesting to me now that I was not offended by the scene, nor by the merchants as they were hawking their wares. The crowds of sales people at special holiday seasons was something I always remembered when I visited the Holy City. We all grow accustomed to things, and do not consider what should be. We assume that if our leaders do not stop something, it must be all right. The priests of the Temple did not object to the vendors and the money changers. Somehow they accepted what they must have considered a necessary part of the Temple sacrifice. Money needed to be changed so only Temple money could be offered to God. Sheep, lambs, and birds needed to be offered as burnt offerings. Someone needed to provide these goods and services. The merchants filled a need.

Lambs were also at the market to be sold as food for the Passover Feast. This special day required a special meal. The Passover lamb was slain to be eaten the night of the first Passover, when the Angel of Death passed over the homes of the Hebrews when they were slaves in Egypt. If the lambs weren't brought to market, each of the families there would have had to bring their own lamb for their part of the celebration. Many who were not farmers or herdsmen, like Simon and me who were fishermen, and who keep no animals, would have had to do without. The people who sold there on the Temple Mount were providing us an important service, a religious necessity.

Jesus walked to the first money changer's table, and tipped it over. It was a surprise for me, as it was for the other disciples, the people about us, and the merchants. Suddenly the crowd that had been moving through the market area with some measure of patience and courtesy, changed itself into an avaricious mob. Coins rolled across the stones beneath our feet, and people dived for them. Jesus walked to another table, and tipped it; then to a third, and a fourth. No one stopped Him. But the money changers at the other tables quickly gathered up their funds and put them in pouches. For them, business was closed, at least for a while.

Then Jesus unfastened one of the ropes that kept the lambs from moving freely. He took the rope in his hand, making a whip of it, and snapped it. The lambs moved out, their owner trying to recapture them. Some of the people in the crowd, seeing an opportunity for a free lamb, took advantage of it. Jesus moved to another rope corral, and then to another, freeing more animals, and then on he went to yet another. It didn't take the other vendors long to see this was not the time or place to display their merchandise. They packed up and moved out quickly, but not soon enough to prevent a melee of animals, and then some birds as well, to crash about among the crowd.

I couldn't help it. I laughed aloud at the discomfort of the merchants, and even at the ridiculous sight of us, Jesus' followers. A few of us tried to capture some of the animals for the merchants, and others tried to recover coins for the money changers. But we were pushed and shoved by the crowds, and had little success.

Jesus continued upsetting tables and freeing animals; confronting merchants. He spoke frequently, saying over and over again, "My Father's House is a House of Prayer. You have made it a den of robbers."

The Temple Courts were cleared of merchants quite rapidly. They took their animals, their birds, and their money, and set up shop outside the city walls. We stood among the pillars, looking out across the stone courtyard to the Temple entrance. Hundreds, even thousands, of people moved about, the disturbance at our entrance unnoticed, or quickly forgotten. I looked to Jesus. He looked about at the scene before Him, His face showing some satisfaction at His accomplishment. Then He turned to us, beckoned us to follow, and we returned to Bethany. On the way, we stopped at the Garden of Gethsemane at the foot of the Mount of

Olives where we rested. There we talked quietly together as Jesus and the twelve, separated out from the other followers and hangers on. Jesus didn't say much to us that evening, nor did we say much to each other. We just sat there under the olive trees, watching the light leave the sky. Lights began to show in windows in Jerusalem. The second day of the week had started. Only Jesus knew the true light of our hope would leave our lives in a few more days.

As the author of the first book of Moses said, "Evening came, and morning came, the first day." I wonder if any on Earth knew then that a second day, and a third, through a whole week of creation, was to follow?

The second day of that week of Passover followed the pattern of the first, except that Jesus didn't ride a donkey into Jerusalem again. We walked from Bethany shortly after we broke our fast, and we came to the same city gate. There we saw many of the merchants who had been on the Temple Mount were selling and trading outside the gate. When they saw Jesus, a few of them shook their fists at Him. As we climbed the stairs, we saw some of the merchants had returned. Temple priests, and a few uniformed Temple guards stood watching for what might happen.

Jesus said nothing. He simply began cleansing the Temple area again just as He had done the day before. The merchants somehow knew Jesus had authority, or they knew He was right, and that they would not have the acceptance of the people if they continued peddling where they were. They left to join the others outside the walls.

But the priests came to Jesus and asked, "By what authority do you do these things? Who gave you this authority?"

He answered them, "I have a question to ask you too; tell me, was the baptism of John from God or from men?"

They walked away from Jesus to discuss this among themselves. I strolled close to them so I could overhear what they were saying.

One said, "If we say, 'From God,' he will say, 'Why did you not believe him?'"

Another said, "If we say, 'from men', the people will all stone us, for they are convinced that John was a prophet."

"All we can say is, 'We don't know,'" said a third.

That is what they brought back. "We don't know."

Jesus said to them, "Then neither will I tell you by what authority I act."

He told a parable against them comparing them to untrustworthy servants. The crowd laughed, and we saw the priests were angry at Jesus. Judas told me later that the priests collected rent from the merchants who wanted to sell their wares closest to the Temple. Because of what Jesus did, money they would have had from this rent was lost to them.

One way to get Jesus in terrible trouble would be to make Him say something that could be called treasonous to Rome. All knew that to oppose publicly the taxes levied by the Roman Government was to invite arrest on a capital charge.

The priests presented Jesus with a question most difficult to answer. "Master," said their spokesman, "We know that why you teach and preach is sound. You pay deference to no one, but teach in all honesty the way of life that God requires. Are we or are we not permitted to pay taxes to the Roman Emperor?"

Jesus looked at them all, and smiled. Even the most stupid of His followers could see through this trick. If He said, "Don't pay the taxes," He would be in trouble with Rome. If He said, "Pay the taxes," He would lose his followers who hated Rome's oppression as well as the oppression of the local government, and of the priests of the Temple. I wonder if there will ever come a time when people will want to pay taxes?

"Show me a silver piece," Jesus said. They handed Him one. He examined it carefully, as if He had never seen one before. "Whose head does it bear, and whose inscription?" He asked.

"Caesar's," they replied. I looked at it. It did have a likeness of Augustus on it. The other side was stamped with symbols of Rome. Jesus handed back the coin.

"Very well then," He said. "Pay Caesar what is due Caesar, and pay God what is due God." He looked at them with a look of compassion, but showed them He was fully aware of their purpose. He waited for them to say more. But in one sentence He had disarmed them. They turned and walked away, shaking their heads. BarTholomew commented to me that head shaking might be a new way of worship for the Pharisees since they did so much of it when Jesus was around.

I have thought about Jesus' answer often as I have continued to live under the authority of Rome. I know now (far more than I did that day) that God is all powerful, having full control over his universe. If Rome is powerful, it is because God permits it to be so. Philip helped me with his Greek thoughts.

"Start with the premise, 'God is all powerful,'" he said. "Follow with 'God has created all things, and all people.' Continue with 'Rome and the emperor are created by God.' Follow again with 'All that God created belongs to God.' And you come to your conclusion. 'Whatever I give to Rome, I give to God.'"

"But does God want us to give to Caesar? Shouldn't we give it directly to the priests in the Temple?"

"What do they do with it?" Philip asked.

"They distribute to the poor. They maintain God's house. They pay stipends to the Temple staff. They pay taxes to Rome."

"God doesn't care if you give to Caesar, or to the Temple, or to the poor directly. What he wants you to do is to give freely. It isn't a matter of law, it is a matter of love."

Philip was very smart.

The third and fourth days of that week passed slowly, and without any major incident happening. Sometimes I would sit with my back against one of the hundreds of columns that surround the Temple square, the area called 'Solomon's Court.' There I would listen to Jesus as he taught. Whenever we crossed the Kidron and came to the Temple square, Jesus was met by people eager to see and to hear Him. Often sick people were with them, and He never failed to touch and to bring them the healing they needed.

You might not believe this, but it is true. Jesus' teaching I had heard, and though I was not able to comprehend it all, I no longer listened when He taught. I had grown accustomed to the voice and appearance and manner of the greatest rabbi the world has ever known, and what I saw and heard appeared so commonplace, and I was so certain I would be able to hear Him speak again, and again over succeeding years, that I no longer paid any attention to His teaching.

There were others among the twelve like me, so three of us determined to stroll through Jerusalem rather than stand by Jesus. A truly golden city, it had been rebuilt by the first King Herod. It took him most of the years he reigned to complete it. We had much to see. We walked down the pillar lined wide avenue that led from Herod's castle, the Citadel, to the Temple. Herod's architects achieved tremendous effects with the massive stones they used for building the walls that surround the Temple. They adorned the Temple Mount with a forest of pillars that supported a protecting roof around the perimeter. Common Jews though we were, we could enter this area, and go into most of the Temple itself to view the artistic perfection that Herod and his priests had demanded. The work was not completed in Herod's time and is not completed even now, but only small details are left to be done. The effect is of man making his best effort to honor God by building God a house more lovely than any other in the world.

Still, Herod did not skimp on his own quarters. They were built for him, and completed while he was still young enough to enjoy them. He lived with his court in extravagant comfort. His baths alone, here, and at the Herodium east of Bethlehem and again at Masada in the heart of the desert where water is more precious than gold, are equaled by none in this country. I wonder if Rome has any better?

My two companions were from Nazareth, Jesus' home town. Their way of life was even more primitive than was ours in the towns by the lake. We had no more than a thousand people living in Bethsaida, and Caphernaum was no larger. Nazareth may have had half as many as we. Our homes were built of rough hewn stones, plastered together by a white mortar. Few of our houses had more than two rooms, one for living, the other for sleeping. When we visited the large cities we had to look about us and stare at the great things man can do.

We walked from the Pool of Siloam to the Pool of Bethsaida, from the south wall to the north wall, over the walls, around the walls, and on most streets in the city. Passover is a festive time, and the local merchants displayed their wares not only in their little stores, but on the streets in front of them. Even the widest avenue was narrowed to an alleyway by the merchants' eagerness to show the largest crowds of the year all the beautiful items they had for sale.

We saw cloth from distant lands, dyed in brilliant colors. There were metal lamps, wrought to look like boats, and beautiful pottery molded in many useful or ornamental shapes, frequently glazed with scenes or designs that made them even more valuable to the prospective shoppers.

We had no money with us. Judas Iscariot kept the purse, and didn't distribute more than was required. Probably there was little in the purse, or we required little, for we never solicited funds. Jesus sent us out to minister, requiring us to expect our heavenly father to care for us, to meet our every need. And we had all we needed on every occasion. We never went hungry, ever. But we were certainly tempted to acquire things we didn't need, and never were we so tempted as then, in Jerusalem, walking by the piles of merchandise.

Still, it was the city itself that impressed us the most. Having no money for wine, we stopped at one of the pools where people came for their water, and drank until our thirst was quenched. Then we strolled on, absorbing the beauty, sharing in the humanity of the moving crowds about us.

Before we returned to Bethany that night, we looked at the Temple, and commented to Jesus about the magnificence of the buildings and columns. "Yes," Jesus said, "Look at it all. I tell you this: not one stone will be left upon another; all will be thrown down."

On our way up the hillside to Bethany, we stopped and sat on a log by the roadside near the top of the Mount of Olives. We looked back at the Temple. I was disturbed by what Jesus had said about it being torn down. "Tell us," I asked, "When will this happen?"

Thomas spoke up, "What will be the signal for your coming, and for the end of the age?"

Jesus spoke several minutes about matters I didn't understand then, and still do not understand now. Still, I remember much of what He said. "Take care that no one misleads you. For many will come claiming my name and saying, 'I am the Messiah,' and many will be misled by them.

The time is coming when you will hear the noise of battle near at hand and the news of battles far away; see that you are not alarmed. Such things are bound to happen; but the end is still to come. For nation will make war upon nation, kingdom upon kingdom, there will be famines and earthquakes in many places. With all these things the birth-pangs of the new age begin.

"You will then be handed over to punishment and execution; and men of all nations will hate you for your allegiance to me. Many will fall from their faith; they will betray one another and hate one another. Many false prophets will arise and will mislead many; and as lawlessness spreads, men's love for one another will grow cold."

That much of what Jesus said that day, I have memorized from a scroll Levi made. He wrote down the things Jesus said, especially the things He said during that week of the Passover. I have a copy of the things Jesus said among my possessions. I will have a copy made for you. I say again, though, that my understanding of Jesus' talk much of the time was not great. I didn't follow Jesus because of what my mind understood from His teaching. I followed Him for another reason. I saw His compassion for people, including myself. I grew to love Him with all my heart.

11

Pontius Pilate

Jerusalem, Spring, Year of Tiberias - XVIII

My father,

I wonder if my last letter reached you? I have received no reply, though it is six months since I wrote. Word has reached us of three ships that were lost in the Mare Nostrum last winter. Perhaps my letter was on one of them. Henceforth I will make at least two copies for you, and one for my files. The two I send to you, I will send on separate ships. With this letter I send a copy of my last epistle. Since these letters are an opening of myself that I want no one but you to know, I have set myself the task of copying them. I have a superb slave, Lucas, a Greek with an excellent education, who handles the writing of most of my official correspondence. But I do not trust him enough to see these meanderings to you.

As you can see from the salutation, I am in Jerusalem as I write this. It has become necessary for me to travel here every year in the spring, as it is here that a festival the Jews call 'Passover' takes place. That is a religious observance of an historical event that took place while they were led by the man, Moshe, I wrote about in my last letter. A tale included in their scrolls that they claim Moshe wrote, reports Jah's angel of death passing over the land of Egypt, killing all first born sons of the Egyptians. Note that first born sons? How much like the god Molluck! But the first born sons of the Haiberews were spared, as were all their people. The Haiberews made good their escape from their slave masters. Apparently their God required them to remember that time their sons were spared. They have a special meal like the one they ate the night the angel passed over. They come to Jerusalem to do this, for it is in Jerusalem that their God's House, the Temple, stands.

Consider a city of ten to fifteen thousand people, and then add to it thirty to forty thousand more for a week, and you have the elements of a riot. That is why I, with about two-thirds of my military force, arrange to be in Jerusalem now. We want to be very visible. We don't want the Jews to think their God is going to help them escape from our rule as he did from that of the Egyptians. This tactic of presenting a visible deterrent has worked in the past for my predecessor, and now for me.

One aspect of the Jews' religion is that their holy scrolls predict again and again that there will come another savior like Moshe. The new one will be even greater than Moshe was, and he will lead the people who obey their God to a new freedom. One difference is that Moshe led the people out of Egypt to the promised land. The new savior will drive the enemy out.

Almost two hundred years ago there was a man named Judas Maccabeas who led the Jews to victory over the Greeks. The land was made free of the Greek rule, and the people remained free until we conquered them some seventy or so years ago. The great grandchildren of Judas Maccabeas are now the puppet kings we allow to rule in the north. My governorship is over the territory traditionally designated the land of Judah. Probably one Jew of every ten in this country is named Judas, either after the founder of the tribe, or after

Maccabeas, or both. Parents keep hoping their children may be blessed by God to be the leader their nation needs to obtain its freedom from us.

There is another name that is often given to boy children on their name day, that is, the day they are circumcised. That name is 'Joshua,' after the first general who led the Haiberew people into the land and fought for it after the death of Moshe. That name isn't as popular as Jude or Judas, but it is still one of the most popular. It is a little like the people in Rome naming their sons Julius after the Caesar you first served.

The reason I mention this to you is that on the first day of the week a 'Messiah' (that is the title of the savior who is to come) rode into town on a donkey. That's right. He rode into town on a donkey with a crowd numbering in the thousands following him and shouting. He is a man we have had an eye on for some time, as he has drawn crowds here in Jerusalem on other occasions. Many who have come under his influence say he has magic powers, that he can heal people, even raise the dead.

Our spies, and the spies of the priests too, have joined the crowds and listened to this Joshua BarJoseph preach. He talks a lot about the 'Kingdom,' that is coming, but he doesn't make much sense. One of my men came back and said, "He said the Kingdom is like a mustard seed." I asked what that meant, but the fellow was just as puzzled as I.

The Jews would be desperate indeed if they chose this Joshua to be their leader. He is more than likely a harmless madman. The donkey riding act was supposed to be so that the people would recognize him. Apparently one of those writers of hundreds of years ago said the King would come riding on a young donkey that had never been ridden before. Apparently the King was to be as inexperienced as the donkey.

This Joshua rode almost into town, and then stopped the donkey and started to cry. Can you imagine a leader doing anything like that? Then he got off the donkey, walked into the Temple grounds, and insulted the Sanhedrin by disrupting their market place on one of the busiest days of their year.

Well, it is good to laugh at the antics of the weird ones. We won't have to watch that Joshua! If their God is sending someone to try to overthrow us, he will pick someone more competent than that. Perhaps we should keep our eyes out for a Judas.

I'll be glad when this week is over. I want to get back to Caesaria, go for a swim in the sea, and pretend for a while that I am living in a world with no problems.

You should know I am thankful to you for one thing, father. Your discipline of me when I was a child is paying off. The training in logic you insisted I master is a most helpful tool in my work as governor of Judea.

In grateful love,

Pontius

12

Andrew

It was the fourth day of the week that I decided I would stay close to Jesus every moment of the day. I remembered when Mary, sister of Martha and Lazarus, had sat near Jesus, listening while Martha prepared the meal. Martha complained and Jesus said, "Mary has chosen the better place." I decided I, too, would choose this better place, and not let myself be distracted by the crowds, the merchants, or the officials, as I had the day before.

We broke our fast simply that morning, eating what was always our customary food when it was available; a little cheese, a little fruit, some goat milk, and a chunk of yesterday's bread. Our meal completed, we strolled together to the city, following the same worn path over the Mount of Olives, through Bethphage, down the hill, and into the valley of the Kidron River. The last of the spring rains had allowed for a light flow of water along the normally dry bed of that stream, and we had to cross on the footbridge that the first King Herod had constructed there. Then on up the other side of the valley we went to the gate of the city that led directly to the Temple Mount. This was our path the day Jesus rode into Jerusalem on the donkey. It was the path of a continuing flow of pilgrims to the city. We walked with Jesus in a small group with men, women, children, and a variety of animals traveling before us, behind us, and beside us.

The city of Jerusalem that has a normal population of perhaps ten to fifteen thousand people, swells to ten times that figure, or even more, when the Holy days arrive, especially this is true at the time of Passover. It was good that the Kidron was flowing, for the water supply of Jerusalem was sorely taxed by the arrival of such crowds. We carried wine skins full of mildly fermented grape juice, part of last year's crop, along with us so that we could slake our thirst throughout the day. We also had some bags of bread and fruit for a light meal in the middle of the day.

As we entered the Temple square, several of the twelve turned away to find diversion for themselves about the city. They were probably planning to do much the same thing I had done the day before. But I was determined not to leave Jesus for a moment. That day I chose the better way. It had been almost three years since Philip and I had followed Jesus and stayed overnight with Him on the other side of the Jordan. I felt a real need to be renewed in my relationship with Him.

I did not sit directly in front of Jesus as Mary had. I am a shy man, and have not, even now, the assurance to put myself so far forward. What I did was find a pillar behind Him, from which place I could sit and watch Him, over His shoulder. Thus He could not see me, but I could see both Him and the people in front of Him. He told many parables that day. Levi was there. He wrote them down and saved them for us to read again and again. Somehow hearing the words of Jesus read to us, or reading them aloud to others, brings Him back more forcefully into our hearts than when we simply try to recall Him.

His parables were about the Kingdom of Heaven, and what it would be like. And as the day wore on, He talked of what it would be like when the 'Son of Man' comes in His glory, with all the angels with Him. I heard Him say those things, and He seemed to be speaking directly to me though His back was still turned.

"He will sit on his throne, with all the nations gathered before him. He will separate men into two groups, as a shepherd separates the sheep from the goats, and he will place the sheep on his right hand and the goats on his left. Then the King will say to those on his right hand, 'You have my Father's blessing; come, enter and possess the kingdom that has been ready for you since the world was made. For when I was hungry, you gave me food; when thirsty, you gave me drink; when I was a stranger, you took me into your home; when naked, you clothed me; when I was ill, you came to my help; when in prison, you visited me.' Then the righteous will reply, 'Lord, when was it that we saw you hungry and fed you, or thirsty and gave you drink, a stranger and took you home or naked and clothed you? When did we see you ill or in prison, and come to visit you?' And the King will answer 'I tell you this; anything you did for one of my brothers here, however humble, you did for me.' Then he will say to those on his left hand, 'The curse is upon you; go from my sight for the eternal fire that is ready for the devil and his angels. For when I was hungry you gave me nothing to eat, when thirsty nothing to drink, when I was a stranger you gave me no home, when naked you did not clothe me, when I was ill and in prison you did not come to my help.' And they too will reply, 'Lord, when was it that we saw you hungry or thirsty or a stranger or naked or ill or in prison, and did nothing for you?' And he will answer, 'I tell you this: anything you did not do for one of these, however humble, you did not do for me.' And they will go away to eternal punishment, but the righteous will enter eternal life."

These words burned themselves into my heart that day, and they have been there ever since. Then, as I watched and listened to Him, I was granted a gift like the one my brother and the Zebedee brothers had on the mountain in Galilee.

Many months before, Jesus took James and John and my brother with Him up a mountain. He often did this, and taught them. Then each of them would teach three of us what He taught them. We, in our turn, were each to take three of the other disciples, and train them. In this way He made us teachers as well as students, and gave us an opportunity to practice our new learnings. Once He sent out the twelve of us plus the ones we had taught, and several they had taught as well, a total of seventy others, altogether 82 of us. He had us all go into the villages of Galilee to teach and to heal. I wonder if He did that to prove the system He used would be effective?

But the day Simon Peter, James, John, and Jesus climbed that mountain, things happened up there that changed those three men. When I saw my brother that evening, I knew he was transported with an experience he wanted to share. But it was one of those things that happened when people were around Jesus that our Master asked them to keep to themselves. We had been busy for a time while Jesus and the other three were gone. We tried to minister to the people in the area, but there was one child we were unable to heal.

When they returned, Jesus healed that child with a word, and the conversation that evening was about why Jesus could do what we could not do. He talked to us then about prayer and fasting.

Simon came to me late that night and awakened me. When we slept out under the stars, I always selected a spot off by myself, feeling somehow that if anyone wanted to be with me, they would find me, and not wanting to impose myself on anyone's unwilling hospitality. Quite frankly, it was my usual experience that when Simon sought me out, it was to be critical of me, as he always had been in the past. But this time he had something to whisper to me that he had to tell someone.

"Andrew," he shook me awake. "Andrew, I have to talk. Will you listen?" I grumbled something that must have sounded like a yes, for he continued immediately as I sat up and leaned my back against a convenient tree trunk.

He began again. "Andrew, we were there on that mountain, with Jesus off praying, as He always does. I am sure He has us there with Him so that we can learn from Him how He prays, and begin to follow His way of seeking regular contact with God. But we never spend His entire time of prayer watching Him. We often relax nearby, even take a short nap. That is what we did today."

He paused a long time, waiting for me to come fully alert to him, so that I would really hear his next statement. Nothing important had been said up to that point, except for his admission that he and the Zebedees were as weak as the rest of us. But his agitation alerted me to the notion something really important was about to be said. "We didn't really fall asleep, you understand. We were just dozing, and we were fully awake when we looked at Jesus. All three of us saw the same sight. When the day comes that Jesus will let us tell what we saw to everyone, the others will bear witness to what I tell you now.

"Jesus was standing in a great light! In fact, somehow He himself was the great light! His body, His very clothes, but especially His head, shone so brilliantly that we were dazzled, and had to shield our eyes with our hands. Then we saw standing beside Jesus two other people. I know they were Moses and Elijah! They and Jesus were talking together about Jesus going up to Jerusalem, and about terrible things that would happen there." Simon was shaking as he told of this vision. I had to believe he thought he saw what he reported. Nothing in our past lives had ever affected Simon this much.

"It was then a cloud came over us, and covered us all. We couldn't see Jesus or the other two, could barely see each other. The cloud was thicker than any fog we ever had on the lake. Out of that cloud came a voice that shook the whole mountain. 'This is my son, my beloved on whom my favor rests; listen to him,' the voice said. We fell on our faces. I have never been so frightened in all my life."

"Why do you tell me this? Why not tell all the others? Is it a secret what you saw and heard?" I was perplexed.

"Jesus told us not to tell anyone until 'The Son of Man has been raised from the dead,'" Simon replied. "I don't know what that means. But I know I was so full of the sight, I had to tell someone."

We talked together for an hour or more that night. I enjoyed my brother's companionship more than I have for years. I liked seeing him as he was that night, and I told him so. Simon seldom wore humble robes. It was good, too, to share Simon's secret. That made me one of the four Apostles who knew Jesus had appeared transfigured when on that mountain.

All of this I remembered as I sat that day in Jerusalem, the day before Passover. There I sat and watched and listened. And as I concentrated on Jesus' presence, I was treated to a vision too. I had no others who witnessed it with me, though there were perhaps hundreds of people there. Since I am the only one who saw this, you must study what I say in your own heart. If you gain more of the truth of Jesus' nature from my recitation of it, good. If not, discard it. But I must witness to my vision.

Jesus sat on the steps in front of me, the steps that led down to the central court where the people gather to hear rabbis teach. Jesus was clothed in his usual rough spun garments one moment, and then He was clothed in beautiful shimmering cloth the next. His face was the face of an ordinary human being one moment, and then it was shining forth in glorious beauty the next. I didn't take my eyes off him, not once. His beauty was greater than the beauty one would see if he were to look at all the vivid sunrises and sunsets he experienced in his entire lifetime, all shining gloriously all at once. My mind and soul were caught up in the true vision of the light and life that was Jesus. But as I looked at Him, I saw that all the Temple area was included in Jesus' beauty. The vivid light made everything stand out in a reality I never knew before. I was fully aware of the power of Him who created all I saw that was not Jesus. At that moment I realized that Jesus was a part, or perhaps all, of the power of the Universe.

Even then the vision was not finished. Hovering about us, over us, around us, even somehow within us all, were other beings. Some may have been people who lived before us. Others I am sure were the angels of heaven, cherubim, seraphim, the living occupants of the heavenly kingdom. They were hanging on Jesus' words as the audience were not. For I could see they were of a higher order than are we, and their intellect was free of the distractions we endure as we try to concentrate.

Yet I was grateful that I had not been concentrating on the words of Jesus, but simply basking in His presence. For I believe I would never have had this vision if I had been trying to grasp the full meaning of His teaching with my mind alone. I had to be trying to grasp it with all of myself, and trying to come to know Him more than ever before.

Even now, as I recollect that experience, I know that it wasn't just my eyes that were opened to deeper reality. My ears heard Jesus speak and His words penetrated so that I would always remember them. That is why I could quote Him so completely a few moments ago. And my ears heard the multitude of sounds available to us every day; the whisper of the wind, the songs of birds in flight, the murmur of the people about me. Above all, I heard the singing of the angels and other spiritual persons that surrounded us. My nostrils caught scents, and I noted them, including the perpetual burnt offerings of sacrifice at the altar a hundred paces from us, and the scent of the perfumes worn by many of the people about me. I was fully alert, fully aware, perhaps for the first time in my life.

Through that experience I found my attitude was changed. I had heard Jesus talking about love often enough. “Love one another,” was His principal theme. I had tried to follow this teaching, but had been singularly unsuccessful. But as I absorbed all the beauty about me, I absorbed something of the Spirit of Love as well. I loved Jesus with all of me right then, and continued in that love from then ’til now. Love for the other people present was a part of my experience at that moment too. Though I can’t say I have always held that love strength as I have the one for Jesus. Love for my fellow man wanes, excepting for the times like this when I remember.

Right now I have a strong love for you, much stronger than when I began this narrative. Think about it. Perhaps hearing me is enough for you to feel some of the strength of Jesus’ and the Father’s love. Look about you. Think of someone you know. How do you feel toward them at this instant?

Where Simon, James, and John had their experience last a few moments and stop with the coming of the cloud and the Heavenly Father’s voice, my experience lasted perhaps the entire day. I don’t know when it began. I don’t know when it ended. Perhaps it was only a few moments for me too. Perhaps none of us can live permanently with that powerful awareness until we live with Jesus in heaven.

It was while I was sitting there, absorbed in Jesus, looking on Him fully revealed, and loving Him, that Philip came up behind me and spoke. “Andrew, there are some Greeks waiting outside who want to see Jesus.” He had to speak to me a second time before I could answer him.

"Tell them to come back another time," I said. But he prevailed on me to go up to Jesus and tell Him of the visitors. I remember asking myself, "How can they possibly see Jesus if it took me three years to see Him as He is?"

When we stood before our Master, my eyes were nearly blinded by the light of His eyes, and the beauty of His face. "Jesus," I said, "Philip has something to say to you." I was so full of awareness of Jesus, I could say no more. Philip gave Him the message.

Jesus turned to dismiss the people He had been instructing, and then turning back to us, He said, "The hour has come for the Son of Man to be glorified..." I was so filled with Him and then whelmed by this statement, I heard no more. Philip told me later that Jesus spoke about grains of wheat dying before they could bear a harvest; of men loving Him enough to be His servants and to follow Him to eternal life. But that is Philip's witness. Mine is that I stood in the face of the full glory of Jesus. I was changed, and I knew it.

Jesus knew it too. He said to me later in the day, after the vision had faded, "Today my Father and yours gave you a special blessing. It is for you to have and remember after the time of testing that is coming. You and all the others will be tested, and will lose courage, and will run away, leaving me alone. But later, you will remember today and will gather with the others, and you will live in hope.

And then came evening. The fourth day ended. The fifth day began.

The morning of the fifth day of the week, Jesus sent me and Judas Iscariot to find the place where we were to eat the Passover feast. Jesus said, "Go to a certain man in the city, and tell him, 'The Master says, 'My appointed time is near; I am to keep Passover with my disciples at your house.'" We found the man, and we told him what Jesus said. The man led us to his home, where we found a spacious upper room large enough for Jesus and we twelve, and for many more of Jesus' followers, including the women.

We then went and found several of the disciples of Jesus, including Mary and Martha and Mary, the mother of Jesus. They brought or bought the things needed for our Passover feast. Passover is always a special time when we remember the angel of death passed over the Hebrew people and took the first born of the Egyptians. We were saved, and provided our freedom through that action. Thirteen hundred years later we celebrate in the same way, obedient to God's decree, knowing that our Roman oppressors are no stronger than was Pharaoh; knowing that God has it in His power to free us.

Passover is a time of singing, dancing, laughing, feasting, rejoicing. We prepared ourselves for the occasion, anticipating the evening would be a time of overwhelming joy. Despite the warnings Jesus had given us, we could not believe anything terrible would happen to him at Passover! When all was in readiness in the upper room, we went to prepare ourselves as well. I bathed at the home of Mary and Martha, put on clean clothes, and walked back into the city with several other disciples. When we entered the upper room, we found Jesus was there ahead of us. My experience of the day before was still strong on me, and I found I had to go forward and embrace Jesus. The others, seeing me do this, knowing I was the most reticent of the twelve, chose to embrace Him too.

Jesus responded with a return embrace for each of us, then did something more He had never done before. He removed His outer garment, wrapped a towel around Himself, and went to each of us, washing our feet. He played the role of slave of the house, washing my feet tenderly and gently, looking me in the eye as He did so. I tell you the emotions of that week were the most powerful I have ever felt. The time I am about to describe now — the rest of the fifth day of the week, and almost all of the sixth day, has been written about by John Mark for my brother Simon, and by Levi. I have their scrolls here. You may read them. My personal experiences have not been written down, though I have witnessed to thousands throughout Asia of the things I have to say to you now.

We ate the Passover meal standing, as has been our custom. For it was to remind us the first Passover was a hurried meal, eaten by slaves who were about to escape their oppressors. The bread we ate was unleavened, just as was theirs. The herbs we ate were bitter. It was after this memorial meal was completed that we sat at low tables, eating specially prepared foods, dipping our bread into bowls. drinking the good sweet juice of the grape. All the old formal prayers had been said. We could, and did relax in good fellowship.

Then it was that Jesus said another prayer of thanksgiving to God, broke another loaf of bread, and passed the pieces to us. "Take this and eat it," He said. "This is my body, broken for you. Do this in remembrance of me." He said it so quietly, and solemnly, that the words pierced our minds as no other words, even words from Him, ever did before. We ate the bread in silence, looking at each other to see if any knew what Jesus meant.

Shortly after, He took a large cup, filled it with wine, and said, "Drink this. All of you, drink all of this. It is my blood of the new covenant. Do this in remembrance of me." We were obedient, passing the cup around the tables, sharing among the twelve and the others present as we had the bread He broke, and the other food at this holy meal.

We were still studying what He had said, and trying to ask each other what He meant when He spoke again. "One of you will betray me," He said. "One of the twelve." We sat about Him as an inner circle as we often had before. Each of us was close enough to ask in our turn, "Lord, is it I?" I asked, and received the same words He said to each of the others — but one. "Watch. Be vigilant." It was as if He had a warning for each of us that we would soon fail as Apostles to our Master.

"Tonight," He said, "you will all fall from your faith on my account; for it is written: 'I will strike the shepherd down and the sheep of his flock will be scattered.' But after I am raised again, I will go on before you into Galilee."

Each of us replied, "Even if I have to die with you, I will never disown you."

He let us have the last word.

It was late when we left the supper, and I know I expected we would go back up the road, over the mountain, and seek a good night's sleep at Lazarus' home. But Jesus took us to the garden of Gethsemane where we often met, and sometimes even slept, when we visited Jerusalem in the warm summertime. But this spring evening under the full moon, it was quite cold. We shivered. Resting under blankets inside a warm house would have been so much better.

At the garden, Jesus took His usual three men with Him, leaving us to sit alone. When the others around me wrapped their coats tight around their bodies and huddled against tree trunks, I did the same. I woke once or twice during the next few hours, but I dozed off most of the time. Others can tell you about that time better than I. Levi and John Mark wrote accounts of that time too.

Late in the night, when the moon was in the west, we were awakened. Jesus was back among us, telling us to get up. I struggled to my feet to find myself facing a crowd of Temple and Roman soldiers. They came into the garden, but stopped, looking at us. We looked back, nobody wanting to do anything, or perhaps nobody knowing what to do.

Judas Iscariot stepped forward out of the crowd of soldiers, and spoke to Jesus. "Master," he said. And Jesus said something back to him I didn't catch. The soldiers stepped forward, and my brother Simon took out a long sword. I remembered then, I had a sword too. I had picked it up after supper. I reached for my sword, thinking this was the time to use it. But a soldier stood at my side, and took my arm so firmly, I couldn't draw the weapon from its sheath.

By this time I was awake, and really frightened. I heard Jesus speak then, quite clearly. "Whom do you seek?" He asked.

"Jesus of Nazareth," was the reply.

"I am he," said Jesus. With that the soldier at my side let go my arm, and fell back. Some of the people near Jesus fell to the ground, as if they had been struck down.

All was confusion. Simon swung his sword. I turned and ran away. I always remember that. I was the first to follow Jesus with Philip being right there too, of course. And I was the first to run away. I may have a right to be proud of the one, but I have a continuing knowledge of deep shame at the cowardice of the other.

I ran to Bethany where I awakened Mary, Martha, and Lazarus. They hadn't had too much sleep, for they had shared the Passover with us, and the women had cleaned up after the meal before going home. It was very late at night when I arrived at their home, you understand. Oh, the confusion of that night! I am still confused as I try to tell you of it. I know Thomas showed up, and a few of the others came in after me. Then we all decided to go see what had happened. I led the way. How foolish of me, and of them, to think we could rescue our Master!

13

Andrew

As we left Lazarus' house and started back to Jerusalem the moon went behind a cloud, and we found ourselves stumbling along the familiar road that led toward the city. As we walked, we talked, and soon we found others joining us. As a precaution, they made me drop the sword I carried. I was surprised I still had it, really. I never was a swordsman, and carrying it would certainly have been a sign of our intent to fight. There was no fight left in any of us.

I thought about the evening, the supper we had together, the foot washing, the eating of specially blessed bread and wine, and of Jesus' talk to us. These thoughts were so strong that other things He had said before were shoved far back in my heart. I thought about His telling us it was all right now to take up swords, and my saying, "Lord, here are two swords,“ and His saying that was enough. Simon took one from me. I wonder why I kept the other. Surely Simon the Zealot would have been glad to have it. But keep it I did, and never used it.

There were no recriminations among us as we walked down into the valley and across the Kidron River. We talked in low voices, not because we didn't want to be heard, but because we felt so small and insecure. There was a good chance the Pharisees and the Romans would be looking for us. By walking toward them, we were making it easy for them to capture us and try us with Jesus.

"Where do you suppose they took our Master?" asked Mary of Magdala. Though she lived at home with Martha and Lazarus, I always thought of her as being from Magdala, the town where we first knew her.

"I think they must have taken Him to Caiaphas' house," James said, and I agreed with him. We turned left down the valley, past the south wall of the Temple, and right again through the narrow gate that led into the old part of the city, where King David once lived. As we began to climb the steps that led up to the mansions on the hillside, we were given a break in the clouds, and could see our destination.

Surrounded by stately trees, with a lovely garden stretching halfway down the hill below it, stood Caiaphas' house. It was large enough to be a small palace in any other city but Jerusalem. There the homes of Herod and Pilate were magnificent proof of where power rested in our country. Still, Caiaphas' home, and that of his father-in-law, Annas, had to be considered mansions. Jesus told us earlier that evening, "In my father's house are many mansions. I go to prepare a place for you." Then and now I wonder if Jesus was thinking about heavenly housing for us that would be as beautiful as Caiaphas' earthly home.

Halfway up a long flight of steps that would bring us to the level of Caiaphas' ground floor, we paused to think about our next move. The moonlight cast the shadow of a large cedar tree over us, and we welcomed the added darkness. Above us I could see someone standing by a marble rail near the side entrance to the courtyard. Watching, I could see it was a man, and I soon saw it was Simon Peter. I left the others and hurried to him.

"What is happening?" I asked.

"Didn't you hear the cock crow?" Simon responded.

"If I did, I didn't give it much thought. It is time for the roosters to waken," I said.

"Oh Andrew," Simon did something I never remembered his doing before. He embraced me, and buried his head on my shoulder. He was sobbing! Something I do not remember him ever doing before. "I denied Jesus!" Simon said. "I denied Jesus." He looked at me, his eyes clouded with tears. "I denied our Master."

"What are you saying?" I asked.

"You remember what He said," Simon was almost angry with me for not understanding him. His anger made him able to speak more clearly. "Jesus said, 'before the rooster crows twice, you will deny me three times.' I swore there would never be another rooster crow heard here on earth. I was so sure of my heart."

He put his head back on my shoulder and sobbed so hard I wasn't sure he could catch his breath. "But I did it," he said. "I denied Him, and when the rooster crowed, Jesus looked at me. He looked right into my eyes." Simon held my shoulders, and looked at me, giving me his idea of how Jesus had looked at him. "That's how He looked at me, as if to say, 'I knew it.' But also to tell me something more. What that something is, I don't know."

I grew irritated. Simon was not my primary concern. "Stop your babbling," I said. "Where is Jesus?" The others had come up behind me, and James said, "Yes. Where is Jesus? What are they doing to Him?"

"He's in there, in Caiaphas' house." Simon's voice sounded terribly dejected. "I don't know what they are doing to Him. But John is inside. If John gets away, he will come out and tell us." Simon was no rock to himself or to us that night.

My brother walked slowly away from us, his head bowed, his shoulders bent, a man lost in his grief. I looked at the others standing there, and again at Simon as he walked up the road that leads to the Temple. I guessed he was going there to pray, and decided to join him. He was so downhearted I was afraid of what he might do to himself. At least that is my excuse as I tell you now of that terrible night. I left the other disciples, walked away from Jesus' time of trial, and went to be with my brother.

"If you love your brother more than me, you aren't worthy of me," Jesus said. I don't know if I loved Simon more, or if I feared being captured by the soldiers more. I know that by leaving, I was moving myself into relative safety. Simon and I walked the open spaces of Solomon's court near the Temple through the balance of the night, and then we sat close to the eastern wall of the Temple mount. From there we watched the sun come up, giving light to that terrible sixth day of the week.

Occasionally people came by us that morning, and we learned of what was happening in the city. We heard of Jesus being taken to the Roman Governor, Pontius Pilate, and then to Herod, and back again to the governor. We heard of the sentence, and then of the walk to Calvary Hill with Jesus carrying his own cross. Still we sat. We sat from the first hour of the day through the sixth hour before we stood and walked heavily up the slowly inclining street that led to the western gate.

We climbed higher, until we could stand with a crowd of people who were watching three men dying on their crosses. We stood there, some hundred or more paces away from Calvary, and looked at our Master hanging on nails driven into His wrists and feet. He hung naked, his back against a roughly hewn log, His arms extended upward, nailed to the cross arm. A sign was fastened over His head that I couldn't read from where we stood. I read it later. It said, 'The King of the Jews.' A thorn wreath was smashed down on Jesus' head, and blood had trickled down His cheeks, drying there and in His beard. There were whip slash marks on His arms and chest that had cut so deep they too had bled.

We watched his life drain away during the next three hours. Sometimes someone spoke to Him. Sometimes Jesus spoke. Others have written about that. I was too far away to hear His words, too far away to look into His eyes, or have Him look into mine. As Simon Peter denied Jesus verbally, I did so by my actions. Some time after supper the evening before, I had stopped being an active disciple, and had become a mere spectator.

I no longer believed Jesus could overcome the world. He no longer appeared to be the Messiah.

When Jesus' head fell forward, clouds covered us, rains fell, an earthquake shook the ground beneath our feet, and I ran away. I didn't even look for Simon. Maybe he stayed. Maybe he found courage again after Jesus breathed His last breath. But I didn't.

Late that Sabbath night I found my way to John Mark's house. I had hidden in the Garden of Gethsemane, under the olive trees, for a time. I had scouted Bethany and Lazarus' house, but there were no lights showing, and I was afraid the house was being watched by soldiers. We had not used John Mark's home as a place to meet before our Passover supper. It was safer for us to hide there. I gave the secret knock on that door, and it opened to admit me. Most of the disciples were there ahead of me, including my brother. As the night wore on, still more joined us.

We wept and fasted and prayed there through the balance of the Sabbath. We were inconsolable, and we were deathly afraid of the authorities. Daylight ended. It was evening of the first day of the week. Darkness covered us.

14

Pontius Pilate

Spring, Year of Tiberias - XVIII

My dear father,

It is only a week since I wrote you, and it may be this letter will reach you before the other. Who knows the speed of ships when powered by shifting winds?

The winds of my life have shifted. That is why I write you now. Grave things have happened, things I cannot understand, things that make me tremble.

It was relatively peaceful here for two days after I wrote you. The crowds were manageable. The zealots and others who agitate for insurrection were quiet. I was enjoying a little peace for myself. Procula walked through the bazaars and made some excellent purchases for our home in Caesaria. But she was not alone on the streets. She was a companion of Ruth, my Centurion's wife. The two of them stopped at least once to listen to that Joshua BarJoseph about whom I wrote you last. Procula told me of him, and I could see she was impressed. She told me she considered the man to be a good teacher with strong moral principles.

Then Thursday came. It was well named after our God of War! For on that day I experienced diplomatic warfare from the Jews, the cunning of which has not been matched, even by our Senators in Rome.

Procula and I retired early, and agreeing we were both tired, we fell asleep, barely touching. This was the night of the Jewish Passover. There would be parties, dining, much drinking of wine, and celebrations that could lead to trouble. I assumed I might be awakened before dawn by someone for some official reason, and I wasn't disappointed.

Some time, at least three or four hours before dawn, the high priest Caiaphas (he succeeded Annas about six months after that dinner party with Antipas), and Annas, and a crowd of other priests of the Sanhedrin, pounded at my door. I invited them in, but they refused. Though they have been guests in my house before, one at a time, they could not come in together. My house is a pagan's house as far as they are concerned. By entering the house of the Governor who has authority from the Emperor of Rome, authority to rule over them with absolute power of life or death, they defile themselves. By being with me in my home they become unclean! They have to purify themselves for weeks before they can function as priests to the people again!

They make me sick!

But they had awakened me, and they insisted they remain outside while we talked. So a chair was brought by one of my Jewish slaves. I make a point of parading those slaves before the priests. It reminds them that no matter how powerful Moshe was, the Jews aren't free of slavery in the most demeaning sense of that word. They are our slaves now, and will probably remain our slaves forever.

It was probably the only point I made for the rest of the day. Caiaphas' Temple guards thrust a man before me. "This man has committed a crime worthy of death," he said. "We want him sentenced, condemned, and executed immediately."

I thought of several cutting things to say, but my wits weren't with me. They were still asleep. Had I been more alert, I would have noted it wasn't just the Temple guards who had the man in custody, but some of my soldiers were present as well! Later, I wondered who had authorized them to be a part of the action.

All I could say was, "Who is he?"

"He is Jesus BarJoseph," Caiaphas said, apparently the appointed spokesman for the Sanhedrin. He pronounced the prisoner's name using our Latin equivalent for Joshua, the name I wrote in my letter of only a week ago. "We found this man subverting our nation, opposing the payment of taxes to Caesar, and claiming to be Messiah, an anointed king."

"Is that the charge you bring against him?" I asked, looking pointedly at the still dark sky above us. There was certainly no reason in bringing Jesus to me at that hour if all they had against him was the madness of thinking himself a king! Preaching against Rome's unfair taxes wasn't peculiar to him. I was sure Caiaphas and his priests could have brought me a dozen who had preached that in the streets of Jerusalem in the past two to three days.

"If he were not a criminal, we would not have brought him before you," Caiaphas said. He pretended to be hurt at my doubting the importance of the case. The others with Caiaphas nodded their agreement with him. I expected nothing less.

"Take him away and try him by your own law," I said, and turned away. But they wouldn't leave me alone.

They clamored after me, making me turn back. "We are not allowed to put any man to death," they reminded me. And I remembered my decree of only a few months before. In an effort to make the Jews aware it is our power and authority that determines life or death for them all, I decreed there would be no more capital sentences in the Jewish courts. They could chastise. They could imprison. They could fine their people up to and including taking all private property. They could even declare a man and/or his family must be sold into slavery to pay debts. But they no longer had the right to kill.

I studied the man, Jesus. He stood quietly before me. This was my first sight of him, though you know I had reports of him for two years. My opinion of him did not change as my eyes examined him. He stood quietly, his arms bound behind him, his head up, face serene, eyes alert. The emotional donkey rider I had heard of was calm at the moment, but I could see he was aware of his circumstances; fully aware.

We looked each other in the eye. There was something compelling there that I seldom see in any of the conquered people. I can't describe it really. It was certainly not defiance. There was no anger there either, at least not at me or the Roman government. There was something of power, and of tremendous assurance. That confidence stood out, though I was painfully aware Jesus had been badly manhandled by his captors. He had a bruise on his face, his hair was awry, his cloak pulled half off his shoulder was trailing on the ground behind him.

I took Jesus inside. That forced his captors to permit me a private interview with the prisoner. Their fastidious laws, especially at Passover, kept them from walking on contaminated land. Jesus didn't seem to object to coming with me. Perhaps he had different ideas about what ground is holy, and what is not.

I looked him in the eye again. I waited for him to say something, but he remained silent. He forced me to speak first. "Are you the king of the Jews?" I asked. Even dirty, tired, and bruised the man did look almost regal. I stand half a head taller than most men, and was taller than this

Jesus too. Still, face to face, I felt I was looking up at him. "Are you a king, then," I asked.

"Is that your own idea?" Jesus asked in return. "Or have others suggested it to you?" I looked for the sound of sarcasm in his voice, but did not find it. He struck me as being exceptionally sincere. Yet I was sure he knew the answer to his own question.

"What! Am I a Jew?" I asked. Such a question to pour from my mouth! There were few Jews I considered equal to any Roman citizen, and none my equal. Their monotheism is an intriguing thought. Their two thousand year history shows their tenacity. But their contentious manners and zealous attacks on us, their betters and their superiors, certainly shows them mentally and physically our inferiors. Perhaps I asked the question to remind myself of my strength, and of the power I do have over these vassals.

Even the Jewish 'kings' are not kings. They are puppets we make function under our authority. My governorship has twice the power of Antipas or Philip, the gutless sons of the first Herod. I asked the necessary question again, sincerely hoping I could help the man. I instinctively liked him, but I couldn't tell you why.

"Your own nation, and their chief priests have brought you before me. What have you done?" His answer confused me.

"My kingdom does not belong to the world. If it did, my followers would be fighting to save me from arrest by the Jews. My kingly authority comes from elsewhere."

"You are a king, then?" I asked. No matter how intelligent and assured he looked, I could see he was demented. His eyes may have carried a regal look, but the rest of him proved him to be a country peasant.

He replied, "The words are yours." I had to smile too. I had tricked myself into calling him 'king.' I took him back to the priests.

I dismissed them. "I find no case for this man to answer."

But they insisted. "His teaching is causing disaffection among the people all through Judea. It started from Galilee and has spread as far as this city."

That gave me an easy way out. I could get rid of Jesus, and his priestly accusers, and get back to bed. "Is the man a Galilean?" I asked. I didn't wait for them to reply. I could see the answer in their faces. "Send him to Antipas." I turned away, paying no attention to the clamor of protest behind me.

But that tactic did me no real good, except to give me an extra hour of rest upon my bed. Within two hours they were back again, and I had to dress in my formal robes to meet them. Jesus BarJoseph stood in front of me, dressed in a purple robe, a humorless gift from Antipas. I found myself admiring the scoundrel. With the little joke made, he passed his authority on to me as an act of subservient courtesy.

"Herod says the decision is yours," Caiaphas almost sneered at me. A closer look at the prisoner showed he had been maltreated by someone in Herod's court. I plan to find out what happened there. One of my spies will tell me. But I could see spittle hanging in Jesus' beard that indicated he had been insulted. A few scratches on the side of his face showed that he had also been hit.

Still his eyes maintained that look of serenity they had when we first looked at each other.

"Very well," I said. "I will interrogate the prisoner. I nodded to the two guards I always keep near me in this treacherous land, indicating that they should bring Jesus into the inner court. There, with the guards out of my hearing, I said, "Tell me about yourself." I realized the question was fatuous when I said it. Even a man in his right mind, expecting to be sentenced to death wouldn't want to stand and chat with his judge. Jesus just looked at me and waited.

I tried to fathom his look, but was not successful. Yet I was disturbed.

Peasant or not, he looked more truly regal than any Caesar I have ever seen.

"Do you not hear all this evidence brought against you by them?" I asked, almost begging him to defend himself. Father, I assure you I have always tried to rule these stiff necked people with compassion and justice. But the following will show what little success I had with this strange man.

He answered me nothing, so I brought him out before the leaders of the Sanhedrin. Before them all I interrogated him.

"You are a king then?" I asked.

"'King' is your word," he replied. I felt some satisfaction that he answered me. But he continued. "My task is to bear witness to the truth. For this I was born: for this I came into the world, and all who are not deaf to truth listen to my voice."

Father, can you imagine the naivete of the man? I tell you there are some really simple people living in the hill country of Galilee north of here. I knew him to be a small town carpenter with two years of open air preaching as a recent hobby. But imagine someone with no formal education, no training under the tutelage of skilled instructors like the Greek slaves you had tutor me, speaking about a mission to bring truth. To whom? I wondered. But I didn't ask that. I exploded with another question.

"What is truth?"

Our eyes locked, and I had to look away, though it took a full seven long deep breaths before I knew he was more able to hold a steady gaze than I. I looked away from him to Caiaphas. "I find no fault in him worthy of death. I will have him flogged, and then release him." I nodded to the guards, and they took Jesus away.

"No. No. We want him crucified." Several shouted, but I was distracted. One of Procula's servants came to me and gave me a message from her.

"Have nothing to do with that innocent man," her note said. "I was much troubled on his account in my dreams last night." Now father, you know Procula. She is as sane a woman as can be found in all of Rome, or in any of the provinces. She doesn't have flighty premonitions. I knew she had listened to this Jesus preach a day or two before, but she had not been so enamored of his presence that she would dream of him.

I was puzzled that she had even known of the trial that was going on. She doesn't pay much attention to the day to day functions of government. She stands at my side when protocol demands it. She entertains beautifully when it is our turn to show Rome's wealth and might to local citizens or occasional visitors. But never before has she attempted to interfere in a trial. I wondered what her dream was. When I had time, I asked her, and she told me. I will add that to my letter on one of the succeeding pages.

I sat looking at the representatives of the Sanhedrin. They stood looking at me. My soldiers may have had the pretender to the Jewish throne for twenty minutes, perhaps for half an hour, certainly no longer. When my soldiers returned Jesus to us, it was obvious they knew their work, and had done it well. The man could barely stand.

His robe hung almost off his shoulders, his bound wrists could easily have been freed, for there was no strength left in the man. They had woven a crown of thorns and thrust it down on his head so hard it stuck in his scalp! Blood trickled down his face, down his arms, and had I been able to see it, I am sure it flowed down his back.

This time he didn't look me in the eye. His head hung down. He was a most pitiful sight. I tell you this father, though I know you have seen such circumstances often. I am not sure why, except that this time I was both impressed and to my surprise, I was grieving, feeling guilty for having directed this torture to occur.

It was now full day. The sun had climbed high enough over the Mount of Olives that it had chased the shadows out of the Kidron valley beneath us. I saw many more people standing behind the priests, watching and waiting for my verdict. The time had come for me to make my best play. "You know it is our custom to deliver a prisoner to you, to set him free, totally pardoned at this season of the year. I offer you this man, Jesus of Nazareth, or I offer you Jesus BarAbbas."

I told you about names in this country, father. At least one in ten is named Judas, and an almost equal number are named Jesus. Whichever one of these men I set free, they would get a Jesus returned to them, a man called 'savior.' And, ironically, whichever they chose they would get a man called 'Son of the Father,' for that is the meaning of the name BarAbbas. The impassioned priests accused Jesus of calling himself equal to God by calling himself the Father's Son.

"Well, which is it? Do you want this man, or BarAbbas?" I really thought I had them, for BarAbbas was a wild member of the Zealot party that had murdered Romans and Pharisaic priests as a part of the insurrection that always foments under the surface here in this terrible country. The priests hated BarAbbas as much as we did, and wanted him dead. I smiled at them as they put their heads together in a quick conference.

Caiaphas stepped forward. "Give us BarAbbas."

I called to the crowd behind him. "Which should I release to you, Jesus BarAbbas, or Jesus called Messiah?" The priests had done their work well, sending the scribes and others among the crowd and urging them to answer, "BarAbbas."

"What then am I to do with Jesus called Messiah?" I asked, and they answered as if with a single voice.

"Crucify him."

"Behold the man," I said. Jesus stood with his head down, very little strength left in him. It seemed impossible to believe anyone would be so vindictive as to ask for more punishment for this man.

"Crucify him!"

"Why? What evil has he done?" I asked. But they shouted even louder.

"Crucify him!"

I looked at Caiaphas and asked, "You want me to crucify your king?"

He smiled a really wicked smile and checkmated me. "We have no king but Caesar," he said.

I knew I had lost, but I tried again. My wife's dream must have been terrible, I felt, or she wouldn't have tried to interfere in my work. "For my part, I find no case against him," I said.

"We have a law, and by that law he ought to die, for he calls himself, 'Son of God.'"

"Son of the Father," I remembered was Jesus name for himself. He believed his father was the God of the Jews, perhaps the God of all creation. Know this, Father, one gets a sick feeling deep in the belly when dealing with the possibility of killing a deity. I walked back into the Praetorium, beckoning the guards to lead Jesus to me. Inside I stopped them and spoke to Jesus privately. "Where have you come from?" But he would not answer. He raised his head and looked at me so I knew he was capable of hearing and understanding the question.

"You refuse to speak to me?" I was becoming angry with him. "Surely you know I have authority to release you, and I have authority to crucify you."

He answered me then. "You would have no authority at all over me if it had not been granted you from above." Then he had the effrontery to offer me pardon for whatever judgment I was about to make! "Therefore," he said, "the deeper guilt lies with the man who handed me over to you."

Can you imagine that father? He implied that his God had given me my assignment of governor here, rather than Caesar? I was affronted! But I was also impressed. "There is no cause for capital punishment, I said, when I had returned with Jesus to the courtyard. He has already been flogged twice." We looked at him standing there in need of a doctor's attention. He looked pitiful to me, but they had no pity. "I will let him go," I said.

Caiaphas is a master politician, and obviously a strong leader of the Sanhedrin. He led a chorus of voices. "If you let this man go, you are no friend to Caesar. Any man who claims to be a king is defying Caesar."

I had Jesus brought to stand on a parapet above them. He looked dreadful. "Behold the man!" I said again. "*Ecce Homo!*"

"Crucify him!" they shouted, though I heard other voices crying, "No!" there was some scuffling in the crowd. A riot could easily begin.

"Here is your king!" I taunted.

"Away with him! Away with him! Crucify!" they shouted back.

"Crucify your king?" I shouted too. "You want me to crucify your king?"

"We have no king but Caesar," Caiaphas mocked me.

Then I called for a basin of water, and washed my hands publicly before them. "I am innocent of the blood of this man," I said.

"His blood be on us, and on our children," Caiaphas said, and the priests behind him said the same.

I nodded to Cornelius, my most trusted centurion, and he led the poor demented Messiah away to his death. Turning to another of the cohort of guards about me, I said, "Have BarAbbas released immediately."

Then I walked away from the priests, not giving them the courtesy of waiting for their bows of subservience. What a drain it is to serve Rome. Some of the things we are asked to do are really quite inhuman. There was no reason for me to kill the madman, Jesus, except political expediency. I have no idea the real reason for Caiaphas to want the man dead, though I suspect it was something Jesus said or did that made the whole Sanhedrin angry.

That wasn't the end of my distress. I went to my room, disrobed, bathed, and lay down to sleep again. Perhaps I had two hours of rest before Procula came to me and asked about Jesus, the man I knew was already hanging on a cross outside the city gates.

Father, the woman unmanned me by the way she wept. As soon as I saw her, I said, "Procula, I tried to save him." She stared at me for several poignant moments, her eyes big and liquid. It was obvious she had been crying before she came to me. I was telling her nothing new about the crucifixion order.

It might have been easier for me if she had let me touch her and try to console her. But she stepped back as I reached for her, crossed her arms over her chest, and sobbed deep and terrible sounds that came from the center of her being. All I could do was sit there on my couch and wait for her to stop.

Finally she said, "Pontius, you have no idea what you have done." She sat on the floor in front of me then, and continued. "Ruth and I listened to him speak only two days ago. We stood in the women's court near the Temple, and the things he said made much sense to me. Of course I don't know the Aramaic language well enough to fully understand his message. But Ruth knows our language, and she helped me with things he said I didn't know. Someday I will try to tell you what he said.

"But this I know. He wasn't a madman. He wasn't a fool. He was perhaps the best teacher I have ever heard. And the message he had was one that carried a new power for all the world's people."

She stared at me, still sobbing occasionally. "I dreamed last night. I suffered in that dream. In it I saw you and me and all of Rome suffering terrible punishment. The world was in the dream, and the world was on fire with no one to put it out. That is no one could stop the fire but this Jesus. The people's faces were turned toward him in that dream, and they had a look of hope. Their mouths were open in anticipation of some blessing he was about to bestow.

"And then I saw you directing that the man who could save us all was to be killed. I saw him led away to die, his body already cut horribly and seriously bruised. And I saw the light of day fading as his life faded." She looked then to the windows. "Just as the light is fading now, my dear husband. My dream is coming true. The light of the world is going out.

"And as I watched him go, and the light fade, my eyes were caught by the eyes of one after another of the people who had looked to Jesus in hope. They stared at me with looks of horror or anguish, or of terrible pain, or a combination of all of them together. Some of them were demonic looks of horrible anger. The anger was directed at you, my husband. Your name will live in history for what you have done today."

"I tried to save him," I repeated.

"And who could have stopped you if you freed him? Are you not the governor of this province? Do you have Caesar's ring seal that makes any word you say the law of this land? My dear husband, you may fool others with that statement. But you can't fool me. I don't know why you wanted Jesus dead, but it was your order that sent him to his death. If you wanted him alive, you could have stopped the execution."

She was right, of course. I thought about what I had done. "You know I had a sign fastened to the top of his cross that said, 'The King of the Jews,'" I said. "I made those priests squirm with that one. I guess that must have been my primary reason for ordering the man's execution. I wanted to hurt those damned priests!"

"Is that reason enough to have an innocent man tortured and killed?" Procula was insistent.

"No," I said. "Finally there is no reason for one human being to do that to another, and certainly never to an innocent victim without cause. But Rome is called to control its vassal states, and I saw no other way today to do that than to direct the death of Jesus."

"You can rescind the order," she said. "Have him taken down."

"Even if I did, he would die." I pride myself as a historian. "No one nailed to a cross and taken down, even a short time later, has lived more than a few days. Something happens to the blood. They die suffering almost as much as those who finish on the cross. What has been done has been done." I looked at the sky. It was completely dark, and we began to hear huge thunder rolls following after barrages of lightning. Rain held off for some reason. I repeated myself. "What has been done has been done. We must live with it."

Procula let me put my arm around her shoulder and we stood together looking out on the empty city below us.

It was then the earth began to shake and tremble. I have felt such tremblers before in Rome, but never here. And the shaking of the earth I have known was not so violent as this. The walls of our home shook, and I feared the roof might fall on us. I am sure, father, that this was coincidence, and had nothing to do with the death of Jesus. Still, the quaking ground affected the Temple area more than any of the rest of Jerusalem, and I am told the Temple's veil was torn in half, allowing the people to see the Holy of Holies was no more than an empty room.

Procula was terrified. She clung to me desperately, and I held her, caressing her, until our bodies proclaimed a more urgent need than the cataclysm outside. In moments the need for balance and peace was restored in the city, and in our bed. Exhausted by our exercise, and by her almost sleepless night, Procula lay sleeping. I arose and dressed. I was certain of further disturbances of my regular routine. I was right, of course.

A man called Joseph of Arimathea was announced. I saw him immediately. "Welcome," I said. "It has been months since our last visit. Have you news of Rome? Have you merchandise I might want?" I was open and warm with this honest merchant with whom I have dealt ever since I arrived in this land. But I was short with him too. The eastern people don't like to be hurried. One has a visit first, a bite to eat, a glass to share, and then one does business as a part of the social ceremony. But today was different for both of us. He too was in a hurry.

"Pontius," he said, "I come to ask a favor of you. Will you permit Cornelius to let me claim the body of the Nazarene?"

I was surprised. "Of course," I said. "I don't want to leave this one hanging, certainly not over the Passover. There would be a riot. You may have his body as soon as he dies. Within the hour the soldiers will break the legs of all three criminals, and they will be dead in minutes after that."

"Jesus of Nazareth is dead already," Joseph's statement surprised me. I knew, of course, that Jesus had suffered much in the tortures Herod and I had ordered. But only six hours to die when a man is young and strong and healthy is most exceptional.

"I will verify that," I said. "You understand, Joseph. I do not doubt your word." He nodded. I sent a servant to call for Cornelius. "Have some bread and wine while we wait," I suggested, but he shook his head.

"Not today, Pontius. I will not eat today. The man I most admired in all the world has just died." He looked at me with such pain and such awareness of my part in that death, that I knew I had sentenced the death of an old friendship when I ordered Jesus killed. I wonder how many other things in my life will change because of this execution?

Cornelius came and reported that Jesus truly was dead, so I directed him to give the carcass to Joseph. "Let this man have the body as soon as all three are dead. Break the others' bones. Do what you have to do to make sure none are resuscitated. Disperse the crowds. Then dismiss your men after you thank them for me. Your cohort does their work well."

They left me. I wrote a copy of the following letter to Tiberias. Both that letter and this leave Jerusalem today. Below is my letter to the Emperor.

Pontius Pilate, Procurator of Judea
to Tiberias Caesar, Emperor:

I have, this date, ordered the execution of three enemies of Rome. Two were insurrectionists, thieves, and murderers. The other was one Jesus of Nazareth, an itinerant carpenter turned preacher, who has been proclaiming himself king of the Jews.

I found this last man, Jesus, to be deluded, with only a small rabble following him — perhaps a dozen, perhaps a hundred, who believed in him and his cause. But I ordered his death because the high priest and his Sanhedrin claimed Jesus had broken their law and deserved to die. As always, I did what I could to maintain good relations with the local religionists, fulfilling the standard of government policy.

Nothing will come of this day's work. This Jesus that died is close to being the least important man in the world. I assure you nothing more will be heard of him, or of his followers.

Pontius Pilate,
Governor of Judea

Farewell, Father. I wonder now why I wrote you all the above. It was probably because of Procula's dream. Her superstition must have troubled me more than I thought. I go to her now. Perhaps the rest she had has done her some good.

Your son,

Pontius

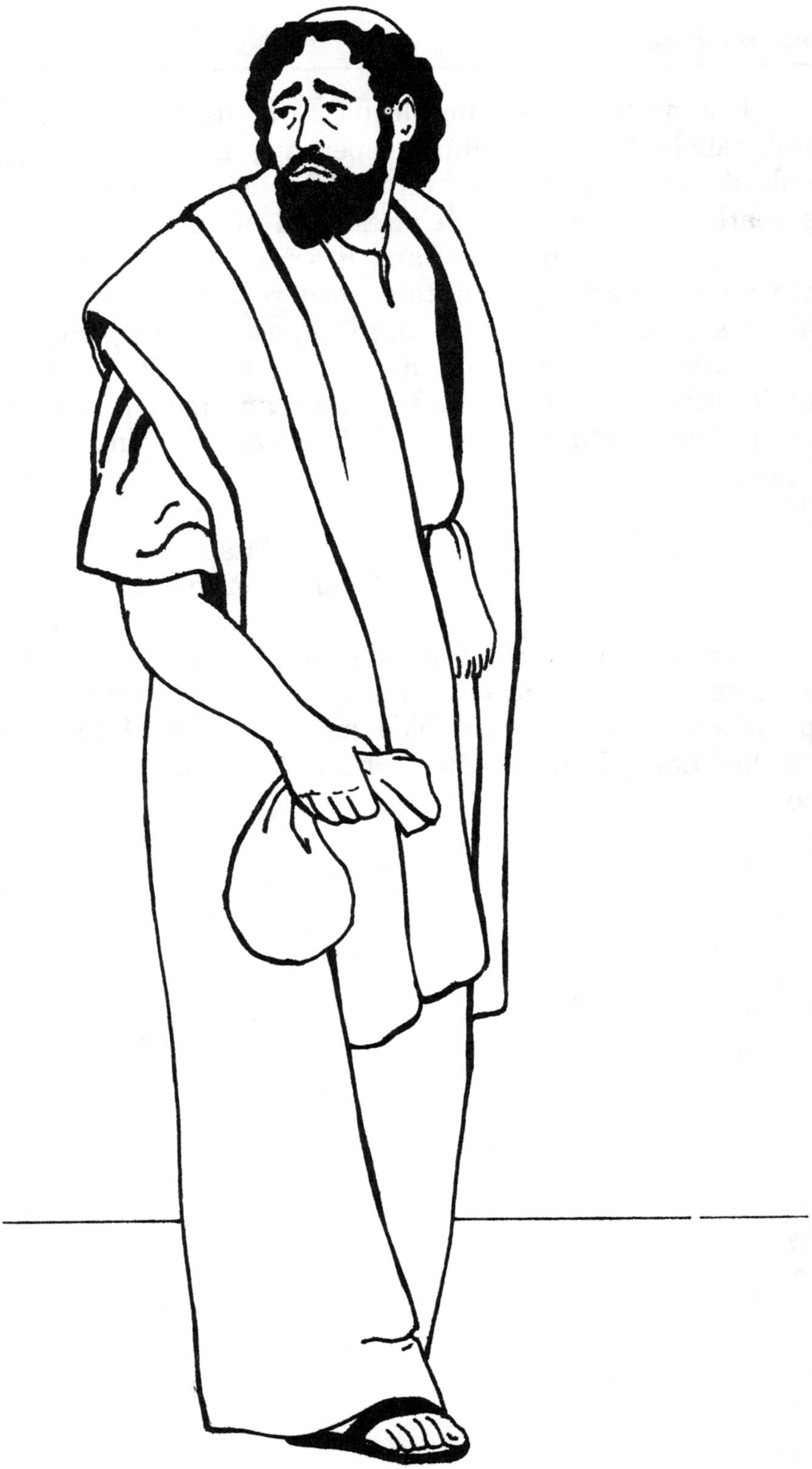

15

Judas Iscariot

My life is over. I write this as a faint hope for someone to read it and learn. Perhaps the wrong choices I made can be avoided by another. Who knows? My name could be remembered with a touch of gratitude. Though tonight is the ultimate end for me, I choose this act of writing as deliberate delay. When I leap from the cliff and the rope tightens around my neck, I will carry hope that this writing will do some poor mortal some good.

Who am I? I am Judas of Kerioth, a town of Judah, a day's walk from Jerusalem. I am a Jew of Judah. I am a man, a member of the Sadducees. I lived a life under the oppressive rule of the Romans. Yet it was a good life. My father Simon is a priest. He serves, even today, in the Temple. He and I are members of the Sanhedrin. After much study, when I had reached maturity, I became a priest. My priesthood in the Temple has been my special role of honor for the past decade. Yet for the last three years, I served as a follower of a man I really thought was our Messiah!

Now that false Messiah is dead. He died here at Calvary nailed on a cross between two thieves. Somehow I know I am to blame for that death. But I see no way to have avoided what happened. Now that Jesus of Nazareth is dead, there is no meaning, no hope for my life. That is why I too shall die.

Still, I must examine my life before I die. Perhaps there is a clue in it somewhere that will show me what God's purpose was for me. I had friends once. Just as my father has friends. One friend in the priesthood with him was Zechariah. Zechariah and Elizabeth were my father's friends. Their son became a good friend of mine.

Zechariah was a priest forty years ago when my father began the work. Father once saw Zechariah come away dumb from the Holy of Holies. That was a miracle that occurred here in Jerusalem. Nine months after that my father was present at the naming of Zechariah and Elizabeth's son. I was a boy of five when that happened. I remember my father and mother talking at dinner and then far into the night about the portent of John BarZechariah's life.

I grew, and John grew. I was educated by Gamaliel in Jerusalem as was John. He left home while still in his youth, and went into the desert. There John joined the Essenes. I became a scribe in the Temple complex, continuing to study for the priesthood.

When we were children, and even in youth, John BarZechariah was my friend. When he visited his home from the desert where he lived, we would sit and talk. The Essenes are a strong sect. They hold firmly to God's Word. They demand strict obedience to the Law. John impressed me then. At fifteen, he had a wild look in his eyes. At twenty the look was still there but there was more, a growing strength. When I became a priest in the party of the Sadducees, I expected John to be happy for me. But he was neither happy nor sad.

"You have a responsibility now," he said. "You have authority. Be sure you learn what God wants. Be sure you obey Him."

When my friend John was in his late twenties, he went alone into the desert. He became almost a wild man. He was what has been termed a Nazirite, one who doesn't drink, or spend time with women; who never has his hair cut or his beard shorn. John ate what the land provided him, often only locusts he caught in his hands as he walked, often on honey and the bees he killed in the honeycombs. He wore animal skins as his clothing. And John talked with God! The Holy Spirit of God was upon him! I know. I went to hear him preach. He was truly a Nazirite. He saw me by the Jordan among the priests. He included me in the attack he made on the priesthood that day. "You brood of vipers!" He called us snakes' children! He looked right at me when he said it. "Who warned you to flee from the coming wrath?"

I was impressed. I listened to John give counsel to people who sought his advice. He spoke of honesty and fair play. I liked what I heard. But my task was to show him to be a fool or a fanatic or both. Friend or not, he knew he had to deal with the establishment.

"Are you the Messiah?" I asked him. He knew I was baiting him. Old playmates never expect much from one another. I knew he wasn't the Messiah. But he answered without showing his awareness of my dishonesty.

"No. I am 'like one crying in the wilderness, preparing the way of the Lord.' There is one who comes after me. I am not worthy of him, not worthy to touch him, even to untie his shoes."

I came under John's spell. Before I knew it, I had stepped into the Jordan and walked to his side. "I will baptize you," John said, and he led me to the center of the stream. We stood knee deep, looking each other in the eye. If I knew John, he knew me too. Better! My guilt as a child, as a man, as a priest, was apparent. His look forced me to acquiesce. "I baptize you with water, the baptism of repentance. I baptize you." Then he poured the water three times over my head. "You are now clean. Your guilt is washed away, down stream it goes to rest in the Dead Sea forever."

Suddenly I felt clean. I felt whole. It was as if a great burden had fallen from me. Joy came to me, and I embraced John in gratitude.

"What more could a Messiah do for me than you have just done?" I asked.

"I baptize with water," he said simply. "He that is coming will baptize with the Holy Ghost and with fire." He said it calmly, but forcefully. It made me want, yet fear, to meet the true Messiah.

All my life I have heard men speaking of a coming Messiah, a great charismatic leader, one who would save us from our enemies, bring in God's Kingdom and make us Hebrews free. Some I have seen who have claimed to be that Messiah. They were soon proven to be too small, too weak, too scheming after personal gain for that role.

I remember what my father said. "Judas, if anyone claims to be the Messiah, put him to severe tests. He must be loving of all the Jews, rich and poor alike. He must care for the poor, love the law and abide by it. He must be just and honorable, self giving even to sacrifice of himself for others. He must be fearless, brilliant, wise. I believe the Messiah is coming. When he comes, he should show himself first by his teaching, second by his healing compassion.

"For centuries we have awaited him. I know that it is now that he is coming. Keep close to John BarZechariah. The Messiah will find John. John will recognize him and point him out to you.

"But don't depend on John's judgment. Test the Messiah yourself. Make sure he is the one you owe your allegiance. Then commit your life to his cause."

After I was baptized, I returned to Jerusalem. Life was much the same, yet it was different. John did something to me when he poured water over me. The old way of life was no more for me. I have remained a bachelor since my wife died in childbirth when I was twenty-five. A bachelor, yes, but I have not slept alone.

Many women have chosen to accept me for an evening or more of intimate companionship. I have satisfied their sexual hungers. Frequently one or another of them satisfied mine. But a Greek slave boy I purchased on a trip to Egypt proved to be a most excellent investment. He was well taught, and he taught me much! His body was beautiful. I enjoyed myself touching, fondling, caressing, kissing, and tasting him. He reciprocated generously.

But after John's baptism, I found everything changed. Much as I knew I would still revel in sexual sins, I found I no longer wanted to do, or even think about, them. It was as if a voice inside me kept asking, "What would the Messiah say? You repented. You are clean. You are ready to meet the Messiah. Do not get dirty again. Be your father's son."

So I stopped having sex. I sold my slave to a pagan for a good profit, and then tithed my income from the transaction. My priestly business I began to conduct with righteous purpose, to the point where I was given assignments of some real trust.

One day Annas, the high priest, asked me to go on a journey to Hyrcania. "Judas," he said. "Herod Antipas has arrested John the Baptizer. The wild man is imprisoned at Herod's winter home. Go there and visit John. Become his confidant, even one of his disciples."

"Of course, Annas," I said. Obedience to the high priest is as important as obedience to God. Whatever he asked, I would do. But because of my inherent curiosity, I had to know my assignment. "But what am I to do in this strange role?"

"You are to learn John's plans. For it is most likely that Antipas will release him soon. You are to find out from John all you can about the Messiah he proclaims is coming.

The only way we can protect ourselves against these fanatics is to infiltrate their organizations, know their plans, and find ways to block them."

I felt a little flattery of my superior was in order. "Annas, you are a genius," I said. "It will be a pleasure to serve under you in this special way." We struck hands after we embraced, and I discovered a substantial sum had been transferred to my palm.

"For expenses," Annas said, and I knew I would have ample funds to live well throughout the time of this assignment. It was only right that this should be so. After all, I had to live outside the civilization of Jerusalem, among religious fanatics in the wilderness. I was due some compensation for that.

As Herod Antipas had been informed of my coming, I met no resistance in visiting John. The first thing I did was to bribe the guards to see that a few comforts were provided my old friend and playmate.

When I entered his cell, I said, "John, why don't you apologize to Herod? Promise not to call him an adulterer again. He will free you from this dungeon." Such an abrupt approach was the best way to handle John. He hated the niceties of small talk; also any light conversation that had no real purpose probably didn't belong in that prison atmosphere.

John looked at me with the same uncompromising fire in his eyes that I had seen so often before. He stared at me until I dropped my eyes. I couldn't think clearly, make the necessary careful steps to achieve my goals, while I was looking into his eyes. His piercing look demanded honesty. It demanded justice. It demanded God's law be obeyed implicitly.

I kept my head up, my body erect, but found a place on the wall just behind John's head where I could focus my eyes. Thus I looked like I was receiving and returning his gaze, but was free of its power to confuse me. Then I presented my argument. "Antipas is a king. You know kings are a law unto themselves. Remember David. He had many wives. He committed adultery with at least two of them. He had concubines as well, and many of them bore him children. Remember Solomon. His record was even worse. Herod's marrying his brother's divorced wife is almost nothing by comparison. Close your eyes to Herod's sin. Then you can come help us." I spoke with deep sincerity. Compromise. Compromise. Compromise. That is the way our nation survived under every oppressor since the Babylonian captivity six long centuries ago. "We need you among us, John."

"Your baptism did you little good," John said, quite mildly for him. "You don't know right from wrong."

"I offer you the right of your being free for preaching, teaching, baptizing again. It is wrong for you to be here!" I argued.

But John had a clear head, and an unchangeable direction. His answer was, as always, straightforward. It cut deep into the facade of truth we priests are prone to accept and practice. "The wrong of my being here is Herod's, not mine. He is accountable for two wrongs, his continuing adultery and his unjust imprisonment of me. I am still only a voice crying in the wilderness. If God wants me to cry here, here I will cry. My jailers will hear me. Herod hears me."

He paused, and knowing he had more to say, and guessing what it would be, I rushed in with a thought of my own. I remembered Annas' directions. I must get closer to John. I could do that, learn more of his plans, by offering to serve him while he was imprisoned. I knew I was the only one permitted to see him. In a sense, John had to choose me to be his spokesman, his courier, to his other disciples.

"John, since you baptized me, I have changed," I said. Then I outlined for him the radical life style changes I had made. I concluded, "John, let me be one of your disciples. Teach me. Let me help you 'prepare the Lord's way!'" I threw that last line in because I knew it to be one of my friend's pet phrases.

John sat down, leaned his back against the wall, stretching his long skinny legs straight out across the floor so his feet nearly touched the opposite wall. He stared up at me. "I thought I had completed my work. I met my cousin, Jesus of Nazareth, while I was baptizing and preaching one day at the Jordan." He stopped talking. I waited for him to go on. I realized he was not thinking of what to say next, but was experiencing again a very moving event in his life. His face took on a softer look. A light of gladness changed his eyes. His lips that spoke such a strong message of righteousness softened into a glad smile.

"I ought to be baptized by you, and yet you come to me?" He paused as if to listen to an answer. Somehow his face brightened even more, and a look of pure joy came over it. His reverie ended, but a part of that look remained as he turned to me.

"I had a revelation from God. He told me I was to prepare the way of the Lord. I asked God, 'How shall I know him?' And I knew. 'The one on whom the Spirit comes and remains, descending like a dove. That will be him.' It was the word of God I heard.

"When I saw Jesus come, something came over me. I already knew in my soul it was he. He made me baptize him. And it was then I saw the dove descend on him. And a voice came from heaven,

"'This is my beloved son with whom I am well pleased.'" John fell silent again. For some time I waited. It was as if he had forgotten I was there.

"What can I do to help you, John?" I made my voice sound deeply sincere. I made it a little subservient. I put a touch of pleading in it. I have had some success at acting. This time I was so good at it I almost believed myself.

John looked deep into my eyes. It was most difficult, but I sustained the force of it. I did not look away. Finally he said the words I needed to hear as Annas' employee, that I needed to hear for myself, knowing this double role was a part of my destiny.

"Yes, Judas, I will use you. Take Jonathan and Simon, my two most trusted disciples. Find Jesus BarJoseph. I hear he is in Galilee preaching a strange doctrine of love and forgiveness. I am confused. My idea of the Messiah's work is vague, but I don't know that what he is doing and saying has anything to do with God's will.

"Is it possible I was mistaken at the Jordan? No, it is not! But what is he doing? What is he saying? What does he say about himself?

"Go ask him. Tell him I must know. Say to him, 'Are you the one, or are we to expect another?'"

I accepted the assignment, and after a few words of wishing John well, I left the dungeon. A few words with Antipas indicating that the Sanhedrin was not unhappy with John's incarceration, assured me my old friend would continue his residence under Herod's demanding hospitality. I knew that would please Annas.

Jonathan and Simon were easy to find. They were camping beside the Jordan near the place of John's successful preaching campaigns. They accepted me as John's emissary without question. If possible, they were even more naive than John. We arranged to start immediately for Galilee.

(An hour has passed since I began to write this account. I read and reread what I have put down on this scroll. It seems so unimportant! Jesus of Nazareth is dead! He let himself be captured. He let himself be tortured. He let himself be tried and sentenced, stripped naked, nailed to a tree. He let himself die. He offered no resistance. He called me his betrayer! "Oh Lord, my God, is there no help.?")

We climbed the winding road out of the Jordan valley. The warm summer sun brought the water from our bodies, almost gushing out of every pore. We climbed in still air, hearing the sounds of creation about us. Growing grasses, buzzing insects, singing birds, bleating sheep. Occasional travelers met us, and a few who were riding horses or donkeys passed us. We seldom spoke to them, or to each other.

Jonathan and Simon were depressed about John's imprisonment. Also, they didn't like me. Few people do. I am not an open person. I am sure, too, that they were secretly plotting against me. John couldn't have been as gullible as he appeared. Somehow he got word to them to keep me under careful watch. John didn't really trust me.

(I wonder what spies Annas has watching me — even now that it is over?)

When we reached the hill country we looked back over the Sea of Tiberias and saw its entire length and width nestling like a beautiful opal in a setting of gold. The Galilee is beautiful and fruitful. We lazily harvested figs and apples from trees along the side of our road. Often we rested in the shade. Twenty miles of climbing the first day was enough for me.

The second day we were off at dawn and were two hours along the road before we met travelers coming toward us. We enquired of them if they had seen Jesus BarJoseph and they told us they had not only seen him but heard him preach. They told of healing he had done. Miracles! Of course we didn't believe them about that. But they told us where they had last seen him.

"He is at Nain," they said. "It is only a day or a day and a half ahead of you." We walked on until just before sundown. Then we stopped to say our Sabbath prayers. We rested by the roadside on the Sabbath, taking short naps, replenishing our energy. I slept only fitfully that night as I dreamed of our mission.

On the first day of the week we arrived at Nain. It was about the sixth hour, mid-day. A crowd was gathered on the edge of town near the cemetery. We walked over and joined them. It was there I first saw Jesus BarJoseph of Nazareth.

Jesus did not impress me then. He stood away from the crowd, his back half turned to me as he looked down the road toward Nain. A number of men and a few women stood near him, looking somehow as if they belonged to him. One woman I recognized. She was Joanna, wife of Chuza, Herod Antipas' chief steward in Tiberias. Joanna was comely and well dressed. Jesus and the others wore cheap rough linen garments, ropes about their waists, peasants' sandals for their feet. Jonathan and Simon beside me looked enough like them to be indistinguishable. Apparently Jesus and John attracted the same kind of followers.

We stood back, not making any effort to do more than observe the scene before us. On the gently rising pasture beside the cemetery many people were encamped. It was obvious they had come to stay for a few days and nights, and by the way they were settled in, most of them had arrived at least two days before. There was an atmosphere of celebration in the camp. We saw people embracing, heard laughing, singing, and shouts of joy. Tears gushed from eyes in faces that were smiling broadly. It was obvious one or more great events had taken place before our arrival.

We looked in the direction Jesus was looking. Then we saw a funeral procession coming out of Nain. Mourners led the bier, weeping, sobbing, carrying on in a manner that was in sharp contrast to the joy filled acclamations about us.

The open bier was carried by four strong men. Behind them walked a woman in early middle age. Behind her walked her community of friends and relatives. We didn't have to enquire. The deceased was hers, husband or child. Also, we could see that with the death her household was reduced to her alone, all alone. Her shoulders slumped. Her eyes looked occasionally in anguish at the determined procession ahead of her, but more often in despair at the ground before her feet. She was like so many bereaved, able to set one foot before another. But that was all.

Jesus waited for the professional mourners to pass. Then he stepped forward and stopped the casket bearers. As a Sadducee priest of the Temple in Jerusalem, I saw the body of a dead young man in that box. ***I certify he was dead!*** Then I watched a miracle.

Jesus touched the bier and spoke to the body. "Young man, I say to you, arise! ***And the body sat up***!

Jesus helped the young man to his feet and, without a word, handed him over to his mother. Then Jesus turned away at a call to him from one of his disciples. I wanted to watch Jesus, but my eyes held to the drama of reunion between a living mother and a newly living — but recently dead — son. The entire funeral party were in a state of shock. They had committed their hearts to force their bodies to do all that was left to do for the young man. That is, to put his body in the ground, and to cover it. Then to walk away, leaving part of their life, their love, behind them.

Now, suddenly, they had to do an about face. They needed to climb from unbelief through doubt and uncertainty to the point of touching the young living body, and listening to him speak. Their joy grew, but the miracle of resurrection is so great that humble awe at majestic godlike power kept its expression subdued.

At last I could turn away to follow Jesus. In so doing, I took the first steps along a road that has led me here. My life of association with Jesus is bracketed by death. There was the one death three years ago that was changed back to life; and now with Calvary, and this barren hillside, two others. Jesus' death and my own.

> *(Oh Jesus, my Lord, I saw you raise three persons from death to life, the man in Nain, the little girl in Caphernaum, and Lazarus, Martha's brother. You had the power! Why did you let yourself die? Why did you not come down from the cross and destroy your enemies and ours? I cry out to emptiness and receive nothing. Not even an echo!)*

Simon, Jonathan, and I stood watching for two full hours as people were brought to the Nazarene. A blind woman was led to him. He spoke to her, she to him. He spoke again, and touched her face.

"I can see! I can see!" she cried out. Then she hurried away without assistance.

A cripple on a stretcher was carried to Jesus. It was obvious the man had terribly deformed feet. Jesus spoke to him, and he stood up to walk away on normal feet!

Deaf were made to hear again. Tongues were untied and harelips healed. A few lepers stood to one side, ringing their bells if anyone came too close. Jesus spoke to them and all were healed at once. I had never seen anything like it before.

I was impressed.

Finally the crowd thinned and we were about to go to Jesus with our greetings from his cousin. But a young woman stood before him speaking terrible disgusting things. Jesus didn't speak to her. Instead, he spoke as if to a spirit within her.

"I command you to tell me," he said, "who are you?"

A voice deep and resonant, but rasping as if it had a severe cold, replied, "I am anger, but I am not the only one here."

"Come out of her now. Leave, and do not come back!"

Something happened to her. She trembled all over, turned white as the angry flush left her face. But Jesus was not finished with her.

"Who are you," he said again.

She looked away, but a voice from her mouth said, "Lust."

Jesus said again, "Leave her." And it was gone. Five more times he did this, each time freeing her from a demon, until at last she was really free of her inner oppression.

The change in the woman was dramatic. I am a competent actor, and I know acting from reality. This woman had been fighting seven powerful spirits and had no way, of herself, to get free of their power.

The woman was one of a very few who showed gratitude. She fell to her knees, bent to the ground, and kissed the Nazarene's feet. "Oh, thank you, Master," she said. He lifted her up, embraced her as if she were his sister, his equal, and then let her go. I saw her walk away, and watched Chuza's wife come up to her to speak. Soon they walked away together, arm in arm, happy smiles on their faces.

As we approached Jesus, I found that for some reason I was shy. That is an emotion I don't recollect having felt before. But because of it I stayed behind Jonathan and Simon as they approached Jesus with John's question.

"Are you the one who was to come, or should we expect someone else?" they asked, and added, "Your cousin, John the Baptizer, sent us to ask."

Jesus looked at them, and a look of love shown forth that made him powerfully attractive. My heart begged for him to look at me in the same way. Then he did look past them to me with an awareness that was total. Instantly I was sure he knew all I knew of myself, and far more, to a depth I could never dare penetrate. He seemed to gasp, and then to recover completely.

He turned again to the others and said, "Go back and report to John what you have seen and heard. The blind receive their sight. The lame walk. Those who have leprosy are cured. The deaf hear. The dead are raised. And the good news is preached to the poor."

Then he looked at me and continued, "Blessed is the man who does not fall away on account of me." He stared deep into my soul for a moment, and then seemed to look inward, staring (perhaps) into his own.

Then he called me by name, even though I am certain it was our first meeting. "Welcome Judas. I've been expecting you. Follow me." He turned and walked toward the peasants I had assumed were his followers. He did not look back. He knew I would come.

And I did, but I stopped long enough to say "Farewell" and "Peace" to Simon and Jonathan. They started back immediately though it was nearly sundown. I assured them that I agreed with their opinion. Jesus BarJoseph was certainly the most remarkable, most powerful, most enigmatic, most magnetic, most charismatic human being any of us had ever seen. "He must be the Messiah," we agreed. They departed, and I walked over to Jesus and his other followers.

Jesus looked at me and said, “Anyone who starts to plow and then keeps looking back is of no use for the Kingdom of God.” The words chilled my heart. Was he rejecting me? Simply because I stopped to say farewell to Jonathan and Simon?

I heard Jesus say the same words to others on other occasions. I believe he used it as a way to remind those who would follow him of the total dedication such a life demanded. The reference to the plow was not lost on me for I was reminded instantly of Elijah’s call to Elisha. The latter had wanted to postpone briefly his new ministry, and had come close to rejection.

Perhaps that is what occurred there at the edge of Nain. Jesus almost rejected me before I joined his disciples. I am sure this had something to do with his knowledge of me. But his decision to accept me came from that knowledge as well. One could say Jesus was ‘tempted’ to send me away. One could say he refused that choice.

I was accepted.

Jesus introduced me to his followers. There were Simon (called Peter) and Andrew BarJonas, his brother; James and John BarZebedee; Philip of Bethsaida, a Greek! One was introduced to me by his last name only, BarTholomew. I asked, “What is your name?”

He responded, “Jesus,” and I understood. It would have been confusing to us all if our leader and one of his principal followers had the same name.

Others introduced to me were James BarAlphaeus; another Simon as often called the Zealot; and Judas BarJames, who they often called Jude, made up the company about Jesus.

Some women nearby seemed busy preparing a meal and Jesus introduced me to them. One I knew, Joanna, the wife of Chuza, Herod’s steward. Another I had seen cured. She was called Mary of Magdala. The third was a lovely girl named Suzanna. I determined to strike up a conversation with that one later.

I was accepted by Jesus' followers without question. He had called me. I had come. They were a part of the community for the very same reason.

Two men came from the town. They brought bread and wine I assumed they had been sent to buy. Jesus welcomed them and introduced them to me. Levi of Capher-naum was also called Matthew. The other was another Judas, this one of Nazareth, who was affectionately called 'Thomas,' the twin. He was amazingly like Jesus in appearance. I was sure they must be cousins or brothers. My first guess was right. They were cousins.

With the fellowship of a shared meal of bread, wine, and some fresh fruit, we cemented our new acquaintance and planted seeds of friendship. I was friendly. I wanted so much to be a friend to all of them.

(Another hour has passed. It is the dawn of the new Sabbath. I have seen Annas and his son-in-law, Caiaphas. "I have betrayed innocent blood!" I cried. And they just laughed at me. That's my problem, they told me. It's not my only problem, I know. But hanging is my total solution. "Oh Jesus, Why?" is my cry.

(What a headache I have. I grow dizzy. It is so long since I have felt any illness! In Jesus' presence we were all well. We even had some of his power to heal.

(Then why am I sick? First, because he is not here. He is dead. Gone forever. Second, because I have made myself sick. I haven't eaten since "The Living Bread" gave me bread. I haven't touched liquid since the 'Vine' gave me wine. I haven't slept since....the first

day of this week when he rode that donkey into this terrible city).

I shall get on with this final exercise. I found myself the only priest among them. Except for Levi, who had a rudimentary education so that he could read, write, and do simple ciphers, as a tax gatherer, I was the only one who could read any other language than Hebrew. It was so obvious that I was their superior that Jesus immediately put me in charge of the money. One of my first expenditures was to pay a messenger to take my report back to Annas. I was certain Annas would be pleased with my progress. I had at least postponed John the Baptizer's release from prison. And I had, with amazing ease, infiltrated the heart of the camp of one called Jesus of Nazareth, an astonishingly charismatic man, and therefore a serious Messianic threat.

No one ever asked me how I used the money. They trusted me. Under Jesus' teaching they trusted everyone. "Be wise as serpents. Be gentle as doves," was one of his wise sayings. However great their combined wisdom, they never suspected I was a spy among them, working for the Sanhedrin.

But they didn't like me. They didn't associate with me. Only Mary of Magdala, who had been a whore, who was formerly from Judah, associated with me. She talked to me often, but it was only out of courtesy when she added funds to our purse for necessities. The other eleven men of the inner circle around Jesus were all Galileans. Except for Levi, the tax collector, and Philip, the Greek, they were old friends, many of them blood relatives of each other and of Jesus. I was an outsider, never accepted.

When Jesus sent us out two by two to minister, no one chose me. I was always the left over selected for whoever else was next to the last.

I laughed when Jesus said, "The last shall be first," and left me in charge while he went off alone to pray. I was also left in charge when Jesus took his slow learners, the stupid fishermen, up a mountain to teach them. Peter, James and John. He always took them. That wasn't fair. But making me first showed his clear thinking, his recognition of my excellence.

I talked with one of the disciples who had a mission. He was Simon, the Zealot, and was looking for a Messiah who would lead our people in a war for independence. I was interested in that possibility too. We could see the growing wave of support from the people. The crowds were impressed by several things Jesus did. First they said, "He does all things well. He makes the deaf hear and the dumb speak." Then they learned he could and would heal all diseases of anyone who asked, whether for themselves, or others. He brought the dead back to life. And, much to my dismay, he asked nothing for this service, but seemed to relish words of thanks. The people liked it when Jesus compared good health to the way things are in the Kingdom of Heaven.

The idea of Jesus becoming our king and leading us to permanent victory over all our oppressors, the Romans, their vassal monarchs, the subservient priesthood, was not long in coming. It became a full blown concept when Jesus began feeding thousands with minimal supplies. On one occasion, five thousand men plus their families, perhaps as many as fifteen thousand people, were fed from some means Jesus had to expand five loaves of bread and two fish.

I was there. I helped distribute the food, watched it grow and double in my hands as I passed it around. After the meal, I carried about a large basket, filling it with full loaves, half loaves, and good sized pieces of fish. Each of the other eleven filled their basket as I filled mine. Thereafter I had the duty of sending those baskets in the hands of lesser disciples to the towns and villages about us to feed the poor.

Imagine an army that doesn't need to carry its supplies! Imagine a nation of well fed people who never have to work for daily bread! Our war could be won with little effort. Our happiness as a people freed from toil was assured. All we needed was the further assurance we could win battles without suffering losses. That was there too. Jesus could heal the wounded and raise up the dead.

Then, when we saw Jesus raise the dead a second and a third time, we knew no army on earth could stand against us. We could enter battle fearlessly, knowing we would not die. Jesus also proved himself invincible. He could and did walk through angry mobs containing men who intended to kill him. He either blinded them temporarily, or was protected by legions of angels. Which I don't know, for either alternative is patently impossible. Yet I saw it. Again and again he walked through danger, and no one laid a hand on him in anger.

Jesus' own righteous power was immense. Just this past week I saw the greatest evidence of that. All alone, using only his voice and a length of rope, he drove out hundreds of businessmen from the Temple. I watched him do that. He didn't raise his voice. He tipped over a few tables, scattering money across the stone floor of the Temple's outer courts. He opened a few cages, releasing perhaps two to three dozen pigeons. Then he calmly walked behind the merchants and money changers as if he were a herdsman. "My Father's House is a house of prayer. You have made it a den of robbers," is what he said. He said it calmly, forcefully, but quietly, and they all obeyed him. Somehow each knew that Jesus had authority to do what he was doing.

The evil of oppression from Rome was, and still is, the chief reason we need a Messiah. Jesus could have evicted the Roman trespassers on our land as easily as he evicted the money changers. Simon the Zealot and I talked of this, knowing all of Jesus' parables of the Kingdom would soon be coming true right where we lived. Jesus would be King. We would be his chief officers, executing his commands over all the land God promised Abraham and his seed. The acceptable time for a Messiah we were sure had come!

I am certain Jesus knew I was a double agent, working for the Sanhedrin and for Herod Antipas even as I served him. I had taken precautions, of course. I had my name deleted from ***The Book of Servants of the Temple***.

Whenever Jesus brought us to Jerusalem, I made a point of moving away from the other disciples, standing among the anonymous crowd. Then, if family, friends, brother priests, or mere casual acquaintances saw me, they could assume other things than my fellowship with this controversial man.

16

Judas Iscariot

One day Jesus chose to send me to John the Baptist with a personal message. I was to go tell my old friend Jesus' statement honoring John that he had often said as he preached. "What did you go out to see when you went to see John? Did you go into the desert to see a reed shaken by the wind? If not, what did you go out to see? A man dressed in fine clothes? No, those who wear expensive clothes and indulge in luxury are in palaces. But what did you go out to see? A prophet? Yes, I tell you, and more than a prophet.

"This is the one about whom it was written, 'I will send my messenger ahead of you, who will prepare your way before you.' I tell you, among those born of women there is no one greater than John; yet the one who is least in the Kingdom of God is greater than he."

That was the message Jesus sent me to tell John. He wanted John to be assured that Jesus knew and deeply appreciated John's hard life of self sacrifice and obedience. Jesus took me aside before he sent me. He looked deep into my troubled eyes, holding my attention. That forced me to look back into his clear mind and recognize the vast difference between us. He was power; I was weakness. He was righteousness; I was treachery. He was selflessness; I was self seeking.

Jesus placed his hands on my shoulders and stood so close I could feel his breath on my face as we talked. I inhaled some of the air he had just had in his lungs. I felt warmth spread through me from deep within, and yet also from my shoulders as well where he held me with his firm but gentle grip. I had been in awe of him before, admired him, respected him, willingly put myself under his authority. But I had had no personal feeling for him.

But from that moment on, I loved him. I loved him more than I have ever loved anyone else, loved him more, indeed, than all else.

(I swear this is so. Rather, I affirm it. He taught us that the word of an honest man is enough. My word on it then, the word of Judas, son of Simon Iscariot. I loved Jesus BarJoseph of Nazareth with my whole heart. I never willed him harm.)

> *(Oh Lord, my God, is there no help for the widow's son? The ritual cry of our temple cult comes back to me as I remember the mother of Jesus. She is the widow of Joseph, mother of a dead son. She is one of the few followers of Jesus I have not seen to seek solace, forgiveness, acceptance, reconciliation. And I remember the widow of Nain whose son was restored to her by Jesus the day I met him. There was help there and then.*
>
> *(Then why is there no hope of help for me or for Jesus here and now? Were Jesus alive, I would be forgiven. Were he alive, I would not have to die.)*

There in Galilee he spoke to me. "John is Elijah come back just as the prophets predicted. Go to him. Tell him what I have said about him. Tell him what I have taught about the Kingdom. Tell my dear cousin I love him. And know this; John is in great danger. Stay with him until you know he no longer needs you. Then come back to us."

Then Jesus embraced me. His Spirit, perhaps the Holy Spirit of God Himself, filled me. My eyes overflowed as I embraced him in return, hugging him to me with all of my strength. I looked honestly into his wet eyes, for he was weeping too, with such a caring love, and I spoke. "Yes, Master," I said. "Yes, Lord," I said. Since that day, though I continued to keep Annas and the rest of the priesthood in Jerusalem well informed of Jesus and his works, his teachings and his movements, I have been Jesus' man. Yet that was the only time I called him, 'Lord.'

"One thing more, Judas," Jesus said to me. I memorized the saying for though I heard him preach it to thousands, he said it first to me. "One thing more. A man cannot serve two masters, for he will either hate the one and love the other, or love the one and despise the other. You cannot serve God and money."

I knew then that nothing got by Jesus. *He knew all about me.* He knew I had been taking funds from the common treasury and setting them aside for my own purposes. I pretended to myself these were for the great future battle against our enemies, or for some other laudable purpose. But I knew, and I knew then that Jesus knew, I was simply accumulating wealth (and therefore, earthly power) for myself.

I looked away, penitent, resolved to change. Jesus rested his hand on my shoulder one more time before I started my assigned journey as his ambassador to John. That touch assured me of his understanding, and of his forgiveness. The power of his love, and of his joy came back to me. I walked away, my heart bursting with gladness.

Three days later I found John still in his dungeon at Hyrcania, Antipas' desert fortress near the Jordan. John and

I talked for several hours. “I knew he would increase, and I decrease,” John said with no jealousy or rancor in his voice. He was pleased to be compared with Elijah; more pleased to be told of Jesus’ deep love for him.

Then I went to Herod Antipas. I decided I would try to do a good deed for my old friend. I would attempt to gain John’s release. “Let him go,” I said. “Imprisonment in that dark stone dungeon is killing him. Give him a warning not to preach against you again, but give him his freedom.”

“Who told you to say that?” Herod responded. The political aspects of keeping John jailed had always been stronger than those for releasing him. The people of power did not love John. Only the weak, the poor, the faithful little people cared for him. He was their champion.

I had to admit that it was only my personal prejudice that I was offering. I represented no one else in this request.

“I’ll think about it,” Herod said, leaving me a courteous exit without a direct denial. Then he offered me the gift of social acceptance on a much higher level than I had ever achieved before. “By the way, I’m giving a banquet next week. It is my birthday celebration. Please stay and be my guest.”

Of course I did stay in Herod’s palace. There I saw two of the women followers of Jesus, Joanna and Suzanna. I spoke to them and they invited me to join their group at the banquet. The preparations were elaborate. Two young fattened oxen were killed and their meat prepared over slow fires. Fish were there, brought in fresh from the great western sea. Grapes, apples, pomegranates, figs, and many kinds of nuts were set out in silver bowls. The selection of wines included the best from Rome, Greece, Babylonia, and Egypt.

Ambassadors and emissaries from every country in the world came. I saw Annas, our high priest, and gave him the sign so that he would not publicly recognize me. With Annas was Caiaphas, his son-in-law, who was next in line for the high priesthood. Pontius Pilate, the governor of Judea was also there.

Two senators were present from Rome. Unlike Pilate, Annas, and Caiaphas who escorted their own wives, the senators surrounded themselves with several attractive young men and women.

The feast was held in the gardens of the palace. Torches lit the scene adequately, especially as they were aided by a nearly full moon. We ate and drank, entertained by several pompous speakers who lauded Herod for his many attributes. Since he had few worth noting, they were forced to be both imaginative and repetitive. Each was applauded for great oratory by an audience growing less competent by the tipping of every glass. I know not the revelry of Rome, but surely Herod must have done well emulating his masters.

As the evening progressed, so did the entertainment. From speeches we went to poetry, from poetry to music, to song, and to the dance. We noted that each dancer was more lovely and each dance more erotic than the last.

I sat beside Suzanna. Joanna and Chuza sat just beyond her, on her right. Chuza had everything under control. Servants came and went, keeping our dishes and glasses filled. Chuza was relaxed and obviously in his cups. Few at the party would notice that, and if they did, they could consider it normal behavior. For almost all present were half drunk or more.

Except for Chuza, our group were the exceptions. Of course we ate, and we enjoyed the wine, and when we watched it, the entertainment. But we were engrossed in conversation. Chuza knew little about Jesus, and the three of us took pleasure in telling him of the wondrous things that man said and did. I was amazed at my own enthusiasm. "He is a great healer," I said. "I have seen him raise the dead!"

Joanna and Suzanna took their turns. "He teaches happiness is the way of the Kingdom of God. Health and happiness."

"He teaches love and sacrificial service are the way to the Kingdom."

"He shows us that way," I said. Despite my interest in the conversation, my interest in Suzanna, my dinner companion, grew greater.

She was lovelier than ever that night. Her dark eyes flashed joy as she spoke with real animation about Jesus. Her cheeks were flushed and her more rapid breathing did things to her nostrils and her chest that reminded me that I had been celibate for a long time. I touched her hand deliberately as she spoke, and she just as deliberately, and with an aware look at me, enclosed my hand in hers as she concluded her statement.

Suzanna and I fell silent as Chuza and his wife continued the conversation. My hand in Suzanna's felt it was where it belonged. She squeezed it occasionally as we listened.

"I grow jealous of the man," Chuza said. "You are away among the crowds listening to him and watching him more than you are at home."

"Oh, my dear, I am your wife," Joanna replied. "Do not be jealous of Jesus. Somehow he is husband and brother and friend to all of us, but he is not a sexual lover of any."

"Jesus is the most righteous man I know," I said. "He teaches all to obey the law of God."

"But does he not break the law of the Sabbath? I heard he did." Chuza's question was valid. We had seen Jesus heal on the Sabbath. We had worked with him on the seventh day of the week. We had been accused of breaking that commandment with him.

I was about to give an answer when another dancer was introduced. It was Antipas' step daughter, Salome, a girl of no more than fourteen, but fully developed. That was apparent to all of us as we saw through her skimpy gossamer costume to her lovely flesh.

However, a beautiful body is no novelty. The dresses of many of the guests and the costumes of most of the earlier performers were nearly as revealing. We were moderately surprised that a member of Herod's immediate household would perform before so important an audience. But a King is a King, and his subjects and guests do not question his taste or his choices.

We watched Salome, fully expecting an amateur to make a fool of herself and then to applaud her, putting her indulgent step father in our debt. We were soon caught up in a performance of consummate skill. A child she was in age, but certainly not in experience. Her dance was sinuous, sensuous, blatantly sexually arousing. I am sure every man in the room felt turmoil in his loins as he watched her. I know that I did.

Salome danced exclusively for Herod. Her eyes held his as if to force his mind and soul into acknowledging her, accepting her, fulfilling her. It was obvious to all of us, the balance of her audience, that she was remarkably successful. She danced close to him, just beyond his reach, making all of her alluring self a tantalizing reality, fully available for even closer exploration at his command.

Antipas' face became a study of all consuming lust. We watched him lean forward, his mouth open, lips wet, his eyes almost out of his head. He reached for her, but she danced inches away from his fingertips, offering, enticing, promising, but elusive.

The dance ended, and she bowed low before Herod, the most beautifully packaged gift he was offered that evening. We all knew she was offering more than the performance we had just witnessed. She offered a private dance with Herod as her partner, a dance that would gratify him at a level beyond description, but well within the imagination.

However, the private performance had a price. Herod knew that, and was willing to pay. "Anything I have is yours, up to half my kingdom!" he exclaimed. Salome grew still, calculating, considering. Then, with a final bow to Herod that included us all, she ran lightly away.

She sank down among a group near us. There she wrapped a slightly less transparent garment about her and spoke quietly to her mother, Herodias. "Mother, he wants me. He offers me anything I want. You heard him say it before all these witnesses. What should I ask of him?" There was no question of the alternative of a refusal. Only the price was in question.

Herodias looked at her. She is an attractive woman, barely thirty-five herself. She knew she would never hold Antipas as her exclusive lover. She had accepted him in her bed while still married to his brother. She knew, too, that she would seek some discreet affairs with other male partners in the future.

"There are many things you could ask for, but you will be able to choose them all later. What he pays tonight will only be a down payment for future favors. This that you contemplate is far worse than adultery in the Hebrew law. Remember that Herod is your father's brother, your uncle. The ancient law against mating with blood relatives is about to be violated. He wants you. You are willing. But I must have my price too. For I am sending my own daughter to the king's bed. Let us ask for something that will give us both our freedom from the awful law of God, or at least from that terrible and disgusting spokesman of that law. If you do this, and I permit it, John's voice will destroy us both. His cry will bring such rebellion that it could mean the end of Herod's reign!

"Ask for John the Baptizer's head!"

Salome had listened carefully. Perhaps only I, sitting near them as I was, overheard their conversation. My respect for Herodias increased. She is a strong, practical, calculating woman. I watched to see their next move. The whole room full of guests waited and watched with me.

Salome arose and walked slowly to a place at Herod's feet. She stood there for a moment, looking him in the eye, and then she removed the outer garment that almost covered her and her costume. Very deliberately she continued disrobing, until she stood bare before him. Legs apart, and though her back was turned toward us, I could imagine she was offering a smile of triumph. In a voice that carried throughout the garden and into the empty desert beyond, she said the fatal words, "Give me John the Baptizer's head now, on a platter."

Herod's lust was quenched. He gasped, looked about, knowing he was well trapped. The Romans in the room, Governor, Senators, and several military officers simply watched. John's life or death meant nothing to them. They were amused at Herod's discomfort. Only a country fool would be forced into executing anyone for so small a reason as gratifying his mistress' whim.

The priests of the Temple leaned slightly forward, in hope. They could soon be free of the terrible accusations of John without having to arrange anything themselves. Annas and Caiaphas looked like vultures, eager to devour dead flesh that some predator destroyed for them. I could guess that their minds envisioned another benefit to the Temple. Their witnessing the event could give them a position of real bargaining power over Herod. I know they expected Herod would be making substantial contributions to the Temple coffers.

All this I saw, or knew inwardly, as I watched Herod and Salome. As she was given little time to name her gift, he was given even less time to accept or reject her demand.

He could not postpone his decision. He couldn't seek wise counsel. His eyes sought for friends. Were there no friends of Herod at his birthday banquet? Finally his eyes caught mine, and held.

I was caught up in the moment. Already I was grieving for John, as I was certain of Herod's choice. I could not speak, of course. I could choose to remain as the others, stone faced and waiting. I could look away, giving him no indication of my opinion. I could nod slightly, approving the choice of execution, or I could shake my head, only a little, rejecting that choice. But the last of these possibilities would have been foolish, for I would have been voting against a choice that had to be made.

I shrugged. That's all. I simply shrugged and smiled slightly. Thus I shared in the decision to kill one of my oldest and dearest friends. I have grieved since for John; grieved for myself and the cruel realities of this world. But, I must say, I never regretted the choice I made that night.

Herod nodded slightly, first in my direction, then at Salome. But the cold look in his eyes as he stared at her showed a far different passion from the one that caused him to be so foolish. He spoke to a guard beside him, who left the garden in the direction of the palace. "Your wish is granted," he said. "Dress yourself."

Salome looked confused and frightened. Suddenly she became a little girl again, a pawn in a deadly game. She blushed as she dressed quickly and tried to step back.

"Wait!" Herod said. "Your gift is coming." She froze at his side.

We sat in silence. Aware my hand was still in Suzanna's, I withdrew it. We looked at each other in anguish. Only a few days before we had been at a meal with Jesus BarJoseph. There love and peace and gladness prevailed.

Such a contrast to this occasion!

I hung my head, remembering the lust I had recently felt for Salome. I recalled Jesus saying, "To think of a woman in such a way is to have already committed adultery with her." I was guilty. In this as well as in murder, I was guilty. Two commandments shattered in one evening!

A loud cry was heard from the bowels of the castle. "Herod! Repent Herod! Repent! Re..." and an awful silence fell on us all.

Soon, too soon, the guard returned with John's head lying on its side on a silver platter. He brought it to Herod. Herod simply looked at it for a few instants, then showing no emotion, he nodded toward Salome.

The child reached out her hands and took the tray from John's executioner. She walked as in a trance to her mother. There, at last, a little of her ancestral spunk showed through. She dumped the head off the tray into her mother's lap, and walked away with her head held high.

No more was said. No more was done. The banquet was over. The final dessert satiated all appetites for some time to come.

In the middle of the night Herod was heard to cry out, "Send for Salome. I want her *now*! God knows I paid enough for her!"

In less than a year she was to bear a deformed brainless son; a fit heir to the throne of Herod.

That night I was not alone. Suzanna was so disturbed by the events of the evening, she sought peace from someone she could trust, someone she respected. As I was one of the twelve, she knew she could trust me! We talked through the night. When the light of dawn came, we were still clothed, still talking. I felt a little cleaner when we parted. Perhaps, I thought, Jesus would approve some part of my time at court.

When morning was fully upon us, I walked into the desert the short distance to the Jordan river. There I found John's disciples and told them of his fate. I went with them to Herod and was present when they asked for and received John's body. The head belonged to Herodias' daughter. It was not delivered to us. I stayed with John's body until it was safely buried. I even said some priestly prayers over it.

Afterwards I returned to Jesus. John needed me no longer.

17

Judas Iscariot

The days of Jesus' ministry followed a pattern. We walked from town to town, enjoying our fellowship with him and with each other. Shortly after I returned to them, finding them in Simon Peter's town of Caphernaum, we walked north to Caesaria Philippi. Along the way Jesus asked, "Who do men say that I am?" After a day's discussion of possibilities, including my suggestion, "John the Baptizer come back!" Simon Peter said,

"You are the Christ! You are the Son of the Living God!"

We all agreed. Though I wasn't the only one who had a few reservations.

Several days later, Jesus took Peter, James, and John with him again up yet another mountain. They left me in charge in the valley.

Before long, a crowd gathered and I divided the other apostles two by two to have them function as healing teams. Soon all were busy, and as usual, they were successful. A man came up to me and asked me to drive out a demon from his son. "Of course," I said.

I turned to the lad. "Come out of him!" I said. I spoke with authority, just as Jesus always did. Nothing happened. I knew I had failed. To emphasize my failure, the demon threw the boy down on the ground where he lay frothing at the mouth.

In true and proper humility, I asked each of the others to help me. It always worked before. Two of us tried; then three; then five; then all together. Still nothing. The demon remained. The boy stopped writhing on the ground, but we could see he had not been freed.

We healed others that day. We drove out other demons that day. But the boy's demon was still there. To prove it, the demon threw the boy on the ground again, made him growl like an animal, and froth foam from his mouth again. The more we tried, the more exhausted we became, the more frustrated, the less confident.

At last Jesus came back with the three. The father immediately went to Jesus and asked for help. "Your disciples tried to drive a demon out of my son, but they failed. I beg you to look at him. He is my only child. When the spirit seizes him, he screams. It throws him into convulsions so that he foams at the mouth."

"Oh, unbelieving and perverse generation," Jesus replied. "How long shall I stay with you and put up with you?" He looked straight at me when he said that, as if my faithlessness were the cause!

I wanted to ask, "What about the other eight?"

The father brought his son to Jesus. Even while the boy was being led to the Master's side, the demon threw the lad to the ground with another convulsion. Jesus rebuked the evil spirit, healed the boy, and gave him back to the father.

Later, when we were alone with him, we asked Jesus, "Why couldn't we do that?"

Jesus replied, looking directly at me, "Some can only be done with prayer!" Jesus knew me. He knew the deepest corners of my soul. He was certain my prayer life was dry and fruitless. I was constantly amazed at him spending time in prayer. Then and now I would pray to God, beg him to answer me, to speak to me. And all I got for my efforts was the feeling of being a fool to talk to an empty sky. Better to have shouted in the mountains! There, at least in some places, an echo might come back.

Jesus often picked on me about prayer. Once he overheard me praying a prayer of heartfelt thanksgiving. I prayed openly in public on a street corner. "I thank you, God, that I am not as other men are." A low down tax collector was standing near me, saying his prayers at the same time. He was saying something like, "God have mercy on me, a sinner." He certainly had that right! I prayed a little louder then, making sure the tax collector had an idea of how much better I was than he. "I obey the laws," I prayed. "I tithe even the smallest things."

Later Jesus told others about my prayer, not mentioning me by name. He said the lowly tax collector's prayer was heard and answered, and mine was not. I know what he was doing. He was making me look bad, and making Levi, the former tax collector, and all his tax collecting friends, happy at my expense. I remember turning and looking at Levi then. He was grinning to himself.

> *(My head hurts. God how it hurts! If only I could sleep! It is almost a whole day since Jesus died. The sun has moved around to the southwest. It is not like the dark cloudy day with its wind and earth shaking thunder when Jesus and the thieves hung here. The sun is warm, but my soul is frozen. I shiver. I tried drinking a little water, but it came back up. My stomach is a solid knot of pain. Oh Lord, My God, is there no help.?)*

I must review the time before we failed at curing the epileptic boy. We were walking for two days up into the hills north of Caphernaum. Jesus wanted to go to Caesaria Philippi, the headwaters of the Jordan River. Along the way he asked, "Who do men say that I am?" The very way he posed the question made us think of the answer he wanted. 'I Am' is God's name.

John said, "Some say you are Moses."

Andrew said, "Some say you are Elijah."

Thomas said, "Some say you are certainly a great prophet."

I said, "Some think you are John the Baptist come back from the dead." It was my way of saying the whole discussion was valueless. Jesus was what he was. He looked at me, remembering that I had brought the news of John's death, remembering his grief, perhaps realizing the path he followed would lead to his own death very soon. When I saw his stricken look, I almost repented those words. I loved Jesus. I followed Jesus until he breathed his last breath.

"And you," he asked, keeping his eyes on mine. "Who do you say that I am?" There was that echo again. We all knew Moses heard God say His Name. "I am that I Am!" said God to Moses. "Tell them, 'I AM has sent you.'"

Simon, the stupid big fisherman from Caphernaum, said first what we all knew Jesus wanted us to say, "You are the anointed Messiah, the Son of the Living God!"

Jesus commended him as if he were the smartest pupil in the synagogue. "Blessed are you, Simon BarJonah, for it was not man who told you this, but God Himself. You will be called Peter (the rock). And it is on this rock that I will build my church, and the gates of Hell shall not overcome it. I will give you the keys of the Kingdom of Heaven. Whatever you bind on earth will be bound in heaven, and whatever you loose on earth will be loosed in heaven."

Simon was so happy that had he been a dog he would have wagged his tail right off his rump!

Interestingly, it was less than an hour later when Jesus was prattling about some gloomy event to come the next time he was in Jerusalem that the new foundation stone said, "Never, Lord. This shall never happen to you!"

Jesus turned on his pet and said, "Out of my sight, Satan!" I felt really pleased about that. Simon can't be the 'rock' if he is 'Satan.'

Simon the Zealot and I had long talks. We understood far better than the others the true mission of the Messiah. We were certain of Jesus being that savior of Israel. But his role in our salvation had to be as an invincible earthly king. His power to bring down angelic legions to overthrow the Romans was what we were counting on. Moses had that power. Thirteen hundred years ago he led his people out of Egypt and fed them in the desert. He did this by using God's power. He defeated kings and their armies by God's power. Moses was God's beloved servant and he had God's overwhelming power at his command. He could not lose.

With Jesus as our leader, we could not lose. But, we needed to help him correct his thinking. He taught pacifism, submission, love of enemies, patience. Such ideas may be a part of a lovely philosophy, but they are not at all practical. He was equally impractical when it came to material things. It wasn't just accumulation of wealth he opposed when he said, "It is easier for a camel to go through the eye of a needle than for a rich man to enter the Kingdom of Heaven." It was everything. When he sent us out as his representatives in Galilee, he made us go without money, and without so much as a spare pair of sandals!

Jesus was a fanatic. He was sure his Father, 'God Almighty,' knew all about each of us, including our every need, and that we could call God our Father too. Jesus was too much like his cousin, John the Baptizer. He didn't feel the need for comfortable housing furnished beautifully, for fine clothing, sumptuous meals. His needs were expressed fully in one phrase of the pattern prayer he taught us. "Give us today our daily bread." Then he implied we didn't even need that if somehow (this was the most confusing and upsetting thing he taught) we fed on him.

The Zealot and I were assured in our hearts that we could bring Jesus around to our way of thinking. We established a method of having one of us, or some one of our associates, in a gathering where authorities were present, ask a controversial question. We knew Jesus' answers would upset the people in power. They would then use their human strength, all of their wealth and influence, against him. They would use their association with Rome, expecting that nation's powerful military machine to stand with them against Jesus. Surely all that was a formidable array. But Jesus' power was so much greater! We knew that once confronted by their attack, he would stop them. The battle lines would be formed, the battle engaged, and Jesus would soon be our victorious king!

We put Jesus face to face with government on the matter of taxes. Once, when I told him we had no money, he sent Simon Peter out to catch a fish. It had a gold coin in its mouth, the exact amount needed to meet our tax obligation. Another time I asked a Pharisee I knew to speak from the crowd, "Is it right to pay taxes to Caesar, or not?"

Jesus called for a coin, looked at it, asked whose image was on it, and said, "Give Caesar what is his, God what is God's."

Since that approach was getting us nowhere, we tried to make Jesus take a stand that would anger at least half of the divided priesthood. Jesus often spoke in favor of life after death, antagonizing my Sadducean party. Then we arranged to have Jesus heard as he spoke against the hypocrisy of all the temple workers, Sadducees, Pharisees, and Scribes. He called Caiaphas, the new High Priest, a 'whited wall,' meaning he was scrubbed clean on the outside, but a rotten stench, putrid as a coffin, within.

That was enough. Annas told me Caiaphas had convinced the Sanhedrin, "It is better for one to die for the people than that the whole nation perish." We began to see the powerful forces were gathering to crush Jesus.

With each passing day, Jesus was more precious to me. I loved him. He was so fair, so kind, so giving, so honest. I wanted to serve him always. But I wanted him elevated to his true position of honor and prestige. He had to become a great king, not just an itinerant, destitute, preacher-healer.

> *(How hard it is to concentrate! The sun has set. The Sabbath is over. We are into the night of the first day of the week, the last night of my life. I won't see the sun rise again. My scroll is lighted by an oil lamp beside me, and the full moon above. I must finish! I must tell of what I did to help Jesus. I must tell why I did it. Thus I will complete my life. How I regret I was ever born! Jesus said his 'betrayer' would say that. But I am not his betrayer! I was his faithful friend. I was guiding priest to Jesus as Aaron was to Moses!)*

A few days ago we were at dinner in Bethany. Mary, Martha and Lazarus' sister, anointed Jesus with very, very expensive oil, a brightly scented perfume. I objected. But Jesus took her side.

"She has anointed me for my death," he said.

Such foolish talk had to stop. If we could just get the army to try to capture him, he would direct his heavenly forces to destroy them. (I had an elaborate plan worked out with the Zealot. I have no time to elaborate now. Anyone finding this can check with the Zealot if they care.)

What I must say again and again is I did not intend to send Jesus to his death. I wanted him to assert himself, to take his rightful place as King; King of Israel; King of the World!

When he rode into Jerusalem on the foal of an ass that I borrowed for him on the first day of last week, I knew he was proclaiming himself King.

When he called himself, 'Son of Man,' I knew he was proclaiming himself King.

When he said to the Pharisees, "Before Abraham was, I AM," he was proclaiming himself God!

Surely he was mad. But it was a madness we could control while we directed his power to overthrow our evil enemy oppressors.

After he let Mary waste the three hundred denarii worth of perfume, I said it could have been sold and the money given to the poor. For over a year now I have been taking from our corporate purse and making gifts to the poor beggars we met all along the way. I have added some of my own capital as well, paying back all I took before; even more. It really troubled me to hear Jesus say, "The poor you will always have with you. You can help them at any time." Today's poor are the ones we had to deal with. How can we know we are not the instruments to deliver daily bread to the hungry?

I knew then that I must speed Jesus' action of calling down angels to destroy the enemy. He was procrastinating, not accepting his responsibility to act.

So I saw Annas again. He paid me my back wages and we agreed on a bonus of thirty pieces of silver; the exact amount of the perfume Mary spilt on Jesus' head. For that sum I was to lead the Temple guards to Jesus at night when there were not any crowds around.

I emphasize this was not betrayal! It was a simple business transaction. Annas and the Sanhedrin were the losers. Let them find Jesus, I thought. Let them bring an army of hundreds! Then they would know what it means to face an invincible foe!

I could visualize the earth opening and swallowing them as the Red Sea swallowed Pharaoh's army when they foolishly pursued God's man, Moses.

The last meal Jesus ate, and my last meal as well, was on the evening of the fifth day of the week. It was our Seder supper, when we remembered the Passover of the Angel of Death in Egypt. That was the beginning of our people's freedom. The night of that dinner was to be a new start in our blessed freedom through the power of God wielded in the hands of Jesus. I was to report to Annas and Caiaphas about midnight. Since I had plenty of time, I relaxed with Jesus and our friends in the room upstairs at John Mark's house.

That was a special time. Jesus washed the feet of each and all of us, beginning with me. Even though he spoke foolishly again about us being servants and the greatest servant as servant of all, it was a moving experience. I loved him even more than before.

During supper he gave us bread and said it was his flesh, his body. We ate it solemnly, not understanding him then any more than we had before when he said he was bread and we had to eat him to live forever. He often said he was bread. He often said he was living bread and that he had for us living water. It never made any sense to me.

Then Jesus started talking about his 'betrayer.' One of us twelve would betray him. How or who he didn't say.

He talked with John for a minute. John always got closest to him. John was the youngest of us, very immature, very insecure. He claimed Jesus loved him as if he were the only one of us Jesus did love. I never really liked John. I know he hated me!

I guess Jesus put him down a little right then. Jesus dipped a piece of bread in one of the common bowls, and then handed it to me! He looked at me with deep love and understanding, but with something else in that look as well. Was it tender compassion? Was it forgiveness? For what?

"Do what you must do," Jesus said. Suddenly I remembered my appointment with Annas. I hurried from the room without looking back.

With renewed purpose I hurried to Caiaphas' house where he and Annas awaited me. They, in turn, directed me to the guard house inside the Temple's outer wall. They sent Malchus along. He is Caiaphas' personal servant, and was my passport through the streets, the one to confirm my message to the captain of the guard. The captain selected fifty of his best men, and chose to lead them himself. For an hour I briefed those soldiers, telling them of the dozen or so peasants they were to round up and imprison.

I wanted Roman legions there too. Jesus' victory over them as well as this flabby local militia would be far more of a telling blow. But Malchus and the captain saw no reason to 'bother' the Romans with so petty a matter as the capture of Jesus of Nazareth.

It was close to two hours after I left Jesus that we left the Golden gate in the northeast wall of the city, and walked downhill to and across the Kidron valley. I was certain Jesus and the others would be in the Garden of Gethsemane, at the foot of the Mount of Olives. That was our regular meeting place. If I was wrong about that, I would be in trouble with Caiaphas. But I knew I was right. The full moon lighted the road for us. We did not need torches. We proceeded under strict orders to maintain silence.

I could scarcely contain myself. I was the instrument to set off the great war for our freedom. Now, I thought, now at last Jesus will act!

As we came into the garden, it was obvious the disciples were there, and all were asleep. No guard had been posted. We stopped and observed the scene from beneath the branches of some olive trees. A man, I was almost certain it was Jesus, came and began to waken the disciples. We watched them struggle to their feet in some confusion.

"The one I kiss. He is the one." I said. I stepped ahead of the guard, and walked toward Jesus. I was more excited than I had ever been at any former moment in my life! I spoke. "Master!" I said. (I never could call him 'Lord.') I reached out to embrace him.

Then he spoke to me. "Judas, do you betray the Son of Man with a kiss?" He looked at me. It was the same look he gave me three hours earlier in the upper room. It was the same look he gave me when we first met in Galilee. But the love was even deeper. The forgiveness was obvious. I cannot understand why, or for what, Jesus was forgiving me.

> *(Now I know, but forgiving others is a lesson none of the other eleven learned. I have not learned it either. For I cannot, indeed I will not, forgive myself.)*

Jesus stepped into my embrace. He embraced me! He kissed me! He breathed his breath into my face. And he said, "Friend, do what you must do." But it was already done.

The guards stepped forward. There were several moments of confusion. Then Jesus asked, "Whom do you seek?"

"Jesus of Nazareth," the captain of the guard replied.

"I am he," Again I heard 'I AM,' the name of God! The entire contingent of the guard fell to the ground! Ah Ha! I thought. The war is well begun. Jesus claims the first victory! But the guards stood again and came forward.

Two of the apostles had swords! They stood between Jesus and the Temple Guards. Somehow a Centurion and a cohort of Roman soldiers was among the guards. I am sure Caiaphas asked for them to be sent to check on me, as well as to be certain of Jesus' capture. They all moved forward with professional purpose, but not in time to stop Simon BarJonah. He took a wild swing with his sword and knocked off the ear of Malchus, Caiaphas' servant. A Roman soldier knocked Simon's sword from his hand and was about to thrust his own sword into the big awkward fisherman's belly.

Things weren't going well. Jesus stepped forward and said with his voice of authority, "Enough of this!" He bent down, picked up Malchus' severed ear, and replaced it. The ear stuck to the head! Malchus was healed.

"Did you have to come out with clubs and swords as if I were an outlaw? I was with you in the Temple every day, and you did not try to arrest me. But, this is your time to act when the power of darkness rules." That was when the eleven scattered and ran with the guard starting to chase them. Again Jesus stopped them. "Who are you looking for?" he asked.

"Jesus of Nazareth," several said.

"I have already told you that I am he. If then, you are looking for me, let these others go." The eleven and a few other disciples were well away by then. It would have been difficult in the dark for the guards to capture any of them.

I stood amazed as Jesus, the one I believed to be the invincible Messiah, permitted the soldiers to bind his arms behind his back and lead him away. I stayed close to him. I was certain he had some plan. "Why did you not call down legions of angels, Jesus?" I asked. "This was your hour to triumph."

He looked at me with an unfathomable look. "You will suffer much in the next few days, Judas. And I see you must suffer alone." I suddenly realized Jesus was going to let the authorities try him, sentence him, kill him!

> *(It is late. Would that I could weep. Would that I could sleep. Oh God! Oh Jesus! What have I done? Let me review. All I did was tell the authorities where Jesus was, lead them to him, point him out, take my pay.*
>
> *(Could they have found him without me? Yes!*
> *(Could he have given himself up so long as he believed he had to die to fulfill prophecy? Yes.*
> *(Was my forcing the issue of his fighting or surrendering so bad? No.*
> *(Wasn't it worse for the others to run away? Absolutely!*
>
> *(I stayed with Jesus through the trial. I found Nicodemus and got him to the meeting of the Sanhedrin. He and I voted 'no' to the resolution to condemn Jesus. I watched Jesus beaten by the soldiers. I watched Jesus spat upon. I saw the crown of thorns smashed down upon his head. I would have followed him up Calvary Hill, but I had to stop that process, somehow.)*

"Take back this money," I shouted. "I have betrayed innocent blood!" They wouldn't listen. They laughed at me. I threw the money down, and I ran.

I ran to Calvary. There I saw Jesus hanging on a cross, the nails holding his healing hands hard against the rough wood, his feet skewered by a huge spike, his body beaten bloody, shivering naked under the cloudy sky. He looked awful! Somehow I remembered the poetry of Isaiah about the suffering servant.

"Father, forgive them..." I heard Jesus' prayer and I knew he looked at me. I could not look back. It was then I decided to seek out any one of Jesus' followers. Perhaps one would understand me. Perhaps one would forgive me.

The Zealot turned his back on me. "Forget it," he said. "Where can we find another?" He looked hopeless.

John stood just beneath the cross. He looked at me with terrible anger. There was no forgiveness there.

Simon Peter was almost fair. "Are you so much worse than I?" he asked. "I denied him. I ran away! Leave me alone, Judas." And I did.

Andrew and Thomas and the James boys, and the other Judas, and BarTholomew and Levi either refused me, or they looked away.

I am already dead in their eyes!

Now it is almost dawn on the first day of the week. I have hope yet that Suzanna or Mary of Magdala will see me, be kind to me, understand me. Or, foolish hope indeed, they will believe the worst in me and still have enough of Jesus in their lives to forgive me.

I know them. They will go to the tomb of Jesus at first light. They will do the last thing anyone can do for the dead, anoint it for final internment, give it a last touch, a final goodby. The spices will mingle with the rotting flesh in the coming days, reducing the offense to the nostrils of passers by. For corruption is inevitable. It is the end of all of us.

I could never believe in a life hereafter in the Kingdom of God. I was content with the years God gave me here; glad to engage in battle for freedom and for justice. Now I am almost glad there is nothing but oblivion before me. There is no one, man or God, that I wish to see again. I am the enemy, enemy of all, enemy even of myself.

Ah, here come Mary and Suzanna...

They passed me by. They looked away. Mary was like a sister to me. Suzanna I had hoped to wed.

I am in total despair...

But I have one last word. It is a word of prophecy. I solemnly declare that no body of believers in Almighty God will ever capture the world for Him until they have learned loving forgiveness. That much I learned from Jesus. Love all. Love even your enemies. Forgive all, especially your enemies.

I prophesy that any who try to follow the teachings of Jesus — even if the miracle came about that he would rise from the dead — they will be doomed to failure, unless they learn forgiveness.

There will be no body of believers until forgiveness is granted to all. Only fragmentation will occur with each small group saying, "Lo, here is Jesus. Here is the anointed one!" They will divide and divide again and stand rigid against union. They will not forgive. They will not love. They will always stand in fear, suspicion, even in anger against every other group of people who profess to believe in, and to love Jesus.

I proclaim this. I was one of the twelve. I must be counted! I was the last to be chosen. Jesus said, "The last shall be first; the first, last." I am the first of the twelve to die.

I heard him speak from the cross. He said, "It is finished." I believe him.

He said, "Father, into your hands I commend my spirit." That I do not believe. Should my spirit live, it would weep forever. How much better oblivion!

I have the rope. I go to the valley of Gehenna, the city dump, where the fires always burn. There is a tree there that will serve.

It is finished!

18

Mary Magdalene

The Sabbath is over. I await the first light. The sun may rise, but it is possible the hours of darkness will continue forever. My bed is drenched with the sweet sweat of sorrow, the stream of my flowing tears. I didn't know I could cry so hard for so long. Why am I not dried up?

Let me be up and on my way. I may as well wait at the garden of Gethsemane as here.

Now I am out of my room and into the hallway that leads past the other bedrooms. I must be very quiet. Martha and Lazarus are as tired as I. Let them sleep.

Here is the door. The latch is stuck! I must remember to ask a servant to repair it.

Now it is free. I step through, and close it behind me, and begin my walk. I see the stars shining in the black sky. It is terribly dark, dark as my hopeless soul. Yet it was full moon only last night! There must be one cloud left to cover that moon tonight. It is good that I know the way. Climb the hill out of Bethany to the southern crest of Olivet. One must stay strong and supple to be able to move about in these Judean hills.

Now I pass the cave where we buried Lazarus. Was that only six weeks ago? Martha and I cried then too. We employed a complete staff of mourners to help us pour out our grief. That grieving lasted four days, more than twice as long as we have endured this loss. That was for our dear blood brother.

Who was this man for whom we weep now?

Let me rest a while. I didn't know I was so weak. No food, no drink, no sleep. No hope. That is what takes the strength out of you. No hope in the world any more.

Oh Master, I loved you so!

Now Mary, be still. Get hold of yourself. Life must be lived out. He taught you that. He taught you to live. Come. Let us go on. Strange how I still talk to myself as if I were more than one person!

The road here is steep. Loose stones bite my feet through the soles of my sandals. I welcome the pain, recalling the brutally torn feet of my beloved Master. My eyes blur again. I must stop until they clear. Though the road is familiar, and the moon has come out again, and though I know this way well, I still stumble. The night and my tears are making me almost totally blind.

The cluster of stone houses I leave behind are my beloved Bethany. Nearly everyone in town is one of my family. We have lived here for centuries, less than a hundred families intermarrying, sharing life together. I can call almost every one of them, 'aunt' or 'uncle' or 'cousin.' We are a strong family in a strong town living on the edge of a strong mountain. I pass the edge of town, climbing the greening side of Olivet. Behind me lies the town, and east of the town lies the desert.

The thinnest line of first light has begun to mark the horizon, the jagged mountains of Edom, Herod's country. If I stood here an hour and my eyes held dry, I could watch the sun rise, touch and turn to rose gold the desert hills this side of the Jordan. If the day were clear I could see the edge of the Dead Sea to the south, the green line of the flow of the

Jordan to the north, the oasis of Jericho twelve miles due east, and five thousand feet below me.

The path leads between two hills, up and over the hump of Olivet, down again into the village of Bethphage. There, to the west, beneath me, lies Zion, Jerusalem, the City of Peace. Such a strange name for a city that has known only warfare for hundreds of years. Only a week ago today we took off our coats and lay them on the back of a donkey and shouted 'Hosanna. Hosanna to the Son of David!' And we watched our Master ride down this road, across the valley beside the garden, and up the hill into the gates of Jerusalem.

My dear, dear friend, my rabbi, was entering into his kingdom. He was to be our beloved benevolent ruler. What terrible changes a few days can bring! Now he is dead. These ointments in the basket I carry, I will rub in his cold dead flesh. Then we will close the grave for the last time, and I will see him no more. Never, never, never, never again.

Get on with it, Mary. Down the hill into the darkest part of the valley. Mary, Clopas' wife, will meet me there. We will go together to do our work. It is down hill now, the walking is easier. The shadows aren't quite so dark. It will soon be dawn.

Wait! What is that? The earth is trembling again. It is like that terrible time on the sixth day of the week after he died. I must sit down. I must lie down, away from the walls, far from the trees. Hug the earth and wait for it to subside. The terror of earthquake was bad enough in the daylight. It is worse here in the dark.

O God! Make the tremors pass, or give my heart courage!

There. It is past. I can walk again. Thank you, God. He told us to call you 'Father.' Thank you, Father.

There are some figures before me near the garden of Gethsemane. “Hello,” I call. “Who is there?”

A familiar voice calls back. “Oh Mary. You’re here early too.”

“Who is that with you,” I ask.

“Suzanna.”

“Yes,” of course. “I’m glad you’re with us, Suzanna.”

“I am here too. It is Joanna.”

“We left his mother sleeping. She is exhausted.”

We stand in silence a moment. They look to me for leadership, I who am so weak. I have no choice. We must get on with the task before us. “Then let us be on our way,” I say.

“Yes,” Mary replies. “Let us be on our way. It is still a long uphill walk to the west side of the city. We will have to walk along the outside wall. The gates won’t be opened until dawn.” She sobs, and we sob with her. “Oh Mary, hold me for a moment. How can we go on? Our hope is dead.”

Did she say it to me? Did I say it to her? We hold each other. She says, “Weep, dear one of Magdala. We have time. We will sit here a moment. Suzanna, Joanna, come back. We have time.”

My overwrought emotions become too strong for me. For a time I loose my tongue and ramble. “Oh Mary. Now that I see the daylight approaching, I see that this is the place our dear Rabbi was captured.” My voice stops, but my thoughts go on. This is the garden of Gethsemane. It is the place where my life was terribly changed, almost destroyed, six years ago. It is the place I first met fear, and was conquered by it.

“Fear was the first of the vicious spirits Jesus drove from me. I haven’t been afraid since. Even now, when I know I will never see him alive again, my fears are gone. I know I will soon die of grief for him. But I am not afraid. Fear has left me since I came to know his love.”

I stop talking, and we remain quiet. Now, sitting here, watching the hills become solid in the new light, my mind watches the night of six years ago unfold and return through my memory. I remember slipping out of the city through the east gate just as they were closing it for the night. The light was fading then, not growing as it is now. By the time I reached the valley here, it was quite dark. It was too late for me to be out. There was a chill in the evening air. I started to run toward Olivet and home.

He came out of the darkest place behind the huge old graves south of the road. He was big and drunk and strong, and he stank of sweat. I was fourteen and slender and weak. A virgin before he caught me. I would have screamed, but he held his hand over my nose and mouth. Terror filled my heart. I couldn't breathe. I knew I was fainting. I knew I was going to die!

"O God! Help me!" I screamed inside myself. But I was alone in there. No one came.

When I came to awareness again, I was all alone. But I was no longer a virgin. My clothes were torn. My body was torn. I crawled back out of Gethsemane, and began to climb the mountain toward my Bethany home. My legs ached. My stomach hurt. I felt blood trickle down between my legs. I hurt so much it took an hour and a half to complete a half hour walk. Then, as I drew closer to home, I found myself walking slower and slower. Fear and shame slowed me, and finally stopped me.

I had been afraid of the brutal soldier. He had caught me and assaulted my body, and had left me with an enemy companion of living fear. That fear attacked my reason. I knew I was ruined. I knew my dear betrothed, Joseph BarJoseph, would be ashamed to marry me. He might make excuses. But however he managed it, the wedding planned for the following spring would not occur.

My loving father, I was sure, would accept me home, but he would hang his head in shame. Old busybody Martha, my insensitive sister, wouldn't be the only spinster in the family. I would join her. She would like that! But she would tell me again and again how I wouldn't have come into my trouble if I had just paid attention to her.

And dear Lazarus. I knew he would be the most foolish of all. He would make me describe the hulk of a man who raped me. Then he would go out alone to declare war on Rome. If I went home, Lazarus' death would be a part of my guilt.

That night I stood in the shadow of the wall above my house, and watched moonlight filter soft beams over the whole town. I was afraid. I feared my father's resigned sadness, my sister's sharp tongue, my brother's quick temper. I feared too much for my future there in my family to be able to stay.

How happy and sure of myself I had been but a short time before; and how frightened, shamed and alone I was then. In confused sorrow I circled the town on a goat path, and started down the long steep hills into the pitiless desert. Perhaps, I hoped, a wild animal would take my life.

Of course fate would not answer such a fond hope. I walked farther and farther, trying to keep warm. The dry desert air turned cold immediately after sunset. My only hope of warmth was to walk. I knew the further down I walked from Olivet the warmer it would become. It is less than a day's walk from Jerusalem in the high hills to Jericho in the deepest valley. In the winter sometimes it snows in Jerusalem. But the winter is always warm in Jericho. I followed the new Roman road, expecting to meet no human traffic, and I was right. The road runs in a straight line almost due east, and almost always down.

Each time I took second thought and started to turn back, three barriers kept me from the decision. It was uphill to home; it would be colder going home than going where I was headed; and there was nothing to hope for but an empty life after hateful explanations once I arrived. As my life was ruined, I thought, I might as well be comfortable while waiting for some additional cruel turn of fate to complete what the drunken soldier had begun.

How ironic that I had been running home to tell my father, sister, and brother of the completion of my wedding plans to Joseph BarJoseph. The nuptials were to have been in three months, right after my fifteenth birthday. I truly liked Joseph. His father, Joseph of Arimathea, I liked so well I found myself glad I would soon have a second father. Sarah, my mother-in-law to be, was a gentle woman who seemed most happy to have me coming into the family as her daughter. All was so good! I had been lifted to a plane of happiness greater than I had ever known. I knew even greater joy awaited me.

But in less than three hundred steps it had all been taken away. I stopped often to weep.

As the night progressed I remembered I had been running home for another reason. It was to have my supper. I was hungry and I soon grew thirsty. The desert was a desolation around me. There would be no food, for the only place for such was the Halfway Inn, and I had no money. My only source of water was two Sabbath walks to the north of the road, the aqueduct Herod had built for his fortress in the hills above Jericho. I chose not to seek the dancing water in that man made stream. I knew I could quench my thirst there if I wished. Instead, I chose to hurry so I could be in Jericho before the heat of the coming day.

Fear grew and led to despair. I wondered if the best choice would be to sit down and wait for the desert heat to destroy me. That would have been quick, but in a sense, it would have been the hardest choice. The decision I made to leave home took all my energy; and I could make no further hard choices. I simply kept walking.

By the middle of the night I found that fear and loneliness and a lack of knowledge of where I was going, or who I would come to for help, added up to a new emotion I had never known. Terror. The night was dark enough without an expectation that each darker shadow would bring me to my end. I was so afraid I had to cry out. I was so afraid I dared not make a sound.

When at last I had walked down far enough to smell the Dead Sea in the distance, I was able to sit down and rest without shivering from the cold. I rested my head against the steep embankment behind me and closed my eyes. My body called for rest, and I chose to grant it. Rest I did.

I awoke to find myself looking into the eyes of a desert nomad. I could see at a glance that he was a Son of Ishmael. It mattered little to me, but I knew I was his captive, and I would soon be someone's slave.

19

Mary Magdalene

The dawn is breaking, and we have started up out of the valley. We are on the way to the tomb Joseph provided for him. The four of us, Mary, Suzanna, Joanna, and I, have a task to perform. We will anoint Jesus' body.

Who will roll away the stone from the tomb? We are not strong enough for that task. When I saw the tomb that afternoon of his death, I was surprised Joseph had made it so small. There was only room enough in it for two, for himself, and for Sarah. With our Master buried there, another tomb will have to be chiseled out of the stone for them. Still, the tomb has a big door, and though the stone is well cut, like a huge wheel, it will take two men to roll it away. Perhaps some of the men who have been set to guard the tomb from grave robbers will help us.

O Jerusalem, Jerusalem, the city of peace. I have sung David's song. I have prayed for your peace. You are my city. You are the holy city of all Jews. We have sung and danced in your streets. We have celebrated all the great festivals of the year within your walls. Those walls will soon turn to gold in the morning light. The sun will melt away the mist from the valleys around you. You will stand proud before us as always. The great Temple will be a jewel set in your midst. And your people will rejoice that they belong to you and to your God. How then can you permit yourself to lie beneath the rule of Caesar? How then can you permit yourself to lie beneath the corruption of the Pharisees?

How are you able to permit false witnesses to destroy the innocent?

A week ago my master wept at your gates. Today I weep as I walk beside your walls. May his prediction come true. May you be destroyed! May the Temple fall, no stone upon another!

O God! Where is the justice and righteousness promised centuries ago by your prophet Amos?

We approach the Damascus gate. How well I remember Damascus. It was there I was brought to be sold by my desert captor. I bore no anger toward him. He and his family were kind to me. They fed me. They let me walk with their shepherds as we made a wandering journey to the north. Up the Jordan valley we went, never seen by the people who dwelt there. The Ishmaelites can make themselves almost invisible when they choose to do so.

The route we followed was all new country for me. I had never been further away from home than Jericho and the Dead Sea. I was accustomed to the desert though. I had played in the desert with my neighborhood friends from Bethany. I had come to know and to respect it, but not to fear it. I knew its dry heat could be a terrible enemy. I knew its dry cold could be another one. But there is little danger from wild beasts there any longer. They are no problem in this time of our modern civilization. The lion and the wolf and the bear of David's time are almost gone forever. Man is now the one remaining dangerous enemy of man.

Who can tell about the Ishmaelites? They are a people with no law, no nation. Each family lives unto itself. They cross borders from nation to nation with impunity. They have been sojourners on the land since before the beginning of time. These wanderers spoke to me in Aramaic, the language I understood the best. But they spoke to each other in a desert tongue I could barely comprehend.

The women of the family took my clothes from me and dressed me to look like them. They kept me with them whenever we stopped for a day or two along our winding way. As they clothed me in their garments, they set me to work at their tasks. This family was one of weavers of rugs; at least the women were. The men worked as shepherds and scavengers. The rugs that were made were both beautiful and durable; and were to be sold in the markets of the cities past which the family traveled. My fingers were clumsy, but they kept me going with the most elementary work, carding wool, dying it, and making threads. After some months I grew adept at all parts of the work, was able to make out the most intricate of designs, and was permitted to work at weaving.

Though I was very homesick for Bethany, my beloved Joseph, my family, and for Jerusalem, I had no desire to return to them. I made no effort at escape. My fear of the role I would play as a spoiled virgin, cast aside by my husband to be, and by his family, was enough to keep me from any hope of joy at home. Keeping alive in the desert with these people who were indifferently kind to me was enough for that time.

Growing within me was a greater emotion than fear. It was anger. I determined in my heart that I would find some way to kill that Roman soldier who had raped me. Someday, some way, I would see him again, and I would destroy him. My mind imagined my seducing him first, then drugging him. Then, while he was helpless, but fully awake, I would carve him and slice him, and finally kill him. His two minutes of lust had destroyed my life. My revenge would cause him infinite pain, and take away his spirit. There would be no breath left in him. Day dreaming over this gave me a physical thrill I could not comprehend. In fascination and disgust, I found my imagination played as delightedly over the seduction of the brute as it did over the destruction of him.

After several months we crossed the Jordan and worked our way along the east shore of Lake Galilee, or the Sea of Tiberias. The ten Grecian towns were easily bypassed, and we turned east past the foothills of Mount Hermon. It was then we made a long trek straight to Damascus. One morning we stood on the outskirts of that city, and I was informed it was time for me to be separated from the family with whom I had dwelt for nearly half a year. I embraced the two children with whom I had become friends, and without saying anything to the six women who lived in the huge tent, I permitted a rope to be tied to me, and walked willingly into the next experience of my life.

Two hours in the Damascus market, a place no more noisy, and with smells no worse than the market in Jerusalem, and I found myself the property of a shrewd looking man of middle age. Ibrahim was his name. He was almost thirty years old, was very rich, and had several girls like me as a part of his business. That business was to provide pleasure to his customers, and his customers were all men.

Ibrahim assumed I was a woman of no experience, which was correct, of course. One rape doesn't make a woman an instrument of love or a tool of lust. He introduced me to good food, and to strong drink. And when I was no longer afraid of him he approached me and touched me in ways that gave great pleasure. I was living in almost a purely animal state at the time. I knew no right, and I knew no wrong. There was only existence. To have existence provide occasional moments of ecstacy was a pleasant surprise. There was something positive about the life. What I was doing I knew I had been created to do. How I was doing it was against the principles of my religion. I knew

God would be angry with me for what I was doing. But I had no fear of Him. He had not stopped the one who raped me. He would not stop me! Thinking about it now, I see that the fear of beloved family members was instilled in my heart, along with hundreds of other unreasoning fears. But the fear of God was taken from me.

When Ibrahim had me fully aware of the gratification a woman can receive from a sexual encounter, he began to teach me ways of making a man fully satisfied by his contact with a woman. It was a most interesting education, often surprising, sometimes briefly disgusting, occasionally mutually satisfying. I learned the entire anatomy of the human male. I came to admire its structure and its function. Ibrahim kept himself scrupulously clean. He also insisted on my maintaining a habit of cleanliness. That was easy, as it had been instilled in me in my childhood.

Satiated with food, drink, and sex, I found it easy to drift. When Ibrahim asked me to show kindness to some of his friends, it was most easy to do so. There was excitement at first in my new role. Once a day was acceptable; twice a day was a pleasure. Three times a day was joy. Four times a day was ecstacy. Five times a day was acceptable. Six times a day was boring. Seven times a day was painful. Eight times a day was tiring. Ten or more times a day was disgusting. A never ending line of hungry men became my steady diet. New unhealthy emotions came to join the others.

Fear came first. Anger followed.

Lust welded herself to me. A single touch from Ibrahim would set me panting for more. When one of my paying partners was inept, I pretended he was Ibrahim. The thought of his expert love making was almost as good as being with him. Lust helped me to gain and to give more satisfaction each time I was with a man.

Then gluttony joined us. One drink was better than none. Two were better than one. And the progression of that indulgence seemed to have no satisfying end. Drinking seemed the only way for the other emotions within me to be satisfied and at rest. For a while in the company of gluttony, I could keep the other emotions at bay, become a casual observer of my life. But before long I was spending all of my waking hours (when I was out of bed) at table with food and drink. There was an emptiness in me no man, meal, or bottle could fill.

Too much of anything satiates. Additional consumption leads to regurgitation. I grew sick of food, sick of drink, sick of sex, sick of myself, and found myself face to face with another neighbor who had moved into me unobserved.

At sixteen I was sure there was nothing new for me. Everything I knew was boring. I was a good professional and could act out the love my customers demanded. But less and less often I found myself really enjoying the experience. Even Ibrahim grew to be as boring as the rest. I could anticipate his every word, his every move, his every demand. Boredom brought on exhaustion, and exhaustion brought on sickness.

A sick whore is no use to her owner. So it was not long before Ibrahim found a way to sell me before I infected the rest of his stable. He sold me as a 'servant' to a Roman Centurion who was headed for Galilee.

The Centurion, Anthony, had been with me often. His needs were elementary, and I had taken pleasure in giving him complete gratification. When he knew he was to be transferred to Tiberias, he sought me out and asked if I would be willing to go with him if he could arrange it. I shrugged my shoulders in acquiescence. He made the arrangements. I wonder if my value had appreciated from the time Ibrahim bought me? I never knew my first or my second purchase price.

When I left, Ibrahim kissed me goodby. I think I missed him for about a week.

The trip to Galilee did me good. I liked Anthony. I liked his soldiers too. They admired me, even flirted with me cautiously, but knew I was off limits to them. I accepted being the woman of one man. Grudgingly, I also accepted his taking control of my diet. With less rich foods, and almost no wine, I found myself feeling better than I had for some time. I was almost happy. The three day trip to Tiberias was uneventful. The thought that I was coming closer to home meant nothing to me. I knew I could be back in Jerusalem and still not be at home. Home was gone. Even to think of it was to have my fear mount within me again, and to make me sick with dread.

If a raped daughter was abhorrent to my father, what would a whore daughter be to him? My spiritual trip downhill from Bethany had continued down long after the road began to climb again.

I loved Tiberias. It was like a jewel. It seemed to hang over the west bank of the lake, white home built above white home, up the bank with Herod's palace standing high and free above all the other buildings. Anthony established me in a nice little house right on the shore. He gave me everything I needed, including two eunuch servants to take care of the household details. Every day I rested, basked in the sun, and swam in the warm sea. Anthony came to me at night, tired and sweaty, from his working day, and I met him refreshed and ready for an evening of pleasure.

How grateful I was for Ibrahim's teaching. I would bathe Anthony, anoint him, give him a glass of good wine to drink, and tease him into desire. On the nights that even this was not enough, I would sit with him, satisfied that he knew he had bought well. Often I would let him sleep an hour or two, and then undress him as he slept. When he was fully nude, I would slowly waken him, arouse his desire, and thus find a way to calm my own lust.

In this way another year went by, and I turned seventeen.

20

Mary Magdalene

We have arrived at the tomb. Daylight has come upon us. The sun's upper half can be seen over the top of Olivet. The air is absolutely still. A few birds have begun their morning song. Even the death of our Master doesn't still their persistent optimism. We look down on the tomb from atop the hill of calvary, the place of a skull. We are surprised by what we see.

"Look," cries Joanna. "What a strange sight that is!"

"The soldiers look like they are all dead!"

"No. They are only sleeping. See! That one has stirred a little."

"Look! The stone has been rolled away already!"

"How strange. The tomb faces west, yet there is light like the sun coming from within it!"

"Oh, I am too frightened to stay!" cries Suzanna, and she starts to run.

"Wait for me," cries Joanna. And she runs too.

Now we two Marys are the only ones left to do the anointing. We step forward, trembling. Fear left me when the Master touched me and healed me. I have never been possessed by it since. But fear can walk beside me from time to time. And this is one of the times. Oh, heavenly Father! Your Kingdom come. Deliver us from evil. Amen. The prayer doesn't calm me.

We stand at the door of the tomb. Two great white personages stand on the right within the grave itself. The place where we lay Jesus is now empty. His body is gone!

"Why do you seek the living among the dead?" The voices do not touch our ears, but reach into the center of our beings! I have never heard such voices! I cannot speak. These creatures are brightness itself. Could they be angels from God?

"Do not be amazed," the other says in a voice like a blast of trumpets, yet not overpowering, simply beautiful and strong. "You seek Jesus of Nazareth who was crucified.

"He has risen!

"He is not here!

"See the place where they laid him!

"But go, tell the disciples and Peter that He is going before you to Galilee where you will see Him, as He told you."

It is too much for me. I cannot hold it! Every emotion I ever had is boiling up in me and bursting forth as an unreasoning hope, an exquisite joy. I must run. My heart will burst if I stand here another instant! Where has the other Mary gone? I don't know.

I must fall here and be still. I will be as still as the soldiers lying about. The Spirit of God is here! I am overwhelmed by heavenly light. Somehow I know the gladness of God in His whole Universe, and of His great anguish for man. And I know it all at once. No human being can contain this much awareness in a single moment.

Yet I do! I must be still.

Lying here, unable to move, I see all of my history at once. The rapist, the Ishmaelite and his family. The city of Damascus; Ibrahim and Anthony. All are there. So also are my childhood in Bethany, my parents, my brother and my sister. All are there. Each moment stands out and all moments meld together. Oh, how I remember! The clarity of every detail is overwhelming me too.

I focus my thoughts on the time when Anthony left me alone for a few days. I sought diversion for myself in the streets of Tiberias. There I saw the soldier who had raped me two years before outside the walls of Jerusalem. I knew the man instantly. Without thought I began to follow the plan of my daydream. Knowing my eunuch servants to be on holiday, I caught the attention of the man, and assured him from look and body movement that following me would give him untold delights. I didn't even look back as I walked the three blocks to my home by the sea.

I felt him close behind me. He came through the door less than half a minute after I entered. He would have caught me and taken me then, as he had before, but for the glass of wine I had already poured and held out to him.

His little eyes looked to me, and then to the glass. He chose the glass. He swallowed it in a second, and reached for me to find that he was handed the bottle.

It took him but three minutes to finish that, and he was coming for me again. This time I came to him, almost eagerly, and gave him what he wanted. He was through with me almost as fast as he had been with the bottle. I smiled at him, caressed his face, crawled from beneath him, and found him another bottle. He drank this one a little more slowly, belched, and stared at me quite stupidly. We still had not spoken to each other.

We never did. I gave him three more bottles, offered myself once more, and as he tried to accept the last offering, he was overcome by the drink.

The reality of my vengeance was far better than my day dream. I pulled the unconscious drunk to the edge of the lake, turned him on his face, and helped him drown. Once he tried to lift his head out of the water, but I simply sat on it. I clutched his head between my bare legs, and gloried in the sensation of his last struggles. I laughed when I felt no more movement beneath me. I rocked his head from side to side against the rocks on the bottom of the lake. And when I was certain the vengeance was complete, I floated the body in the Galilee and walked away.

North was the direction I walked, and I walked that way for no good reason except that it was out of town, and perhaps that it was away from Bethany. There was plenty of money in the house. Anthony always left me enough to pay the household expenses. He was always generous. I took what I needed, and left everything else behind.

The next town north was Magdala. I assumed, correctly, that should Anthony look for me he would look far, and he would scour with diligence in distant places. But he would not look for me close by his station. Magdala has an unsavory atmosphere. It is a place for drying, smoking, and salting the fish that are caught by the fishermen of the Galilee. This dried produce is a commodity that can be carried great distances, and is of real commercial value.

The people who live in Magdala have to live with the aroma of the business. On a still day, the stench of dead fish fills your nostrils almost to the point of making you sick. The workers there are well paid, but most of those who live there are bachelors. It was a good place for me to come. My trade was welcomed there. I earned a good living by providing my services.

For two years I worked in Magdala, coming to know almost every man who lived there, and most of the fishermen who brought in their catches. I ate well, drank better, and had plenty of exercise.

And my hatred for everything and everyone grew. There was no more pleasure in anything. I grew sick of the harlot's disease. I came to fear everything, but especially each new day. The women of the town who were married, and the young girls in the town who were pure, were objects of jealous hate for me. At eighteen I was wealthy. At nineteen I was sick and losing weight, but still wealthy. Men who had first come to me because I was pretty continued to come because I was all that was available. They could close their eyes and pretend. I watched them do it. I wished them dead.

I wished myself dead.

And then I found myself facing a man who looked more like the man I had killed than anyone I had ever seen before. I watched him come into my house, watched him through the process of close contact, and watched him leave. I forgot to charge him!

O God! Had I killed the wrong man?

In my ears reverberated the command, "Thou shalt not kill!"

I was suddenly aware of another commandment that I was breaking several times a day.

Then remorse drove me the rest of the way to madness. I was not insane all of the time, only often enough and long enough to live each day through. Reality in my house was perhaps a little like madness if it had been in the home of any other. My personal madness simply made my reality livable.

A day came when the town grew absolutely quiet. No one came down the street. No one knocked at my door. I dressed and went out to see what was the matter. There was no one in town. It was deserted except for Silas, the town beggar. He sat on his mat at the corner of the town square, his usual station. I asked him, "Silas, where is everyone?"

"Gone to hear the new rabbi," he answered.

"Who?"

"You know. This Jesus, the Nazarene, the cousin of the Zebedee brothers. He has been teaching and preaching in the hills above Caphernaum. Now he has come to preach along the shore just outside of town."

I had never heard of him. I stayed away from rabbis and synagogues, and from talk about them. They would remind me of the laws of my society, and I had made my choice to be a lawbreaker. If someone had mentioned Jesus in my presence, I would have ignored them. I knew what conversations to listen to, to share in, and which to ignore. It seems that everyone in Magdala knew of this Jesus except for the town whore, except for me.

I went back home. The house wasn't empty. My thoughts were there, and they wouldn't leave me alone. "Mary, you're a no good whore," my mind told me. And that wasn't the worst thing I was told. "You're sick. You're dirty. You're a killer." When your accuser is yourself, you have no defense. My fear of everything was focused on the fear of being left alone with myself. My anger had turned on me. I was the most despicable person I knew, the one human being I could not stand. I hated myself.

Though it was not yet the middle of the day, I went and opened my third bottle of wine and took a big drink. At least my appetite for wine was still a friend. The wine would eventually make me unconscious. But before it could take hold, I found myself fondling me. My lust turned inward. No other human being could satisfy my eroticism. I sought the release of an orgasm.

And I failed myself...

And the wine failed me.

And I determined that the time had come for me to destroy the life of another person. I had come to this decision before, even acted on it. But I was always divided inside myself. Some part of me always stopped me, or made me fail in my resolve. This time I was sure I knew what I was about. I would walk out to the lake, dive in, and swim toward the center. I would swim to the point of exhaustion.

Then, no matter what the one within me who wanted to live would try to do, she would not make me capable of swimming back to shore. I would drown, drown like the man I had killed, and that would be the end of it. That would be the end of me.

As I walked past Silas the beggar, I threw him several pieces of silver, the equivalent of many day's wages for a well man. He called his thanks. After I had walked on quite a distance, I looked back over my shoulder. To my surprise I saw Silas pick up his mat and then turn and walk away without so much as a limp. "The little faker," I thought. "Damn him, too."

At the lake shore, I was beginning to remove my sandals when I became aware of a crowd less than half a mile away to the north. Two things turned me to them. The first was my curiosity. The second was the knowledge that if I could see them, they could see me. Suicide should be a private activity. I merely postponed my plan for my last day. One last swim under the stars that night would be a fitting way to end my darkened life. I walked toward the crowd.

The closer I came to them, the more I could see my determination to postpone killing myself had been unnecessary. The people were listening to a man, and they seemed to be hanging on every word the speaker was saying. He sat in a fishing boat I recognized as belonging to Simon BarJonah. He spoke quietly, but his voice carried clearly across the water to me. "Be not anxious for tomorrow," he was saying. I smiled to myself. That was one thing I was no longer anxious for. "Sufficient unto the day is its evil." I could see the wisdom there. Every day had a full plenty of evil. As I began to listen, I became as absorbed in him and his teaching as the rest of the crowd.

"Blessed are you poor, for yours is the kingdom of God.

"Blessed are you that hunger now, for you shall be satisfied.

"Blessed are you that weep now, for you shall laugh." My ears listened to the sound of his voice while my mind dwelt on this last statement. My life had gone through hills of joy and valleys of sadness before. I knew that new moods took the place of old ones. Even the desperate states, the times I acted on my suicidal decisions, were supplanted by periods of frantic merriment. Could that be what he meant?

"But I say to you, love your enemies, do good to those who hate you, bless those who curse you, pray for those who abuse you. To him who strikes you on the cheek, offer the other also; and from him who takes away your coat do not withhold even your shirt. Give to every one who begs from you; and of him who takes away your goods do not ask them again. And as you wish that men would do to you, do so to them."

I thought of the cheating beggar of Magdala. I hated him. I hated the rabbi.

"Judge not, and you will not be judged; condemn not, and you will not be condemned; forgive, and you will be forgiven; give, and it will be given to you; good measure, pressed down, shaken together, running over, will be put into your lap. For the measure you give will be the measure you get back."

He didn't sound like the priests I had heard in Jerusalem. He didn't sound like the local rabbi I remembered in Bethany. He sounded a little like Ibrahim! Only when the rabbi spoke of loving, he was talking about really caring, not just taking care of sex needs. I pushed my way through the crowd. I wanted to get closer. This must be some naive boy who was preaching to us. How nice it all sounded. How totally impractical it was. Live the way he taught, and it might make you happy, but it certainly would make you broke.

"Give, and it will be given to you...Good measure."

The words echoed again in my mind. Then I stood less than twenty feet from him. I stood on the shore. He sat in the boat. He continued to talk to the whole crowd. But his eyes found mine. It might have been for a moment. It might have been an eternity, but our eyes were locked on each other's. I saw depth upon depth upon depth, opening ever wider in perception. No human being has ever had eyes like this, though sometimes I have caught a reflection of such in the eyes of a newborn baby. The questioning that was there, was what I saw in a baby's eyes. But the absolute complete knowledge his eyes revealed was uniquely his.

I could see reflected in his eyes my entire lifetime. The innocent hopeful fourteen year old girl was there. All that I had become was there also. He looked into every part of my soul! I braced myself for what I knew would come next, the look of distaste, of disgust, or worse, the shrewd look of lustful and assured anticipation. But it didn't come. This rabbi, this Jesus, knew me. I didn't know how, but he knew me. And he accepted me. If he had been a fool, or if he had been an idiot, his acceptance would have meant nothing. But he was a brilliant teacher. His illustrations had a clarity that made his points quickly.

"Can a blind man lead a blind man? Will not both fall into a pit?

"A disciple is not above his teacher, but every one when he is fully taught will be like his teacher.

"Why do you see the speck that is in your brother's eye, but do not notice the log that is in your own eye?"

Before Jesus' eyes turned to look with the same intimate knowledge on the others in the crowd, they let me know of an accepting love that he had for me. They let me know they knew I had a beam in my eye that was absolutely visible to him, and that he was certain I could not remove it myself. I closed my eyes, sat down by the shore, and let hopeful tears cool those burning eyes of mine. His voice went on, touching my heart, and opening it.

"No good tree bears bad fruit, nor again does a bad tree bear good fruit; for each tree is known by its own fruit. Figs are not gathered from thorns, nor grapes from a bramble bush. The good man out of the good treasure of his heart produces good, and the evil man out of his evil treasure produces evil; for out of the abundance of his heart his mouth speaks."

I remembered Ibrahim who was evil.

I remembered Anthony who was good.

I remembered the rapist soldier, who may only have been drunk.

I remembered myself, possessed by powerful emotions that drove me from producing anything pure or good.

Yet I saw that even with the wicked twisted emotions that kept me from fulfillment of my destiny as one of God's creatures, I was still showing forth gifts of love. The twisted men who came to me received a gift, more than they had paid for. I had tenderness and compassion for them. I understood them, and felt their loneliness, even as I felt their lust overpower them, even as I shared in the coupling.

Jesus' eyes fell on mine again as I opened them, remembering my profession. I knew he knew. It was as if he had been with me each moment of my existence. I came to feel that nothing I had ever been, and nothing I could ever become, would keep him from accepting me. It was beyond belief, but I could see he accepted me as if I were pure, clean, lovely, and fully whole.

He finished speaking, started to step ashore, and I was gripped again by fear. I turned and ran blindly down the shore line, back to my home. I locked my door, for I didn't want any business that afternoon or evening. I know that all my customers had been in that crowd. Once, unknowingly, I had stood within arm's reach of Anthony, and even though he recognized me, he made no effort to capture me. (I learned this much later from him.) All of the people who had been there had been fed words that made them full of contentment and peace. Such do not make good customers for women in my profession.

Plans for suicide vanished from my mind. I lay down on my bed to think about the man, Jesus, and what he had said. I remembered his eyes, and felt that I was being observed again in their black light. I stared at the imagined sight, and refused to blink. In moments my little mind was caught up and held by some universal power, and I simply ceased to know anything.

A persistent quiet knock on my door brought me awake. I went to open it, still groggy, but remarkably refreshed from twelve or more hours of sleep. There at the door was a young woman I remembered having seen in Tiberias. "I am Joanna," she said. "The Master has asked for me to bring you to him."

I knew who she meant by the master. I wasn't going to go. I had seen enough of him the day before. My fear mounted, and I played for time. "Don't I know you?" I asked. "You live at Herod's castle in Tiberias!"

"I am Chuza's wife," she said. That meant nothing to me. "He is Herod's steward," she said. The wife of the second most powerful man in Galilee was standing inside the door of the house of the whore of Magdala! And she seemed to be treating me as her equal! What could possibly happen next?

She stood patiently in front of me, letting me absorb this new knowledge "You mean that your husband, Chuza, wishes to see me?" I asked, knowing that it was not he, but Jesus, who had called for me to come. She didn't reply in words, but simply shook her head and smiled at me. She gave me a tender smile, as if to a retarded but beloved sister.

No excuses came to my mind. I found myself changing clothes, picking up the house, closing the shutters, as if I expected to be gone for some time. I packed a lunch and a second set of clean clothing. When there seemed nothing more to do, I turned to Joanna, and she led me out the door. I forgot to lock it as I left.

We walked to the docks, and boarded Simon's fishing boat. He and his brother, Andrew, had never been my customers. But I knew them when I saw them, for they were prosperous fishermen who were often at Magdala. Often I had entertained one or more of their crew. This day there was no one on board but the two brothers, Joanna, and me. We set out immediately, and I could see we were driving for the north shore, probably for Simon's home city, Caphernaum. I was right. We arrived there to hear crowds speaking with awe and astonishment. It seems that Jesus had told a centurion that his servant would get better, and the servant had. Instantly! It was a remarkable coincidence.

After Andrew and Simon had secured the boat, they found Joanna and me on the edge of the crowd and told us we were to follow Jesus westward to the city of Nain. That was to be a two day journey. There were several men in the group, including Jesus. Four of them I knew; Simon and Andrew, James and John. All four of these were fishermen. I didn't get acquainted with the others right away. They seemed to ignore all of us women. For Joanna and I weren't the only women in the group. James' and John's mother, Mary, was with us. There was also Suzanna, a shy girl, almost a child, and several others. We climbed the hills to the west out of the deep valley where our Galilean lake nestles, and found a place to camp near a spring.

It was late afternoon. We had walked through a field of grain and harvested the nutty kernels as we strolled along. We weren't hungry. A sip of the spring water slaked our thirst. I found myself stretching out on the ground, and considering the flowers that danced lazily just above my head.

His words came back to me.

"Be not anxious for the morrow.

"Consider the lilies...Sufficient unto the day. I slept. When I awoke I found Jesus was sitting beside me, and we were alone.

(Now I am resting in a garden again, near Jesus' tomb. Now I am alone. Only brief moments have gone by since I threw myself on the ground here. If I am more calm now, it is because I have looked back to the time I met Jesus, rather than to this frightening time here. Does God want me to remember? How will it help? But what else can I do?)

My companion sat there beside me staring into the sunset, so I had an opportunity to watch him unobserved. His features were strong. His dark brown hair hung to his shoulders. His beard and mustache looked as if they had been recently trimmed. I had heard that he was in his late twenties or early thirties, but he looked both younger and older. There was a vitality about him that proclaimed his youth. A joy seemed to emanate from him like an aura. At the same time the total awareness he had of each of us human beings seemed to make him almost ancient. All of this I knew from having stood by the sea and watched him as he taught.

Then the man beside me turned and spoke. Instantly I knew this was not Jesus. His eyes were clouded over with something like physical pain. When he looked directly at me, he looked no deeper than any other man had done, and it was without recognition.

"Hello," he said. "You're new among us. Why have you joined us?"

"You're not Jesus," I said.

"No. I am Jude, a close cousin of his. They call me 'Didymus,' the twin. Many have mistaken me for Jesus. Some say that all who come from Nazareth look alike." He asked again, "Why have you joined us?"

"Joanna came to my home and told me he had sent for me. I had to come." There was no need to explain further. Jude nodded his head and assured me that such was true for everyone there.

"He says, Follow me,' and people stop what they are doing, and turn away from home, career, friends and family, and they follow him. We men who he calls his disciples were the first. We walk where he leads us. We hang on his every word. We watch him heal the sick, doing absolutely impossible things. We believe him when he tells us we will do these things too, and even greater, as our faith grows stronger."

I asked him about the healings. "You'll see," he said. "You'll see."

Everything in me demanded that I turn back. Voices spoke to my mind.

"Let us leave this man. He is a holy one of God. I am afraid."

"You are a dirty whore, Mary."

"You are a murderer, Mary."

"What do you want to do, go to be with the holy man, Mary?"

"You're sick, Mary. You're dying of the whore's disease. You're worse than a leper."

"Look what you have become. You are right to hate yourself. No one can love you."

"There is still time, Mary. Walk away from these fanatics. Walk back by the sea. Swim out into the darkness. The only cure to this life is to end it."

I screamed and ran from the voices as fast as I could run. I ran until I was exhausted, and ran further until I fell on the ground. The voices were still with me, but so also was Jude.

He reached out and touched my shoulder. Something of his calm reached me. I noted that he was not even breathing hard while I was panting for each precious breath.

"Be still," Jude said. "Tomorrow Jesus will heal you."

The screaming went on inside. But I could not run any more. I let Jude take my hand and lead me back to the camp.

The next day we walked on to Nain. It is a pretty little town on the south side of a low mountain, about half a day's walk from Jesus' home town of Nazareth. We camped outside the town, by the well, and rested again. It is good that we did, for shortly after rising the next morning Jesus was busy with a crowd of people who had come to be healed. If they came to hear him preach too, it was a secondary purpose. The need for wholeness was far greater. He worked the whole day speaking to some, and touching others. Then we met a funeral procession coming out of the town. A great crowd had gathered around Jesus, and the crowd from the funeral made the road almost impassable.

Jesus came face to face with the woman who was mother of the man who had died. She was a widow with no other sons, no one to care for her in her old age, no one to bury her when she died. I stood close by and watched Jesus look on her. He looked so much like my father when I was a little girl! He looked just like daddy looked when I was sad, or hurt, or lonely. There was a tenderness about him that seemed to envelope the poor widow.

"Do not weep," he said.

Then he walked over and touched the bier. The bearers stopped still. Then Jesus said, "Young man, I say to you, arise."

The young man sat up and began to speak!

Jesus took the man's hand, helped him out of the bier, and put the mother's hand in that of her son!

We were struck with awe! We had just seen a dead man come to life! Some said, "A great prophet has arisen among us." I remembered the story of Elijah raising a dead boy for his mother. Perhaps that is what the people there remembered as well.

No one dared say anything to Jesus. Several began to come to him with their hurts, and their illnesses. He went back to the work with a vigor that was surprising since he had been at it all day. I watched the people healed one after another. Diseases and plagues were healed. Blind people were led to him and after being touched, they walked away shouting that they could see again.

All this time I stood close by, but behind him, watching, hoping, but unable to move toward him. All the guilty past stood in my way. His absolute purity stood out against my absolute guilt. I loathed and hated myself, and knew I was unworthy of his attention. I wanted to run again, but my legs seemed to be rooted to the ground.

"Come to me all of you who labor under heavy burdens, and I will refresh you. I will give you rest," he said. As he said it, he turned and looked at me.

"Fear not," he said to me. "Come to me, my child," he said. A cold lump inside of me began to melt, and I took a faltering step forward.

"Love your enemy," Jesus said. And I knew he meant I must love myself, for I was my own enemy, and I hated myself with a terrible hatred. "Don't be angry with yourself,"

Jesus said. "Don't call yourself names." He smiled. I took another step toward him, then fell at his feet.

He started talking to someone else, but kept looking at me. The voices inside me answered him.

"Who are you?" he asked.

"I am afraid," came the answer.

"Leave her, and never come back to her. Never again make your home in her heart." Jesus' words were spoken with absolute authority. The fear that had been within me half a decade melted away, and it was gone. I understand now that the mental attitude that weighs and balances choices before making a decision was not the kind of fear that I had. My fear was not caution. It was unreasoning emotional bindings that kept me from having any right relationship with anyone, including myself. Any time I tried to be free of it, and to meet others in true human friendship, the fear mounted in my throat, and I found it to be totally uncontrollable terror.

This vicious emotion was now gone from me. Where it had been was now an empty place. The person I am had room to move, but chose not to do so. Better to watch and see what Jesus did with my other unwelcome guests.

"Who are you?" he asked.

"I am angry," came the answer. And I felt that anger well up within me. Who was he to make me grovel here at his feet? What a stupid person I was to let this happen to me! The whole of the area within sight of me began to fade as my anger mounted. I saw everything through a haze of red. There was no way to reason. My heart pounded. I found myself ready to strike out at Jesus. I would kill him!

"Leave her!" he said. "Leave her now, and never come back!" I felt the anger resisting, and caught sight of Jesus' eyes. He wasn't looking at me, though he was looking right into my eyes. He was looking at something evil within me. Eyes locked, and anger was instantly defeated by godly wrath. Another empty place opened within me. I felt lighter, almost better.

Suddenly I found myself capable of forgiving. With anger gone, I had no weapon against the memories of people who had harmed me. I had to declare a truce with myself too, and to stop my activities of self destruction. I could look back and see the Ishmaelite, Ibrahim, Anthony, the drunken soldier, the long line of my former customers, and even my own self, and find compassion for each of us.

I felt something like gratitude toward Jesus. But it grew and became desire for him. I looked up at him out of slut's eyes, pursed my lips, took a deep breath, forcing my breasts to stand out against my clothes. My lips smiled the smile of invitation. I wanted him.. I wanted him to want me.

"Oh Jesus," I said. "Thank you." I crawled closer to him. "I am so grateful. Let me..."

"Who are you?" He required an answer.

"A natural physical need," my voice equivocated.

"Who are you?" he repeated. A truthful answer was required.

"Hunger for fulfillment," I responded. "An offering of gratitude," tumbled from my lips. His look required the truth. "Lust! All consuming adulterous lust!" cried a hoarse voice that sounded something like my own.

Again Jesus said, "Go. Leave her alone." Immediately I felt washed, cleaner than I had felt when Anthony and I were two alone, and I had the entire Galilean lake to swim in every morning.

"Oh thank you, Jesus," I cried. And I looked at him as at a friend. I was most assuredly a female person, and glad that I was. But I had control over my bodily desires. They were no longer my masters, or so I thought.

Now that he was finished with me, I wanted to back away and give myself a little reward. After all, I had stood up under this attack rather well. Fear, anger, and lust were conquered. My own dear self was free now! I would go and get hold of a nice skin of old wine, and rejoice. How nice it would be to sit back, sip the beverage, take a few hearty swallows, get mellow, and tell anyone who was within earshot of the great operation Jesus had performed on me.

"Who are you?" Jesus was persistent. I wept.

"Gluttony," I whispered the response. I recognized this as my own voice. Gluttony and I were one. The soldier had given me fear. Ibrahim had given me lust. Several had given me anger. I had no one to blame but myself for my gluttony. I lived to eat and drink, to indulge myself. Food and drink and sexual encounters were not my tools for existence, they *were* my existence. Gluttony and I were very closely associated. I was not at all sure that Jesus could remove gluttony and leave anything that I would recognize as myself.

Yet, without hesitation, he said, "Leave her." And the spirit of gluttony obeyed.

Now I thought I was truly empty. But he did the same to three more spirits. These were more subtle, and had been with me far longer than the others. Envy had two names. Her other one was Covetousness. They are distortions of ambition, as lust and gluttony are distortions of other God given desires. Good ambition makes you want to work with and to support your neighbor. The vicious spirit of envy makes you hate and distrust him. Jesus set himself the task of driving Envy out of me.

Envy was a secret enemy. She had been with me long before I ran from home. My brother Lazarus I envied. I coveted his manhood. I knew he must be my father's favorite. But I envied Martha too. She had the honored place as 'the woman of the house,' the manager. My life there seemed to be only that of a subservient satellite.

Once Jesus drove out Envy, I saw she had sided with fear from the moment I thought of running from home. "Why stay," she had whispered. "You are not important to them. They won't even miss you."

With Envy dislodged, I was aware at last of the deep love my family had for me. I grieved at their loss and mine. I inhaled a deep breath, and for the first time in years a spirit of hope returned to my heart. Jesus watching me saw my eyes clear for a few moments, and then grow clouded again.

"Who are you?" His knowledge and authority knew I was not free of all my old companions. I yawned in his face.

"This has gone far enough. There is no need to trouble you further. Relax with me. We can celebrate your success. Give me another treatment tomorrow. Take a rest."

"Who are you?" Jesus was persistent. He kept working.

"Let well enough alone," my familiar responded. He asked again.

"Nobody's perfect!" Hiding places were getting harder to find in the bright light of his presence.

He held my eyes and waited. "Tomorrow is another day!" I tried to turn from him. Inside a voice whispered, "Don't let him send me away! If he does, you'll have to go to work!" My eyes implored him to stop. But he looked with such love, such tenderness, such understanding, I felt I could trust him. I let go of my sixth familiar enemy, allowing Jesus to take her place.

"Sloth," she answered. Thus the spirit of laziness left me. How fine I felt. Miss Sloth had been within me since I was a very little girl.

These spirits had eaten on my heart. They were, together, the cause of my loneliness, my feelings of despair. There was only one left, and Jesus knew it.

I knew I was better, except for the whore's sickness, and I knew he need but speak, and all physical ailments would fall away from me. My body was already so much better without the weight of my enemies within it, that it was doing an excellent job of fighting my infection on its own. After all, God had created my body. Why would He not create it strong enough to conquer physical illness?

I could visualize myself as a whole woman. Life would be sweet now. I could follow this Jesus, and remain with the crowd of disciples. There would be things for me to do, and food and shelter for the doing of them. From the sickest of whores to the most needed disciple, I was changed. From the superlative of evil to the saintly, almost angelic superlative of good, that was me! Mary of Magdala! Hallelujah! Praise the Lord!

"Tell me who you are?" Jesus demanded a response.

"Forget it Jesus. They are all gone now. I am most satisfied with the results of your labor. You took six times as long with me as you did with the blind, the deaf, the lepers. Look what you have now! Here I am, a splendid, beautiful, obedient disciple who will follow you and show the others how to do it!

"You deserve a lot of credit, Jesus. You did a lot quicker job than I could have. Though, of course, you know I could have handled the whole situation myself. I have always been me, Mary of Bethany, the Jewess with the glowing jewel for an innermost heart. Nothing has ever touched that pure center..."

Jesus interrupted me!! "Tell me who you are," he said. His authority was unmistakable. It was complete. My last tenant responded honestly, but with absolutely no humility...

"Pride."

"Leave her. Follow the others. Do not return." Then I was really free. Jesus reached down and helped me to my feet. As he lifted me up, I felt the fever leave me, and the smelly discharge that had plagued me for months was simply dried up and gone. He embraced me for a moment, then stepped back, holding my hands in his. He smiled, and I had to smile back. But he spoke quite seriously.

"Now, Mary, you are whole. But you are empty. You must begin to fill yourself with fruits that last. Follow me. Lose your life for my sake. Let me show you how to be a joyful servant of my Father, and of all of the people He created."

I didn't understand him. But I knew he had something special, and that what he had was the most powerful energy I had ever seen in a person. As long as he touched me, I felt that power. Even when he let me go, it lingered. I could feel it for days afterwards.

Disciples of John the Baptist came to Jesus then, and he turned away from me to answer their questions. They had been sent by John who was in prison in Hyrcania, Herod's desert fortress. John had heard that Jesus was breaking some of the laws of the Jews, especially the Law of the Sabbath. He was afraid Jesus was not the promised Messiah.

Jesus answered these men by pointing out the miracles that had occurred in Nain. The dead man had been raised. Blind people could see again. Deaf could hear again. Lame could walk. And some of us had been freed from terrible debilitating spirits that had been ruining our lives.

John's disciples went away, apparently satisfied.

I followed Jesus. A week after I was cured I followed him into the home of a Pharisee who had invited Jesus to dinner. My heart overflowed with gratitude, and I chose to bring a jar of my favorite perfume and to pour it on Jesus. It was my personal act of saying "Thank you!" I poured out the oil. Then I bent down and kissed his feet. I couldn't stop crying, so I spilled my tears on his skin, and used my own hair to wipe his feet.

Simon, the Pharisee, recognized me for what I had been. He may have been one of my former customers. I cannot remember. There were so many. Jesus reminded Simon that he had been a poor host, and then pointed out that my service was an act of love. I was grateful.

He said to Simon, "Those who have loved much will have much forgiven them." Something like that. Then he looked at me and said, "Your sins are forgiven you."

Imagine my peace! My demons were gone. My health was returned. And now my guilt for all my years, even those early ones when I had hated my sister, Martha; all of my adulterous acts; and the one murder were all wiped out. It was as if I had never done any of them! Then he said something more to me I have yet to understand. "Your faith has saved you. Go in peace."

21

Mary Magdalene

Dear Jesus. It is full light, and I have been lying here for several long minutes. Someone is running. It is more than one. They are coming here. I see them now. It is Peter and John.

"Mary came to us and told us the soldiers are all dead, and that the tomb is open," cries Peter, as they run past me.

"They have taken our Lord out of the tomb, and we do not know where they have laid him," I try to say more, but they have kept running toward the tomb. John gets there first and stands looking in. Peter steps in front of him, and goes inside. There they find things as Mary and I had found them. The wrappings are there, the head cloth in a different place from the others.

Peter and John talk for a moment or two, and then turn back. I have followed them to the tomb, so I stand there. How confused and overwrought I am!

The angels appear again. Nothing more can happen to me, I am sure. I just stand here looking at them, and continuing to cry.

"Woman, why are you weeping?" I think it was the angels who said that to me. Their voices seem to come through my heart, rather than through my hearing.

I respond without speaking, "Because they have taken away my Lord, and I do not know where they have laid him." They know what I said, though I did not open my mouth.

I feel the presence of another, and I turn around.

There is a man standing there. The gardener? I cannot see through my tears. "Woman, why are you weeping?" he asks. "Whom do you seek?" My ears hear this person.

"Sir," I say, "If you have carried him away, tell me where you have laid him, and I will take him away."

He says nothing. He stands and looks at me until I wipe my eyes and look back. I begin to recognize him, but I can't believe it is he! Jude, my dear Thomas, 'The Twin,' and Jesus look so much alike! He speaks again. I know I will know his voice.

"Mary."

"Rabboni!" I fall on my knees before my beloved teacher, and reach out to clasp him by the knees.

"Do not hold me, for I have not yet ascended to the Father; but go to my brothers and tell them, I am ascending to my Father and your Father, to my God and your God."

Now he is gone! He isn't here in front of me. He is nowhere to be seen. The angels have gone. I stand alone. But -

I have seen the Lord.

I HAVE SEEN THE LORD.

I HAVE SEEN THE LORD!

I run after Peter and John. I find them with the other disciples at the home of John Mark. "I HAVE SEEN THE LORD! I HAVE SEEN THE LORD! I HAVE SEEN THE LORD!"

They make me sit down. They want to believe me, but they don't. They give me something to eat. I'm not hungry. I sit with them and remember. I HAVE SEEN THE LORD! MY BELOVED TEACHER LIVES! THANK GOD! THANK GOD! THANK GOD!!!

I try to tell them what happened at the tomb, about talking with Jesus, but the people about me don't believe me.

They think I am mad with grief, that I am hallucinating. Still they can't explain the fact that the tomb is empty, the stone rolled away.

It isn't long before we hear that the soldiers who were set to guard the tomb from us are claiming that we must have stolen the body while they were asleep. We know that none of us did such a thing. Peter and John were the first disciples to see the empty tomb. The others have been there since, one and two at a time they have gone. When they come back, they are silent. The women who were with me saw the empty tomb too. Mary saw the angels as I did.

Yet they will not believe me when I say, "I HAVE SEEN JESUS!"

But I know I have seen him. He is alive! I shall sit here hugging that knowledge to me, and think about other times when I followed him.

I think about Joanna, Chuza's wife, and Suzanna, the wealthy young widow of Caphernaum. We and other women followers of Jesus found quiet ways to minister unto the disciples, and to our Master. Jesus gave himself to his teaching and his healing ministry and taught his disciples to do the same. None but Judas Iscariot seemed to care about where the funds for daily living were to come from. It was probably right for Judas to worry, as the others expected him to be able to purchase all of our necessities, except when Jesus performed one of his miracles of feeding us and the crowds. We women quietly saw to it that the purse was kept full.

Often I found myself visiting with one or another of the disciples. Though I had known the fishermen by sight, it was good to come to know them as friends. We did come to know and to respect one another as we traveled about the land with Jesus. I recall now one of the journeys we took. We walked north from Caphernaum to Caesaria Philippi.

During the three days it took to walk there, Jesus set us the task of reporting the opinions we had heard of him.

"Who do men say that I am?" he asked. Each of us came up with reports we had heard. Some of them were quite bizarre. John the Baptizer had been beheaded shortly before, and some people really thought that John's spirit had come to dwell inside of Jesus! The disciples had all known John. Some had been John's disciples before they met Jesus. John was a powerful and important man. God created him for a powerful purpose. Most of us believed that purpose had something to do with Jesus, our Master. Jesus' ministry really began when he was baptized by John.

Jude became a particularly good friend of mine on that journey. More and more often I came to call him 'Thomas the twin,' as the others did. He did look very much like Jesus. Often Jude and I would walk along at the end of the line, behind the other disciples and the other women. We would talk about things that interested all of us as well as about the things the group discussed.

"Could he be the Messiah?" I asked Jude.

"What makes you think that?" We Jews always answer questions with questions.

"Well, look at the miracles he has performed." Surely that was proof enough for me.

"Every one of them can be explained away," Thomas replied. "Even the dead man could have been a fake. Jesus could have set it up just to build a reputation for himself."

"The changing of water into wine?" I had not seen that miracle, but had heard of it often.

"A substitution. A few bribed servants."

"The cripples who were healed?"

"What about the crippled beggar in your town of Magdalla?" Thomas' cynicism and grave doubts troubled me. Still, I remembered that old faker very well. Others could have been faking their suffering.

"What about the feeding of thousands? How could he fake that?"

"What if many of the people brought food baskets and were just shamed into sharing?"

"The blind man?"

"...could see before Jesus touched him."

"The deaf man?"

"...could hear! The lame could walk. The leper was just dirty, and looked better as soon as he was washed." Thomas was really disturbed. "I question everything I see. I especially question things I don't understand. I seek out the people Jesus has cured, and I talk to them afterward. Most of them discount the illness they had. Most of them continue the way of life they lived before."

"What about me? What about my healing?"

"Jesus does have great gifts of persuasion. He convinced you that your fears and angers and other emotions were hurting you, and you obeyed his orders to set them aside. You told me yourself that you felt your body getting well as soon as the anger and fear left you. He didn't heal you. He talked to you, and you healed yourself."

"What about his forgiving my sins?" I felt fear closing in on me again as I waited for Thomas to reply to that question. "If he is not the Messiah, he does not have the power to forgive my sins. All of my guilt for all of the evil thoughts and acts of the past would still be with me." My voice was beginning to rise.

"He could be the Messiah," he said. "Yet I lived in the same town with him from the day of my birth. We played together as little boys, though he was a few years older. When we grew up, I worked in the vineyards, while he became an apprentice in Joseph's shop. He didn't appear very different from the rest of us then."

"Very different?" I pounced on the opening.

"Well, there were some things about him. He would go off by himself more often than any of us. Sometimes he seemed to know things he had never been taught. Once, when he came home from Jerusalem when he was twelve, his parents told how he had sat and confounded the wisest of the priests at the Temple. The time he may have turned water into wine that I told you about, when we were at the wedding in Cana? His mother told him to do that. So he must have done things like that around home. Why else would she expect him to do it?"

"Do you love him?" I asked.

He seemed shocked. "Love him?" He was silent for a very long time. "I am following him. He is living a reckless life. Many people in high places are already jealous of him. We put out lives in danger by being his disciples. I guess I must love him."

That evening around the campfire Jesus asked us again, "Who do men say that I am?" The responses were the same.

"A great prophet."

"One sent by God."

"Moses re-incarnated."

"Elijah re-incarnated."

"The spirit of John the Baptist is in you."

Jesus stopped them with a gesture. We waited in silence. It was his turn to speak. "And you? Who do you say that I am?"

We remained silent. "A beautiful person. A generous person. A compassionate person. A living angel." All of these came to my lips, and I said nothing. Others told me later they had thoughts too. "A healer. A great teacher. The greatest of teachers."

Simon spoke up. "You are the Christ! You are the Son of the Living God!" We all gasped. Each of us had begun to think this, and each of us had discarded the thought, and picked it up again, and set it down, and walked around it, and worried it, and worried about it. But none of us had set it outright in public as a statement of our faith.

How many understand that the Christ, the anointed one of God, God's true Son, is something far more powerful than the Messiah? God can choose to do what He wishes, of course. A savior of the people was all we had ever asked for. The prophets had promised us this, a Messiah who would come to lead his people, and to care for his people. I had been talking that day with Jude about Jesus being the Messiah. Jude had studied the possibility, and had studied Jesus' work, and was not sure enough to say, "Yes! He is the Messiah we have been promised!" Yet he was unable to say, "No! He is not the Messiah, and I will no longer follow him!" Jesus, we all knew, was very powerful. He was more powerful than anyone we had ever seen in any of our separate lives. He was much shorter of stature than Simon the fisherman. He and my friend, Jude, not only looked alike, they were of the same height as well, rather short in stature, really. I stand almost as tall as Jude.

The silence continued. We all waited with deep anticipation for Jesus to answer Simon.

"Blessed are you, Simon, son of Jonah. For no human being revealed this to you. Heaven revealed it to you. From now on I will call you 'Peter,' the rock. And on this rock I will build my church."

We remained silent. He had not said, "Yes, I am the Son of God. I am the Christ." But he said heaven had revealed the answer to Simon! He must have meant that Simon had the true answer!

"I will give you the keys of the Kingdom of Heaven," Jesus said. We looked at Simon, now Peter, and knew that Jesus had made him the second in line of authority among us.

That night, late, my look like Jesus friend, Thomas, and I sat up very long after all the rest of the company were asleep. We talked and talked. If Jesus is God's Son, what does it mean for the Jews? What does it mean for mankind? What does it mean for Thomas? What does it mean for Mary of Magdala?

If Jesus is not what Peter called him, and if Jesus thinks himself to be God's Son, what does it mean to us to be following a charlatan or a madman? I found it easier to believe in Jesus than to torture myself with doubts as Thomas did. I knew I was grateful to Jesus. I knew I loved Jesus with a love that was different from the love I bore for any other human being I had ever known.

I knew that my love for Jesus was a love that included my being a person created by the Father to have sexual needs. In this knowledge I was certain that Jesus would meet my needs for his love but in a way that was not physical, or rather a way that was both physical and spiritual, greater than any love making between two bodies. In Jesus' presence I could sit still and feel a greater glow of well being flowing to me than I could ever feel from a million caresses from another man.

I could see my love for Jesus was a major part of the reason I believed him to be who Peter said he was, the Son of God.

My dear friend Thomas was quite close to me. We were in the foothills of Mount Hermon. It was a cool night. Loving Jesus as I did, I found myself loving Thomas too. His questioning, studying, fearful yet hopeful attitude toward Jesus aroused something like a mother's tenderness for him. I kissed him with a mother's or a sister's kiss. Or so I thought.

He kissed me back with a kiss that I could interpret very well. We separated quickly. We were both a little surprised. We said, Goodnight,' and found our own places of rest.

That night I found myself taken up into a dream experience of love with God that included Jesus and Thomas. Jesus seemed to be holding Thomas and me in a tender embrace that gave us more awareness and satisfaction with our separate selves than any one could ever hope to have. And as Jesus held us, we seemed to be held together by Him in a way that made us a part of each other. From that night on I found that the pain of Jesus was my pain, and the pain of Thomas was my pain. But so was the joy of either my joy. Yet I was more than a mirror of them. For I found that my sadness was their sadness, and my happiness theirs in this same great binding of our selves to each other.

Thomas, much later, told me that he had the same dreamlike, but absolutely real, experience I had had. We both knew we were from that time forth, fully bound to each other. Yet we had a quiet shyness, and we found no need for courtship. The day might come when we would mate. We both knew that without speaking about it. But we could wait for the right day, the day that would be our day of love.

I walked in a time of timeless happiness.

22

Mary Magdalene

The day came when Jesus set his face toward Jerusalem. We continued to follow, though I became quite reluctant. The thought of returning to my home town brought to mind my family, and my former fiance and his family. By going to Jerusalem, I would be so close to home! The road we followed would lead right through Bethany, over the Mount of Olives, through the Kidron Valley, and into the gates of the holy city. Even though I had been healed by Jesus, my imagination of what a reunion with my family would be like always indicated that I would be tried and judged by them. Their judgment could only determine me to be an unworthy person. I visualized them looking at me, recognizing me, hesitating for the briefest of moments, and then turning and walking away from me with a finality of steady tread that would leave me crushed. The picture was bad enough. What would the reality be like?

We walked from Caphernaum down the west bank of the Sea of Tiberias. Thus, staying on the main road, we skirted Magdala, and walked through the heart of Herod's city that he had named for Tiberias the Emperor. A few miles further south we came to the lovely spot where our lake empties into the Jordan River, and then followed that river into the desert.

Ever southward, ever downward, we walked for a period of four days, until we came to Jericho. Some of the sights we saw along the way, I recalled from my time of captivity with the Ishmaelites. Fresh water was available to us all along the way, both from wells, and from the river itself. As we neared Jericho the disciples pointed out the place in the Jordan where John baptized Jesus. The day we were there, the river moved slowly by, meandering in a great ark along the wide valley. The water was no more than waist deep, and it was quite dirty. Still we used it for drinking as well as for bathing, and even for a meal or two of fresh fish. We carried our bread with us.

After a time we were a part of a caravan of travelers. We were glad of their company, for the more there were of us, the less danger we were in from bandits. When we arrived at Jericho, we relaxed for a day or two in that beautiful oasis. We rested, swam in the Jordan, ate dates, sang beautiful songs. Jesus was always joyful with us, and we with him. Still, there were times I saw he was pensive, and I often saw him walk out into the desert to be alone. He would climb one of the many hills about us, and we wouldn't see him again for several hours. When he returned, he was joyful again, loving and supporting of all of us.

This was a festive time for us. We sang mostly from the psalms of David. We laughed and we played like little children. But we were never cruel to each other as little children often are. Our life was a festival, as if we were walking with a bridegroom on his way to the wedding, as if we were already at the wedding, and the festival was at its peak. At night we would dance around the campfire. Jesus would laugh with us, and encourage us to greater activities of joy. We would often fall asleep exhausted after a day and an evening of joyful fellowship. We would expect to arise the next day too tired to travel. But that never happened. When we awoke, we had a new energy. We would break our fast on fish left over from the night before, and fresh fruit from irrigated orchards nearby. Then a drink from the river to quaff our thirst, and we set forth singing as if there had been no interruption in our merriment. This abundance of energy, I am sure, flowed from Jesus. I know I never had such resources within myself.

Along the way Jesus spoke to us often about the Kingdom of God. His descriptions of that Kingdom were always in parables, and always indicated he knew it better than we knew Galilee, Samaria, or Judea. Heaven, he assured us, is a most wonderful place, and the King of Heaven is so loving we are to speak of him as we would our own fathers. Whenever Jesus spoke of God as Father, I remembered my own father in Bethany and grew pensive and homesick for him. Was this the way Jesus felt about his absence from heaven?

When I left home, I made the trip down from Bethany to Jericho in one night. It is an easy one day journey. From Jericho to Jerusalem is a different story, especially in the hot summer. It is hot and arduous, and takes more than a day and a half. The road is steep, and the weather as you leave the valley is quite humid. By the end of the first day we climbed to the half way inn. Jesus told one of his parables about that place. It had to do with a Samaritan helping someone.

We were conservative with our funds. We did not pay for lodging indoors. Instead, we slept near the walls of the inn for protection against possible robbers. We kept each other company with stories and songs until sleep overtook us. The stars overhead we saw as a sign of the immensity of God's love for us. Yet they showed us nothing by comparison with the beauty and power and tenderness that was in Jesus, our friend and companion.

We were tied to our master by bonds of love we thought inseparable. He had taught each of us, healed several of us, become a rabbi and friend like none we had ever known. In turn, each of us had sacrificed the way of life we had known, and come to an attitude of trust, so that we could become followers of this itinerant teacher. We showed forth our faith in him, and in his powers, by our actions. He showed forth his faith in us by calling us specifically to follow him, to be his companions.

That night I stayed awake, my eyes searching the road that led to the west. Only a few more miles to Bethany. As the moon set, it went down behind the Mount of Olives. The black shadow covered my home town. I stared and stared at that shadow. I couldn't see my future, but my imagination continued to visualize rejection and emptiness.

The reality was nothing like the imagination had predicted. I suppose it seldom is. Only my murder of the soldier had been a little like my dream of it. When we came to Bethany, we walked through the town without seeing anyone I knew. An hour later we had entered the gates of Jerusalem.

We stood on Solomon's Porch, among the double rows of pillars in the portico on the east side of the great open space in front of the Temple. There we saw the people of Jerusalem and the pilgrims from the country coming and going. Money changers and sellers of pigeons and larger sacrificial animals were doing a slow and dull business. It was the middle of summer, a few weeks after Pentecost. There are no significant festivals at that time of the year. No festivals meant fewer pilgrims, and fewer pilgrims meant less sacrifices, so there was less need for sacrificial animals. Still the sounds and smell of the market were there as they would be on all but Sabbath days. Yet they were muted, almost acceptable.

As we stood there, we watched a Pharisee come to Jesus. I recognized Nicodemus. He was an old friend of my father, and of Joseph of Arimathea. Jude and I were standing close together as usual, and I noticed how tense he was. We had both grown tense as we entered the city. Now, as

Nicodemus approached, it was obvious that Jude was even more nervous.

"What is bothering you, Thomas?" I asked. He led me around a pillar so we could not be seen by the others, including Nicodemus.

"That is a Pharisee. And he holds much power in the Sanhedrin," he said.

I nodded. "Of course. I know Nicodemus. He and my father are close friends." Jude looked at me with something like a new respect in his glance.

"Your family has influence then?" And when I nodded again, he went on, "Perhaps you will be of help to Jesus where none of the rest of us can do anything. He is reckless in the things he says, and in the places where he says them. He has visited with Nicodemus in the middle of the night, and told him he was terribly ignorant for a leader of the Jews. He told Nicodemus he would have to be born again to be able to understand the things that the Spirit of God would teach him. He told that old man that he, Jesus, is God's son. That thing that Simon Peter said about Jesus on the road to Caesaria-Philippi, Jesus had already told to Nicodemus."

"How do you know this?" I asked.

"Because I look so much like Jesus. Nicodemus caught me in the market a few days later and started in to review the whole conversation he had with Jesus. I knew almost everything they had said to each other before he realized I was 'the twin.'" He was silent, thinking about that time, and I waited for him to speak again if he wanted to do so. We looked back across the Kidron valley to the Mount of Olives. The hills about Jerusalem provide a serenity of timelessness that is helpful to us. My heart recalled again the song of David, I will lift up my eyes to the hills. From where does my help come?'

Jude spoke again. “I talked it over later with John BarZebedee, and he visited with Jesus about it. I stood with them and listened.”

“And...” I prompted.

“And I was as ignorant of what Jesus meant as was old Nicodemus. I guess I will have to be born again too to understand.”

I squeezed his hand, stepped forward to embrace him, and my tender offering of understanding and kindness was mistaken. Or his love for me was growing. Or unconsciously I truly intended more to be offered. We were locked quickly into an embrace that set our hearts to racing and our thoughts to finding an even closer union.

“Oh Jude,” I breathed, and stepped away from him. We came around the post to see Jesus was engaged in conversation not only with Nicodemus, but with Joseph of Arimathea. Joseph was less than two paces from me. Apparently the three of them had been walking slowly toward us as they talked. Joseph recognized me immediately. The look on his face registered surprise and something else. Perhaps it was shock that I was with Jesus and his followers.

“Mary?” he asked. “Aren't you Mary?” As I nodded my head, my eyes filled so that his face blurred. He stepped forward to embrace me, and I accepted his offering. Had I met him before Jesus healed me, I could not have done so. But healed as I was, I found myself fully clean and worthy. Joseph spoke again. “Wait a moment, Mary. I must finish my conversation with this man. Then you can tell me the many things I must know about you.”

We waited. The conversation between Jesus and these two prominent citizens of Jerusalem lasted only a few more minutes. We couldn't help overhearing part of it.

“Jesus, your sermon at Caphernaum has been reported here.” Nicodemus said. “Please don't expose yourself too much at this time. The high priest has spies out. Some of them have joined your followers. Everything you say and do gets back to Annas."

"The way I travel is mine," answered Jesus. "It is straight, and it is narrow. There is no turning to right or left. There is no looking back."

Joseph approached him from a different position. "Much good can be accomplished through trading and diplomacy. Compromise achieves far more than absolute obstinacy. The priests have had to learn to live with their oppressors, and with the puppet government of Herod. Your teaching that demands absolute obedience to the law causes them real embarrassment. They will stop you. They will use any means to do it."

Jesus looked at each of these men with real appreciation and real affection. "Thank you," he said. "You are close to the Kingdom of God. I know your concern for me. I know your love for me. You know Love is the Law. It cannot be compromised."

"Prepare yourself to be tested," said Nicodemus. He and Jesus looked in each other's eyes, rested their hands on each other's shoulders for a moment, then walked away from each other and from us.

Joseph of Arimathea turned toward me. Jude stepped out of earshot, but stayed near us. "Mary," Joseph said, "We have thought you dead these many years. And now I find you in the company of the Nazarene rabbi." He didn't say anything more. He held my hands and searched my eyes. His eyes were the same as always, intelligent, kind, searching for the truth.

"Oh Abba Joseph," I said, and started to cry. He let me lean on his chest and sob. My heart was so full! After a few minutes I regained control and stepped back. The outline of the life I had led for five years tumbled from my lips. I was raped. I ran away. I was kidnapped and sold into slavery. I met Jesus. He brought me back to my home.

Joseph listened, nodded, and accepted. He did not question. I didn't have to tell him about my years as a whore. He was a man of the world. He knew what women had to do if they lived outside the protection of their families. As I talked, I watched him carefully for any sign of rejection. There was none.

"And my family, Abba Joseph?" The question had to be asked. "And my dear Joseph, your son?"

"Your brother and sister still live in your house in Bethany," he replied. "My son has married, and moved to Caesaria. There he keeps an eye on our shipments."

I found myself glad for Joseph, and not grieving at my loss. I was happy to hear that Martha and Lazarus were all right. But my father? Why had he not mentioned my father? I looked at him and opened my lips to speak.

"Your father died four years ago," he said. "An illness came upon him. He didn't seem to want to live. And so he died."

Again I wept. Again he let me have his shoulder. I turned to find Jude. I introduced him to Joseph. "Dear Thomas," I said. "I am going to my home in Bethany now. I must see my brother and sister. Will you go with me?"

He shook his head. "I will stay near Jesus. But I will see you later." We agreed to meet at the pool of Siloam at noon the next day. Joseph of Arimathea accompanied me to Bethany. I needed him to provide me courage for that meeting.

The reunion with Lazarus and Martha was good. At first it was terribly strained, even after the initial embrace. I had to tell my story in far too much detail under the critical eyes of Martha. She asked so many questions! But at last Joseph and Lazarus put a stop to that. They all accepted my return, and it was obvious they rejoiced that I was there. They began to plan a feast for the town. "This our sister was dead, and she is alive again. She was lost, and is found," said Lazarus. We embraced again, all of us, and there was much less strain in the air. Joseph of Arimathea left us shortly after that, rejoicing that he had helped return me to the bosom of my family.

That night I found myself sleeping in my own room again, in my own home. So much for the fears that kept me from home for all those long years!

Home, a second womb for each of us, the safe place, the place of acceptance, of love, of tenderness, of provision of simple things. There is none who can grasp the meaning of home until one has had a good one, and then has gone without it for a long period of time. I was sure my home was truly the best home a person could have. There was love in my home. My sister loved me. My brother loved me. The continuing memory of our parents having loved us in this particular place fills us with warmth. The simple walls and furnishings, the sights from each of the windows and doors, the individually waving branches of the tree in our center garden; each and all signal a reflected gladness that this member of the family, this Mary, is home at last.

All the next morning I basked in the old patterns of living in my home. The sunlight awakened me as soon as it crossed the Jordan touching the hills. It glanced in my room, saw that I was there, and welcomed me back with a flood of golden beams. Its radiant light seemed to flow clear through me, and to take away the last remnant of concern I had held that I might not be accepted by my family. I ran down the stairs from my room, through the center garden, and into the kitchen.

Martha was there first, of course. Martha is always the first up, and the last down, and she remains busy every waking moment. Though she had annoyed me with such diligence before, especially when she chided me for not following her example, I loved her for being herself that day. We made the breakfast for our brother, and for ourselves. Bread and cheese and fruit and goat's milk, and a few bright vegetables, some eggs, and some more bread. Our larder was full as always. We ate, and we talked.

We talked and we ate. It seemed that neither words nor food would fill us, following the long and foolish famine we had endured. As we talked of what each had been doing, and of the loss we had experienced in our father's death, I studied Martha and Lazarus. She was plain and healthy, a strong spinster of twenty-five. She knew her role of homemaker, and she performed her function well.

Yet Lazarus looked tired and drawn. There was a sick yellow look to his skin. His eyes revealed that he lived with an internal pain. He moved with care. Though he appeared to eat as much of the food as we did, his plate did not empty, and he did not put more on it. He was alert to all we said. And he absorbed our words like a thirsty man absorbs cool water. But he had little to say. He showed his interest and his love by the attention he paid to us, and to the conversation that was important to us.

His apparent illness made me think of Jesus, and of his healing of so many persons, including myself. "Do you know Jesus of Nazareth?" I asked. "It is with Jesus I have been traveling. He it was who rescued me from my bondage. He is wonderful! I love him more than anyone I have ever known!"

Martha looked at Lazarus. After an exchange of glances they made no attempt to hide from me, Lazarus spoke carefully. "We have heard of Jesus, of course. We have even seen him. We heard him speak once early in his ministry. He came to Jerusalem, and he drove the merchants from the Temple grounds back into the open ground outside the city walls. Then he spoke with authority that God's house is a house of prayer. I was impressed by him."

Martha said, "We have gone to hear him several times. He always seems to draw crowds. He speaks of God as his

Father! That is exciting, for though we all know we are God's children, in that we are created by Him, we hear Jesus speak as though God were his daddy, the one who sired him. Jesus speaks with the assurance of one who is the firstborn son of a king. I often watch the Pharisees as Jesus talks. They don't like what he has to say. He could be getting himself into trouble!"

"Have you seen him heal anyone?" I asked.

"No. But he healed a man I have known all my life, you know him too, Mary, it is John of Bethlehem. He used to be brought to Jerusalem in a cart. Jesus healed him by the pool of Bethsaida. John told me so himself. He had been brought there for almost forty years because he believed the story about the angels stirring the water there, and he hoped to be the first one in, and thus be cured. But he never made it. One Sabbath about a year ago, Jesus walked up to him and told him to get up."

"Did he?" I knew the answer.

"Yes! And he walked away carrying his pallet. The Pharisees got after him for working on the Sabbath. Then they were angry with Jesus for healing on that day of rest. Jesus told them his Father works every day, so he does too!" Lazarus paused. "I don't mind if Jesus and God work every day, but I am glad we have our Sabbath day of rest!"

"Lazarus!" Martha exclaimed. "Be serious! We know that this Jesus merely spoke the words, 'Stand up and walk, and that the old cripple did just what he was told!"

I couldn't help remembering my old beggar in Magdala. But I held my tongue. Surely John of Bethlehem had been a real cripple. I had seen him, and I don't remember him making a living as a beggar. His family supported him. Would Jude believe that healing? I wondered.

"Would you like to meet Jesus?" I asked. "I could invite him and the disciples here for our evening meal?" It was so arranged, but not for that day. Martha didn't have time to prepare properly. She needed three more days. I excused myself, and went to find my friend Jude by the pool of Siloam. On the way I thought of my dear brother. How ill he looked. It was good that I would be introducing him to Jesus soon.

Jesus accepted the invitation, and he came with all of his disciples. We had a real banquet. Martha outdid herself with her preparations. Lazarus must have opened his purse and told her to spend as much as she wished, for I do not remember so fine a meal in our house. As she served, Jesus and the disciples sat enjoying the food, the wine, and the conversation with Lazarus. I sat at Jesus' feet, absorbing all that was being said. It made me happy to see that Jesus and my brother were making friends so quickly. The joy of life that was in Jesus seemed to spread throughout the household, and my home that was warm and tender to me upon my return began to vibrate and reflect a mood approaching perfect harmony as it accepted the blessing of Jesus' presence.

Suddenly the mood changed. Martha exploded in anger that I had not done any of the work of serving. She demanded of Jesus that he instruct me to be of help to her.

Nicodemus and Joseph of Arimathea should have been there. They would have seen Jesus at his diplomatic best. He replied in a way that won Martha as a friend, yet exonerated me and blessed me for having chosen to feed on his presence, and his words.

When the evening came to an end, Jesus and his friends slept in our home! It was the first of many nights that we were so honored. Our home became the center for people who sought our Master. Days we would sit and listen to him talk, and watch him as he ministered to people, freeing them from the burden of their troubles. Evenings were filled with songs and laughter. Martha had several of us women to share in the housework. Jesus trained the men to perform the ministry of healing, and of proclamation of the coming of his Father's Kingdom.

Then one day I discovered that my companionship with Jude had grown way beyond friendship. We walked together daily, seeking out quiet places where we could be alone. One such place was a private grove of olive trees in the valley outside of Jerusalem. We were very much alone, and we were both suddenly aware of it. I sat down in some deep shade beside a stone wall. Jude sat down beside me. He was so close I could feel the warmth of his body making my body heat increase. We were both talking, but neither of us was listening to the other, even to ourselves.

As I chattered, I found myself looking at Jude with a growing love, a love like nothing I had ever known before. The love I had for my parents was beautiful. The love I once had for my fiance may have anticipated this moment, but was like a budding flower by comparison. The love I had for my brother and sister was entirely different. The love I had for Jesus was infinitely greater, but somehow it was included, and somehow it blessed this love I felt for Jude.

Long ago I had been able to distinguish between these look alikes. They were of the same stature. Their faces in repose were often exactly the same. There was almost the same timbre in their voices, and their Galilean accent was the same. But Jesus always walked fully erect, fully balanced. His eyes were always clear, and were always piercing to the depths of anyone who dared look into them. My Jude was burdened. His shoulders were stooped. His brow was often furrowed. His eyes were clouded, and they looked inward, trying to examine puzzles, searching for missing pieces. My love for Jesus is as a student toward a teacher, a child toward a parent or protector, a patient toward her doctor healer, even as that of a creature toward her creator.

It is in this latter love of Jesus as creator that I find a blending of love with Jude. For I must love my creator as I see the beauty of the person created. This is especially true when I see Jude in almost the exact image of Jesus. I love the creator more as I see that the created person of Jude sees my created beauty, and is excited by it.

My love for Jude grew. I knew somehow that when he was with me most of his doubts faded. I wanted to touch my beloved friend. I wanted to kiss him. And I wanted Jude to love and kiss me. All of the awakened awareness of my former life made me tingle with anticipation of the moment of Jude's touch. Deep within me I knew that this experience that was coming with Jude was right for each of us, and was right in the eyes of God.

I knew Jude would touch me. I leaned forward, straining in anticipation, yet demanding that he be the first to reach out, to place his hand on my body.

He touched. Then I touched. We touched again. Our lips touched, and touched again, and clung, and separated, and touched.

He cradled me in his arm, bent over me and kissed my lips, ever so tenderly. Then he pulled open the loose folds of my garment, and fondled my breast. I held his head between my two hands, and kissed his mouth, and his eyes, and his mouth again. As I did so, he lowered me gently to the ground and leaned over me. This fond possession of me was a love experience I never knew. I opened my mouth to speak and he covered it with his. The moment of choice had long passed. I lay there anticipating the next moments and reveling in them before they occurred. I am one of the best dancers in the dance of love, though I had never before put my whole heart into the music. Now I was rejoicing that I had been healed by Jesus, made clean by Jesus. Now I was worthy of the love of one of his disciples.

Suddenly Jude stopped. He was still touching me, but he was absolutely still. He turned, looked back over his shoulder, and leaped to his feet. He ran away through the trees, leaving me on the ground with most of my body exposed. I looked up into the faces of three pop eyed leering Pharisees.

"Well, my friends," said one. "We have caught ourselves an adulteress."

"So we have," said another. "She is lovely. Perhaps we could accept the gifts we see for ourselves."

"No," said the third. My ears heard, as I quickly adjusted my garments to cover myself, that he regretted having to say that negative word. "No. We will take her to the judgment. This is the opportunity we have been looking for. This is the reason we were set to spy on this woman." It was then I learned from them that they had been watching me ever since Jude and I kissed among the columns near the Temple courtyard.

They took me firmly by the arms, and led me through the gates of the city, back to the Temple courtyard, and brought me through a crowd. Suddenly I realized they were bringing me to Jesus! Why were they doing that? What purpose did they have?

Caught in adultery. I knew the law. If proven guilty, I was to be sentenced to death, and publicly stoned. The Law of Moses is explicit in this. Jude, too, would have been punished if he had been caught. But Jude ran away. He left me alone with my captors. I was numb! I was ashamed! My Master was to hear of my private affair with one of his chosen twelve. I, who had been cleansed by Jesus, freed from the life of a whore, and permitted to be a regular member of the traveling company, a trusted participant in the Master's life, had betrayed that trust.

It didn't matter that Jude was guilty too.

It didn't matter that neither of us was married. The charge would be 'adultery,' and who could prove otherwise if Jude were not there?

It didn't matter that we were parties to an overpowering emotion of true love, the drawing together of a man and woman that seemed to be a true part of God's plan.

What did matter was that I was before Jesus, and my actions were to be an embarrassment for Him. "Oh Jesus," I thought. "I am so sorry!"

The Pharisees shoved me, and I fell. I lay on the stones before Jesus. "We caught this woman in the very act of adultery," said one of my captors. "What should we do with her?"

I looked up, and the three who had brought me to Jesus were now joined by an assortment of many scribes, Pharisees, and Sadducees. It seemed as if all of the officials of the Temple had congregated to hear how Jesus would reply to the accusation of the witnesses. Somehow all of Judaism had become my accuser.

"Moses, in the Law," said one of them, "commanded us that such should be stoned. What do you say?"

Jesus looked at me, and I looked down. I knew he knew everything about what had happened, and with whom I had been. He didn't have to ask where my partner was. He knew that too. The law says that both have to die. The Pharisees could have caught Jude, but they made no effort to do so. Every town in our land has harlots. Jerusalem is no exception. No effort is made to control the traffic. Women ply their trade in the market, even on the steps that lead to the Temple courts. As I was led to Jesus, I saw three women and two men stop working their territory to watch our little parade. I was certain that this was no morality drive by the Sanhedrin. My arrest had not been for sexual activity. It was so that I would be led to Jesus, and he would have to make a ruling.

However he ruled, it would be an embarrassment to him. If he directed that the law was to be obeyed, and I was killed, it would be one of his own people that was stoned. In addition, it would be a breach of Roman rule. For it is only our Roman masters who have the right to slay us. Capital punishment is not the right of our people while Rome governs us.

If Jesus ruled I was to be forgiven my adulterous act, he would drive away the deeply committed religious people who, throughout their lives, had maintained their chastity. Poor Jesus! I was the instrument of an insoluble dilemma. He looked down at the ground. He squatted down. He took a stick and began to write in the dust that had accumulated over the stones of the temple court.

A silence fell on us. The silence extended. I could feel the discomfort of everyone but Jesus. I love him so! I wanted to tell him. He could condemn me to death, and I would not hold it against him. But I couldn't open my mouth to speak.

Jesus remained totally at ease.

Then he spoke. "Let the one who is without sin cast the first rock."

He continued to write in the sand. I don't know for certain what he wrote. Some told me they saw the words of the ten commandments scrawled in the sand. Others said they saw their own particular sins underlined in the dusty writing. The silence continued. I couldn't bear it. I had to look up.

The scribes and most of the Pharisees and Sadducees were leaving. Jesus had not fallen into their trap. It was their law. It was their responsibility to uphold it. Perhaps there was a pure one there. But if so, he wasn't brave enough to become my judge and executioner. Or, being pure, he was also kind, gentle, forgiving, and compassionate? Yet all knew that to be the one to cast the first stone was to be the one who would have to stand before the Roman court for murder.

My three accusers drifted away in separate directions.

All the people who had gathered to hear Jesus teach seemed to know that their schooling was interrupted for the balance of the day. They walked off in little clusters, shaking their heads at the new lessons they had heard from the Master.

We were alone, Jesus and I. The silence deepened. Finally he looked in my eyes, and I could not look down.

I knew again that Jesus loved me. Jesus accepted me as I was. Jesus forgave me for what I was, and for what I had been, and for what I had been doing with Jude.

"Where are your accusers, woman? Has no one condemned you?" When Jesus spoke the word, 'woman,' it was with tender knowledge that every woman is like a beautiful Eve, the first of us, in his sight, and in the sight of his Father.

"No man, Lord," I said. My emphasis on the masculine was not lost on the Master. As we looked at each other, he forgave me that too.

"Neither do I condemn you," he said. "Go, and sin no more."

Jesus knew it was Jude with whom I had been. He knew the embrace had brought us close, but that our love had not been consummated. He knew that we had both already consented in our minds to do this. Without words from him, I knew that our sin was in not proclaiming our exclusive union with one another before joining as one flesh. Though we were to each other as one body, we were a part of the community's body as well. We were answerable to that community.

The months since that day have not provided me any revelation of conversations between Jesus and Jude. If they did speak to each other about this event, and Jude's part in it, the conversation was fully private.

I forgave Jude for running away, and I told him so. There was nothing for me to forgive him for in his love making to me. He was no more responsible than I. I am certain that my willingness had encouraged him, for he is a pensive and shy man. It was his running off and leaving me that needed forgiveness.

Whether it was that I only said, "I forgive," and signaled something else, or whether it was that he did not forgive himself, I do not know. But the opportunity to sin with Jude did not come again. I arranged to stay home in Bethany when Jesus and the disciples left Jerusalem. I knew that temptation to be with Jude would come upon me. And I wasn't sure I could find strength in me to withstand it when it came.

Still, I was disappointed when Jude didn't urge me to change my mind!

1

23

Mary Magdalene

The day wears on. The time approaches for the evening meal. The twelve disciples are here together. No, that is not true. Judas Iscariot is not among them. He too has died, but by his own hand.

My dear Jude is not with us either. I am the only one in the group who is happy and assured. I have seen the Lord! I know He is risen! Yet my happiness makes me as unwilling to eat of the meal as are the rest. I find that happiness, extreme happiness, can make one forget hunger. I remember Jesus once said, "I have other food that is not of this world." I understand that now. The others are in an opposite condition. We all know deep sadness kills hunger.

As the sun sets, we look to each other to see what we will do this night. And as we do so, we find another one in our midst. I am not surprised.

IT IS THE LORD!

But the others, seeing him, still do not believe! The doors are locked. No one could get in the usual way. Yet, here he is in our midst.

"Peace be with you," He speaks. "Shalom." I weep with joy. The disciples wonder, and still refuse to believe.

"Give me something to eat," he says. "I am not a ghost." We feed him bread and fish, and he blesses us.

Now we all know that Jesus lives. Then he leaves us....

We rejoice and sing. We dance and sing. We laugh and sing. We leap for joy. Though Jesus is not seen in our presence, we find ourselves speaking to him.

"Oh Jesus! You are alive! We love you. We know that all is well for us. As you have overcome death for others, you and your Father overcame death for you!" We turn to each other. "Rejoice, rejoice and sing. Alleluia, praise the Lord. Praise the Lord, Alleluia!!"

As we cavort in a wild ecstacy of overwhelming feelings of immense gladness, dear Jude, 'the twin,' comes in and looks at us as if we have all gone mad. "What in the world has happened?" he asks, quite reasonably. The other disciples crowd around him to tell him.

Jude listens, and the same incredulous look comes into his eyes that I have seen hundreds of times before. Jude can't believe it. He searches for reasons to doubt. He falls back on the known fact that he and Jesus are look alikes. He has been mistaken for Jesus before. It must be that someone else has been mistaken for Jesus now.

"I won't believe it until I have put my finger in the wounds in his hands," he announces. "I won't believe it until I have placed my fist in the wound in his side." Then he storms out. He is the only living disciple who does not *know* of Jesus' Resurrection from the dead.

I follow Jude. We sit through the night talking. I tell him of seeing and talking to Jesus that morning. My happiness, my faithful reporting of the great truth of visiting with two angels, and of touching Jesus, my beloved Rabboni, does not affect Jude. He does not budge. He will not believe.

I find there is no communication between people when one is in despair and the other is ecstatic. Jude cannot dampen my spirits. I cannot raise his. Dawn comes upon us, heralding the second day of the week of a new world. We are now living in a world in which the dead have overcome death. Now life appears eternal.

24

Pontius Pilate

Late spring, Year of Tiberias — XVII

My dear father,

I should have held my last letter to you, for what I write now is on the same subject, the same persons I wrote about just a week ago.

Those damned priests came by on their Sabbath, the day they aren't supposed to work, to tell me they wanted my soldiers to guard the grave of the Nazarene, Jesus. Imagine that! One of their chief arguments against Jesus was that he worked miracles of healing on their Sabbath. Then they break their own rule to come see me!

Why did they want the grave guarded, you might ask. The answer was given by Caiaphas. "Your excellency," he fawned, "we recall that this imposter said, while he was still alive, 'After three days I shall rise again.' Therefore, give the order to have the sepulcher kept secure until the third day, for fear his disciples come and steal him away and tell the people, 'He has risen from the dead.' This last piece of fraud would be worse than what went before."

"You may have your guard," I told them, sneering at them for fearing a man already dead. "Go and make all as secure as you know how."

So they went and made the sepulcher secure, putting seals on the stone, and mounting the guard. I had let Cornelius and his cohort return to Caesaria after the crucifixion. Cornelius was terribly disturbed by the experience. He told me of the man's death, and it was certainly remarkably noble considering the ignominious show of totally helpless nudity displayed to a gawking public. (Except that it is much more bloody; beheading has a lot to be said for it.) Cornelius told me that Jesus didn't rant and rave, or beg or plead. He simply hung there, saying to God, "Forgive them, they don't know what they are doing." Once he said, "My power, my power, why have you forsaken me?" Perhaps then he was trying what the mockers beneath him called for him to do.

"Come down from the cross," they cried.

You know that most men die worse than animals when crucified. Jesus died a man. Cornelius was highly impressed. He is reported to me as saying, "Surely this was a son of God." I can't use him until he has his head clear and he is free of any guilt for having obeyed his commander. So I sent Magnus to guard the grave with a half dozen men. They watched until dawn on Sunday.

Apparently they all fell asleep, for the tomb was open and empty that morning. Magnus reported to me a strange tale that they were all struck down by some strange power, and were unable to move. They put a story together they all agreed on. The story is that the stone that covered the tomb was rolled away by that same unseen force, and the tomb was empty. No one came out. No one went in, not until some of the women who had been Jesus' followers came to look for his body.

I sent Magnus and his men to the chief priests, expecting their interrogation would produce truth. It did. When Magnus came back, he said the disciples must have come by and removed the body while he and his men were all asleep. These men are all under severe discipline, of course. They will lose a month's pay and be confined to barracks for the same period of time. Magnus admitted to me he and is men thought it a joke to be asked to guard a tomb. From what? Who would want a body, especially one so badly bruised as that of Jesus? They considered the assignment a time for getting drunk, and were all in a stupor most of the night the body disappeared.

I have instituted a search for the body, and expect that it will be found soon. The priests have their spies out looking for it too.

I am having trouble with Procula. We have returned to Caesaria with her still distressed about her dream and Jesus' execution. I hoped the calming effect of endless waves rolling up on the beach near our home would sooth her, perhaps help her to put the petty events of this petty principality in proper perspective.

To my surprise, she not only became well, but very excited. She visited with Cornelius' wife, Ruth, one day. When she returned, she had a look of joyful wonder on her face. She told me we didn't have to feel guilt any longer over the death of the Nazarene, for he was no longer dead! Several disciples had seen him, and word is spreading that the man is indeed risen!

Of course, I am pleased that Procula's depression is gone, but I fear for her sanity when she discovers the truth. Once the body is discovered, and the proclamations of resurrection are proven false, will she not grieve even more than before?

Before I left Jerusalem, I made the Sanhedrin produce the debate of the council that met to determine the fate of Jesus. This meeting was at least four days before he died, and may have been held several weeks earlier. I am trying to learn the exact date. Apparently the priests have made a dupe of us, forcing us to do their killing for them. I enclose this copy for you:

1.	Simon Lepros:	By what right is a rebellious man condemned?
2.	Rabam:	I know not why laws are made when they are not kept.
3.	Achias:	One must first have a true and correct report before he passes a sentence of death.
4.	Subath:	By virtue of Divine and human statutes, no one should be condemned, unless he is guilty. Therefore, what has he done?
5.	Rosnophin:	Why are laws made, if they are not kept?
6.	Phutiphares:	An imposter is not good for the country, by whom a sedition would be made among the common people.
7.	Ryphar:	The statutes only punish the guilty ones; therefore, if he is a transgressor, make him confess his own deed, without which sentence him not.
8.	Joseph of Arimathea	O how shameful and disdainful, that in a city not one should be found, who protects the innocent.
9.	Joram:	Why do we allow this righteous man to die on account of his righteousness?
10.	Ehiberis:	Though he is righteous, yet shall he be killed; because the common people become rebellious by his speeches.
11.	Nicodemus:	Does our law judge a man before he is heard, and it is known what he did?

12.	Diarabias:	Because he is accused before a council, is he worthy of death?
13.	Sereas:	A rebellious man is detrimental to the country, therefore he must be taken from the people.
14.	Rabinth:	Whether just or unjust, because he is against the ancient laws, we can neither tolerate nor suffer him.
15.	Josephat:	Keep him chained with iron chains in prison.
16.	Ptolemy:	Since he is neither just nor unjust, why do we tarry so long, before we condemn him to death, or banish him from the country?
17.	Jeras:	It is much better and more advisable to remove him from the country, or to send him to the Emperor.
18.	Mesa:	If he is just, let us turn ourselves to him; but if he is unjust, let us put him away from us.
19.	Samech:	Let us have peace, that he resist us not; and if he is unjust, let us put him away from us.
20.	Caiaphas:	You all know not what you say; it is expedient for us, that one man should die, and that the whole nation perish not.

Father, as I study this obviously abbreviated copy of the proceedings of the council, I come to two conclusions:

1. The Sanhedrin was greatly divided until Caiaphas spoke. They agreed on no cause to have Jesus killed according to their law or to ours.
2. It was the high priest who wanted Jesus dead.

I asked Joseph of Arimathea about this, and he told me Jesus had once insulted the high priest, implying he was as rotten inside as a dead body in a grave. I asked Joseph also why he was at the meeting of the Sanhedrin, since he is not one of the priesthood. He said he had been invited to speak, but that he had no authority to vote.

Well, the high priest got his way. Jesus was killed.

I am sure Jesus is very dead, stinking up some grave somewhere in this stinking land.

But if I knew last Friday what I know now, he would be alive. Procula and Ruth wouldn't have to live out this foolish fantasy, and my own heart would be at rest.

Here is a copy of the proclamation of sentence of death of Jesus of Nazareth. Note how the Sanhedrin's spokesman, Caiaphas controlled the evidence:

"In the seventeenth year of the reign of Tiberias Caesar, and on the 25th day of March, in the city of Jerusalem, when Annas and Caiaphas were chief priests of the people, Pontius Pilate, Governor in Lower Galilee, sitting in the chair of the Praetor, sentences Jesus of Nazareth to die on the cross between two murderers. After the chief of the people and notorious witnesses say:

1. Jesus is a seducer.
2. He is a rebel.
3. He is an enemy of the Law.
4. He falsely pretends to be the King of Israel.
5. He entered into the Temple, followed by a multitude, which carried palms in the hands.

Pilate orders the first Centurion, Quirilus Cornelius, to lead him to the place of execution, forbidding all poor or rich persons to prevent the death of Jesus.

The witnesses who signed the sentence against Jesus are:

1.	Daniel Robani	3.	Raphael Robani
2.	John Zarababel	4.	Kapet

Jesus will pass through Jerusalem by the gate, Struene."

I understand Caiaphas is having copies made of the above, and is having them distributed to every tribe.

I can't say positively that we have heard the last of the Nazarene, father. But I hope that is so.

Farewell.

Pontius Pilate.

25

Mary Magdalene

I have seen Jesus alive twice since the day we buried him. The days go by as they always have, one at a time. The sun rises. It sets. We go about our daily tasks. It seems as if there is no change. Yet there must be a change. Jesus lives! We don't know where He is just now. But he lives! Therefore, there is no reason for mourning him. It is as if he were away again on one of his many trips throughout our land. I spend these days resting at home in Bethany. Waiting for what? I don't know, but waiting, nevertheless. I have ample time to daydream about the past.

I remember especially the time after he left with the twelve, and I remained behind with Martha and Lazarus. We all stood in the doorway and watched and waved as they descended the hillside down into the desert. They were on their way to Jericho, and then north along the Jordan, back to Peter's home and family in Caphernaum. Peter's wife and mother-in-law certainly saw little of him. It must have been hard on him to be a family man and to follow Jesus. Yet following Jesus requires everyone to sacrifice. Wives sacrifice the time they would have with their husbands. Husbands, the time they would have with their wives and children. As I watched, Jude turned to look back. I think it was Jude. They were so far away, and he and Jesus were walking close together. That day even their clothing looked a lot alike, loose fitting tunics, white scarves upon their heads. The one who turned waved at me. I waved back.

If Jude asked me, would I marry him? I rejoiced in his presence. My body cried out for him. In the night my dreams were of him, and when I was close to sleep my dreams let me do what my waking controls would not permit. Dream time became more satisfying than the hours when I was awake.

Days passed into weeks, and we didn't hear from them. Martha and I watched Lazarus grow thinner, almost emaciated. His skin turned a deeper yellow, yet it was nearly transparent, like old parchment, and he was quite lifeless. Martha urged food on him. I sat with him, sometimes holding his cup to his lips, loving him into taking another sip.

We sat together in the central garden of our home, the three of us, and we talked. Sometimes Lazarus would read to us from the Scriptures. He seemed to know of my deep love for Jude, though I did not tell him. He knew my past, for I had told him all of that. (I never told everything to Martha. I think she knew she didn't want all the details of my past. It is probable that anything I told her would be less than she imagined, and would spoil her vision of the terrible life I had led.) Both knew of my near execution for adultery.

They were shamed by that. But they stood with me. And our neighbors, the people of Bethany, stood with them.

The evening I was exonerated by Jesus... (That is not right. He simply refused to condemn me, for he told me to sin no more.) Rather, the evening of the day I had been brought before Jesus, he had come to our house, and had sat with the three of us. He spoke with us as if no untoward thing had occurred. He was as open and courteous with me as he was with Martha and Lazarus. Somehow we learned through his silence on the subject that adultery was no worse than avarice, and certainly far less evil than unforgiveness or lack of love within a family. Before Jesus went to his pallet in our garden that night, Lazarus embraced me, and Martha touched my arm. It was only the second time she had touched me deliberately since I came home. Their touch spoke of love and acceptance. I was still one of them.

The scriptures that Lazarus often chose to read were from the Song of Solomon. Martha often blushed as Lazarus read those physical passages of Solomon's love for Sheba and of her love for him. I leaned back in the shade and let my imagination have full reign, with Jude as my Solomon and me as his Sheba. It was certain that I had come to a conclusion about that man. If what Jesus said was true (and everything else I ever heard him say was certainly true), my thoughts of adulterous experience with Jude were as if I had committed the act, then I was still as sinning and sinful as I had been the day I was caught in the garden near the East Gate.

It took me some time to realize that Lazarus knew what I was dreaming about. And it took even longer to realize that he knew such reading would make Martha dream the same dreams. Though she was probably still physically a virgin, and had no specific man in mind as her lover, she was still a woman created to function fully as a woman. One day as we came to really know each other well, I asked Lazarus about this.

"We are created by God," he answered. "As creatures who should mate. I am an incomplete man because I am not married to a woman. You and Martha are incomplete women because you are not married to your own men. Since we have become adults we have all had vague dreams of touching other persons, and of being touched. We have been led by God through those dreams to be open to a way to complete ourselves. Martha is not too old to marry and have children. Certainly you are ready for that experience. As for me, if I were well, I would seek a wife, and thus permit our God to complete me."

I tried to interrupt, but he continued. "Let me say one thing more. The male and female relationship is not only a part of God's plan, but it helps us to understand our personal relationship to God. He is, as Jesus says, our Father, for he is our creator. But somehow, he is our lover as well. Hosea tells us of this, and surely our Song of Songs tells us more than the story of Solomon and his beloved. It tells of God and of his love for us, his beloved. I know God loves me with a tenderness that is that of the leader in a love duet. I return his love. God loves you in the same way. And somehow, the two of us, the three of us (he nodded at Martha, including her) are enveloped into a love relationship together as a part of one another, and loved as a whole by our God. Solomon in the Song of Solomon is a lover, and he plays God's role. Sheba is a beloved, and plays the people role. We are God's people, a part of the Sheba experience of being fully and completely loved by our God."

"That is the kind of love I experience from Jesus," I responded. "There is something total about his love that I cannot express. Now I see Solomon's Song is like a love song to all mankind. Individually, and all together, we are the King's beloved."

"Yes," Lazarus said. "That is it." He leaned back and rested. He seemed exhausted, and I insisted that he take to his bed and rest. He didn't argue. And he didn't get up again.

Two days later Martha was certain that Lazarus was dying, and urged me to send for Jesus. I did not hesitate.

Four days later, Lazarus stopped breathing. His body turned cold. Martha and I called for the mourners, anointed our dear brother's body, and had him carried to our family grave cave on the outskirts of Bethany. As we placed his body there, we saw the grave clothes about the dried and deteriorated body of our father who had been buried there four years before. Beside him we saw the remains of the linens not quite covering the skeleton of our mother who had died when I was a little girl.

We rubbed additional ointments into the skin of Lazarus' body, wrapped the grave clothes about him again, completed our prayers at the grave site, and had the stone rolled across the entrance. We returned to our home, desolate. Family and friends came to see us, and they stayed and took care of us. They supported us, wept with us, and waited for us to come to the point where we could accept Lazarus' death. Thank God for friends! Joseph of Arimathea came by as did Nicodemas. Food was brought to us by almost everyone.

From time to time Martha would slip away to the grave and pray. From time to time I would do so too. Two days went by, and then three, and we were as disconsolate as ever. Our fellow mourners began to urge us to complete our grief and look out for our own lives. The old saying, "To grieve for two or three days is good, but to mourn longer leads you to the grave as well," was what they quoted to us. We didn't hear them.

The sixth hour of the fourth day brought more visitors. Martha went out to see them. Then she returned and came to me. "The Master is here," she said. "He wants to see you."

I leaped to my feet and ran to him. I fell at his feet and clung to him. "Oh Jesus...Jesus... if you had been here, my brother would not have died!" He lifted me up and held me close. I could feel the power of his love calming me, and I broke away. I didn't want to stop crying. My sorrow was my sorrow. It was all I had left after the death of my dear brother. Cruel death utterly destroys everything. Father dead. Now Lazarus dead. All see corruption. The Sadducees are right, I thought. One need only visit the home of the dead, see the dried up remains of persons who were once warm and living, and then one can easily proclaim, 'Death is the end. There is no more.'

Jesus said, "Where have you laid him?" And I led him and the disciples to the grave site. Martha and all the people who had been supporting us in our grief joined us there.

Jesus wept.

"Take away the stone," he said.

Martha demurred. "He has been dead four days, Lord. By this time he stinks!"

"Did I not tell you that if you would but believe, you would see the glory of God?" Jesus asked. He looked at her with such force that she made no further objection.

Then Jesus looked up, directly into the brilliant blue sky. He spoke quietly, yet his voice projected into the consciousness of each one of us. "Father," he said, "I thank you that you have heard me. I know you always hear me, but I have said this on account of the people standing by, that they may believe that you did send me."

When he stopped speaking, we were all hushed. There was not the sound of a bird, not even the gentle buzz of an insect. The wind didn't blow, and the leaves were still.

Jesus said, "Lazarus, come out!" He shouted it as if Lazarus were deaf, or perhaps far, far away.

None of us believed anything except that perhaps Jesus was mad with grief at the loss of his friend. Yet each of us looked at the door to the grave. Did we expect something? Or were we under the spell of Jesus' powerful influence over each of our minds?

As we looked, Lazarus walked out of the grave! His grave clothes still bound him. Jesus said, "Unbind him, and let him go." Martha and I leaped to do Jesus' bidding. As we unwrapped Lazarus, we saw that his skin looked healthy again. With the bandages off his face, we could see his eyes were clear and bright, and they had a new depth of understanding in them I had never seen in the eyes of anyone, except those of Jesus himself.

Our friends all returned with us and with Lazarus, and we changed our mourning into joy. We rejoiced until our emotions were totally exhausted, and then we found a place to rest. When we were strong enough, we arose and rejoiced again. Martha and Lazarus and I celebrated in this way until the middle of the following month, the time just before Passover, when Jesus was arrested and sentenced to die.

Yet now I remember that Lazarus' happiness was different than ours. It was as if he had been celebrating longer than the rest of us. It was as if he had come back to provide us happiness, to alleviate our sorrow. His trip into death provided him the ability to see across horizons which still blocked our vision. In the midst of our celebration I would see him sitting very still, and I would study his face. Always a quietly gentle contemplative man, he has an ability to sit still for long periods. But now, even when he is still, he seems to bubble over with assured joy and new energy we never saw in him before.

Jude visited me often during the days immediately following Lazarus' return. Jesus made our home his headquarters. It was in our home that he spent long hours teaching the twelve. It was in our home that he ate and slept. One day he told his disciples he had a new commandment for them.

"Love one another."

He taught that commandment first when he was in our house.

We liked to listen to Jesus' teaching. Jude, who had been a vine dresser in Nazareth, was especially instructed and edified when Jesus taught, "I am the vine, and you are the branches. No one can bear fruit, unless they are in me.

The bad branches are lopped off and cast into the fire. The good branches are pruned so that they will bear even more fruit. You have been pruned already." This teaching made good sense to Jude. To him it was far more clear than when Jesus spoke of being the good shepherd, or when he spoke of being the living bread that came from heaven.

As for me, I liked the idea of Jesus being the Shepherd, and me being one of his sheep. Growing up in Bethany meant growing up in a community where many of the citizens were sheep owners and shepherds. Often as a little girl, I had gone into the hills between Bethany and Bethlehem and had spent hours sitting and talking with the shepherds.

It was from one of the old shepherds from Bethlehem that I first heard the story of the night the angels sang, and of the shepherds going to see the Messiah in the grotto stable near the inn. "I was only twelve years old then," old Jacob said. "I wasn't even married, though I was engaged. I married Rebeccah two years later when she was fourteen. I didn't mind waiting the extra time for her. She was the oldest daughter and her mother wasn't very well." Old Jacob was a rambler. I helped him back to the subject.

"Tell me about the angels," I said.

"Well, we were all together by the sheepfold," Jacob continued. "My father took the gate, and lay across it. The rest of us sat and visited and looked at the stars. One of them seemed brighter than we had ever seen it, and we were talking about that. Then an angel came and stood right in front of us."

"How did you know it was an angel?" I asked. Now that I have seen two angels for myself, I am better able to understand what he told me.

"He was bigger than a man." Jacob thought for several minutes. "And he looked stronger. And he had a way of coming and going like he was right there all of a sudden. He seemed to have a light coming out through him. His face glowed so we had trouble seeing his features." He became quiet, remembering.

This time I didn't hurry him. Shepherds have plenty of time. Their listeners must learn to take their time too. He looked out over the flock and counted them. He counted again. "There's a lamb missing," he said, and stood up.

The lamb was behind a rock, and he saw it instantly. He gave a low call, and all of the sheep moved closer to him. The lamb came from behind the rock, and found a green morsel closer to the flock. Jacob sat down again. The silence continued. I was almost rude, but I determined to wait for him. It was his story.

"The angel really surprised us," he said. "I never saw one before. In fact, I never saw one again, not since that night." Silence again. "But now I don't need to. Now I know what they look like." Silence again. "They are really very good looking." Silence again....a long silence. I had to ask.

"What did the angel say? What did the angel do?"

"Oh. Why he said, 'Don't be afraid.' And he sounded so nice and friendly we stopped being afraid right away. Then he said, 'I bring you good news that will be news of real joy for everybody everywhere. Unto you is born today a savior. He is born in the City of David. You will find him wrapped in a diaper and lying in a manger.' Well, you know some people think David's City is Jerusalem because he was king there. Some people think it is Hebron because he was king there first. But we know it was Bethlehem, for he was born there."

He looked at me and smiled. "I was born there. David is one of my ancestors!"

Everyone knows that David and Solomon had so many children that all of the children of Judah for the last five hundred years can claim David as their ancestor. I can claim him too. "What happened next?" I begged.

"Why the angels sang! All of a sudden the whole sky lit up and there were angels everywhere, and they were singing the most beautiful song. 'Glory to God in the highest! Peace to his people on Earth!'" Jacob sang the words softly. "Again and again they sang it, chorus after chorus. And we sat and listened and looked. We might have fallen on our faces. We might have stood up. But I think we were frozen in the position we were in when the angel first came and spoke to us." Jacob was silent again for a while.

"And then they weren't there any more. We decided to see the savior. We all got up and left the sheep unattended! Just think of that. We all left the sheep and we all went to town, and the sheep were without a shepherd while we were gone!"

"What did you see when you got to Bethlehem?" I asked.

"A baby wrapped in a diaper, in a manger." I had pushed Jacob too far. He would tell the story in his own way, and at his own speed. It took me months before he would tell me more about the baby and the parents. That day he concluded, "And the sheep were all right when we came back. But these sheep need me now." He stood up, called to them, and led them away to what he determined was better pasture.

"A shepherd knows his sheep," Jesus told us. "He calls them by name. He is known by them. They recognize his voice, and come to him." I could see myself as a trusting lamb in Jesus' flock. That idea made me feel safe. I remembered how Jesus had cured me, and the memory flooded back, and I went to my room. There I found a jar of expensive perfume and brought it to Jesus, broke the jar and let the perfume pour down over his head. It dripped through his hair, over his cheeks, into his beard, and down onto his robe. He sat and looked at me and loved me.

Then I knelt before him and washed his feet again. We both remembered.

Judas, the treasurer, spoke. "Why did you let her do that, Jesus?" He was irritated and really spoke in anger. "That jar of perfume could have been sold for a lot of money, and many poor people could have been fed."

"Be patient," Jesus spoke with patience, and with understanding. "What she has done is to anoint me for my burial." I was too shocked to breathe, much less speak. My rabbi, anointed for burial? Surely he was joking! But there was no trace of humor in his voice, or in his look. Our life with him was almost constantly a life of joy and laughter. But this was not a time for laughter. What he said was not a thing to laugh about. Nothing more was said that night. We embraced, all of us, and we went to our separate places of rest.

No, that is not true. Jude and I spoke together for a few minutes. He told me that it had been he who urged the disciples to return with Jesus to Bethany when they knew Jesus was coming back to help Lazarus.

Jude looked hard at me. "I said then, and I say now, 'we are here to die with Jesus.' For surely he will be killed by his enemies in Jerusalem. Surely we, his followers, will be sentenced to die with him."

"Don't say that, Jude," I begged. I started to weep. But he was stiff, and did not reach out to console me. A cool breeze touched my heart, and I turned away. I was frightened and very much alone.

26

Mary Magdalene

The last five days of Jesus' life were very busy. The morning of the first day of that week, he sent Judas Iscariot and Andrew to find a donkey he could ride into Jerusalem. We knew that this was to proclaim to all of Judea that he was king. "Behold your king comes, riding on a young donkey," so wrote a prophet. The crowds were beginning to arrive to fill the city for Passover. As many as four or five thousand people a day climb through our town at the beginning of Passover week, and then they walk back down through the desert to their homes in the North a week later. Many of the pilgrims led several young lambs. One was to kill for their Passover meal, the others to sell to help pay the expenses of the journey. The road was crowded, and the crowd was in a festive mood.

Judas led the donkey back to Jesus. "We had a little trouble getting her," he said. "But we told them you needed her, and they loaned her to us." Then we threw some of our cloaks over the back of the donkey. Jesus stepped up and sat down on her. We all became excited and began to shout and cheer. Soon the visiting pilgrims took up the shout. Some cut down fronds from the trees and threw them in the way. All of us shouted again and again, "Hosanna! Hosanna to the Son of David! The highest heavens are shouting! Hosanna!"

Over the west side of Olivet we marched, accompanying our king. Jesus maintained his dignity sitting on the jenny. He sat absolutely still, saying nothing, acknowledging the crowd with the smallest of nods of his head. I walked in front of him, looking back to see his sensitive face. His eyes looked different than I had ever seen them. Surrounded by acclamations of his royalty, looking royal, he looked as though he were in deep pain, as if the weight of the world was on his shoulders. The thought came to me, "If there is a burden to power, is there an ultimate burden to ultimate power?" I wanted to help him, and there was no way I could do so. Surrounded by the largest crowd he had ever experienced in his ministry, he was totally alone.

Once we stopped when we were halfway down the mountain, still above the distant roof of the Temple. "Jerusalem," Jesus said. "I have wanted to take you to me as a mother hen gathers in her brood. But you would not." He spoke with the sadness of God Himself. Only a few of us heard this musing, for he didn't pronounce it as a teaching for a crowd. He spoke as a man already homesick for his favorite place on Earth as he is about to be sent into exile.

He rode on. Pharisees met him as we crossed the valley. "Make the people stop shouting!" they said. "You are disturbing the peace."

"If I made them stop," said Jesus, "The stones would begin to shout." He rode into the gates, dismounted, and went into the Temple.

The gates of every entrance to the Temple were almost totally blocked. Merchants stood on the stairs shouting the items they had for sale, and the bargain prices they claimed. Sheep and goats stood tethered around our feet. Their droppings and urine made the stones slick.

Cages of doves and pigeons were stacked so close there was only the narrowest of passages between them. In that narrow passage the tradesmen stood, deliberately forcing all of the pilgrims to pause in their approach to God's House.

Money changers had their booths set up, offering Temple money in exchange for the foreign currency visitors brought. Only Temple money could be given as offering to God.

The pilgrims did not object to any of this. They were there for the festival, and the objects for sale were necessary. It was really a convenience to them to be able to buy there. Those who had been there before knew that this is the way that Passover had always been, at least during their lifetime. The merchants gathered at dawn on the first day of the week, and sold right up until dusk of the day of Passover. This is always the time of biggest profit for them. It makes up for the lean times. Each year there seems to be more merchants than the year before. This year they encroached the courtyard of the Temple itself!

Jesus walked up the stairs between the people and the animals, and stood in the center of the court. There he stood and looked at all that was going on. He had gathered a few of the fronds we had thrown down before him, and using these as an extension of his arm, he began to drive the sheep and goats from the Temple court. He moved with such authority that few questioned him. To those who did, he spoke quietly but firmly, "It is written, 'My House shall be a house of prayer,' but you have made it a merchant's market." The owners of the animals followed their property. Jesus spoke to the sales people who owned the doves and pigeons. "Get them out of here." He spoke as if he owned the place. "This is my Father's House," he said. The money changers were slow to obey him. They were under the protection of the Temple priests. But he overturned a few of their tables, and as the people scrambled after the rolling money, the others packed up and moved away.

They didn't go far. They simply moved out of the range of Jesus. They set up shop again in the market place, and outside the walls of the city. I am certain they made as much money there. With them gone, the Temple Court became relatively much more quiet, a place where Jesus could teach. It was there he taught on the second, third, and fourth days of the week.

In the evenings we gathered in the Garden of Gethsemane to hear him teach us. We women were permitted to sit in the circle among the twelve men Jesus had selected as his chief disciples, and several other men who followed as we did. Jesus taught as if he didn't have time enough to tell us everything. Several times he said he was about to leave us.

"Where I go you know, and the way you know," he said.

My Jude replied, "Lord, we don't know where you are going. How can we know the way?"

He held silence for a long time. He reminded me of my old shepherd friend from Bethlehem. "I am the way," he said.

"I am the truth," he said.

"I am the life," he said.

We were confused. He was so still. He wanted us to understand him so much. "No one comes to the Father but by me." he said.

He saw we didn't understand. And he knew his time was running out. He said to us who were his close companions for this long time, "If you had known me, you would have known my Father also," and we looked at him, and realized we had not really tried to know Jesus. Each of us had come to lean on him, to trust him, to love him for the things he did for us. But we had not tried to *know* him.

Who was he?

What did Jesus want?

He spoke again. He repeated himself. "If you had known me, you would have known my Father also; from henceforth you know Him and have seen Him."

Philip, the only Greek Jew from among the disciples, said to Jesus, "Lord, show us the Father, and we shall be satisfied." It took courage for him to say what we had all been thinking.

Jesus was so patient with us! He spoke again, "Have I been with you so long, and yet you do not know me, Philip? He who has seen me has seen the Father." He stopped speaking, and looked at us, knowing that Philip had been our spokesman. "How can you say, 'Show us the Father?' Do you not believe that I am in the Father, and the Father in me?" We hung on each word. We knew it was important. He spoke very slowly, and he emphasized each word. It was as if we were little children and he was the Father telling us a very important message.

My Jude asked him, "Lord, how is it that you will manifest yourself to us, and not to the world?"

Jesus answered, "If a man loves me, he will keep my word, and my Father will love him, and we will come to him and make our home with him. He who does not love me does not keep my words; and the word which you hear is not mine but the Father's who sent me.

"These things I have spoken to you, while I am still with you. But the Counselor, the Holy Spirit, whom the Father will send in my name, he will teach you all things, and bring to remembrance all that I have said to you. Peace I leave with you; my peace I give to you; not as the world gives do I give to you."

He spoke of peace, yet we could see He was troubled. He left us then, and we didn't see him until after dawn of the next day.

That was the day he directed Matthew and Judas Iscariot to make arrangements for the Passover supper. A room was found and prepared, and he and his disciples gathered together in the old part of Jerusalem, where King David lived centuries ago.

Several of us women arranged to serve them. It was a festive occasion. Passover always is. To remember the time when Moses and his people were protected as the Angel of Death passed over them and struck down the first born of the Egyptians, is to look back through all of our ancestors and see God's love for us. The Angel of Death has been stopped from destroying our people. We are God's children. We were created by Him. We live forever under His protection. Moses was a great prophet and leader. Indeed he was.

Other great prophets have arisen and shown us God's light. Elijah, Elisha, Isaiah, Jeremiah, Ezekiel, Daniel, have been giants in their time. And each has walked with God. This night we knew we were in the presence of God in a way that none of them had ever been. Jesus was sitting in our midst.

As supper began, he took the loaf of bread, gave thanks to the Father, and broke it. Then he passed it around to the disciples, and said, "Take and eat this. It is my body which is broken for you. Do this to remember me."

Suddenly the memories of his ministry with us came rushing back. We remembered the bread he had broken that had multiplied to feed thousands who had come to hear him preach. Greater than Moses, he was, and the crowds followed him, expecting him to do it again and again. But he told them they would have to eat him! He told them he was living bread. Now this bread that he had blessed and broken was passed from one disciple to another, and the leftovers we women ate reverently and gratefully.

A thought came to me then that we and Jesus were somehow united in a single body. Each of us who had eaten of the bread was part of the total loaf. All of us together were the body of Jesus. Yet he was sitting there among us, enjoying our fellowship with him.

Then he shocked us. "One of you will betray me," he said. The disciples looked into themselves, and each knew that he was capable of doing just that. Each asked the same question of Jesus.

"Is it I? Lord, is it I?"

Jesus did not reply. He talked of the great desire he had had to celebrate this Passover with us. "I was born for this," he said. None of us could understand him.

John, the younger son of Zebedee, the youngest of the disciples, leaned against Jesus and rested his head on Jesus' shoulder. "It is good to be here with you, Rabbi," he said.

Simon Peter motioned to John. "Get him to tell you who is his betrayer," he said.

John asked, and received an answer. "The one who dips his hand in the dish with me," Jesus said. John told us that later on. He said he saw Judas Iscariot dip his piece of bread in the dish with Jesus. This was not the bread Jesus had broken before.

I always liked Judas Iscariot. He was the only one of the twelve who was not a Galilean. He came from Kerios, a city here in Judah. Perhaps my being from Judah made me more friendly with him. Judas was a quiet man, and he watched Jesus more closely than did any of us. He seemed to have been waiting for something. Once Jesus declared himself the 'Son of God' and accepted Simon Peter's statement that he was the 'Christ,' the anointed one, the holy one of God, it seemed that Judas was more and more excited by an inner knowledge of his own.

Judas and Simon the Zealot, who have worked diligently with the Zealot party to overthrow the Roman enemy, had surely been expecting Jesus to step forward as their general. The talk he has given us of his being killed by his enemies did not set well with Judas and Simon. Though it may be that Simon considered Jesus could prove himself even greater by dying and rising to life than he has by raising Lazarus.

Jesus surprised us again. He stood up, and interrupted the meal by setting out to wash the feet of each of his disciples. This is a servant's role, and though it had not been performed by anyone as they entered, that was the time it should have been done. Feet that have walked the dusty unclean streets of the city should be washed clean before they walk on the floors of a clean house. Jesus seemed to be rebuking the host of the house for not having provided this kindness to all of the guests. But he didn't say that. He simply removed the sandals of each of the disciples in turn, and carefully washed their feet in the basin of water we women provided him. Equally carefully, and gently, he dried those feet that had grown callouses following him in mountain and desert across our land.

We were especially quiet throughout the time of Jesus' performing this work. Each disciple looked glad, yet terribly uncomfortable as Jesus washed him. Each watched the others receive the gift. Judas nearly broke down.

Simon Peter refused at first. "Lord, do you wash my feet?"

"What I am doing you don't know now, but afterward you will understand," Jesus replied.

"You will never wash my feet," blustered Simon.

"If I do not wash you, you have no part of me," Jesus paused and waited. He has never done anything for us unless we have agreed to let him do it. He looked into Simon Peter's eyes and waited.

It didn't take long. This was the disciple who had long ago said, "Lord, to whom shall we go? You have the words of eternal life." To have no part of Jesus, and to have Jesus have no part of us? It is impossible to contemplate. Yet for the forty hours he was in the grave, we contemplated nothing else.

Simon Peter capitulated. He came all the way. If washing his feet made him a part of Jesus, total immersion would make him completely with Jesus, give him a totality of Jesus. "Lord, not my feet only, but also my hands and my head!"

Jesus knew that each of the disciples had prepared himself for Passover. All were bathed, and all had on their cleanest and best clothing. This that he was doing was a ritual offering. "He who has bathed," he said, "does not need to wash, except for his feet, but he is clean all over. And you are clean, but not all of you."

A spirit of pride entered into me, and I welcomed it. All of the disciples had received a gift from Jesus that he had not given me. He washed their feet. But I had the blessing of having washed Jesus' feet twice. Not one of them had ever performed such a service to Jesus. Jesus did not ask this of them.

Jesus said to them, "You call me teacher and Lord; and you are right, for so I am. If I then, your Lord and teacher, have washed your feet, you also ought to wash one another's feet. For I have given you an example, that you should do as I have done to you."

Then I remembered. I have never washed the feet of any of the disciples. My pride collapsed!

"If you know those things, blessed are you if you do them," said Jesus. All of us followers have work to do before that blessing comes.

Still, I believe I am the only one of Jesus' followers who has washed his feet. The joy I had in serving him thus has remained with me every day since. Oh how I love Jesus!

After supper Jesus took a large cup of wine, gave thanks, and then gave it to his disciples. "Drink this!" he said. He spoke with such power and authority that they all stopped their private conversations and looked at him.

"Drink this, all of you," he said. "It is my blood of the new agreement, the new Covenant. It is shed for you, and for many. It is poured out for the forgiveness of sins, yours, everyone's, all sin." They looked at him with no understanding. I looked at him in the same way.

Jews don't drink blood!

Jews are not cannibals! Eat his flesh! Drink his blood! How can anyone understand that? We loved him and we knew he was in terrible distress over something. His teaching that whole evening was impassioned. Each word burned into our hearts.

But none of us could understand this saying.

And Jesus knew it. He said the same thing about the wine that he had said about the bread. "Do this in remembrance of me." "Do this as often as you drink it to remember me."

That we could understand a little. Every time we drink wine, we will recollect Jesus. Every time we eat bread we will recollect Jesus. That way, when he is away from us, we will have a living memory of him with us. When two or three of us gather together and break bread we will think about Jesus. We will talk about Jesus. Such activity will bring us happiness.

Shortly after supper Judas Iscariot left. Jesus said something to him just before he went out, but I didn't hear what he said. I have seen Judas only once since that night. He was standing beside the road that led to Jesus' tomb when Mary, Joanna, Suzanna and I were on our way to anoint Jesus' body. He stood there and watched us as we walked by, but he didn't say anything to us. We were too absorbed in our mission to say anything to him. Someone found his body a few hours later in the valley of Gehenna, near the city dump. He had hung himself there.

Then Jesus left with the other eleven. I knew where they were going, to the garden of Gethsemane. But I chose not to follow them. Jesus' mother, Salome, and I stayed to clean up after the meal, and then we left for our homes, each to her own place. The night was chill, and I shivered a little, drawing my cloak around me as I walked down the hill, through the Kidron valley, across the ancient cemetery, and wound my way up the pathway that leads over Olivet to my home. I passed within a hundred cubits of the garden where they were resting, and might have stopped. But something told me to go on home. I climbed wearily, glad that there was but one more day before the Sabbath rest.

27

Mary Magdalene

The worst day of my life, perhaps for the life of all mankind, began with a pounding on our door. Pounding! Pounding! I awoke and saw it was still dark outside. Who was the importunate intruder? I heard Lazarus call.

"Yes? What is it? Who is it?"

A muffled voice responded. The door opened and shut. A whispered conversation loud enough for me to know there was terrible tension brought me fully awake. Then there was someone at my door!

"Mary! Mary! Wake up! Its urgent!" Lazarus called me. Was it Jude I heard with him? I covered my body in a loose wrap, and opened my door.

"What is it?" I waited impatiently for an answer.
I saw that it was Jude standing behind Lazarus.

Lazarus waited for Jude to speak.

Jude worked to catch his breath. It was obvious that he had been running, running hard. "Oh Mary, Mary!" He paused and took another slightly less pained breath. "The soldiers came to the garden. Temple soldiers came. Roman soldiers came. There was a fight, and I ran away. Jesus and the others are killed or captured!" He slumped down, and placed his head in his hands. His fear was contagious. It flooded our hearts.

Questions filled my mind. "What has happened? What shall we do? Shall we run? Shall we hide? Shall we fight?"

Martha joined us. Practical woman that she is, she led us to the kitchen and set out some bread and cheese. Martha can make anything livable by performing her function as hostess. But before we could compose ourselves, there was another knock on the door.

This time we opened to Andrew. He rushed in and cried, "They have taken Jesus captive!" He looked at us wildly, and said it again. "They have taken Jesus captive!"

Lazarus took charge. "Tell us what happened," he said. Andrew began, only to be interrupted by a third knock. James and Matthew came in together. Young John Mark, the son of a good friend in Jerusalem, slipped in behind them. He was naked! Lazarus found him a garment.

"I woke up and there were soldiers all around me," said John Mark. "I jumped and started to run, and they caught me! But I wriggled out of my shirt and ran away."

They each told of their experience, and we added them together. We grew sure of but one thing. Those who were with us in our kitchen were alive. It was difficult to piece together what else happened. But we did learn that Judas Iscariot came to the garden leading the Temple guards.

We learned too, that most of the disciples ran away.

We were fairly sure that Jesus had been arrested and taken somewhere.

But we didn't know what we should do. We were afraid to venture out, and we were afraid to remain in our house. If Jesus had been arrested, would they not come and arrest us all? We decided to go out and to enter the streets of the city as soon as the gates opened. We would go in groups of two and three, and seek news of the Master, and of the others. We chose a place to meet, the Damascus gate, whenever we knew something about what had happened.

Andrew, Martha, Jude, and I left first. We were well on our way before the dawn, and we made our way to the south side of Jerusalem. We found a place where we could watch Caiaphas' house. We knew the Temple guards would be coming and going from there, reporting to him, the High Priest.

As we arrived, we heard the crowing of a rooster, proclaiming the beginning of a new day, the sixth day of the week, the day God created man in His own image.

Someone ran toward us. We stopped and slipped in among some bushes behind the road. The footsteps slowed to a walk, and then stopped altogether. We saw the figure of a man leaning over the wall, looking down into the black valley below. The man was weeping. He sobbed as if his heart would break. I recognized him, and stepped from our hiding place. "Peter?" I asked.

"Simon," he replied. "I have betrayed him! Just as he predicted, I have betrayed him! I have denied him three times! Three times in the last hour! I am a miserable coward." He walked away, leaving me. Andrew and Jude followed after him.

Martha and I crept closer to the house. I was amazed at my sister's bravery. We were soon standing on the edge of a gathering of onlookers. As we arrived, we saw Jesus, bound with ropes, being led away by the Temple guards. John bar Zebedee followed behind with the crowd of curious onlookers. There was a little light in the east, but a number of people were carrying lamps or torches to light the way. We became a part of what looked like a lovely string of fire flies that wound its way toward the Temple and Herod's palace. We fell in behind John. He was crying.

"They hit him in the face!" he said. "They blindfolded him, and they hit him again and again. They mocked him. Caiaphas let them!"

"Where are they taking him now?" I asked.

"To a trial by the council."

"But it is barely dawn! It is two hours before breakfast!"

"There will be enough Pharisees and Sadducees to convict him," John said. "There is to be no justice here. This is to be a convenient and quickly completed execution. They don't want to try him. They want to kill him." John is so young. Yet he understood the wickedness of the priests in power.

We followed behind our Master. In only a few minutes we were standing with the crowd in front of the council chambers. Jesus was led in. John, apparently fearless, surely foolhardy, followed. Somehow he gained access.

In moments John returned. He shrugged his shoulders in silent eloquence. Jesus had already been tried, convicted, and sentenced. We walked to the governor's quarters near the Praetorium.

This time we were ahead of the crowd. We watched Caiaphas and Annas, his father-in-law, walking ahead of Jesus. The Master walked between two guards, who walked ahead of a growing number of onlookers. When they reached Pontius Pilate's house, they knocked on his door. They spent some time convincing a servant that he should waken the Governor. Then, after a time, Pontius Pilate appeared. His hair was uncombed, his eyes filled with sleep.

"Now what?" he growled.

The high priest and Pilate argued for several minutes, and then the parade started out again, this time for the Jerusalem home of Herod Antipas of Galilee. Jesus' home is in Galilee; therefore, it was Herod's function to try him. Such must have been the reasoning of Pilate. Though everyone knew Herod had no more authority in Jerusalem than do the priests. The decision would have to come back to Pilate.

The sun rose as we walked to Herod's palace. Jerusalem appeared again in the dawn to be built of burnished gold, its stones absorbing and then reflecting the sunlight. But we didn't notice the beauty that morning. We had eyes and minds for nothing but the terrible drama being played out before us. We stood in Herod's court, and watched him tease our Master.

A party had been going on at Herod's palace through the entire night. Herod's guests were still with him when Jesus was led into his court. "At last I meet you, Jesus," Herod said. "Perform a little miracle for me. Entertain my guests before we break our fast."

Jesus remained silent.

Herod's men practiced a cruel persecution. They placed a robe of Herod's on Jesus, the purple robe of royalty. Someone put a reed scepter in Jesus' hand. Someone else spit in Jesus' face.

Jesus remained silent, and Herod grew tired of the game. He had no fun playing with the man before him. I saw Jesus look directly at Herod. I know what Jesus' eyes can do. They can look right through you. Perhaps Herod suddenly remembered how he had John the Baptizer, Jesus' cousin, beheaded. Herod looked uncomfortable, and he sent Jesus back to Pilate.

Back we trudged. We walked miles already that day, and had little sleep the night before. For the moment, my fears overcame my fatigue, and I assume that is true for the others who walked with me. I didn't even notice that Jude had come back to us, and that he held my hand as we walked. Yet, in time, I did notice, and wondered which of us was giving strength, and which receiving it through that contact.

Jude told me that Andrew was looking out for Simon Peter. I accepted that, but had no room in me to think about anyone but Jesus.

Pontius Pilate was very short tempered with the priests. He took Jesus into a private room to talk with him. In only a few moments he came back. "I find no fault in this man," he said. "I will have him flogged, and let him go." I cringed at the thought, yet found myself hopeful that such would be the end of the event. A Roman flogging is brutal, but one can take a beaten breathing body and nurse it back to health.

The priests wouldn't accept that. "Crucify him," they demanded. Several people in the crowd began to chant the same terrible phrase. "Crucify him. Crucify him."

Pilate remained seated in his judgment seat and had Jesus sent in to his soldiers. They sent him back in about half an hour, almost dead. He was wearing a circlet of thorns on his brow. Blood trickled into his beard. His clothing covered his body, but around the neck and shoulders we saw deep cuts and severe bruises. It was obvious Jesus could barely stand. I saw him blurred through my tears.

"Behold the man," Pilate said. He sneered at us all.

"Crucify him," the priests said again.

"I will give you a choice," said Pilate. "Here is Bar Abbas, a robber, a killer, one who practices sedition against our government, and here is Christ your King. I will set one free today. Which will you have?"

"Give us Bar Abbas!" the people shouted.

"And the king of the Jews?" Pilate mocked us again.

"Crucify him!" The cry grew more vehement.

"Save him," we cried. I was struck across the mouth by a Temple guard who was standing near us. The same happened to several disciples in the crowd. We looked, and each of Jesus' followers in the crowd had a contingent of priests, scribes, or Temple guards standing by. Our hearts were filled again with fear. The plotters had worked out the plan for Jesus' execution to the smallest detail. We could well be arrested in the next moments.

Pilate spoke again. "What evil has he done?"

"Crucify him," they shouted. We didn't dare cry our protests.

"Crucify your king?" Pilate played with them.

"We have no king but Caesar." They mocked him in return.

He called for a basin of water. "I am innocent of the blood of this man," he said. Then he ordered Jesus to be led away.

For the first hundred steps Jesus staggered along, carrying his cross beam on his shoulders. Then he fell.

I was close to him. I reached down to him and helped lift him to his feet. "Oh Jesus," I murmured, and burst into tears. Perhaps I am the cryingest woman who ever lived. Yet others about me were crying too. I don't know who they were. I had no idea of who walked beside me up that hill.

Jesus spoke to all of us then, though he looked right into my eyes. "Weep not for me. Weep for yourselves. The day will come when you will say to the mountains, 'Fall on us.' If they do this to a green tree, what will they do when it becomes dry? The day will come when those who have born no children, who have suckled no young, will be the ones who consider themselves fortunate."

The soldiers chose a stranger to the city, a man named Simon from Cyrene (we learned later), and made him carry Jesus' cross bar. Jesus looked his thanks at that man, and staggered along behind him, two steps ahead of the indifferent soldiers.

Jude disappeared again. I couldn't help thinking he was very good at running away! I found myself walking beside John. On his other side was Jesus' mother. Only recently had Mary, Jesus' mother, and I come to the point where we have had anything to say to each other. Surely there are no other women in the world who love Jesus more than we two. Yet our love for him had not made it fully possible for us to love and trust each other. She is a strong and courageous woman. All through Jesus' ministry she has known somehow that he was in terrible danger. At times she tried to dissuade him. That day she walked behind him on the way to Calvary Hill to witness his execution. Neither of us could believe it was happening. But it was! I knew her pain exceeded mine.

We arrived at the place of the skull, a cruel joke of a name for Calvary. The little rise just outside the west gate of the city affords a view of the Temple, of Mount Olivet, of the vast desert to the east of us. The hillside has several 'trees,' uprights standing stark and stained with bloody warning to us Roman subjects. Already two of the 'trees' had 'branches.' Two thieves, arms tied to their crossbars, and feet nailed to the post, hung there and watched us arrive.

The soldiers stopped us from walking further. Simon and Jesus ascended the little hill a few steps. Simon dropped his burden, and stepped back. He was a free man again.

Jesus, our Master, Mary's son, was stripped of his clothing. Naked, he was thrown down. His right arm was grasped in the strong hands of two soldiers. They held it against the rough wood. Another took a huge spike and a mallet. Five hard blows, and they released the arm. The spike held it fast.

It took even less time for them to impale the other arm. Then two men lifted and supported Jesus' body while two others lifted the cross piece and set it firmly on the upright. The center 'tree' had its 'branch.' Its ripe fruit was fastened securely to it. They placed Jesus' right foot over his left, and another large spike was driven through them both, deep into the wood. Jesus' blood flowed around the nails, dripped down the wood, and into the thirsty ground.

I watched every act. I did not turn away. I sensed that John had turned Jesus' mother's head into his shoulder, and that he held her there, protecting her from seeing what he and I witnessed.

Jesus hung there, almost unconscious, for several minutes. Then he spoke. "Father forgive them." He looked out at the soldiers who had just hurt him so, who had executed him already, though he still lived. He looked at the priests who managed the whole event, and who were sure they had won the day.

I thought, "They have won the game, maintained their positions of power, eliminated his threat of... of what?"

Jesus' look at them, said that he forgave. He looked at his mother, and at John, and implied that they were forgiven, and that they should forgive all. His prayer that he taught us came to mind. There on the cross was the ultimate challenge. Even as this was happening to him, Jesus forgave all his enemies.

Jesus looked at me. He expected me to forgive his enemies as I have forgiven my own. I lowered my eyes. This was asking too much. But I had to look back at him. He looked with such love at me, demanding the act of forgiveness. Hanging there naked, all of his wounds exposed, nailed firmly to his 'tree,' he continued to be in full control of himself. He continued to teach me.

"I thirst," he said. Rivers of living water are to pour out of our hearts. He has said so. Yet he thirsted there on his cross. A foolish soldier rushed up to give him some wine in a sponge. He moistened his lips, but did not drink. It was not liquid for which he thirsted. He thirsted for our obedience. If we forgive as he forgives, we will always be whole. But we will always be as vulnerable as he was. We will become sacrifices for men as he has done. There is no strength in me for that. I wonder if there is anyone strong enough to follow Jesus?

"Take your cross, and follow me," he said long ago. We didn't understand then. Now we understand, we cannot obey. It is too much.

I wept for Jesus. I wept for myself. My weakness was what separated us at last. I could not forgive as he forgave. I could die as he died. But as I go, I know I will hate my executioners.

A storm seemed to come out of nowhere. It grew dark. Jesus spoke again. "My God! Why have you forsaken me?" His eyes became wild and sick. They searched us. They searched the hills. They searched the sky.

The clouds boiled blacker still. A roll of thunder seemed to answer Jesus.

"It is finished," he breathed. He said one more thing, a child's prayer, "Father, into your hands I commend my spirit." Then he stopped breathing.

For a moment there was no movement. It was as if all life were gone and all had turned to stone. As Jesus stopped breathing, I stopped breathing.

When I inhaled again, everything moved at once. The earth trembled and shook. We all fell down to the ground. The crosses holding the dead and the dying shook above us. Lightning flashes crossed the sky. The wind rose. I was aware of all this, and not aware of it at all. I found I no longer cared. My heart was dead inside me. My Master was dead.

The quake ended. The storm stopped. An hour passed, and then another. Jesus' body hung limp on His cross. The hour grew late, perhaps the eleventh hour of the day. The soldiers came and broke the legs of the other two. They died quickly after that. The earth shook again, briefly, as the soldiers approached the body of Jesus. They looked at him and saw that he was dead. One of them, the Centurion, speared Jesus' side. He turned the head of the spear in the chest, and then withdrew it. The blood that flowed from this final wound stopped quickly. The heart had stopped. Indeed, it had no blood left to pump. Jesus' blood had been poured out in love for us all.

I stood there and wept alone. The soldiers were gone. John took away the Master's mother some time before. I watched as friends of the thieves came and took down their bodies. Jesus' body hung alone before me. It was as if I was paralyzed and could never move again.

But then Joseph of Arimathea came with his servants and they carefully took down the last body. I watched them, unable to do anything to help. Less than a hundred steps away lay the grave of Joseph, prepared for his body after his last day. Jesus' body was carried there. They wrapped it in grave clothes, provided by Joseph. Before they covered Jesus' head, I kissed it. Before they covered his feet, I washed them once more with my tears.

The mourning time we had for Lazarus was like unto a festival compared to the time of despair we experienced after Jesus' death. The night came on, and we let our Passover meal turn cold. We tasted no food. We drank no wine. The angel of death that passed over the Hebrew people had come back to take the most wonderful Hebrew in all history. We watched the night through. We said nothing of consolation to anyone. No one had anything to say in consolation to us. The thought came to me during the night.

"Pharaoh can rest in peace. God's first born son has died too. The angel of death plays no favorites."

The bright Sabbath dawn brought no light to us. We saw the light of the sun, and the beauty of the world it warmed, but we sat in darkness. Though we remembered Jesus statement, "Consider the lilies of the field... Consider the birds of the air." The lilies and the birds remained there, but we had no consideration of them. God may be the provider for them, and for us, but we saw it all as a sham. All would die whether he counts them or not. They would die no matter how beautiful their present looks, nor how bright their song. They would die without reason, just as Jesus had died.

The day passed. The Sabbath ended. The hours of darkness passed.

And now, the time of memory has passed.

It is the time of rejoicing again. How good it is to recall the day of Jesus' resurrection!

28

Mary Magdalene

Seven days have come and gone, and we have decided to meet again in the upper room where Jesus ate his last supper with us, and where we last saw him. It is the evening, the sun has set on the end of the first day of the week. The second day of the week has begun. It is now ten days since Jesus died on a cross on Calvary Hill.

All eleven apostles are gathered, including Jude. We women are there too, as are several men who were not chosen by Jesus, but have been followers of our Master.

We recount again and again our experiences with Jesus. Peter has seen Jesus. Two disciples who walked to Emmaus don't tire of telling their story of Jesus appearing and walking with them. All are courteous to me as I tell over and over again of my seeing him first, and knowing him when he spoke my name! We know he is alive. We know he loves us. We know he will fulfill his promise to us.

We enjoy our supper together, sing a few psalms, and rejoice in our fellowship. It grows dark outside, and we lock the doors. Our fear of the Pharisees grows less, but it is still there. We grow quiet. Each in his or her own way enters into contemplation, into recollection. Peace invades our hearts.

"Oh Jesus," I think. "Oh Jesus, I love you." My eyes rest on the face of my dear Jude, and I note his distress. There is no way for him to believe that all of us are deluded.

Yet there is not a way for him to believe that Jesus lives. Jude had stood and watched the events of nine days ago from a hillside some distance from us, but close enough to observe every detail. Jude knew Jesus had died. He knew the spear had pierced Jesus' side. He knew nothing comes back to life after its life blood has been poured out on the ground.

Now Jude sits among us as the only one who does not know Jesus is alive. He does sit with us though. He loves us, and wants to believe as we do. I walk over to him and sit down beside him. I place my hand on his shoulder.

"Oh Mary," he says. "Oh Mary, oh Mary, oh Mary." I want to hug his head against my breast and hold him tight. But he is rigid, locked in his unbelief.

We look up. Someone has come to stand beside us. Someone else has reached out to touch Jude. One of the others in the room? It must be. Yet, we know that no one else has moved. Jude looks up into the face of Jesus, and he gasps in awe — and yet — in unbelief.

Jesus holds out his hands. The bloody holes make me shudder and I close my eyes. But I must open them again. For I must see Jesus. He is fully aware of each of us in the room, but for this moment he concentrates on Jude. "Thomas," he says, "Twin. Reach out and put your finger here."

Jude does! He puts his finger into the hole in the wrist of Jesus, the place the nail was driven through Jesus' right arm. He takes his finger out, sees the blood on it, and puts it in the hole of the left arm.

"Put your hand in my side!" Jesus commands. He opens his robe. The hand of Jude is extended and enters Jesus' body almost up to the wrist. We know that no one can live with a wound like that! Yet Jesus is standing alive before us. Jesus looks with love on Jude as he does this. Jude takes his hand out, covered with moisture from Jesus' body. Jude falls forward on his knees.

"My Lord, and My God!" he says. "My Lord and my God! My Lord and my GOD!"

"You believe because you have seen and touched me," Jesus says. "Blessed are those who will believe who do not see or touch me."

But Jude is blessed right now as are we. For Jude is in the presence of our living Lord as are we. We all see Jesus before us. We can all touch him. We rejoice together with a great rejoicing. We sing. We sing more. Jesus sits among us, and loves us. He teaches us again what he taught before he died.

But now we understand so much more. For Jesus there is no more death. For us who believe in him and who love him there is no death. There is no way to understand such a thing with our minds. Yet our hearts now know. Death has always been a part of life. Death has always been around us. Aging, sickness, suffering, weakness, accidents, and battle lead us to death. But our friend Jesus has gone through death, and we are suddenly living without fear.

Jude looks at his reddened hand. He looks at Jesus. Adoration lights his eyes. Jesus looks at him and smiles. "You drank the wine I called my blood at the last supper I ate with you. Now taste and see! Taste and be a part of me!"

Poor Thomas Jude is pained. Jesus, his Lord has commanded him. Yet he has a dilemma. Though he loves Jesus, he has been taught to hate blood, to hate cannibalism. His love and obedience win. He puts his finger to his mouth. He touches the tip of his tongue to the tip of his finger.

Later Jude claims it was this moment that brought the greatest permanent change in him. I believe it.

After Jude does this awful thing of tasting the blood of Jesus, he stands up. His eyes become clear. He looks with great and assured calmness into the eyes of Jesus. "I will serve you and the Father forever," he says quietly.

Jesus smiles at Jude and loves him. Jesus smiles at each of us, and we know he loves us, the body of believers. Then he is gone again from our sight. But now Jude is in our midst, a living reminder of our Master. We are comforted.

29

Andrew

Dawn of the first day of the week was no better than the Sabbath had been. We knew our group would be breaking up that day. On old friend, Cleopas, talked of returning to his home west of Emmaus, on the coastal plain. He planned to leave before the sixth hour of the day so he could get home before dark. Another, Isaac of Jaffa, volunteered him company, and they packed their few belongings. Simon and I talked of returning to the fishing business. The Zebedee brothers listened, but were silent.

A pounding on the door after daybreak, and the first signal of the permanent change in our lives was heard. I opened the door myself, though I was trembling with fear when I did so. Before me were Mary, James' mother, and Joanna. Looking carefully about to see if there were any others outside, and assuring myself that they were alone, I let them enter.

"The tomb where they laid Jesus is empty!" Mary said.

Joanna added, "We saw angels at the tomb. They told us Jesus was not there; that he lives!"

"You're hysterical," one of the disciples said. I think it was Bar Tholomew. "Calm down. Tell us what happened."

"We went to the tomb this morning at sunrise to anoint Jesus' body," Joanna said. "We were worried that we wouldn't be strong enough to roll the stone away. But it was rolled back, and the entrance to the tomb was open. Oh, I was terribly afraid.

"But Mary Magdalene looked in, and we followed, and then was when the angels said Jesus was not there."

"What did the angels say," I asked. I wanted to believe.

"'Why seek the living among the dead?' they asked us. Then they reminded us of what Jesus told us before he died that he would rise on the third day after he was crucified."

I stood there amazed at what the women said. I couldn't think of anything to do with what they had told us. But Simon Peter and John jumped out the door and ran toward the cemetery. We sat down to await their return, very excited, but very confused.

When they returned, they said, "It is as the women said, the tomb is empty, and the linen cloths that covered him were still there."

"Did you see anyone there?" I asked.

"There were some guards moving about, and looking pretty worried about the body being gone. But they didn't try to stop us," John said.

"Mary of Magdala was there. She stayed behind," said Simon.

"What could it mean?"

"Who has taken the body?"

"Where would they put it?"

"Why would they take it?"

"I'm afraid!"

We were all talking at once, and growing more disturbed.

Then Mary Magdalene arrived. She was sobbing, hardly able to walk. Joanna and Suzanna pulled her inside. We stood around Mary, waiting for her to speak. But none of us was prepared to hear what she said.

"I have seen the Lord!" Her face was radiant. "I have seen the Lord!" she repeated.

"She's hysterical," I said. I turned away, But John took my arm and turned me back.

"Tell us about it, Mary," he said.

"The others left, and I turned away from the angels, and a man came up to me. I thought it was the gardener. He asked me the same thing the angels asked. 'Who is it you are looking for?' I said, 'If it is you, sir, who removed him, tell me where you have laid him, and I will take him away.' Then he said, 'Mary!' He called me by name. Then I knew him. I embraced him. But he made me let go. 'Do not cling to me, for I have not yet ascended to the Father. But go to my brothers and tell them that I am now ascending to my Father and your Father, my God and your God.'"

I remember her words as if she were saying them again in my ear at this moment. Though I am not sure if she told us that all at once, or if we learned it from her over an hour or so. She seemed to be in a trance. Her sorrow was gone, and an aura of joyful peace surrounded her.

A few of the disciples believed her, and some remembered something of what Jesus said about rising again on the third day. But I wasn't in a believing mood. "It is hysteria," I repeated. "She must be crazy with grief."

Several others agreed with me, but some began to believe, and there was a mixture of faith and knowledge, and hope and despair in that room for the next several hours. Around the sixth hour Cleopas and Isaac left us, heading home. I got my things together, and so did Philip. We were the first of Jesus' disciples. But we were nearly the last to believe he was risen from the dead.

But of course I knew he was risen when he appeared among us that night. Then I gave him some fish to eat, and I touched him, and I testify that Jesus bar Joseph was dead, but that he was alive again. I saw him several times during the next six weeks, talked with him, heard him tell us what we were to do with our lives.

"This is what is written," he said. "The Messiah is to suffer death and to rise again on the third day, and that in his name repentance bringing the forgiveness of sins is to be proclaimed to all nations. Begin with Jerusalem. It is you who are witnesses to it all."

I know I was glad he lived. I was glad, too, that he trusted me with such an assignment. But I knew I wasn't man enough to do it. I looked at him, about to ask, "How? How can we poor fishermen and tax collectors and artisans and farmers do this thing you direct?"

But he knew my mind as always. He answered before I could ask. Probably all the others had the same question in their hearts. "Mark this: I am sending you my Father's promised gift; so stay here in this city until you are armed with the power from above." We didn't know what he meant. But we believed his promise.

Then he left us again. One day we were with him on the eastern side of the Mount of Olives. Then he spoke to each of us, embracing us. One moment he was with us. The next he was gone. Some of the disciples say that two angels asked us why we were looking up, and promised Jesus would come back as he had left. But I didn't see or hear them.

For the next several days we rejoiced together, praying and praising God in the Temple, and feasting with one another at Mary and Martha's house. But sometimes we were in the upper room at John Mark's home. As Jesus told us to stay in the city, we made John Mark's house our headquarters. If he and his parents objected, they didn't say so.

Then one morning, the day of Pentecost, fifty days after Passover, we were praying together and rejoicing in the same upper room where Jesus broke the bread, gave the cup, washed our feet, before he died. As we sang and prayed, something awesome happened. A wind blew through the house, and a bright light shone over all our heads. We became so excited, so thrilled, so full of gladness we couldn't express ourselves. Still we had to shout out our joy! Words tumbled from our mouths in torrents.

God came to dwell in each of our hearts that day. He has remained in mine. The questions I asked about how I could do the work Jesus gave me to do were answered. God's spirit now works with me and within me, giving me power, giving me confidence.

As you know, I have served Jesus ever since, traveling through strange countries far to the north of our small land. God has given me a voice to speak, and hands to touch and to heal the afflicted. People hear my preaching, and they seek to know the Lord. When they are baptized, and I lay hands on them, they are blessed as we were that first morning of Pentecost.

It is joy for us to know the Lord. He is our life. The Kingdom of God casts its power over all the kingdoms of the Earth, and those of us who are citizens of God's Kingdom, with Jesus Christ our monarch, need fear no one or any thing.

Jesus is the living Christ. He is my Lord, and my Savior. Accept him by faith, my friend. Let him dwell with you. Let His and our Father's Kingdom come to you. Live with me the joyful life!

30

Mary Magdalene

Two weeks go by. None of us see Jesus. Peter grows restless. He says, "I'm going fishing," which means much more than that. We know he is thinking again of his home and family in Caphernaum. Several of the disciples choose to go with him. My dear Thomas Jude is one of them.

Lazarus, Martha, and I stay at home and wave goodby to them. Summer is fast approaching and they decide the desert route will be too warm. So they choose to walk north to Shechem. There they plan to pause for a few days to report to the people of Sychar who met Jesus and had him stay with them a year ago. What a story they will have to tell! Then they will go on up the valley of Sharon to the Jordan valley, to the Lake of Tiberias. They will be gone a long time. It will be five days' walk each way, and perhaps weeks of working there.

We settle into our household routine and wait. For what, we do not know. But we wait joyfully and patiently. We know now that the priests are not after us. They know of Jesus' rising from the dead, but they are claiming we stole his body and hid it somewhere else. And though we know they are looking for Jesus, alive or dead, we know that they can never kill him again.

It is good to have this one friend who cannot die.

Lazarus, Martha, and I spend many hours talking of this. "What was it like, Lazarus?" I ask. He smiles and teases me. In that way death did not change him. He loves us and twinkles his tenderness as he parries our queries.

"What was what like?"

"What was your dying like? What was death like? Please tell us."

He pretends reluctance, but soon begins. "It was a little like a dream at first. I knew you were about me and caring for me, and I couldn't respond to you. I felt I was leaving, and I wanted to say 'goodby.' For some reason I wanted to comfort you." He pauses and sits in contemplation, and Martha and I wait for him to go on. We see he is caught up in remembering, and we know this is significant, for it seemed that he had an experience to remember.

"I left my body, I remember that. I saw you weeping, and knew you were weeping for yourselves, and not for me. I saw you preparing my body for burial. But then I seemed to stop watching you. There was a bright light, and it approached me. I turned toward it, and felt myself glad. I didn't walk, but I went into that light. That light went into me and through me. I was a part of that light, and yet I was separate from it."

Martha and I sit and let his words flow through us. Is that a little like the light that flowed through him? There is comfort there. There is peace there. Lazarus seems to have no fear. The light he speaks of seems to be present in him now.

Martha remembers. "Jesus said, 'I am the light of the world.'"

Lazarus nods. "When I came back, it was at the call of Jesus. But I didn't seem to be coming back. I seemed to have been here all along. I didn't seem to be leaving someone else to be coming to Jesus' call. I seemed to be released by the same person as the one who called me. I believe I am the only one of us followers of Jesus who was not surprised to see him risen from the dead."

"But Lazarus," Martha said, "You mourned him with us!"

"Yes."

"Then why do you say you were not surprised?"

"Because I wasn't. From the time of his death to the time of his return was more a time of waiting than of mourning for me. That is what we are doing together here. We are waiting, for how long we don't know, but we are waiting. We are not mourning. I know that now. I didn't know it then."

"Yes," I exclaimed. "We are waiting like that now!" It is a real revelation to me.

"Yes and no," he hurries on to explain. "Now we know he is alive. We wait for him as we wait for our friends who have gone to Galilee. That was a waiting of stillness for me, I knew that Jesus' death had meaning too. I think I was simply waiting for the next evidence to piece that meaning together."

"And now that evidence is in?" Martha asked, looking like she was tired of the conversation and ready to return to practical housework again. "Now that evidence is in, what do you think his death and rising mean?"

"That he has power over death. That we, who are his friends have that power to protect us." Lazarus was as ready as Martha to end the conversation. "I am now waiting in assured anticipation that something even more meaningful will soon be happening to us all."

Now it is thirty-five days since Jesus rose. It is again the first day of the week, and we find our joy in Jesus' resurrection has dissipated. We haven't seen him since he joined us a week after his resurrection. The daily routine of living drains away our assurance. The priests continue in the Temple, unashamed at their complicity in the death of innocence. The Roman soldiers maintain their insolent occupation of our holy city. We see no change in our lives.

I begin to doubt. Even my own senses doubt. How could I see him and touch him and know him if he wasn't there? How could he have come through walls to be with us on the two evenings we saw him?

No one can come through walls.

Is it possible that we were all deluded?

But what of Thomas Jude's touching the wounds? What of all of us touching Jesus? What of our standing and watching him consume food in our midst? What of our hearing his voice saying, "Peace be with you?" What of our feeling that peace descend on us as we had never felt it before?

My faith wrestles my doubts. I stand as an observer, not knowing which will win.

Suddenly, running in the gate, all out of breath, is Jude. "We saw him again," he shouts, giving us the last clue we need to know that we are not seeing him now! Jude never looked more like Jesus. "We saw him again. We had breakfast with him by the Sea of Galilee just five days ago."

We gather around Jude, and while we are waiting for the other disciples to climb out of the valley to join us, he tells his story. Jesus met them beside the calm lake we have all known and loved. He fed them fish and bread. He broke bread with them. He queried Simon Peter about love again and again. This time Jude knew it was Jesus with whom they were talking, and so did John and Peter. But some of the others doubted until the breaking of the bread. Then all knew. And all sat at his feet and listened to him teach again.

Jesus told Peter to feed his lambs and sheep. He warned Peter that he would not always have control over his life, but would have to accept a leading at the end that would be most difficult. Jesus took John aside, and talked with him in private.

Then again Jesus left them. But they knew they must return to Jerusalem. The next visit, they were assured, is to be here.

We spend so much time in waiting! The eleven are with us, and many of the others who have followed Jesus have gathered here in Jerusalem. Now so many have seen him and talked with him that we know Jesus has something else that is special about him. Peter estimates that five hundred have talked with Jesus since his resurrection day. No one disagrees. Yet Jesus has been seen in western Galilee by the ocean, and by the Sea of Tiberias, by witnesses who claim they saw him at the same time on the same day! He has been seen in Jerusalem and in Jericho on the same day. The first day of his resurrection, he was seen in Jerusalem and a day's walk west of here at exactly the same time. Jesus is with us in his body in two places at once! Or if he isn't, he is able to traverse great distances in so short a time that it appears he can be a multiple person.

We talk of such things as we wait. While together in this way we grow more understanding and accepting of each other. None of us is jealous any more of anyone else. I remember how the disciples used to envy young John for being so close to Jesus. I remember how they all complained secretly about Peter being called Peter, having his name changed from Simon. They had asked, "What did Jesus mean calling that man a 'rock,' trustworthy enough to be built upon?" Such statements and questions are no longer heard. We all recognize each other's love and faith in Jesus, and we find that our love for each other grows each day.

Our waiting for Jesus is rewarded on the fifth day of the week. It is exactly forty days since he rose from the dead, and he is with us in body again. I don't stay with the group. I whisper to Jude to invite Jesus to my house for supper, and I hurry home to Martha. We begin to prepare a feast, and I help with all the energy that comes with joyful excitement. "Jesus is coming to our house," I tell myself. "He is coming to dine here." We scour the house in preparation. We prepare a sumptuous meal.

Then when all is ready, we climb the hill to the top of Olivet, to the very edge of our town of Bethany. There we watch Jesus and the eleven climbing past the garden where he prayed, and where once I suffered too. Up through the olive groves they walk. They seem so slow in coming. He is talking to them. They appear to hang on his every word.

They stop less than a hundred steps from us. Jesus embraces each of them. He holds the head of each between his two pierced hands, looks each in the eye, and breathes in his face. He then steps back, looks to the top of the hill to the three of us, for Lazarus has joined us, and he waves to us. He turns back to the eleven, raises both his hands, palms extended, pouring out a radiant blessing I swear I can see. Then he simply rises up out of their midst, floats into a cloud, and disappears from our sight.

We run down the hill to the disciples. But before we arrive, two great tall men, dressed in white, are standing there with them. We arrive to hear them speak.

"Why are you standing here gazing up into heaven?"

No one is brave enough to speak to them.

"This Jesus whom you saw taken into heaven will return in the same way from heaven."

The angels disappear without leaving. They are gone. I turn to Jude.

"He breathed on us," Jude says. "He told each of us to receive the Holy Ghost. He told us to wait here in Jerusalem until the Holy Ghost comes upon us all." Jude stops talking, and the other disciples take their turns.

"He is gone, but I feel he is still here. Something warms my heart, stirs in me with a gladness that I have only felt when in Jesus' presence."

"Let us return to the upper room and break bread there." And that is what we do. Martha and I pack up the feast to take to the upper room where we share the meal. The disciples break the bread, and are quiet for a moment as we all recall Jesus doing this simple act. Then they begin to laugh and sing, rejoicing as we have never seen them do before. Martha and Lazarus and I sit and watch in amazement. The disciples' happiness is as great as on any evening when Jesus was physically present. Somehow even more joy is expressed!

Those of us who are not among their number; my family, and others who join us as the evening progresses, are all pensive. We are a little jealous that the disciples have something we have not been given. We find ourselves still waiting; waiting for something, just as we waited before.

One would think these dear men were all drunk. We can't seem to get them to do anything but rejoice and sing. Finally their spirit is catching. We must laugh and sing with them.

Still...they have something we don't have, and we give up on the evening, heading home early....

Each day now we wait, and we await whatever we are waiting for in two separate groups. The eleven wait with some inner knowledge, some inner presence. They go off to the Temple every morning and return home every night. They pray and they praise. They praise and they pray. They seem never to tire of talking to God. They recall together things that Jesus said and did with them from the beginning of his ministry. They quote whole sermons he has given! They repeat his parables, and then repeat the special explanations he gave them.

I don't know this, of course, from being with them. I have to stop in the women's court as they go into the temple. But Lazarus can go in with them, and he does. He repeats to us what was said and done. "They review the scriptures. They search the scriptures. They find evidence of the prophecy of Jesus on almost every section of almost every scroll. Apparently Moses, Elijah, Isaiah, Daniel, and the minor prophets as well, all knew and predicted the coming of our Lord to dwell with us."

The disciples propose to replace Judas Iscariot. They seem certain that Jesus appointed twelve to judge the twelve tribes of Israel, and since Judas hanged himself the morning Jesus rose from the dead, they must replace him with one who has been with them from the start. Lots are cast between Justus BarSabbas, and Matthias. Matthias is selected, and they are twelve again.

It is wonderful that we have been permitted to be a part of the selection of Matthias. All hundred and twenty of us shared in the discussion and prayers before he was chosen. Each of us has an assurance that we are special close friends of Jesus. Some are of the seventy that he sent out two by two to visit the towns of Galilee. Some are the twelve, and some are members of their families. Some are the blood family of Jesus, and of the community of Nazareth. And some are important people in this community. Nicodemus and Joseph of Arimathea, and Joanna and Salome with a part of Herod's court. And the balance of us are a part of the community of the ones he has healed. Former lepers, and formerly blind persons, and formerly deaf people, and former adulterers, along with some who were raised from the dead. We all share a part of the life of this body of believers.

Two of our number have died and not come back. Judas, who left us and then committed suicide, we feel we have lost forever. The thief on the cross, Dismas, was known by many of us, and he knew of Jesus' work. He spoke to Jesus before he died, and Jesus comforted him, even then. Since Jesus is resurrected, we feel we may see Dismas again.

We just don't know when.

We don't know when we will see Jesus again either. But we know we want to see him. And we know he has promised to send his spirit upon us, to do something special for us here in Jerusalem. We gather together each day and enjoy the fellowship of one another. We are all in one accord in that we want Jesus back among us. We love him.

31

Mary Magdalene

Now fifty days have gone by, and it is the day of Pentecost. We are having a big feast, so we have arranged to meet in the upper room again. We gather together, some hundred twenty of us, to celebrate together. The room is crowded. We stand or recline with our bodies close to one another. Jude is close to me, on one side. Lazarus is in front of me, Martha beside me. Peter is directly in front of us, several steps away. Jude and Peter visit quietly as we listen.

"It is ten days," Peter is saying.

"Yes." The answer comes quietly, and with assurance. "I feel his breath in my face as much now as I did that day he ascended." Thomas is so much at peace with himself. I love him now as never before. I reach out and touch his sleeve. He smiles at me most tenderly, and my heart beats faster.

"I don't feel anything any more," Peter says. "But you experienced something different from the rest of us the day you put your hand in his side. You touched him at the very heart of his being. I saw you touch your tongue to the moisture on your hand thereafter. We all see that you have been different since that day." Peter looks around at the others. Eleven of our number received the breath of Jesus, and inhaled that breath into their lungs. Another one, Matthias added to their number only a day or so ago, has something more than the rest of us too. The eleven have each touched Matthias, and he has received something of their gift by the touch of their hands. I don't know why or how that happens, but it seems to happen as the disciples touch, as it did when Jesus touched the sick, or when they touched him.

"Gradually that feeling of well-being, of power in ourselves, has gone from me," Peter admits. "I know Jesus is alive. I know that God is with us, though invisible. But I am becoming nothing more than my own weak self again. As each day passes, I become less a part of Jesus, less a part of the twelve, and more my lonely and cowardly self. Something must happen soon."

We listen to Peter and the chill of fear begins to oppress our hearts. It is uncomfortable being with the disciples when they are so much more joyful than we are. But it is better to have that joy of theirs bothering us than to have them become empty as they were before any of us knew Jesus.

"Why don't we get everyone to join us in prayer," I say. "We need to feel that we are doing something special, talking to our God together."

"Let us break some bread as Jesus did," suggests Jude. "My brothers and sisters," he calls to the entire assembly. "Look, here is some bread. On the night our Master, Jesus, who we know is the Anointed Son of God, was betrayed, he took bread, gave thanks, and broke it." Here Jude breaks the bread into two pieces, hands one to Peter, and breaks off a piece from the other and hands the rest of it to me. Each of us breaks off a piece and hands the remainder of the loaf on to the one near us. As we do, we hold our portion in one hand, waiting for something.

"He gave thanks," Jude says again, and we begin to say our own thanksgivings under our breath, and begin to pray louder as our hearts are filled with the gratitude we have for having known Jesus. Then we are quiet.

Peter says, "He gave it to each of us and said, 'Take and eat this. It is my body that is broken for you.'" Tears well up in my eyes. I choke in memory of the broken body on the cross. "Oh Jesus, Jesus, Jesus," I moan. Others are weeping too.

"Do this in remembrance. Eat this in remembrance of me." Peter says this first. Then John and James and Andrew and the other ones who were with Jesus, who ate of that one broken loaf that night, say it in turn. And each eats it in turn. Each of us who served that meal that night, we four women who were there, each of us eats our piece of the broken body.

The others follow. All have been told of what happened that night of Passover. They have been told of Clopas and his friend who met Jesus and knew him in the breaking of the bread. They each eat their piece faithfully. It makes them one with us. It makes us one with them.

Jude pours some wine in a large cup. Peter does the same. "He also took the cup after supper and blessed it, and gave thanks for it," Jude says. Andrew continues, "He gave that to us too, and said, 'Drink all of this.'"

James, John's brother, says, "He said, 'All of you drink it.'"

We believe them both.

Simon the Zealot says, "Jesus told us, 'Do this in remembrance of me.'" We wait in silence a moment or two while the cups are passed. As each of us receives, we fall on our knees, or we raise up our hands, or we begin to sing, or we reach out and touch a neighbor with a fellowship that wasn't the same a moment before. We are all affected, every one of us.

A sound comes into the room that is not of our making. We listen to it, and we become a part of it. We listen to it, and it becomes a part of us. We participate in it, making our own sounds with it.

A gladness fills me such as I have never known before. I look at Jude and he seems to have fire rising right out of the top of his head! I almost scream, but there is no such thing as fright any more.

The others have tongues of fire too! We make more noise. Then we make more. We can't help but shout! Jesus said that if he stopped the people shouting the day he rode into Jerusalem on the donkey, the stones would shout instead. I believe that in this moment all of the stones of Jerusalem are shouting with us!

The space in that upper room is too confining. The noise is too deafening. We leap in the air, so many of us leaping up and down that we shake the building to its foundations. We pour out onto the street where we meet the festival crowds who have come running to see what disturbance we are causing, and why.

There we dance and leap and laugh and hug one another and we sing and we shout. There is absolutely no reason in any of us. We boil over with living waters of love for each other, for ourselves, for our God, for Jesus.

Oh yes! For Jesus!!! We bubble and boil over with love for Jesus. Someone asks me what has happened. I respond, "God is so wonderful. God has sent His son, Jesus, into the world. Jesus is the Christ, the Anointed one! He has saved us from our sins, from suffering, from death! Oh God! Thank you Jesus! Oh God! Thank you Jesus! He died for us! He rose for us! He is our dear and personal friend, and he and we will live forever!" I am out of breath, and have to stop for a moment.

"Are you from Libya?" the stranger asks.

I am stopped in mid shout. "No, of course not," I reply in surprised love. "I am from right here." The person walks off, looking puzzled.

Others come up to us. "What is it all about?" they ask. They are smiling at us. They can't help but be infected by our happiness.

Each of us tells someone. We have to talk! The more we talk of God, the more we find ourselves in the presence of Jesus.

"Oh Jesus. Jesus. Jesus. How I love you. How we love you!!!" The ***we*** of our love seems to make our individual love stronger.

There is something even more powerful than an awareness of an invisible Jesus with us. It is the same feeling we have always had in the Temple courts. Jahweh, our God Himself, is with us. He is loving us. He is filling us with Himself.

Jesus is right! He and the Father are one!

"This is amazing," someone says. "Several of them are talking in my native tongue."

"Mine too," says another. "And mine." "And mine." It is repeated by several. "How can this be?"

"They are just a bunch of drunks!" someone else says, and turns to walk away. I hear this man, and so does Peter.

He shouts louder than all of us. We stop making noise, and give him the opportunity to speak alone. But this in no way diminishes our overwhelming joy. We simply determine to stand together, without direction from any of us, we all stop and look at Peter, and listen to him, and support him as he speaks the mind of all of us.

The other eleven move to stand behind Peter to give him something of their courage, and of the Spirit they have. Peter has become the mouth, the spokesman for us all, the body.

Peter begins, "Fellow Jews, and all of you who live in Jerusalem, listen to me and let me tell you what this means. There men are not drunk as you suppose; it is only the third hour of the morning." Then he begins to quote scripture and to relate it to the life and death and resurrection of Jesus, our Christ. I have never seen Peter like this. He is strong and commanding, and exciting! He speaks with such strength and authority, and his voice carries to the farthest persons in the crowd. They listen to him. They pay attention!

They are concerned for their own lives, enough of them to say, "And what are we to do, then?"

Peter tells them, "Turn away from your sins, each one of you, and be baptized in the name of Jesus Christ, so that your sins will be forgiven, and you will receive God's gift, the Holy Spirit. For God's promise was made to you and your children, and to all who are far away - all whom the Lord our God calls to Himself."

That is it. God has sent His Holy Spirit, just as Jesus promised. Each of us has the Spirit of God with us now. God is right here. And I know it! I *know* He loves me! I feel Him telling me that! The wholeness I felt when Jesus drew out the demons from me and sent them away forever is the wholeness I feel again now. And more than that. *And more than that!*

As Peter finishes speaking, we find ourselves speaking to each of the people who comes forward to ask about Jesus. We tell of Him again and again. We lead people to be baptized. We use water from pitchers and water jugs near by. I know I baptized twenty or thirty people myself.

As this day ends, Peter estimates, "We must have baptized three thousand people!" We each walk to the place where we will rest that night. But each of us has the Spirit of God as our companion. Not one of us is alone. All of us rejoice. We are three thousand people who each has Immanuel, God with us, and we know that number can be multiplied indefinitely. Our Lord Jesus Christ is freed now to remain with each of us, always, as he said, "Even unto the end of the world."

Tonight I am alone in my home room with Jesus, and my heart continues to sing.

"Oh Jesus, Jesus, Jesus, I pray.
I sing in the morning. I sing all the day.
You're now here beside me. You're now deep within
I sing in pure happiness, Freed from my sin.

Oh Jesus, dear Jesus, good Jesus, my friend.
Will I find this happiness comes to an end?
How splendid this moment! How great is this day.
Oh Jesus, in Jesus, with Jesus I pray.

Oh Father in heaven, Holy your name!!
I know your dear Son! He calls me by name.
My love's in the open, no hiding at all.
Your love, it supports me, I know I can't fall.

Oh Jesus, Oh Father, your Spirit's in me.
I'm now without bondage. I'm now truly free.
Oh God, you do love me! Oh God, you are real.
How bear I this gladness? For strength I appeal.

Oh Jesus, Oh Father, Oh Spirit, with me.
We all are now one. My mind comes to see.
Your image created; your daughter, your friend.
To whom shall we go? Spread our love without end?"

I sing. I pray. I create with my Lord. The next day others come by here and we pray. We laugh together. We talk of the life Jesus has had with us, and the life he has with us now. We go throughout Bethany and proclaim Jesus risen from the dead. That surprises no one.

After all, Bethany saw the resurrection of my brother, Lazarus. They also see the glad faces on all of us. They know we cannot be pretending that Jesus is alive.

Most of our neighbors join us. They are baptized in the name of our Lord Jesus. The Holy Spirit descends on our town. Hallelujah!

Peter arrives. He takes me aside. "Mary," he says, "Thomas has left us. He has been called to go tell the world about Jesus."

"Which way did he go?" I cry out.

"To the East, several hours ago," he says. He looks at me with compassion. "You will never catch him."

"Oh, but I will, I will," I cry. For I know the Spirit has spoken to Jude as well. I know we are to minister together. I run to prepare for my departure.

I sing as I gather together the few simple things I will need for my journey. I will not be alone as I set forth to find Jude. Our Lord will be with me every step of the way. I know my life of service to the Father and to Jesus will be filled with joy.

32

Pontius Pilate

Autumn, Year of Tiberias — XXIII

Dear father,

Thank you for your recent letter. It came only yesterday, and I choose to take time to respond immediately. There is a ship leaving day after tomorrow, and I want to speed this epistle on its way.

The news you send of the untimely death of my step mother, and of your recent illness distresses me. Of course there is always danger of food poisoning happening accidentally, but surely you know how important it is to check the staff. You should surely know if it is possible someone is plotting against you. I wonder about the fortunes of my younger brother whom you have indulged all his life, forgiving him the most flagrant of pranks. Is it possible he had anything to do with the 'accident' of the poisoning?

Don't, please don't, let your heart rule your head in this matter, Father. Employ some trustworthy investigators. Torture a few of the slaves. Get to the bottom of this. Should it be 'only' accidental food poisoning, discipline the guilty cooks or vendors. But should it be as I suspect, let your wrath have free rein. Even if it is my brother who is the guilty man, have him executed — on the cross — as a public example.

Now, to the rest of your letter. You asked some questions about the trial and execution of the Nazarene several years ago. Did we finally find the body? No. We didn't. But you must recognize this is a very ancient land, Father. There are tombs in this country that date back thousands of years. The body of Jesus of Nazareth could have been taken to one of those ancient tombs, and laid to rest there. If that were so, none of us would ever have known its final resting place. In addition, there is a vast open land east of Jerusalem, a terrain that is so desolate and forbidding that only the wandering bedouin can find their way through it. Any dead body could be taken into that wasteland and deposited in a cave, the cave sealed over, and it might be centuries before a few undisturbed bones would be found.

Perhaps I could compare the problem of finding a dead body here to trying to find one in Rome. Were a body moved from its first grave in the catacombs, for instance, and placed in another location in that maze of corridors and rooms that have been occupied by the dead for centuries, who would be able to find it? Except by chance? The first weeks, of course, one would have the help of one's nose. But once the putrefaction process was complete, what then? Only interrogation of possible conspirators could be used effectively.

So, my father, since the body was never found, we must assume the body was transported away and hidden. Many of the man's disciples were questioned thoroughly, using our best methods of interrogation, and we learned nothing helpful. They maintained what the Priests said would be claimed, that the Nazarene rose from the dead.

You asked if Procula regained her mental balance. Yes and no. She has been a wonderful wife to me these past six years. She has not imposed the foolishness of the resurrectionists' teaching on me. But she has assured me she believes what she told me six years ago. She acts as if she is certain the Nazarene did rise from the dead.

Once I asked her to produce him for me. "If he is alive, then have him come and stand before me. He need not fear I will sentence him again." But she said something about his having ascended into heaven before the witnessing eyes of his most dedicated disciples.

Now isn't that convenient? The one place we could never look for him is in the clouds of heaven! She says the promise of angels is that Jesus will return from heaven, and then he will sit on his throne here forever.

I have not feared his return enough to notify Rome of the threat.

Still there have been some amazing things happening among the men and women who followed the Nazarene. Let me tell you of two that have affected our town of Caesaria, even the cohort of troops under my command. One has to do with a man called Philip who moved here to Caesaria about a year after Jesus was executed. This Philip is a Jew of Greek descent. Apparently he was an early follower of Jesus, but was never part of the inner circle of some dozen men.

About two months after Jesus was executed, on a day the Jews call Pentecost as it is fifty days after their Passover, there was a disturbance in Jerusalem. My chief centurion there, Magnus, reported that during the morning hours that day some hundred twenty of the Nazarene's followers were subject to a mass hysteria that seemed to affect crowds who gathered to hear them. Magnus reported that it was simply a reveling crowd who got started drinking at sunrise, or more likely, continued a wild party that began the night before.

Drunk or sober, they found courage to speak loudly and clearly of the crucifixion of Jesus. They blamed the priests! We were not accused! Only the Sanhedrin were called guilty, but of course the guilt was spread to all the people as they permitted themselves to be ruled by their priests. A large number of converts to the Nazarene's group were made that day. Some say as many as three thousand joined them. That is enough for us to pay attention, and we have watched them ever since.

With large numbers in their membership, the twelve principals began an organization. All were expected to contribute all they owned to be accepted as disciples. Even with that requirement, more and more people joined. As inequities developed in the distribution of food to the membership, especially to the widows, men were appointed to help. These men are called 'deacons,' or servants. They 'wait on table.' Apparently the twelve who are called 'apostles,' have more holy work to do, like praying and preaching.

Philip was one of the men appointed deacon, but as soon as he received the commission to wait on table, he went off to be a missionary. First he went to Samaria where he stirred the people enough to make us very nervous. Then he traveled to the south and east, eventually moving here. He chose to settle here. He is circumspect, a good citizen. But he preaches about a risen Jesus to anyone who will listen, and he has enough listeners to fill his house and his garden every seventh day.

There is no disturbance from him or his people. On the contrary, they are diligent workers, and act as if they really care for everybody. Procula has taken to going there, as has Ruth, the wife of my faithful centurion, Cornelius. Both women frequent the local synagogue too. Apparently a number of Jews here have come to believe in the resurrection of Jesus, with Philip the chief spokesman of that belief in this area.

I have questioned Cornelius at length, and find that he is most hopeful that Jesus is not dead. Cornelius still carries a feeling of great guilt at having been the instrument of death of a splendid human being, one who was totally innocent. Still, he doesn't strike me as having the blind faith in that impossibility that Ruth and Procula seem to have.

That is, he didn't until a few weeks ago. It was then that a man called Simon or Peter showed up here. The story is that Cornelius sent for the man when he heard of him in Joppa, the major city twenty miles south of here.

This Simon Peter came with six friends. (A possible bodyguard?) He preached about Jesus to Cornelius and his household. I know Procula was not there at that time, Whether Philip was there, I don't know, but I assume he could have been. It has been reported to me that something strange happened to the people while Simon Peter was speaking. I know that Cornelius was a changed man after that meeting. He changed radically from being an obedient and unquestioning soldier of Rome to being a man full of personal confidence, and with an assurance about him, as if he had a deep, inner power.

I called for Cornelius to come to my chambers for a private interview. You know that for him to be a member of our military, and a follower of another God than Caesar could cause a problem. I include a copy of that interview. I would appreciate it if you would give me your comments about it.

Pilate: Cornelius. This must be a formal inquiry. You understand that? Very well, we will proceed. Tell us for the record, your name, age, and function as a Roman Citizen.

Cornelius: My name is Quirilus Cornelius. I am thirty-seven years old, and have served faithfully as a soldier of Rome for the past twenty years. Ten of those years have been as Centurion, eight of them have been here in the land of the Jews.

Pilate: This inquiry is about your knowledge of a sect of Jews who believe a Nararene, one Jesus, is their king. What do you know of them?

Cornelius: I first heard of the Nazarene, Jesus BarJoseph, when I was traveling through Galilee and stopped at our barracks in Caphernaum. We were a cohort assigned to guard Philip, the Tetrarch of Caesaria Philippi, and the ten towns east of the lake of Tiberias. Claudius Silvus, the commander of the garrison at Caphernaum, told me of Jesus. The Nazarene was already a known healer among the Jews. Claudius told me that when one of his servants was ill to the point of death, he sent for Jesus, and asked for a healing of the servant. I am told a miracle occurred and the servant was made well immediately, though Jesus never touched, or even saw Claudius or the servant.

Pilate: When did you first see Jesus?

Cornelius: I never saw Jesus BarJoseph before the day I had him tortured and crucified at your order, your excellency. Though I know my wife, Ruth, saw and heard Jesus on at least two occasions.

Pilate: When you had him flogged and then crucified, did you note anything about the man that made him appear different from other condemned men?

Cornelius: Yes. He died better than any other.

Pilate: Tell me more.

Cornelius: At first he didn't impress me. He appeared despondent as any other man condemned to severe punishment. But my men and I noted

Jesus did not cry out when he was struck with the lash. He did groan, of course. And his flesh quivered as each blow was struck, and as the lash was withdrawn the lead tore skin and muscle away. We noted too that Jesus remained conscious throughout the beating, and that he looked at each of us whenever we stood in front of him.

Perhaps it was his eyes looking at us that made us work harder at the flogging. I even took a few flicks at him! Though that is not my regular practice. When we beat him a second time and one of my men braided a crown of thorns, I not only permitted it to be thrust down on the prisoner's head, I tapped the crown a few times with my sword. The thorns dug deep, and Jesus looked me in the eye as he received my blows.

Your excellency, Jesus was a man! He took the toughest of beatings without begging for mercy, and without once cursing any of us. Later, when we had him hanging on the cross, he actually spoke of forgiveness for us. You know how shaken I was by that event, sir. I needed the rest you ordered me to take. It may have been months before I was a good soldier of Rome again.

Pilate: Cornelius, you have served Rome well. You have been among the most trusted of my Centurions. Now we come to the more difficult questions. Will you answer me truthfully?

Cornelius: My word as a Roman Citizen!

Pilate: I am no longer sure what that means. But your word as a man whom I have known and respected since I became governor will do. What do you know of this Joshua of Nazareth or his followers since the day of his crucifixion?

Cornelius: Your excellency, I have heard much. For some time now my wife has been a part of a sect of the Jews who believe Jesus of Nazareth is a living Messiah; that he rose from the dead, and that his spirit is still with them. Those of this sect who live in Caesaria meet in the home of a man named Philip. He has brought his family here from Jerusalem, and he works for his living as a stone mason. At present he is working on the government building you ordered erected.

Philip, following the custom of the Jews, does not work on the seventh day of the week, their Sabbath. He and his family spend that day in rest and prayer. Frequently he worships at Synagogue on that day, but not always. In the evening, when their Sabbath is over, people gather at his home to talk about Jesus of Nazareth, and to pray together. I have attended those gatherings with my wife, and I have been welcomed there.

Pilate: Don't they know you were the one who executed Jesus? Don't they know you were the one who drove your spear into his side?

Cornelius: They know. But these are strange people. They seem to have no anger toward me, or toward you. They believe we were simply obeying God by following God's plan.

Pilate: Their god planned, then, to have Jesus killed? Did this god hate or fear this Jesus?

Cornelius: I can't explain these things to you. I am just beginning to learn of Jesus and of the Jews' God. But they claim Jesus is, or was, God's son. They claim that Jesus died so we could live.

Pilate: That is most difficult. Can you explain that to us? He died so who could live? The only life I know he saved was that of BarAbbas! I had something to do with that!

Cornelius: Perhaps Philip could explain that, sir. I only know a little of the faith of the Nazarene sect, though I now number myself as one of them. I can tell you that prophets from hundreds of years ago predicted the Messiah's suffering and death, and Jesus' punishment and crucifixion appear to be described by them as if they were witnesses. I have memorized some of their scriptures that were translated into our Latin language. May I quote them?

Pilate: (I nodded my acquiescence.)

Cornelius: A prophet named Isaias said, "Here is my servant, whom I strengthen — the one I have chosen, with whom I am pleased. I have filled him with my spirit, and he will bring justice to every nation. He will not shout or raise his voice or make loud speeches in the streets. He will not break off a bent reed, nor put out a flickering lamp. He will bring lasting justice to all. He will not lose hope or courage; he will establish justice on the earth. Distant lands eagerly wait for his teaching."

Again the same prophet says, "The Lord says, 'my servant will succeed in his task; he will be highly honored.' Many were shocked when they saw him; he was so disfigured that he hardly looked human. But now many nations will marvel at him, and kings will be speechless with amazement. They will see and understand something they had never known.

"The people reply, 'who would have believed such a report? Who would have seen the Lord's hand in this?' It was the will of the Lord that his servant grow like a plant taking root in dry ground. He had no dignity or beauty to make us take notice of him. There was nothing attractive about him, nothing that would draw us to him. We despised him and rejected him; he endured suffering and pain. No one would even look at him — we ignored him as if he were nothing.

"But he endured the suffering that should have been ours, the pain that we should have borne. All the while we thought that his suffering was punishment by God. But because of our sins he was wounded, beaten because of the evil we did. We are healed by the punishment he suffered, made whole by the blows he received. All of us were like sheep that were lost, each of us going his own way. But the Lord made the punishment fall on him, the punishment all of us deserved.

"He was treated harshly but endured it humbly; he never said a word. Like a lamb about to be slaughtered, a sheep about to be sheared, he never said a word. He was arrested and sentenced and led off to die, and no one cared about his fate. He was put to death for the sins of our people. He was placed in a grave with evil men, he was buried with the rich, even though he had never committed a crime, or even told a lie.

"The Lord says, 'It was my will that he should suffer; his death was a sacrifice to bring forgiveness. And so he will see his descendants; he will live a long life, and through him my purpose will succeed. After a life of suffering he will again have joy; he will know that he did not suffer in vain. My devoted servant with whom I am pleased, will bear the punishment of many and for his sake I will forgive them. And so I will give him a place of honor, a place among great and powerful men. He willingly gave his life and shared the fate of evil men. He took the place of many sinners and prayed that they might be forgiven.'"

Pilate: Perhaps you can have a copy of that made for us, Cornelius. We would study it. Now tell us. You say you have joined the sect of Nazarenes. What occurred that you would do such a thing? Surely you have gods enough in Rome. This God of the Jews has been powerless against us.

Cornelius: I thought that, sir, until I began to pray with my wife at the Synagogue, and to read their scriptures. The God of the Jews has been their God for over two thousand years. He has been with them through feast and famine, war and siege, peace and harvest. Their God has been with them. He has not abandoned them. He chose them to be his people long before there was a civilization on our peninsula, before there was a village on the hills where Rome now stands.

Pilate: So their God is old. He is also impotent. He offers them no protection, no strength. Our gods are young and powerful. They have shown us we have a destiny.

Cornelius: You forget, your excellency, that we both saw the power of their God on a certain Friday six years ago. When Jesus died, the earth and the heavens were shaken by that power.

Pilate: Yes. I had forgotten. It was a remarkable coincidence that the Nazarene should die just as the earthquake occurred and the severe storm broke over the city. If that is evidence of the power of their God, we must concede he does control winds, rain, and the heart of the earth. But we question his having or using his power in the affairs of mankind! Continue. We will listen. Tell us more of how and why you have become a Nazarene.

Cornelius: I often prayed with my wife in Synagogue. Then I began to pray with her and with our children in our home. It was during this time I came to know that the Lord of all creation, including all mankind, was the Lord to whom I prayed. His law for all his people is that they are to love and serve one another, as well as to love and serve him. As we people of the Earth come to obey that command, we will find it a peaceful place, free of the terrible troubles we note all about us.

My prayer time increased, and I found myself praying alone in my room for at least two hours a day. I did not neglect my work or my family. But I found I could not stop basking in an awareness of God's presence.

Then one day as I was praying, I was given a message. It was about the ninth hour of the day. I distinctly saw the angel of God come into the house and call out to me. He called me by name. 'Cornelius.' I stared at the vision in terror, and exclaimed, 'What is it, Lord?' 'Your offering of prayers and alms,' the angel said, 'has been accepted by God. Now you must send someone to Jaffa and fetch a man called Simon, known as Peter, who is lodging with Simon the tanner whose house is by the sea.' Then the angel left me.

Pilate: What then did you do? You know, Cornelius, that you sound mad. Still you look sane enough. But I do note that there is an aura about you, a change in your manner, that commands attention.

Cornelius: I called for two of my slaves, and for my second in command, who is a devout Jew we inducted into the army ten years ago. You know him. He is Alpheus BarJoseph. I sent them to Jaffa to find this Simon called Peter.

Pilate: Did you tell them an angel spoke to you?

Cornelius: Yes, I did. They didn't say what they thought of that. They obeyed my order immediately however. They found Simon Peter the next day. He was on the roof of Simon the tanner's house where he had been praying. When the men arrived, Simon Peter told me later, the same angel of the Lord, or Spirit of God, spoke to him. 'Hurry down,' the spirit said. 'And do not hesitate about going with them. It is I who told them to come.'

The next day Peter was ready to come with them, and he chose to bring along six of the Nazarene sect from Jaffa. They reached here the following day, and I was waiting for them. I had my family and close friends waiting there with me. When Peter came, I went out to meet him, knelt at his feet, prostrating myself.

Pilate: You did what? You, a Centurion of Rome, knelt before a Jew of Israel? You prostrated yourself before him? Well! We'll have something to say about that later. Go on now. What did Simon Peter say?

Cornelius: He helped me to my feet. He said, 'Stand up. I am only a man after all!' He came with me into my home. There he said, 'You know it is forbidden for Jews to mix with people of another race, and visit them. But God has made it clear to me that I must not call anyone profane or unclean. That is why I made no objection to coming when I was sent for; but I should like to know exactly why you sent for me.' I told him, 'Three days ago I was praying in my house at the ninth hour, when I suddenly saw a man in front of me in shining robes. He said, 'Cornelius, your prayer has been heard and your alms have been accepted as a sacrifice in the sight of God; so now you must send to Jaffa and fetch Simon known as Peter who is lodging in the house of Simon the tanner, by the sea.' So I sent for you at once, and you have been kind enough to come. Here we all are, assembled in front of you to hear what message God has given you for us.'

Then Peter addressed us: 'The truth I have now come to realize,' he said, 'is that God does not have favorites, but that anybody of any nationality who fears God and does what is right is acceptable to him. It is true, God sent his word to the people of Israel, and it was to them that the good news of peace was brought by Jesus Christ — but Jesus Christ is Lord of all men.' He then went on to tell of the ministry, death, and resurrection of Jesus Christ. He proclaimed, 'All who believe in Jesus will have their sins forgiven through his name.'

It was that statement of forgiveness that struck me, your excellency. I have been haunted these six years since crucifying Jesus knowing what was my part in his death. I obeyed orders, of course. But I shared in the cruelty of the beatings, as I shared in casting lots for his clothing. Though I heard him speak of forgiveness from the cross, I did not feel forgiven. Knowing that I had done many other terrible things in the past, I couldn't believe a righteous God would ever forgive me.

But as Peter spoke, the Holy Spirit came down on all of us listeners. The people who came with Peter from Jaffa were astonished that the Holy spirit would fall on us. But they heard us speaking ecstatically of the greatness of God! It wasn't just me, your excellency. It was Ruth, my dear wife. And it was our children, and our slaves, and our servants as well as our friends among the soldiers, and their wives. We were all overwhelmed by the presence of God. We all experienced a feeling of love, a feeling of joy, a feeling of immense peace and of powerful assurance.

Peter said, 'Could anyone refuse the water of baptism to these people, now they have received the Holy spirit just as much as we have?' We were all baptized then, in the name of Jesus Christ.

Pilate: What is this baptism. What is this Holy Spirit? What did these Nazarenes do to you? Did you let yourself be cut as they do their infants?

Cornelius: We were not circumcised. We were baptized. Water was poured over us, drenching us. I am a new member of the sect, your excellency. I can't explain what was done, or why, except that Jesus Christ declared his followers must be baptized with water and the Spirit. Since we already had the Spirit, Simon Peter gave us the water baptism as well.

Pilate: You know that Jesus died. You know the grave was opened and the body stolen early the first day of the following week?

Cornelius: I know the grave was open. I believe Jesus BarJoseph rose from the dead.

Pilate: Did you, after Jesus died, call him the Son of God?

Cornelius: I did then. I do now.

Pilate: Is he your king then?

Cornelius: Yes sir. My king and my God!

Pilate: One thing more. You speak of Jesus of Nazareth as Jesus Christ. What does that name imply?

Cornelius: The Christ name means 'The anointed one.' God anointed Jesus as his son. That makes Jesus the same as God. Your excellency, we didn't know it. But you ordered God's son to die, and I executed him as I obeyed your order.

Pilate: If that is true, my guilt is greater than yours. But the same Jesus told me that the greatest guilt is in the one who betrayed him, whoever that person is. I wonder why a God would permit it? Perhaps the guilt is his?

But what must be decided is if your reception of this 'Spirit of Jesus,' and your baptism, has affected your work. Can you continue as a Centurion for Rome and be a Nazarene? Answer that question honestly for us.

Cornelius: I am a man under authority, your excellency. But the authority is not yours or Caesar's any longer. It is the authority of Jesus Christ. I can obey directions from Rome through you, or your directions as my superior, if those directions seem to be what the Lord requires. But I could well refuse to obey if commanded to break one of the Lord's commandments to his people.

Pilate: Tell me the commandments you fear you might break if you obey Rome.

Cornelius: Love God as the only God with all my heart, mind, soul, strength. Love all mankind as neighbors. Give my life in love as Jesus did for us. Do not kill...

Pilate: It is enough. You are relieved of your command.

Father, you see I had no choice. I dismissed Cornelius from our military force, giving him a full pension for his twenty years of service. I also gave him a tract of land here in Caesaria so he can build a home of his own, and live out his days here.

Much of that decision came after a conversation with Procula. She urged me to be as lenient with Cornelius as possible. She and Ruth are good friends, and I know Procula doesn't want them to move away.

I think Procula has acquired something of the same assurance Cornelius has. I have asked her about it, and she has not denied that she believes in Jesus as the son of the Jews' God. She says more. She believes what the Jews say that there is only one God, and that all of our gods in Rome and all of the gods in Greece, and all gods over the rest of the world, are not gods at all.

Perhaps it is because of the change I have seen in Cornelius and Procula. They have a happiness that I envy. They have a patience beyond my capacity to understand. Whatever the reasons, I have decided to investigate the cult of Jesus' followers more closely.

I know there is little purpose in my life, and I keep recalling that man Jesus as he stood before me the day I condemned him. When I picture his eyes, I recall that he was not condemning me in return.

Rather, he was forgiving me!

Was he calling on me to seek the truth through him?

What is truth?

Perhaps at last, and soon, I may find that out.

In filial love,

Pontius.

Glossary

Abraham	An *Old Testament* person who can be found in the *Book of Genesis*, beginning with Chapter 11, verse 26. Abraham was known for his faith in God, and for his obedience to God. He is the father of all the Hebrew people, and of all the Arab tribes as well.
Andrew	One of the first two Apostles to follow Jesus Christ. Brother of Simon. A fisherman on the Sea of Galilee. Resident of the city of Bethsaida.
Apostles	Twelve men selected by Jesus Christ to be his principal followers.
Asphaltus	Roman name for the Dead Sea, a body of water that is so salty that nothing can live in it. The aroma of this sea may have given it this name.
Assyrians	A northern kingdom that overpowered the Israelites in the eighth century, BC, and sent 10 of the 12 tribes into exile.
Bar Tholomew	One of the twelve Apostles appointed by Jesus. The name means, Son of Tholomew, much like a surname today. This is the only Apostle who is called by his father's name; scholarly

work I have followed offers the possibility that this Apostle had the same first name as the Messiah. Others believe BarTholomew was Nathaniel, the man who was led to Jesus by Philip in the *Gospel of John*. (*John 1:44-51*)

Bedouin — A desert people who have lived in and near the holy land for thousands of years. Bedouin burial sites have been dated by archaeologists as early as six thousand years before Christ. Bedouin have lived in tents, moving to new grazing lands several times a year. A very independent people, they do not easily accept governmental controls.

Benjamin — The twelfth son of Jacob, brother of Joseph. One of the twelve tribes of Israel. Benjaminites were descended from Benjamin. The first king of Israel, Saul, was a Benjaminite.

Bethsaida — A small town on the north shore of the Sea of Galilee. Reputed to be the home of two Apostles, Andrew and Philip.

Bethshean — City near the Jordan River in the lower valley of Jezreel. Bethshean or Bethshan is the ancient Hebrew name for this city. Scythopolis was the Greek name given it about two hundred years before Christ.

Books of Moses — The first five books of the Holy Bible: *Genesis, Exodus, Leviticus, Numbers,* and *Deuteronomy*. These books are reputed to have been written by Moses. They tell the story of the beginnings of the Universe, the Earth, life on the

Earth, including human life. They also tell the story of the escape of the Hebrew people from Egypt under the leadership of Moses.

Caesaria — A city that was built by Herod the Great on the Mediterranean Sea. A small harbor was built there of huge stones imbedded in the sea bottom. Caesaria became the seat of government for Roman governors of the area, including Pontius Pilate. The city has not been occupied for centuries. But at the time of Pilate, there were probably as many as twenty thousand people living there.

Cana — A town about five miles from Nazareth along the Galilee road that leads from the Mediterranean through Nazareth to Tiberias. Cana was a place where Jesus performed miracles that are narrated in the Gospels.

Canaan — An ancient name for the land that became the promised land for the Israelites.

Caphernaum — Probable spelling for a city on the north shore of the Sea of Galilee. Today that city is called Capernaum by Christians who visit there. It was the home of Peter, one of the Apostles.

Caravansary — A building designed to house travelers and their animals. Divided into two sections, the animals were kept on one side, the travelers slept on the other. Such a building may have been the 'Inn' referred to as the place where there was no room for Mary and Joseph in Bethlehem when Jesus was born.

Chorazim — A small town north of Caphernaum where Jesus preached, taught, and performed miracles.

Christ — The anointed one. God's anointed could be another name for the Messiah, but it probably meant something far more important. Jesus acknowledged himself the Christ, and also the Son of God, the King of Heaven with his Father.

Church — When Jesus spoke of his church, he was speaking of the body of believers who would follow his teaching, and his way of life. It was on the rock of faith exhibited by Simon Peter that the church would be built. After Pentecost, those who received the Baptism of the Holy Spirit were united as the Church, the body of Jesus Christ.

Citadel — A fortress within the city of Jerusalem that was Herod's home as well.

Cubit — A unit of measure, approximately 16 inches long. The distance from the elbow to the knuckles of a man's closed fist.

David — Second King of Israel. A great warrior with the ability to band together the twelve tribes under his leadership. David had several wives and concubines, and sired many children. Jesus' ancestry goes back through King David to Abraham in the *Gospel of Matthew*, and to Adam in the *Gospel of Luke*.

Deacons — Men, selected by the Church to perform services, particularly waiting on table, and distribution of aid to the poor. One deacon mentioned in the narrative is Philip of Caesaria.

Dead Sea — A body of water twelve hundred feet below sea level. The Jordan River empties into this sea that has no outlet. The waters evaporate in the desert heat, leaving this long narrow lake so polluted with salts that it will not support life.

Devil(s) — The principal Devil was a fallen archangel. One of the names given him by Jesus and others of that time was Beelzebub. This demon was head over many more that could invade the bodies of people, making them sick or mad. Jesus frequently healed people by driving out these demons. Many modern psychologists and psychiatrists report multiple personality disorders using similar language to that of the *New Testament*.

Disciples — Men and women who followed Jesus Christ. The twelve Apostles are sometimes called Disciples, as they did not lose that title when that of Apostle was added. Approximately 120 men and women were Jesus' disciples in Jerusalem after his resurrection. *The Acts of the Apostles*, Chapter 2, states that 3,000 more disciples were added to their number on the Day of Pentecost.

Elijah	An *Old Testament* prophet, noted for his love of the people, and bravery in speaking unpleasant prophecies to their rulers. Some people thought Jesus was Elijah returned. Jesus maintained that John the Baptist was that returned prophet.
Eliud	The name of Jesus Christ's great grandfather on Joseph's side. This name is part of the list of ancestors of Jesus in the *Gospel of Matthew*. The story of his having been a famous man in Nazareth with his grave on the top of a high hill adjacent to that city is fiction. There is no information available about most of the ancestors of Jesus.
Essenes	Deeply religious cult of Jews who set up a semi-monastic way of life for themselves in Qumran, a community by the Dead Sea. Jesus, John the Baptist, and John the Apostle are all reputed to have been a part of this community during their lives. There is no historical data to prove these theories.
Firkin	A liquid measure used in Jesus' time. It is about ten gallons. The miracle of changing water into wine (*John 2*), tells of six water jars filled, each containing two to three firkins, or twenty to thirty gallons.
Galilee	A very fertile land, except for the coastal plain, perhaps the best farming land in the entire land of Israel.

Gideon — One of the men who 'judged' the twelve tribes of Israel after the time of Moses and Joshua. Gideon led his people in a successful raid on their enemies, taking only 300 men to do battle against thousands.

Haifa — A city on the coast of Israel. One of the few ports along that coastline. This is a large industrial city in Israel today. There were probably as many as 30,000 inhabitants there at the time of this narrative.

Herod — In this narrative, Herod Antipas is most often the person meant when the name 'Herod' is used. His brothers were also called by that name. Herod the Great, their father, was the man who Matthew tells us killed innocent babies in and near Bethlehem while trying to kill the predicted new King of Israel. Herod Antipas reigned in Tiberias, under the control of the Roman Empire.

Herodium — A fortress home built by Herod the Great southeast of Bethlehem. Constructed as a home within a man made hill, it was elaborately furnished, and had its own water supply from cisterns.

Israel — The name God gave to Jacob, the grandson of Abraham, after wrestling all night with the man and not prevailing against him. Also the name given to the land that the children of Israel occupied for at least twelve centuries before the Romans expelled them in approximately 130 A.D. Now the name of the land again since it was reestablished in 1948.

Israelites — People who claimed to be descended from the Patriarch, Jacob (Israel).

James — The name of two of the Apostles, and of one of Jesus' brothers. The James mentioned first in the lists of the Apostles is James, brother of John, a son of Zebedee. The second James is mentioned but once in the narrative. He is often called James, the Less, for there is no mention of his words or deeds in the four Gospels. James, the brother of Jesus, is also mentioned only briefly in the narrative. Later he became the Bishop of Jerusalem, and a leader among the Christians.

Jericho — A city on the Jordan River near the Dead Sea. It is a large oasis in the desert, with a complex irrigation system. This may be one of the oldest cities in the world. Archaeologists have found buildings there that they have dated as early as 8,000 BC.

Jezreel — Fertile valley that was part of an ancient trade route from Egypt to the east.

Jesus — A man born approximately 5 B.C., in Judea. Attributed by many millions of people to be the begotten Son of God.

John — Brother of James, son of Zebedee. Probable author of the *Gospel of John* and *Epistles of John*. Possible author of *Revelations*. Probably the youngest of the Apostles, John was also a fisherman with his father and brother before he met Jesus Christ. Estimates as to his age when he first followed Jesus run as young as fifteen.

John Mark — The probable name of the author of the second Gospel in the *New Testament*. Many scholars believe John Mark functioned as a scribe for Simon Peter; therefore, the *Gospel of Mark* might possibly could have been called the *Gospel of Peter*.

John the Baptist — A cousin of Jesus Christ, and a prophet whose primary teaching was that the people of Israel should repent and be baptized so they would be free from sin and ready for the coming of the Messiah. Christians believe John was sent to prepare the way for the coming of Jesus Christ.

Jordan — A river that flows from the north of Israel to the Dead Sea through the Sea of Galilee. It begins at approximately 5,000 feet above sea level, and empties into the Dead Sea at 1,000 feet below Sea Level.

Judah — One of the twelve tribes of Israel. Jesus was descended from Judah through David. Judah is also the name of the land where Jerusalem was the capital city.

Judas Iscariot	One of the twelve Apostles. The only one who was not a Galilean. This narrative portrays Judas as the son of a Sadducean priest, and a Sadducean priest himself. There is no historical basis for such an assumption.
Judas Maccabeas	The leader of a rebellion against the Greeks about two hundred years before the beginning of this narrative. The Greeks were beaten, and the Hebrew people enjoyed freedom for almost a hundred years before the Romans conquered them.
Jude	One of the twelve Apostles. Probably there were three Apostles with that given name. Jude, Judas, and Thomas. Two of the three probably lived in Nazareth, and knew Jesus all their lives.
Lamb of God	A name given to Jesus by John the Baptist. It implies that Jesus will become the sacrifice to save the world from sin. The Jews sacrificed animals as sin offerings at the Temple in Jerusalem. That practice was stopped after the Temple was destroyed about forty years after Jesus died on a cross in Jerusalem.
Lebanon	The land due north of the Holy Land. This land was occupied by the Romans.
Levi	One of the twelve tribes of Israel. Levi was a direct ancestor of Moses. This tribe became the priestly tribe of the Hebrew people. Levi is also the name of one of the twelve selected

	by Jesus to be Apostles. He was also called Matthew.
Malachi	*Old Testament* prophet priest. Wrote the last book in the *Old Testament*. Name is derivation of the name, Melchizedek, the priest from Salem (probably the site of Jerusalem) who blessed Abraham, and to whom Abraham gave his tithes.
Mare Nostrum	The name for the body of water we know as the Mediterranean Sea. It was also known as the Sea of the Philistines, and the Great Western Sea.
Mary of Bethany	Sister of Martha and Lazarus, this woman lived in Bethany and knew Jesus Christ. In this narrative I equate her with Mary Magdalene, following the concepts of Roman and Orthodox Christianity over the twenty centuries of Christianity.
Mary of Magdala	This woman lived for part of her life in a town by the Sea of Galilee just north of Tiberias. A tell there has been identified as Magdala, but it has yet to be excavated by archaeologists. Some evidence indicates that it was a city engaged in preservation and sale of fish. Mary of Magdala was the first person to see Jesus Christ alive after his resurrection from the dead.

Mary of Nazareth — Wife of Joseph; mother of Jesus Christ. May have been as young as thirteen when she was told by an angel she would conceive and bear a son and call his name, 'Jesus.'

Masada — Desert fortress reconstructed by Herod the Great. The last place of resistance by the Jews in their war against Rome that ended forty years after Jesus' death and resurrection.

Matthias — Man who was chosen by lot to be the twelfth Apostle after the death of Judas Iscariot. Not mentioned in any of the four Gospels, and never mentioned again after his selection in Chapter One of *Acts*. In this narrative I equate Matthias with the rich young man who walks away after Jesus tells him to sell all he has, give it to the poor, and then come to follow the Master.

Matthew — One of the twelve Apostles (see also Levi).

Melchizedek — Priest King of Salem (probably the site of Jerusalem). When Abraham was victorious, Melchizedek celebrated the victory using bread and wine. (See *Genesis 14*.) The *New Testament* letter to the *Hebrews* (Chapters 6 and 7) proclaims Jesus Christ as "Priest forever after the order of Melchizedek."

Messiah — A person the prophets of *Old Testament* times predicted would come and save the Hebrew people. Many of the Jews of today believe the Messiah will come to fulfill those prophecies. Christians believe that Jesus of Nazareth is that Messiah, and that he came to save all mankind.

Moses — The greatest of the prophets and leaders of the Jews. Moses was a priest of Egypt, though born to Hebrew parents. He lived in the wilderness for a long period after escaping Pharoah's justice. He had killed one of the overseers of the Hebrews. In the wilderness of Sinai, Moses met God, and was directed to lead his people out of Egypt to the promised land.

Nathaniel — One of the disciples who met Jesus and declared Him to be Son of God almost immediately. Many scholars believe Nathaniel to be one of the twelve Apostles, most likely BarTholomew. In this narrative I follow other scholarly arguments that BarTholomew was not Nathaniel, but another man named Jesus. (Jesus was a very popular name at that time.)

Nazareth — A city today of some 80,000 people in the North of Israel. Was probably a city of 2,000 when Jesus lived there with his parents. He and his 'father,' Joseph, were carpenters. Nazareth is about a five day walk from Jerusalem.

Nazirite — An especially religious person who takes a vow not to cut his hair, nor to consume any alcoholic beverages in his lifetime. John the Baptist was a Nazirite.

Passover — A special holy time for the Hebrew people. It commemorates the time Moses led them from their slavery in Egypt toward the promised land. The 'Passover' was what the angel of death did for the chosen people of God. The angel passed over their homes, and visited the homes of the Egyptians, killing their firstborn sons.

Pentecost — A feast of the Hebrew people that occurs fifty days after Passover. It was on the day of Pentecost that the Holy Spirit descended on the people who believed Jesus was the Christ.

Peter — The name of the Apostle who is always listed as first in the Gospels. Jesus changed the man's name to Peter from Simon either when they first met after Jesus proclaimed himself Messiah, or after Simon Peter proclaimed Jesus the Son of the Most High God. The name means 'rock.' Jesus said, "I call you Peter, and on this rock I will build my Church." Roman Catholics believe Peter was the first Pope, and that all Bishops of Rome since have been Simon Peter's successors.

Pharisees — Priests of Jerusalem. The party of the Pharisees believed in life after death. Jesus spoke against the Pharisees often. The high priests, Annas and Caiaphas, were Pharisees, as was Nicodemus. *The Acts of the Apostles* states that many Pharisees came to believe in Jesus as the Christ after his resurrection.

Pharaoh	King of Egypt. The most famous of the Pharaohs mentioned in the *Old Testament*, was the one who reigned during the time of Moses.
Philip	One of the first two Apostles to follow Jesus Christ. Philip was probably a Greek Jew who lived in the city of Bethsaida. It is probable that he and Andrew were disciples of John the Baptist.
Philip of Caesaria	A Greek Jew selected by the Apostles as one of seven to be deacons. Became a traveling evangelist, finally settling with his family in Caesaria.
Philistines	One tribe that lived in the Promised Land before the Hebrew people claimed it. They were a strong people who lived along the coastal plain, as well as in the most fertile valleys of Galilee. David subdued this tribe, but never eliminated them. Modern Palestinians claim the Philistines as a part of their ancestry. Note the similarity of the name. The Emperor of Rome changed the name of the country to Palestine near the end of the first century of this era, after almost totally eliminating all the Jews in that land.
Romans	Rome was a city in what is now Italy. Its leaders had captured all of the Mediterranean, most of Europe, and most of the Near East almost a century before this narrative begins.
Sadducees	Priests of the Temple in Jerusalem. The Sadducean party claims its heritage from Zaddok,

a priest who served King David a thousand years before the time of Christ.

Samaria — This is the name of a city, the capital of the country north of Judah. Samaria was the home of ten of the tribes of Israel that broke away from the king of Judah and his people after the death of Solomon. Two centuries later, Samaria was defeated by the Assyrians, and its people scattered. New peoples were moved into the area, and the Jews in Jerusalem believed the religion of the Samaritans was polluted by association with foreign gods. Jesus was accused of being a Samaritan, and one of his most famous stories is of the Good Samaritan who was neighbor to a man in need.

Sanhedrin — The governing body of priests who served God in the Temple at Jerusalem. This body was made up of Pharisees and Sadducees, with the majority probably with the Pharisees.

Satan — One name for the fallen archangel. Other names include Devil, or Beelzebub (see Devil(s)).

Sea of Galilee — A lake ten miles long by three miles wide in the north of Israel, the part called Galilee.

Sea of Genessaret — Another name for the Sea of Galilee, and for the Sea of Tiberias. A very early name for this lake. The lake is approximately thirteen miles long, and eight miles wide.

Sea of Tiberias	A name given to the Sea of Galilee by Herod Antipas.
Solomon	Son of David who inherited his father's throne. Solomon was a man of peace living in the city of peace. He was also a great administrator and builder. He built the first Temple in Jerusalem. He had hundreds of wives and more concubines. His wisdom, and perhaps some of his writings (*Ecclesiastes*, *Song of Solomon*) made him a man of great renown.
Sons of Thunder	James and John, sons of Zebedee Jesus called by this name. The Gospels give us no explanation for it. Some think it is because they would work at fishing even during a rain storm. Others, that James and John had quick tempers.
Synagogue	A place for meeting, prayers, and worship of God by Jews. One or more synagogues could be found in every town in the land where this story takes place.
Tell	Word in Glossary. A term from Archeology that means a man-created hill that has grown for centuries. Layers of civilizations lie beneath the surface of a tell.
Temple	The Temple in Jerusalem was considered the House of God. The first Temple was built by King Solomon in the Tenth Century, BC. The Temple Jesus and his disciples knew was one that had been almost totally rebuilt during the

time of Herod the Great, father of Herod Antipas.

Tiberias — The name of the Emperor of Rome during the time of this narrative. Also the name of the city built by Herod Antipas on the Sea of Galilee.

Yahweh — The holy and unpronounceable name of God. The *Old Testament* spells this name YHWH. The vowels were not written, and the true pronunciation of that name has been lost. Some believe the name is as written here. The name is also the present form of the verb, 'to be.' In the book of *Exodus*, God spoke to Moses and said His Name was I AM THAT I AM!

Zealots — The Zealot party were insurrectionists who wanted to overthrow the Roman government by force. One of their number, Simon, was among the twelve Apostles selected by Jesus.

Zebedee — The given name of the father of two of Jesus' Apostles, John and James. Zebedee was in the fishing business on the Sea of Galilee.

Appendix

I. ***Andrew:*** According to St. John's Gospel, Andrew is the first one of the twelve Apostles to follow Jesus Christ *(John 1: 35-51)*. Andrew and Philip have Jesus pointed out to them by John the Baptist near the Jordan River where John had baptized Jesus and perhaps hundreds or even thousands of others. The traditional place where John baptized is only a few miles north of Jericho, at least three days walk from the north shore of the Sea of Galilee where Andrew worked as a fisherman.

If we assume the chronology of the fourth Gospel is accurate, we learn that Andrew and Philip spent that first evening with Jesus. The next day Andrew found his brother, Simon, and brought him to meet Jesus. This would indicate that Andrew, Philip, Simon, and Nathaniel were either followers of John the Baptist, or had come on 'holiday' to hear the wild man preach.

John 1:35 tells us that at least Andrew and Philip were disciples of John the Baptist, so it might be safe to assume that Simon and Nathaniel were John's disciples also. I make that assumption in this presentation of Andrew's story of his personal relationship with Jesus Christ.

Of the twelve Apostles, there are more references to Andrew in the Gospels than to any others except for Simon Peter, John, and Judas Iscariot. Andrew is sometimes listed as the second of the twelve, with Simon Peter as the only one having precedence over him. That could well be because of their relationship, and not a sign of his relative importance among the Apostles. We know him to be the first of the twelve (with Philip) to follow Jesus. But we do not know him to be second in authority after Simon Peter.

The places in the Holy Bible where Andrew is named are:

Mt.	4.18	is called Peter and A. his brother.
	10.02	called Peter, and A. his brother;
Mk.	1.16	saw Simon and A. the brother of
	1.29	entered the house of Simon and A.
	3.18	A. and Philip, and Bartholomew,
	13.03	and John and A. asked him privately
Lk.	6.14	and A. his bother, and James
Jn.	1.40	was A., Simon Peter's brother
	1.44	Bethsaida, the city of A. and Peter.
	6.08	A., Simon Peter's brother, said
	12.22	A. went with Philip, and they told
Ac.	1.13	Peter and John and James and A.

This doesn't give us enough material for so much as a skeletal examination of Andrew's life. We do know he was a man who lived in the holy land on the Sea of Tiberias. His home was either in Bethsaida or Caphernaum, which were two towns situated on either side of the Jordan River where it emptied into the lake where they fished for a living. Whether Andrew lived in the home where Simon Peter lived with his wife and mother-in-law, we cannot tell, though that house is called Simon and Andrew's home.

Harper's Bible Dictionary states, "Andrew's character was revealed when in contrast to the perplexed Philip, he thought it worth while to tell the Lord of the lad's five loaves and two fishes (*John 6:5 ff*) and again when he helped the hesitant Philip to inform Jesus of the presence of the inquiring Greeks (*John 12:22*). Andrew thus qualifies as the first home missionary (*John 1:41*), and also the first foreign missionary, (*John 12:22*)."

Andrew is not mentioned in the *New Testament* after his name is listed as one of the twelve in the first Chapter of the Acts of the Apostles. Neither is he mentioned in any historical work in the secular world. It is only in the ancient traditions of the Church that we gain a nebulous vision of this Apostle going into the world as a missionary.

Tradition in the Orthodox Churches is that Andrew was a missionary to Greece and to Asia, and had a ministry that included many miracles of healing. That tradition and the Roman Catholic tradition agree that Andrew was crucified on an ***crux decussata*** (X) at Patrae in Achaia.

In this fictional work, I portray Andrew as a bachelor with little formal education. I make him a seeker after the meaning of life, first following John the Baptist, then with John's blessing, following Jesus Christ. I believe Andrew believed that John the Baptist and Jesus Christ knew Almighty God. I believe that Andrew followed first the one, then the other, so that he would also know God. Surely he was an ordinary man in that he lived a life as a fisherman in a small town in Galilee. Surely he was extra-ordinary in that he chose to accept the call to follow two visionary leaders of his time.

II. ***Pontius Pilate:*** When we Christians say the Apostles' or the Nicene Creed, we name God and two other persons. They are Mary, the mother of Jesus, and Pontius Pilate. Much has been written about Mary. Little about Pilate. The Gospels portray Pilate as a reluctant judge of Jesus. The little history we have of him shows him an enemy of the Jews, but, perhaps surprisingly, quite possibly a convert to Christianity.

There is little in secular history about Pontius Pilate. The four Gospels name him in nine verses of Matthew, Chapter 27; ten in *Mark*, Chapter 15; twelve in Luke, Chapter 3, verse 1, Chapter 13, verse 1, and ten in Chapter 23. Twenty-one verses in John's Gospel, Chapters 18 and 19. *The Acts of the Apostles* name him three times in 3.13, 4.27, and 13.28. *First Timothy* 6.13 names him as well. This totals fifty-four verses. That makes him a far more prominent figure in terms of the written coverage of his function as an important person in the *New Testament*, than most of the Apostles.

The only Roman source of information on Pilate is provided in a brief historical note by Tacitus who wrote about a hundred years after the event of Jesus' execution by Pontius Pilate in the reign of Tiberias. In that note Tacitus says nothing of Pilate's role in our Lord's death.

Two Jewish authors refer to Pilate's activity during his administration, but neither of them mention him in connection with the trial and execution of Jesus. Philo tells of an incident in which Pilate had shields hung in his palace in Jerusalem on which the Emperor's name was written. Pilate was ordered by the Emperor to remove the shields. Philo characterizes Pilate by attributing to him the crimes of rape and murder, and accuses him also of insult and inhumanity.

Josephus tells of a similar incident when attendants carried into Jerusalem standards bearing the Emperor's image. Pilate bowed to public opinion after a crowd surrounded his palace in Caesaria in protest. Josephus also shows Pilate's power and willingness to confront the powerful Temple priests by taking funds from their Temple treasury to complete an aqueduct system supplying much needed water for Jerusalem. Josephus reported a third incident in which Pilate fought the Samaritans and executed some of their leaders. Josephus reported that complaint was made to the Roman legate in Syria, resulting in Pilate's recall to Rome.

Pilate in the New Testament gets a mixed review of his part in the trial and execution of the Christ. Pilate is spoken of by Jesus Himself in Luke as the killer of Galileans, mixing their blood with an animal sacrifice. The narratives of the trial of Jesus, and of Pilate's talks with Jesus at that time indicate the Governor was reluctant to have Jesus executed, and that he tried to have him freed.

Third and fourth century writings show Pilate a man forced by circumstances to sentence Jesus to death. They have Pilate and his wife (who had a dream about Jesus the night of the Passion, *Matthew 27.19*) converted to Christianity. The Coptic Church has a day honoring Pilate and his wife, Procula, on June 25th. They have made Pilate both a saint and a martyr. The Eastern Orthodox Church has beatified Procula, and her date of honoring is October 27th.

In the imaginative presentation of Pilate's story of his encounter with Jesus that I have created in the meditation in this book, I use quotations from scripture and several apocryphal writings. Part of the Appendix to the *Apocryphal Gospels* include letters from Pilate to Tiberias and to Herod about the events of Jesus' death and resurrection. Thus I have chosen to present Pilate through a series of letters to someone he can trust, his father in Rome.

We are assured by historians that Pontius Pilate really existed, and did serve in Judea as Governor. The science of Archeology has provided us absolute proof of Pilate's existence and place in history in first century Judea. In Caesaria, an archeological expedition found a corner stone to a government building bearing the name of Pontius Pilate. That building lay in ruins under the accumulated dust of nineteen centuries until it was discovered relatively recently.

How would a minor official of the most powerful government in the world react to a confrontation with the Son of the Creator and Ruler of the Universe? That was my question as I chose to include Pilate, the man who spoke the title words of this collection, (*Behold the Man*), on the fateful day he sentenced God's Son to death. As with the other meditations, I present much that is known fact about the principal characters, but more that is conjecture. Out of the blending of fact and fiction I hope to show from many angles the face of the Christ, perhaps to make real to some readers the glorious reality of Immanuel, God with us.

III. ***Judas, The Twelfth Apostle:*** I began writing the meditation on Judas Iscariot as an exercise in understanding myself several years ago. It was at that time I was told by one of the Apostles' successors, my Bishop, that I was worse than Judas Iscariot. All my life I have hoped I might be able to emulate a famous person, to take on a quality of gentle benevolence perhaps, like the man in Washington Irving's "The Great Stone Face." Somehow Lincoln or Santa Claus, or St. Francis of Assisi were people I hoped to be compared to, not Judas Iscariot!

However, my Bishop's statement did stimulate thinking, not only about one's own life, motives, and choices, but also about the ones with whom we may be compared. The parts of this book, the meditations that were trying to make my thoughts like Judas Iscariot's, are the result of much meditation, and a little research. I found that the source material on the life of Judas Iscariot was confined almost solely to the first five books of the *New Testament*. Bible commentaries offered little elaboration on Judas, and none of them made any effort to understand or condone Judas' actions.

The four Gospel authors were unanimous in their condemnation, John being the most venomous, followed by Luke. Yet it became obvious that of the twelve Apostles only Simon Peter received more mention, and much that was written about Peter showed him to be a blustering coward; a denier of Jesus at a critical moment. Surely that was a mixed review.

What good had the Gospels to say about Judas? First and foremost, Judas was chosen as one of the twelve by Jesus Christ. Second, the Gospels all state that Jesus always knew it was Judas who would betray him, yet he did not drive Judas out of the company. Instead, on the last night of Jesus' life He washed Judas' feet, fed him by hand, gave him a part of the very first communion of bread (and perhaps of wine). He gave or accepted a kiss in the garden; calling this twelfth Apostle, 'Friend,' at the moment of betrayal.

We must assume Jesus included Judas in his prayer for the forgiveness of "them" when he prayed from the cross, for it is obvious Judas did not know what he had done. (Witness the paying back of the thirty pieces of silver, the "I have sinned" speech to the priests.)

In this book I have placed Judas' home in Kiriath in Judah. This follows the rationale of most modern commentaries. They list all of the other Apostles as Galileans, including Philip of Bethsaida. One ponders this choice of so many Galileans, recognizing Jesus was of the tribe of Judah, the house and lineage of David. Surely some of Jesus' Galilean disciples had mixed descent with ancestry of different Hebrew tribes mixed with the ancestry of other cultures that were part of the Samaritan melting pot heritage from the preceding eight centuries.

One recalls that when the priests accused Jesus of being a Samaritan and having a demon, he refuted the demonic charge only. Still his comment to the Samaritan woman that "Salvation is of the Jews" indicates his continued association with the city of Zion, not Samaria and Mount Gerizim.

It is quite easy to build a case for Jesus to choose one Apostle from Judah. The logic of making that Apostle Judas Iscariot follows. What is purely visionary or speculative in the account is making Judas an educated Sadducean priest. I used the evidence of his function as 'keeper of the purse,' as one part of that assumption. Then I allowed for the epithet, “Judas Priest!” to color my mind. I have not the training in history or languages nor the inclination of cautious scholarship to explore this avenue back to the first century. But, all my life I have heard, “Judas Priest!” used as an exclamation, and I see no reason to doubt Jesus’ choice of a priest as one of his Apostles.

Have we not ever since chosen our succeeding apostolate from the church’s priesthood? Would we do better to recruit from the IRS? One of Jesus’ Apostles was a tax collector. Jesus attacking the priesthood does not negate this possibility, for he surely attacked tax collectors after choosing Matthew to be one of the twelve. Jesus attacked adulterers after healing harlots. Some may say he has the power yet today to heal the priests, even the bishops, of this century.

Were Judas Iscariot the son of a priest, it would follow that he be one as well. The priesthood was an inherited profession. So, also, it would follow that the reverse would be true. If Judas was, then surely Simon Iscariot would be, a priest. If Simon was, then surely Judas Iscariot would be a priest.

Making Judas’ family priests enabled me to come through with the device of Judas Iscariot knowing John the Baptist as well as of Judas being able to function as a double agent.

You, as reader, may make your own judgment as to the reality of my Judas and his relationship to the other people portrayed in this book.

As I turned to the narrative of the Gospels, again and again I saw Judas loved and accepted by Jesus Christ. Judas was sent out to preach and heal with another Apostle. He was under the close supervision, brilliant teaching, tender touch of Jesus Christ for nearly three years. Would not that influence have made him worthy of our attention?

Would not Jesus' teaching on forgiveness cause us to have to include Judas Iscariot as one forgiven and eternally redeemed by God the Father? Was not the direct result of Judas' leading the Temple Guard to Jesus, the shedding of our Savior's blood? Do we not regularly thank God for that gift?

Who are we to say that Judas was not covered by so much as a drop of that blood?

We remember too, that Jesus said sin against him would be forgiven. But our unforgiveness would not be forgiven. It would seem we have no choice but to include Judas in our forgiving, or to be rejected eternally ourselves!

Did Judas sin against the Holy Spirit by suicide? I don't know. If you know, tell me. But, I know my duty is to love and forgive all - Judas Iscariot included - praying to my Lord that as one charged with being even worse, I can be an eternal occupant of the Kingdom! There, by His Grace, I will behold His face. There I will live eternally in glorious, ecstatic, joyful, union with Him and with all the redeemed of His Church.

It has been said that when all was said and done, more was said than done. Perhaps that is true of the first century apostolate. They may have said more about not forgiving Judas than they accomplished in their hearts. Surely each remembered his own faults and failures on that awful night of Christ's passion, and the dreadful succeeding day. Self forgiveness could only come with forgiveness of all the apostolate.

Still, with only the Scripture narrative at hand for the twelve, and only my personal experience of the succession in view in this century, it is possible I will see but one Apostle in all of Heaven. Judas Iscariot, the last and the first, Omega returned to Alpha.

Of course I know I will be chosen to dwell eternally in Jesus' Father's house. If you forgive my presumption, perhaps you will be there too.

IV. ***Mary Magdalene:*** The parts of this book that are written as if Mary Magdalene were thinking aloud are based on the Gospel narratives. This meditation tries to emphasize the life of Mary Magdalene as one who came to love Jesus Christ. I first began to write this as a part of a series of verbal meditations I was using to make the Gospel 'come to life' among the people of my parish in South St. Paul, Minnesota. Other characters I wrote about I was able to contain in about twenty pages. But this one on Mary Magdalene took on an independent personality almost immediately, and I found I had to expand the story to cover all the interrelated stories of the life of one or more of the Marys named in the Gospels.

For the sake of the story, I have combined two or, possibly three, lives into one. The Gospels speak of so many women with the name of Mary! We know that Mary of Bethany lived in that small town outside of Jerusalem with her sister Martha and her brother, Lazarus. This Mary knew Jesus and loved him, but there seems to be no evidence of her being present at the crucifixion, or at the tomb on the day of resurrection.

Mary of Magdala, on the other hand, lived for some part of her life by the Sea of Tiberias, and was cured by Jesus, in all probability, while in the northern part of the Holy Land, near Nazareth, Nain, Cana, or Caphernaum.

A third person, quite possibly one of the above ladies, was taken 'in the very act of adultery.' This one was not given a name in the Gospel narrative (*John 7:53-8:11*). I used broad literary license to include this incident as a part of the life and experience of Mary Magdalene and Jesus

Christ. However, I note in my defense, that other writers have done the same. Though I am not the first to take this position, it must be said that there are many scholars who say this person was neither Mary of Bethany, nor Mary Magdalene, and that these two Marys are not the same person. Some say that the story of the adulterous woman does not even belong in the Gospel narrative. They maintain that it is a story added to the *Gospel of John* as late as two centuries after the Gospel was written.

Scripture quotations I have taken from different translations, as I have in other sections of the book. I have felt free to add lines for each of the characters that have no scriptural source at all. Other writers of fiction have taken this liberty, and I have chosen to follow their example. The Gospels are available to any who want to read them to see what was actually written there.

Mary of Magdala and Mary of Bethany are not mentioned after the four Gospels. What their lives were like, whether or not they married, whether they lived out their days in or near Jerusalem, no one knows. There seems to be no tradition of their functioning as Christian workers in the Holy Land, or elsewhere in the world. This might appear surprising to 20th Century Christians, but it shouldn't be. Neither Peter's wife, nor his mother-in-law, nor his children, are named in the *New Testament*.

V. ***Thomas 'Jude':*** Though I have not included his comments directly in the book as a separate meditation, I have mentioned him frequently. This is especially true in the section attributed to Mary Magdalene. It would be a valuable exercise for readers to look up the list of Apostles in each of the first three Gospels, and find the name, Thomas. In the *Gospel of John*, he is called, 'Didymas,' the Greek word for twin. The Hebrew for twin is 'Thomas.' So John's Gospel, broadly translated, says, 'The twin called the twin.'

Much conjecture through the centuries has been on the real name of this Apostle. I chose 'Jude' following the line of reasoning of one scholar I read while I was visiting in Jerusalem. That author, whose name I cannot recall (but his book is probably still in the library at St. George's College), concluded that Thomas was a younger brother of Jesus, and that he looked very much like our Lord. As the brothers of Jesus are all named in one passage in Mark's Gospel (*Mark 6:3*) "...the brother of James, and Joseph, and Judas, and Simon?" I simply chose one of the four names. James the Less and Simon the Zealot are often considered brothers of Jesus as well. It is also reasonable to call one of the disciples by a nickname when two others have the same name; Jude, and Judas Iscariot. Still, I have stepped away from the concept of Thomas being blood brother of Jesus, as I did from another author who offered the theory that Thomas was an identical twin of Jesus. The Roman Catholic tradition is that Jesus is an only child of Mary, and that the 'brothers' listed are sons of Joseph, or adopted brothers who were raised by Mary and Joseph.

I give Thomas the name, 'Jude.' I call him a cousin of Jesus, one who lived in Nazareth. As I have a second cousin who looked enough like me when I was twelve to be spanked by my mother who thought she was spanking me, I believe it is possible for Jesus to have had a cousin who looked enough like him to be called his 'twin.'

Many have wondered as I have about the confrontation between Jesus and Thomas after the resurrection. Did Thomas obey Jesus and touch the wounds? Or did he, upon seeing the resurrected Christ, simply exclaim, "My Lord and my God?" There are good reasons to assume either position. The actions are not revealed in the story. All we have is the dialogue. I chose to have Thomas touch the wounds in the hands, and to put his hand in the side, both out of obedience, and out of his own deep need to be certain. He, being the man I believe he was, much like most of us, would have regretted not having touched the wounds, when doubt returned.

Tradition gives us much about the life of Thomas after the New Testament writings were complete. He is reported to have lived in Egypt, and to have written a book, "The Sayings of Jesus," while there. A copy of that document was found several decades ago, and has been translated from the Coptic. Harper Brothers of New York published *The Gospel According to Thomas*, in 1959. From Egypt, Thomas traveled East, according to strong tradition, arriving in India some thirty years after Jesus' resurrection. There he founded the Christian Church, and some three percent of India's natives today are members of this Christian denomination.

Whether Thomas married and took a wife along in his travels, we do not know. In verse 114 of *The Gospel According to Thomas*, we find the following:

Simon Peter said, "Let Mary go out from us, because women are not worthy of the Life."

Jesus said, "See, I shall lead her, so that I will make her male, that she too may become a living spirit, resembling you males. For every woman who makes herself male will enter the Kingdom of Heaven."

Such statements are very difficult to interpret. Yet if we accept the possibility that the source of these sayings has validity, we may accept also that there was a real difference among the Apostles about the role of women in the early Church. For Thomas to have included these quotations at the very end of his 'Gospel,' might indicate that he was willing to share a ministry with Mary. On that thin thread, I offer the conclusion of Mary's running thoughts. Surely, too, she would want to live out her life proclaiming the reality of a living Christ.